LOST CHILDREN

LOST CHILDREN

Edith Pargeter

WARNER FUTURA

A *Warner Futura* Book

First published in Great Britain by Heinemann in 1951
Published by Little, Brown in 1993
This edition published by Warner Books in 1994

A CIP catalogue record for this book
is available from the British Library.

ISBN 0 7515 0369 X

Printed in England by Clays Ltd, St Ives plc

Warner Books
A Division of
Little, Brown and Company (UK) Limited
Brettenham House
Lancaster Place
London WC2E 7EN

CONTENTS

CHAPTER ONE:

Rosalba

1

ROSE'S FOLLY covers the highest rocky outcrop of the heathland as the cloud covers Table Mountain, sagging, wallowing, permanent, and yet for ever quivering and changing to the varying lights of day and evening, the metamorphosis of weather, and every atmospheric caprice of the open uplands, so that in a day it is a thousand different places, each more monstrous than the last, while its essential nature remains aggressive and inescapable. It has a certain femininity, in that the more it changes the more it remains the same. It is volatile, but only to display the innumerable facets of the same solid, resentful, determined singleness. All round it for miles the warrens and coppices and rolling wilderness of the Rose estates fend off the rest of the world; the woods depleted, the edges nibbled away by fields, but the encroaching sea of reality still held fast from over-running it by something of willpower, more of luck, and most of all by the sheer weight of habit and security of possession. As it was in the beginning, is now, and ever shall be, world without end, Amen! Or if not without end, still without visible or readily conceivable end.

The railway line between Crocksford and Bredington, one of the earliest in England, skirts the estate and looks up across the lightly lifting miles of heath to a watch-tower placed high between fits of woodland, to suggest the fourteenth century, though it belongs to the nineteenth. Distance makes almost beautiful the shifting levels of land, bluish-black churning of trees and light-play of grasses, from which the house emerges on its shallow table of rock. The crag is not high, so the Folly compensates with towers of improbable height and ferocity, shot with slit arrow-windows bordered with three-coloured brick of the railway age, slag-blue, raw-clay-yellow and russet-red. Between the towers the complicated roofs run all ways in panic from their turreted Gothic corners, curly-crested, scalloped, battlemented to bewilderment, unsure of everything on earth but their own rightness and permanence. Every kind of window shuts out light from, rather than lets it into, the half miles of corridor and acres of hall within. You could get lost in the attics and wait days for a search-party. Among the twisted, towering, convoluted chimney-pots you could imagine yourself in a new Cheddar, laced with leaner stalagmites, and petrified from the beginning of the world. This monstrous erection, so huge that even across a waste of seven miles it seems to topple over you, ought to be self-conscious about its appearance; and what terrifies is that it sits there with no sense of guilt whatever, so assured, so fixed, so indifferent to your astonishment, that it achieves a formidable personality of its own. You are afraid even to shudder at it. For the truth is that Rose's Folly, for all its artificiality and newness, is only the latest facet of something old, genuine and immense, no more capable of awkwardness in this fresh guise than a woman in a new dress.

There have always been Roses. In the remote Norman and Saxon mists from which they came they do not smell any sweeter than the rest of their kind, perhaps, but they acquired the patina and the permanence of all antiques, and something of the value, before the end of the eighteenth century recoiled with them into a languor and uselessness which is also the frequent fate of *objets d'art*. There was a decent Queen Anne house on the uplands then, the latest of many, reasonably sized for a family with blood far older than

8

the Plantagenets and pride beyond titles. But there was little energy left to prop up the walls of it, until the late explosion of Richard Rose, with his head full of iron and his heart worked by steam, and a length of railway track in either hand.

Richard was as obsessed by railways as Wilkinson was by iron, and showed the same courage and genius in backing his ominous fancy. Which is why the railway line from Crocksford to Bredington is one of the oldest in England, and also why the Roses grew for a time fabulously rich again, rich enough to tear down the Queen Anne house and create a reality out of his Gothic nightmare, a mad masterpiece of vigour and eccentricity from which he could gloat upon his kingdom. He threw up on one hill the sham Norman watch-tower, and on another a bogus abbey in a picturesque state of ruin, spilled four romantic pools among the debris, twisted a river out of its small inoffensive course and made it cascade over manufactured rocks and through concrete grottoes, built himself a fabulous tomb halfway through his lifetime, and spent the rest of it watching with satisfaction the growth of his yews and cypresses, the success of his imaginings, and the uneasiness of his contemporaries in the presence of an egotism they could not match.

But he died, and there were no more such Roses. It may be that he was only a last protest by the old, exhausted blood before it thinned and dwindled away into insignificant veins, and left a shell of pride standing where there was no vitality to fill it. For the Roses withered away again as they had done before him, and their fortunes with them, until the survivors gave up all pretence at coping with a world which was too much for them, and recoiled into their earthworks to stand off the advancing waves of time and change upon the smaller island of their own possessions. And even there, pebble by pebble, grain by grain, the rims of the kingdom began to be eaten away.

The Folly was an expensive indulgence, impossible to be maintained, impossible to be surrendered. They bought off the storm by bequeathing it to the nation, which staggered under the shock of the gift, but could not deny its immensity. There were treasures there, jealously kept; there was history there, even in the curly crests and restless chimneys, not to be refused. Therefore the National Trust put in a custodian, and opened the labyrinth to the public upon payment of a small fee, and the last Rose of this or any summer retired to the south lodge, far, far away from the scene of her glory; to the extreme edge of the estates, looking toward Crocksford's distant factory chimneys; to a house big enough only for a platoon, instead of her customary accommodation for a regiment.

She was born, as well as married, a Rose; a first cousin of her husband, who had less of Rose spirit and Rose fire than she. Inter-breeding had made of them all by then a physical type so exact that it could not be found anywhere else, even in half-relatives, who in any case were scarce; the old blood had never been diluted with the thin stuff of the newer nobility, or the cold metallic flow of tradesmen's veins. But somehow the type had not run, in the women at least, to bone and barrenness and length of foot; and Martine widowed was still and emphatically beautiful. Even then they spoke wistfully of what she had been in her youth, and said that you should have seen her before her marriage. And Martine driven to the lodge at last, even Martine in her eightieth year, clung to the fossil of her beauty as she clung to the rags of her circumstance, with a religious devotion, absorbed all into a flame-like memory of splendour. It dazzled and scorched others who came near it; but she lived in it, and it ate her alive.

There was only one more Rose, no more than a bud, and a little blemished at that. Martine had had a nephew who had married a girl from some nameless family in trade. She might as well have been from the stews by the revulsion she caused; but happily they were both killed in a car smash before the world could take very much interest in their case, and the small girl they left behind could hardly yet be fairly judged. She might be all Martine feared, but by God's grace she might not, and she was a Rose of sorts, and the last; so

10

she was brought to the Folly, and grew up where her steps echoed and re-echoed back to her from aching distances at every move, and every sound must take into account its own unmanageable ghosts, and every action its impact upon the stem and flower of the immemorial Rose.

Her name – nobody knows now whether it was a concession to the offended gods, or a tribute to Thackeray, for her mother chose it, and the few thoughts her mother thought about the match are gone with her – her name was Rosalba. She was beautifully brought up. Duty, duty and duty made her day, and reverence her night; but it was duty to the tradition, the name, the blood, and reverence for the holiness of a God who was almost a Rose. The very essence of all she learned was that she was a Rose, and her every act and word must conform to that standard; and she learned well, and willingly, and they did conform, and took pleasure in it. Other people were different. But sometimes some infantile memory obscurely reminded her that these different people had different pleasures, and she even wondered what they could be, and what kind of taste they had, but being civilised could not admit to such a curiosity. By the time she was seventeen she did not feel very much pain from her wondering. Another year, and she might have felt none, for faculties which are not used take themselves off finally.

But change has no fixed rate, and after centuries of creeping can leap no less incalculably. Stars disintegrate in the twinkling of an eye. Nothing is safe. The rarity of these cataclysms gives them a more bludgeoning quality of astonishment. Nothing is safe.

It might be better to begin: Rose's Folly covered the highest rocky outcrop of the heath-land—

Read it all in the past. Things do pass.

2

Every morning the old man took his bunch of keys, large as

11

daggers, and went clanking up the long drive from the east lodge on an old upright bicycle, his peaked cap set dead straight on the bright patriarchal hair, his back so erect that it was said among the village youths that he steered by the stars. Every morning he set out the visitors' book, the quill pens, the brass inkstand large as a vegetable dish, the monumental blotter, dusted the glass over the most precious cases of documents, wiped an experimental finger over the less loving dusting of the cleaners from the town, saw them off the premises, and tasted, smelled, drank the vast quiet after their going, before the visitors came, before even Martine, whose spirit inhabited and filled the whole even in its emptiness, came in the flesh to re-stamp her image upon everything.

Every evening, after visiting hours, he locked every door gently behind him, passing through the house unwearied after hours of growing weary, loving the stillness and the space and the dark, exceeding cathedrals and tombs and all vast, hushed places. Then he could hear the floors between earth and heaven, earth and hell, creaking softly to unseen feet, and his spirit was ravished with awareness of demons and angels within touch of his hands, and his ears waited for the horn. One day he might walk through one more door at the end of the many, and feel no change; lock it behind him, and turn into the judgment.

Once he had had a wife, but she was dead a long time ago, and a family, but they were grown up and gone, one to America, one to the dogs, one to Littlehampton to keep a boarding-house and add subtle halfpennies to bills; and all of them were gone from him without any feeling of loss, as the years had passed from his head, until there was no time as there were no possessions, and he was the custodian of one portal of eternity, listening to many voices, none of which had a face to it, none of which carried memories. He loved simpler things than human now, simpler but less crude, the strange texture of old wood, with shapes in it not yet found, and struggling to break out between his hands, and be; the feeling of vellum from which writing has been erased, where

12

thoughts have revealed and withdrawn themselves again without capture; the music of old instruments which no one now could play. He loved the curly beard of the self-portrait of the man who built the organ in the enormous gallery, a beard like the sea; and his writhed and wrinkled face, as if the first music made on it was wry to his ears; and the faded colours in the English tapestries, green woodland colours grown amber in decay, dyes five hundred years older than the house. But most of all he loved the feeling of great things about to enter in, when no one but himself was left in the echoing, aware emptiness of the folly at night. Sometimes he did not go home until late in the evening, but sat making willow pipes in one lit corner of the infinity of hallway, and listening for the knocking on the door or the call outside the window.

He did not love Martine, she would not have permitted it. But he felt an artist's reverence and a devotee's gratitude to her. In the disturbing years of the alien war he had rested his eyes in her always, when the frenzied activity of Martians had sometimes shaken even this security with rumours of impossibilities, and tremors from a tide of change; but these had subsided, and what was, was still. Chaos receded, Martine remained.

Rarely he found a like mind among the many visitors who came to be shown round, but more often they were picnic parties from Crocksford, day-tripping families, courting couples gaping and giggling at antiquity, or troops of gawky young men in uniform, from the air bases and training camps round the margin of the heath. Eighteen-year-old boys on National Service, or whatever title they used now to add decency to conscription. Hobbledehoys who sat down on the tapestry chairs, or took the short way down the grand staircase from the gallery when one's back was turned, and marked the exquisite black polish of the oak floor with their clumsy nailed boots on landing. Children who made sticky finger-marks from lollipops and toffee-apples on the banisters, and spread whole ghostly hand-prints upon the glass cases. They were not so much hateful to him as unreal;

13

he was not equipped to hate, he could only be saddened, like the saints by the visitations of devils.

'Marvellous-looking old geezer!' said the youngest soldier, leaning on the rail of the gallery at the edge of the gaping group. 'How'd you suppose he got to look like that?'

'Living in this bloody place too long,' said the scarcely older corporal. 'Gives you the willies to look at it. Let's get out of here, I've had enough.'

'We'd never find the way out. Anyhow, I want my tanner's worth.'

'Please yourself. But I don't reckon to pay to go on route-marches.' The corporal yawned into the face of a Rose who had bloomed before York and Lancaster fought over his species, and caught the reproachful eye of the custodian fixed on him over the heads of staring children.

'His name's Cedarwood,' said the youngest soldier, under his breath. 'Believe it or not!'

'Go on!'

'True enough! I know a girl who used to work up here. That's his honest to God name.'

'It ain't possible!'

'Anything's possible. Look at this lot round the walls. Well, they're Roses. So what?'

'Got the greenfly bad, then,' said the corporal sulkily, and wandered away to experiment quietly with the fastenings of certain small arms on the wall, out of range of the ancient eyes.

The armoury had certainly been something to see, and a few of his fellows were still there, tinkering with the visors of old helmets and sniggering over some incredible gadget called a chastity belt. If they didn't have the thumb-screws on some simpleton before he got 'em out it would be a miracle. He supposed he ought to sneak back and haul them away, but when he peeped over the edge of the gallery he saw them just creeping up the stairs in a hurry, tumbling over themselves and 'hushing' sibilantly at one another, and grinning in a pink and guilty fashion which made it clear some unauthorised activities had been going on. They

14

always waited until his back was turned. Seale, and Tomkins, and Toole – that's the lot, he thought; not that he was responsible for them, but a stripe is a stripe.

'This,' said Cedarwood, in his wide warm voice which had caught from long acquaintance some echoes of the organ, 'is the Humphrey Rose who sat in the parliament of Simon de Montfort. His seal you have already seen, below in the first case. And here opposite him, in the best light we can give it, is Sargent's early portrait of the present Mrs. Rose. A beautiful work! A very beautiful lady!' He spoke as if Martine's magical age had still been twenty. There was never any need to say very much about this picture; one stood back and let them gaze, as that boy in khaki was gazing now. Yes, the day had budded. There was a mind there which could be reached, a set of sensibilities which could feel beauty and urgency. One success in his day was all he could hope to find, and it came marvellously, out of the least probable material, the black-browed young man with ill-fitting uniform and sulky eyes, and an insolent, fierce mouth ready to curl and sneer. But here it was, within this face, that the white, magnificent, wand-straight creature in the portrait fixed her aquamarine stare under the great blanched brow, and smiled. A discomforting smile, it is true, across miles of icy distance which severed her from common flesh such as his; but satisfied, but appreciated.

Eugene Seale gazed, and frowned, wondering what sort of voice she had had; voices, in his experience, most often betrayed people. Probably squawked like a peahen. And her assurance was so insulting that he would have liked to see if it was also brittle. But she was a beauty, all right. How much of the loveliness, he wondered, was in the painting, how much in the flesh? The ice was all her own.

'Nice bit of stuff,' said the youngest soldier. 'They say she's still living in one of the lodges. Must be about ninety by now, though.'

'Looks a bitch to me,' said the corporal candidly.

'Well, I've heard she is. There's a girl here, too, some sort of poor relation, or something. Blimey, what a life for a girl, in this mausoleum! Drive you to drink, wouldn't it?'

15

'Gives me the creeps, fair enough. Come on, old Noah's off again. Let's get it over.'

Onward streamed the procession on Cedarwood's heels, out of the lofty double doors at the far end of the gallery, along an echoing corridor, and up a winding stair into the wilderness of the towers, with clamour of many gaits, and a spray of children skittering on the edge of its advancing wave. The hubbub of feet passed from hearing round the curve of the stair, and Eugene Seale still stood in front of Martine Rose's portrait, admiring and detesting her, liking the panache of the painting, and the encrusted swirls of impasto standing on the froth of her white skirt. She'd frozen out the painter as well as everyone who looked at it since. He thought he could have made quite another picture of her, without changing the truth of her face, made her mean, withered and repellent; but he knew that she was not quite any of these things. That circumstances made her, as she went on making circumstances, he did not consider; he was eighteen, and not yet able to make many allowances.

When he had stared enough he suddenly made a wicked face at her, like a baby reacting to dislike with dislike, and went on after the others. But the gallery was vast, and ended in a wider aisle with no less than four doors opening from it, and he had paid no attention to the guide's exit, and did not know which way to go. It didn't matter very much. Everything was quiet, and he could go where he liked, he'd paid his sixpence with the rest. He tried one door, and stared into a dark-panelled room with a great oriel looking out on sudden sunny courtyards. No stairway there. A second showed him an empty room with a painted ceiling, a little faded and cracked. A third opened upon flooding light and a long wall of windows, a little gallery running the length of both these rooms, and then turning a corner out of sight. At this corner, looking out into the day, stood an old woman leaning upon an ivory-headed stick.

He meant to go away quietly and close the door between them, but he knew her, and halted to stare against his will. How two things so unlike could be so like was a mystery and

16

a paradox which caught his fancy and held him still. The same height and slenderness, but shrivelled all away to angles and hardness of skin and bone, dry as immortelle, dead and not able to rest like that horrible flower. Who says there is a beautiful, clean line to bone? Not, at least, when it still carried withered flesh on it, without a single possibility remaining of grace or subtlety, but all hard and obvious. The hand that clutched the straight head of her cane was long and narrow, but that made it now a more repulsive claw. Her face in profile was old in a protected, not a weathered way; he had seen old women, countrywomen, who had wrinkled like russet apples rosily and merrily, but this one had shrunk hard with few lines, like mummified flesh, cured and stuck to the bone. Her nose kept its bold, patrician line, only a little crooked like a hawk's bill; but her jaw was a witch's, sunken above, contracted below, like a rat-trap hinged on her skinny neck.

But the most terrible thing was that she still had about her the rags of that early beauty. White hair, blue-white and shining, was piled high on her head, and the weight of it bent her neck a little more, and made her quiver as she moved; its coils were dressed like the blazing gold hair of the portrait, wide like heraldic wings half-spread above the great, bland, assured brow. And the brow, but for an ivory yellowing and texture of dryness, was not greatly changed, the hair-line as lofty and as proud. Her eyes were watching some movement below in the courtyard, and he could not judge their quality, but he felt that they could intimidate. And besides these recollections of loveliness, she had kept something, a fearful ghost, of the movements of her youth, an arrogance which had not chosen to age, a pride as erect as the girl in the picture; and with these she wore improbable finery, and jewels in her ears and on her hands.

He made no sound, but his withdrawal was delayed too long, and with some uneasy sense she detected him, and writhed herself round on her stick to launch at him the impersonal stare of the aquamarine eyes, blanched now to an opaque dullness for their lost brilliance. But in shadow,

17

as she suddenly hobbled at him along the gallery, they looked bluely still, hard steel-blue like the points of unbuttoned foils, under thin arched brows repelling him wordlessly from her world. Except as a sort of myth dependent upon the presence of Cedarwood, there were not such people.

'What do you want here, young man?' she demanded. 'This part of the house is not shown to visitors.'

He was so astonished by her voice that he stuttered over answering. It had suffered, too, lost perhaps the lowest and the highest of its range, shrunk like the rest of her; but it must have been like cream once, and even now it was like cream gone a little sour. Even in youth that creature should have had utterance like a smitten glass, brittle, piercing and sharply sweet.

'From the gallery,' she said, one hand unconsciously gathering her skirts from too near an approach, 'people go always along the corridor there, and up the tower.' The thin cane pointed, quivering.

'I missed the others,' he said clumsily. He would have liked to shake the assurance of this ancient aristocrat, to have heaved at her not only his defiance of her kind, but his shameless satisfaction in his own at its most vulgar and earthy; but he looked back at her instead with a strained, withdrawn civility which hated her more. The old, porcelain eyes in the shadow bit at him. He looked back with young eyes like brook pebbles, as opaque and as cold, and said in his smoothest voice: 'I stopped to look at the pictures. I'll go after them.' And inclined his head to her as if his spine were no more pliable than hers, and went away directly, closing the door after him without any sound.

Trudging up the spiral staircase of the tower, round and round on the tapered, unworn treads past the deep shot-windows, he thought: 'A girl in this house! Some sort of poor relation! My God, poor little devil!' And he dug his hands deep into his empty pockets, and kicked with the toes of his clumsy boots at the edges of the stairs, and wondered for a little what she was like, this pale late echo of that

18

blue-blooded, cold-blooded, stagnant race, and what she did all day long and every day under the shadow of the appalling old woman. 'Might as well be in the bloody Army!' he said to himself, and for him that was the last damnation.

3

'The Bretherton girls ride there,' said Rosalba mildly, in the middle of her small hope and smaller anxiety noticing the single rose fallen sideways out of the bowl, and reaching out a dutiful hand to restore it to the water.

'The Bretherton girls may. You are not quite in the same position.'

'After being at school with them,' said Rosalba, sighing, 'naturally I feel a little interest in the things they do. I – it would be rather nice to have their company – and to ride would be fun. I've heard Mrs. Fenton describe how splendidly you used to ride.'

Great-Aunt Martine could not quiver nor warm to praise; not to any inflection of admiration, the subtlest shade of reverence or the crudest flattery. Or was it only that no such offering from Rosalba, of all people in the world, could touch her? Her pale eyes in full sunlight stared coldly under thin lifted brows, rejecting the sweet.

'Our circumstances, I admit, Rosalba, are not what I could have wished them to be. I apologise for the modern heresies, but I am not responsible for them, and I cannot change them. For what subjects I could I have given you proper tuition. I deplore the fact that the rest of your education has had to be entrusted to an inexpensive school among the daughters of tradespeople. Birth is an accident, perhaps; perhaps a providence; certainly a fact. But if you have had to share your working hours with very mixed company, it surprises me that you should accept that as a criterion for your leisure, too.' Her talon of a hand tightened on the head of her stick. 'Or perhaps I do wrong to feel any surprise, in the same breath as admitting that birth is a fact.'

The ghost of the unknown mother, all the little ghosts of her father's shops, had haunted Rosalba rather more frequently during the last year; she didn't understand why, even when her face in the mirror accidentally burned white and young beside the ashy cheeks of her great-aunt. But she looked only at the roses, and said submissively:

'I want to be guided by you, of course. You know I have always tried to do what you wished. But I have no society here—'

'Have I any? I have not tried to suggest it is easy for you. I have never allowed you to believe that it would be easy. Lack of money is also a fact – one with which we have both had to become familiar.'

'But perhaps one could adjust oneself to facts – a little—'

The once-full lips, thinned now to parings of brownish skin, curled silently. Roses do not adjust themselves; they only withdraw, fighting every step of the way.

'I know we can't afford to entertain like the Saxbys do, and all the rest of – our own people; and of course if we can't hold our own with them, we can't possibly attempt to share their sort of life, or accept hospitality, or anything of that kind. But surely there could be no harm in the kind of company we *can* afford? Some of those girls were rather nice.' But her own voice sounded undistressed, because it had never been hopeful; and therefore argument and pleading were alike unreal. She sensed it, and was silent. An odd feeling this, of walking round and round Danae's brazen tower, trying to find a way in; and not even a shower of gold could have penetrated into this tower, because it was brazen right through, it had no inside at all. Only lately had she had such queer thoughts; for most of her mind agreed with Great-Aunt Martine, and to tell truth she had always found it a little awkward to make common ground with the Bretherton girls, and preferred often to avoid such difficulties of adjustment; only some little piece of her being, far inside, cried out indignantly that she was lonely, that where there had been so much of silence a human voice was a human voice.

'I do not dispute,' said Great-Aunt Martine, with curling lips, 'the virtues of the Brethertons in their own sphere. I have no doubt they are excellent tradesmen. Why not? I have no doubt that to be a Bretherton is a very much easier, perhaps a very much pleasanter, thing than to be a Rose. That alters nothing. You are a Rose. It may be unfortunate. It is certainly past cure.'

Often at such a moment Rosalba had said, and truly, that she was proud of it; but she did not say anything now, except quietly: 'Of course, I shall be guided by you. I realise that there are obligations.'

'You realise them from many repetitions,' said Martine, very deliberately, 'not from any conviction. It is scarcely your fault, I suppose, that my nephew chose to import into the family the tastes of a barmaid.'

'Please!' said Rosalba in the stillest of voices, for it would have been rather artificial to defend with indignation someone of whom she had not even a fantasy memory, much less a real one. 'I'm sorry I disappoint you, but we need not speak of it again.' She took her hands from the roses which had given her a focus for her eyes and even her thoughts through this quite usual encounter, and for a moment almost felt in herself her terrible resemblance to the old woman. Even in opposition they played the same hand with the same gestures.

'It would certainly relieve me,' said Martine, as softly, 'not to have to repeat yet again what is so obvious to me, at least.'

'I shall try not to make it necessary.'

Yes, the very phrases they chose sounded the same, the pitch of their voices was like. When Rosalba walked the length of the picture gallery on occasional errands or the dutiful pilgrimage with the old woman on her arm, she saw rows and rows of varying versions of her own face staring back at her from the walls. Like a hall of mirrors; men, women, children, all with her eyes and her forehead and the shape of her face, all fixing her with their measuring gaze, and considering whether she was fit to be a Rose. These

21

were companions enough, she must not look for others. Only sometimes, perhaps, one might walk round with Cedarwood when he made his rounds in the evening, or exchange a few words with some of the more respectable cleaners who scrubbed and dusted in the mornings before the public came. But friendships are something more than this. You may enquire after the charwoman's bad leg, but you cannot confide in her daughter. If you are a Rose, you must not bed with lesser flowers; and while there are none beyond your scope by the measure of blood, all those who can be considered your equals are now too dear for your possessing.

She went out into the heath-land, and when that offered her only early evening storm-clouds hanging ominously low, turned back along the uplands to the Folly, to see the last visitors of the day leaving. Lots of children, chattering and fighting in bursts of affection and enmity, like a litter of puppies; a bunch of soldiers from the camps which everywhere marked the countryside around Crocksford, two American Army airmen from the flying-field near Bredington, some youths and girls twined arm-in-arm, a few respectable middle-aged couples, a scholarly-looking old man with a notebook, some student of human eccentricity. And then, standing a moment quite still in the centre of the inner courtyard, only Cedarwood, looking after them gladly, waiting for the last footstep to recede from hearing, so that the immense quiet may come in.

'Who is the old man?' she asked him, looking after them too.

'A Professor Saint, from Birmingham, Miss Rosalba. He's been studying the diaries of Richard Rose while the others went round. Some book he's writing, I believe. I have to take the books back to the document-room in the tower now, and then I can lock up.'

'I'll come up with you,' she said, and halfway through the gallery wished she had not suggested it, for today the rows and rows of measuring eyes oppressed her strangely, weighing her down with their doubts of her fitness to carry

22

the same name. But up there among the chimneys it was different; up there walking round and round the conical Gothic roof of the tower, leaning into the embrasures to look across four counties through the blue, cloud-streaked evening, she could rid herself of the burden of eyes, and stare for herself, and breathe deeply.

Behind her the nightmare jumble of roofs, chimneys, gutterings, copings, fire-escapes and cowls; before her the woods and gardens first, then the heath, distant the double bluish haze of towns, and the dapplings of farms between, patterned, quilted and green with deepening spring, a glimmer of river threading the lower ground in silver loops, a small bland pool shadowy under the lea of the watch-tower.

'Do you know what it makes me think of?' she said, turning to smile at Cedarwood as he came out through the low door after her, the enormous keys bristling in his hand. 'The devil taking him up into a high place, and offering him all the kingdoms of the earth.'

'That's blasphemous talk,' he said weightily, 'not for you, Miss Rosalba.'

'Oh, yes, it makes sense. These were all the kingdoms of our earth, you see.' And for these, she thought but did not say, generations of us have fallen down and worshipped ourselves. 'You love this place, don't you?' she said suddenly, but not as needing an answer. 'Were you never afraid – a few years ago, when the bombers used to come over – didn't you ever think that you might wake up some morning, and find the Folly gone? Gone, or ruined, or burning. So many things changed then. Didn't you ever fear it might reach even us?'

She could see his fevered dark eyes, bright between the grizzling hairiness of brows and hair and beard, staring back into the memory of flashing, noisy nights when the sky trembled and the earth shook, and everything outside the magic miles of heath and park was in constant passionate flux; but she could see, too, that for him the stones here had never been shaken.

'Plenty such places have gone,' he said, staring bac

23

steadily, 'plenty of them. But the spirit inside them was gone first. That's what stands sturdy here – not this!' Striking his hand against the battlements, as if he would make them gush with miraculous water. 'Another sort of stone keeps the spines of these houses stiff and holds the roofs up. Oh, there's change, there's change! I know it very well. These catastrophes come, and what's gone inside, that falls. But the Folly doesn't fall – not yet. We shall feel the stone inside crumbling before the outside goes down. This is nothing, this hard stuff we're a-leaning on. Only put there – what, not much over a hundred years ago, that was. But look inside it, what it's built over – ah, centuries of adamant there. That's what the Folly means. Not what it says, mark you, to look at it, but that's what it means. That's still there. You'll feel – or if you don't, I shall – when that begins to crumble.'

'But it will go,' she said, convinced and half afraid; for if it went, what was left that she knew the sound or the touch of?

'That hadn't ought to worry us, miss. That things pass, that's ordered, that's providence. There ain't a seed grows but from a head that's ripened already and died. We think in a few years; but when you think in centuries, what's change? Like a night and a day passing, that's all.'

'You don't *mind*?' said Rosalba, marvelling.

'Lord, no, miss! Why mind it? As well mind dying, when we know if it wasn't for that we couldn't reckon up what to do with life.'

'And do you think it will last our lifetime? Great-Aunt Martine does. She always says: "It will last my time, and yours, too, and when it passes we and our kind shall have passed with it." And then she says: "Thank God!" Do you think it's something to thank God for, Cedarwood?'

'Not more,' he said, gazing under the gilded rim of the deep clouds, 'than it might be to live to see what happens next. It isn't for us to take thought, not for the morrow nor for yesterday. The more you look at everything, the more marvellous it gets, and exchanging one thing for another is a sort of art – not to grab too soon, and not to hold on too late, that's a thing you can learn if you stop taking thought. I

24

don't calculate it, miss. I only wait for it, and listen a bit. If you know what I mean.'

But she did not know what he meant; she was seventeen.

Wind stirred her hair, and the sinking cloud began to fray in the middle and break in pieces, letting the sunset through in filtered gold. Beneath, far along the tawny drive, the departing visitors straggled, tiny as ladybirds.

'But we sit up here so much,' she said, in sudden protest, 'looking down from a sort of roof, just like this, where nothing grows; and the people below look like ants. But they're not ants! And they're not just waiting and listening, and opening and shutting their hands on whatever comes. They're trying to make things come, trying to make things happen – not the way they may, but the way they ought to.'

'You can do a lot of damage that way,' he said simply.

'I know. Yes, you can — but perhaps you could do a lot of good, too.' She hung far out in the deep embrasure, following the last strayed few into the shadow of the trees; and last of all a little soldier, small and clumsy and alone as a thoughtful little boy going home separate from his fellows. 'That boy, for instance! We get things all wrong from up here. He looks like some speck you could flatten out with your thumb, but for all we know the spark is in him that could burn away all that adamant you spoke about just now, and bring the house down under us.'

She had raised her voice, and her hand in exasperation was actually shaken from its repose into a gesture of seizing and toppling down, Samson-like, the imaginary towers of her life. But from below the voice could not have been heard, nor the gesture seen. Why, then, did the distant, small, foreshortened khaki figure turn instantly, and lift its head, and stare upward intently at the dizzy skyline of turrets, as if he had received the message as Cedarwood trusted to receive the first note of the trumpet?

4

Every day the cleaners from Crocksford got off the bus at the south lodge gates, and walked all the way up the miles of drive, to scrub and sweep and polish the acres of floor and walls of show-case in the public rooms. Rosalba often watched them pass when she was cutting flowers in the garden, or weeding neatly with her gloves and her kneeling mat at the borders near the hedge. Often they called good morning to her, and she answered them politely, and even looked after them for a while as they bounced on up the drive with a great deal of chatter and laughing. It made her marvel that they laughed so much, sometimes the echo of the youngest girl's mirth made her want to laugh, too, it was so fresh and gay; but she had never exchanged many more words with them than this good morning. And after they had passed from earshot they talked about her, as often as not, though it never occurred to her to wonder about that.

'Stuck-up little bitch!' said one of them dispassionately. 'She'll have to come off her high horse one of these days, mark my words.'

'Didn't have no choice about being on it, though,' said the youngest, who was only eighteen herself, and had red hair. 'Not a chance, poor little devil! When you've seen the old girl you know who calls all the tunes around here. Not that I've got any brief, as you might say, for the young one, neither. I can't say as I've ever noticed her wanting to swop her lot for any cottage life. But you have to admit there'd be hell to pay if she did.'

'Oh, you don't have to make excuses for her,' said the other confidently. 'She's got it in the blood, all right. Can't hardly be bothered to see us, much less speak. Don't waste no soft feeling on her!'

'Still,' said the redhead thoughtfully. 'I wouldn't have her life, not for something I wouldn't.'

But Rosalba, who did not discuss people because she knew none, and had in any case no confidante with whom

26

she could dissect them, never guessed that she was discussed. She went about her gardening with some pleasure, but always an incomplete one because no one shared it; she cut roses even when she was not asked, and put them in bowls in Great-Aunt Martine's fabulous room, hoping for some word or even look of surprise at their beauty. But things of beauty entered there only to burn out into the pyre of the lost beauty which inhabited it. It was a treasure-house for a heap of ashes now just warm to the touch, no more. And the cold, faded face had long ago over-civilised its reactions beyond surprise, and far beyond appreciation of any but its own colour and line.

The rest of the lodge was modestly furnished, but Martine's room was splendid, with a monstrous draped Empire bed, and a white glitter of silver mirrors, among which she sat for hours regarding herself. She did not fear mirrors, like the ageing Elizabeth; what threatened her she hated and defied, but she did not fear it. Out of a perversity of self-torment and smouldering hope she loved mirrors, and whenever she sat long among them, dressing her hair, decorating herself with jewels, she was two people: one who saw the remnants of loveliness still warm, still to be cherished, and one who contemplated the outlines which had once been the truth of her, and sat over their grave drinking her own poisoned regrets, until she was all gall within. Sometimes as these two embraced in her the door would open, and Rosalba would come in with fresh flowers, or the morning papers, or the mail, and flame among the silver surfaces, doubled and redoubled, flashing all ways about the old, blue-white death's-head. Sometimes during this last year, almost a woman, she would even catch the glint of the poniard eyes following her all about, all about the shrine out of the motionless face.

A child has no beauty, only a sort of animal charm. Even now the girl moved awkwardly, with sudden angular starts and stops, and sometimes had imperfect control of her hands and feet, and hunched or sagged her shoulders reassuringly. She had been well taught in the matter of what a well-bred girl should wear, and had not yet envisaged anything beyond it; tailored suits, tweed skirts, sweaters of neutral colours, beyond reproach, schoolgirl's wear. Her hair was up already, in a coil on the back of her head; she balanced it badly, but kept it neatly. Her teeth were perfectly regular, the only glasses she ever needed were sun-glasses. The hair would some day find its true place, low on the nape of the so white, so slender neck, with coiled reclining lines caressing relaxed shoulders, and she would straighten herself, and the young breasts would advance proudly and accept the fingers of the light as she moved. Within every movement now another movement flashed and faded – the same gesture, two years onward, perfected, confident, beautiful.

Down the curve of the young cheek in the mirror, across the deep, bluish lids lowered over the bluer eyes, under the taut, tentative chin, Great-Aunt Martine's eyes drew deliberate knife-marks. And every now and again some new nerve in Rosalba quivered, feeling the wound.

But she did not understand. If she had understood she would never have halted behind the chair after the letters were laid ready to hand on the table, and the morning tray retrieved from beside the bed. She would have stood somewhere less conspicuous, where the mirrors could not find her colouring in the full sunlight, and show how fresh and smooth she was.

'Do you want me this afternoon, Great-Aunt Martine?'

'I think not particularly,' said the dry lips, moving slowly upon thin words. The eyes said, but in a language not yet clear: 'I have never wanted you. I don't want you now. Do you think I take any pleasure in being reminded that you live?'

'Where are you going?' she asked.

'I want to take a dress over to Mrs. Crane's to be altered; and I thought I'd come back through the park, and perhaps take the dogs.'

'Very well. But avoid the path by the camps. There are ways enough through the park without using that one.'

'I never go there,' said Rosalba dutifully.

28

When she left the room all the images of her drew together for a moment, shining silverly in the flat bright surfaces of the mirrors, and the eyes, turning when the head did not turn, watched her go. Growing tall now, a Rose in build if no other way. Too thin, but at that age one is too thin or too fat, and she had chosen the lesser disaster; fair, with pale, smooth gold hair and bright cheeks only faintly flushed with a honeyed pink, like a tea-rose. It needed only that she should begin to know what she carried; but as yet her eyes were quite unaware. Was not the freshness enough, more than enough, without that clarity of line and warming fire of colour? There are ugly girls; even the young can be repulsive, heavy as dough, dull as porridge. But this one – the unfinished, awkward gestures sometimes started and floated in the air as fine blue smoke starts and curls, tenuous upon the drift of an unsuspected wind; and the long dark gold lashes, when she lowered her lids, made fringed amber shadows on her spare cheekbones, like sunlight through silk, and the eyes, sapphire in a high light, darkened to cobalt or ultramarine. They could not for ever go on in blindness, those eyes.

Rosalba crossed the park with the dress under her arm, and delivered it at Mrs. Crane's cottage. It was halfway through May, and already summer by the foliage and the sun. When she came up the crest of the heath she saw that for the first time the hills had a low, dancing haze, and the tremor of their excitement warmed her as the sun warms the flower. Grasses flowed over the flowing uplands whitely, ripening early. She did not go to the kennels for the dogs. She did not go back through the park. She wanted to be where nothing could be seen of the Folly or any of its creatures, in an unpeopled place, alone. She did not know why it was so urgent that she should escape into warm, instinctive, unreflecting quietness, but at the back of her eyes there was still a spiky glittering of mirrors, and her mind was jagged with their uneasy, brittle reduplication of herself and Great-Aunt Martine. She went quickly up the narrow, winding path through the terraced coppices to the

29

watch-tower on the headland, artistically fourteenth century in yellowish-grey brick, and beyond it to the gardens of Richard's favourite artifice among so many, and the broad oval shield of the pool, with its shores of shaven turf and wings of rhododendrons, silver and green and clean in its sterile concrete bed.

It was not because of any beauty that she liked this place, though it was not displeasing; she came here because it was the most remote point of Rose land from the Folly. Rose land it was still in some strange way, though the National Trust owned it, and the War Office were busy prising it from under their indignant fingers inch by inch, with Crocksford City Council hovering on the outskirts of the dispute for any falling crumbs, and uttering faint protesting outcries on behalf of their deprived citizens, who never used it.

Below the gradual slope the war-time growths of chestnut-roofed Army huts still smoked busily and were populous with pygmies, and in the end they would reach their arms up the hill and take all, and the long-projected bombing-range would come into being. Like some hungry lichen which sprawls over the rim of its proper bed and eats the whole garden away, the Army sprawled out of the edge of Crocksford and ate its way steadily into the heath. Down there lived those young soldiers who came clattering round Cedarwood's exquisite polished floors with their loud boots, and prised duelling pistols off the wall to examine their mechanism, and made ugly button-scars down the banisters when his back was turned and his recital in full flow. They came there at eighteen, when willy-nilly they were hauled into this business of defending their country. They grew a lot, and acquired an air of assurance and a degree of smartness, and on the whole seemed to be able to enjoy it in a way. But it stopped short of satisfaction, somehow, like taking half a breath. Rosalba had seen them standing about the street corners in Crocksford sometimes, a little loud, a little lost, as if they had come from nowhere into this not particularly uncomfortable moment, and were going nowhere out of it.

Over there beyond, where she could just see arise from it the minute silver flashing of wings, was the flying-field, where the fabulous Americans were. And between the field and the Folly, wide of the margins of the town, was another big camp site, dilapidated and empty, a perforated scar in the levels of grass.

She sat by the pool for a long time. No one came there, ever. Once today she thought she heard a stirring of the bushes, across the water from her, and looked up quickly in the belief that her solitude was about to be cut in two; but no one appeared there, and the quiet came back greenly, and the stillness. She looked over the edge of the turf into the water, and saw herself dimly mirrored, shadowy as twilight in the hot afternoon. Her face was alien by this light, cold and calm, with a great bland brow and pools for eyes.

Great-Aunt Martine's eyes had never been pools, always jewels; but the forehead was hers, just as in the painting. Rosalba put her finger into the image and sent it shivering away into the grass, circle upon silver circle shattering the disquieting face. Then she went on beyond, into the woods; but she went by the path, and not inch-deep in needles among the belts of pines, and straddling the brambles and bilberries between. She had always been taught to walk on paths.

She walked a long way, but she knew that she would have to turn back at last, for the afternoon was passing, and the south lodge lay directly behind her. Only when it came to the point where she must turn did she understand how much she wanted to go on. Only when the first glimpse of the water rose pale through the branches again, quivering as it had quivered from the reflection of her face as she shattered it, did she assure herself that Great-Aunt Martine hated her. The knowledge rose to the surface of her mind from some deep place where it had lain perfectly understood, perhaps for a long time. She recognised it for truth because there was no puzzling place in their relationship where it did not fit like the single missing piece of a jigsaw puzzle, locking every-thing together.

31

In the rhododendrons she stopped, because there was someone in the pool. First only a head, with wet dark brown hair which flowed over in a heavy, plunging wave as he turned and changed his stroke, then a long, rather thin arm reaching forward beyond the head, and a curved hand taking fierce hold on the green water, then an arched shoulder emerging, and a small bounding fountain of spray, and the upper part of a man's body rising, shaking off water as he stood waist-deep in the pool. As he revealed himself he changed, dwindling, to a lean, string boy, only half filled out yet to match his frame, lumpy at the joints and hollow inside the bones of chest and shoulder. He was smiling, faintly as people smile for pleasure when they are alone, and filling his hands with water as he waded slowly up out of the concrete shallows into the grass, and stretched himself out there in the sun, and flexed his body in its warmth with luxurious sounds of pleasure, half-articulate. Then she heard him laughing gently, a sly, sweet, self-congratulatory laughter confided closely to the grass.

When people believe themselves to be alone they become visible, articulate, disenchanted, like the human stones of the fairy-tales when the spell is broken. Rosalba was the first person who ever really saw Eugene Seale.

CHAPTER TWO:

Eugene

1

WHEN HIS mother first set eyes on him she contemplated the wonder without astonishment, and made the classical comment: 'What an ugly little bastard!' Possibly she was using the words literally, for she had an exact mind, and no one knew the facts of his origin better than she did, though it must be admitted that she herself was not absolutely sure of them. Her later relations with him were all marked by much the same note, though without ill-will; the worst she thought of her offspring was that he was a tedious nuisance, and the most compassion she ever offered him was when, out of his hearing, she pitied him for having blundered in where he had. She knew that he could hardly have chosen a worse attachment.

Afterwards, long afterwards, he could just remember her. Moira Seale: diminuendo through a draggled series of alliances, tending all one way and that downhill, she had kept a kind of heartless, humorous charm, sharp to the taste. She began in a respectable suburban household, decently educated, more than averagely intelligent, and in training for a career in business; but her turning aside into more curious paths was no conventional matter, for which some half-baked man could be blamed comfortably in the family records. Moira did what she liked, and never regretted any of it except the fact that eventually it proved a financial dead-end. She chose men; they did not choose her. At first tentatively, tasting to see if this was what she really wanted, then, discarding the typewriter and the commercial school, wholeheartedly and in a wholesale way; and which of three was Eugene's father she could never be quite sure.

Up to then she had been doing pretty well, but after fate and Eugene caught up with her she was no longer quite so good a bargain, and some sort of continuity began to be a matter of urgency. The trouble was that just when she needed a steady income and a settled life, her version of it began to be less attractive to the people who were expected to foot the bill. Men will stand a great deal, generally speaking, from children, even from children who are not their own; but they tire of it in time, and with each successive trial run the time shortened.

Moira never quite reached the point of popping Eugene under a hedge and walking away, or depositing him in a basket upon some hospitable doorstep; but there were times when she almost considered it. She kept him for no known reason, except that in her whole life yet she had never admitted regret or defeat, and never asked any favour except from an ally. She had no affection for him, except when he began to develop a little of her own personality and to make her laugh. She knew he had a lousy time of it, but after all, she had never invited him. She went her way without regard for him, but without letting him go, and on the end of her train of belongings, themselves diminishing, he went comet-like down the incline from respectable lodgings to soiled single rooms, to dirty hotel apartments and even dingier streets, for the first five and a half years of his young but knowing life.

He learned a lot during these years, and understood a great deal more of it than might have been expected. He got no appreciable respect for either men or women out of the contemplation of those of the species whom he had known, but he found them interesting, and learned in small ways to manipulate them. He had to, for he got no guidance from

Moira. Himself he weighed up each of her dubious partners in his day, and probed to discover which of them hit out when drunk, and which slobbered over him and gave him things, which liked to be thought of as his bleared and temporary father, and which resented the reminder that he existed. His calculations were not always exact, and at least one migrant went to prison for marking him in the face, where it showed; but Moira made herself so neat and scandalised and revengeful on that occasion that she escaped implication, and emerged from the court no more soiled than she already was, and still with a child in tow.

When she got him home, and reflected that she had parted company with a steady earner, if an incalculable temper, she swore at him indifferently, grinned, and said to herself: 'Now why the hell did I do that? Wouldn't I have done better to get them to put you in gaol and turn him loose?'

The next venture was less satisfactory from her point of view, but at least he did not get fighting drunk quite so regularly, and never did worse than slap peevishly at Eugene when his head was bad afterwards. On the other hand, he was not fond of work, and it became necessary for Moira to supplement their income, which she did by a little distasteful cleaning in the mornings, and later a little more congenial shop-lifting among the open market stalls when the crowd was thickest. She was not expert after it ceased to amuse her – Moira could never take much interest in a steady job – and there was a conviction, but it was her first, and she still looked quite nice when got up for an occasion, and escaped lightly. Things were much worse with her when the second case came along, for it was not shop-lifting, but a drunken fight in the street, and another woman lost a great deal of hair in it and not a little blood.

So the authorities, shocked by the conditions in which they found the small Eugene living – though he wondered scornfully where they had spent their lives, to be so horrified about it, for it was rather better than usual after some kind ministrations by the woman from upstairs – decreed very truthfully that Moira was not a fit person to be in charge of him, and took him away to a receiving home to be cleaned up.

He never saw her again. She would never have given him up uncompelled, but she was none the less glad to be rid of him. In a few years he ought to have forgotten her, and perhaps the truth of her did leave him completely; but he retained something, a picture, whether made within his own head or from the fragments of a true memory, which kept her vivid for him all the time that he was growing up. And it was not all of one dull colour, by any means. It could not be said that she had ever in her life been actively kind to him or personally unkind; as far as lay in her power she had ignored him, and that was worse than any contrary storms of affection and detestation. This absolute indifference was what chiefly filled his recollection, and because of it he hated her memory; but the medal had a brighter reverse for which there was less obvious authority. Moira had got a measure of wry fun out of even the less pleasant periods of her life, had laughed a lot, and at the most unexpected moments, and had kept a curious distinction in speech and bearing which scandalised the commentators of her downfall, but strangely reconciled Eugene. If one must for one's satisfaction indulge in all the dirtiest of delights, one may as well do it in the grand manner for good measure; and hate her as he did, he felt tugging at his memory this contrary pull of reluctant admiration.

A boy in a Home of the kind which must be spelled with a capital needs some memories of his own, something to talk about which belongs to none of the others, and can be imparted. The worst of Moira, her indifference to him, could not be shown to other people, it was too hurtful; but the best of her, that lively relish for evil, the taste for grimy adventure, and manipulation of the gullible, about that he presently began to confide tentative anecdotes, and when they were well received, even to boast about her exploits. For this was what he saw as the best of her, having only the standards he had managed to discern for himself in circumstances where a laugh and a gesture of bravado were

36

the only things which could conceivably be seen as admirable.

But it could not be said that it was a good foundation for his later education, or made life with him any easier, or his own stunted prospects any more spacious.

2

From five years old to fourteen, Eugene lived in Homes. They were good Homes in their handicapped fashion, but none of them at all resembled a home. First there was the receiving home, where harassed foster-parents and visiting officials were expected, in theory, to study the individual make-up of each child coming new into this communal life. They never did, because there was never the remotest possibility that they should; there were always twice as many children as had been foreseen, and no chance of reducing the numbers because there was literally nowhere else to put them. To observe individuals was out of the question; one fed and tidied, nursed and bathed masses of children, and that was what it amounted to; and in time one became discouraged, and did it in an automatic fashion, each face becoming a blank because they were so many. If you could get them all up and off to school on time, rush through the necessary house jobs and be ready to feed them again when they returned, bath them, and get them to bed at a reasonable hour, do their mending and begin preparations for the next day before you fell asleep from exhaustion, you had done all that could humanly be expected of anyone.

Then there was the permanent Home. It was an old orphanage building, brightened up as much as possible inside, but the outside was long past brightening. The rooms were not convenient by modern standards, and the sleeping accommodation was in long dormitories not too well supplied with windows. More than fifty children lived there regularly, with, in theory, four adults to be responsible for them, apart from domestic help; but in practice it was seldom that the four appointments were filled, and never for long did they remain so. Three was the most that could be hoped, frequently two had to cope with the situation. Staff came and went bewilderingly, dubious even on arrival, soon overworked to breakdown point in the case of the conscientious, and soon fed up and heading for easier pastures in the case of the less devoted. The only numbers which could be relied upon to remain steady or to rise were the numbers of those strange creatures, the deprived children.

Eugene fed regularly and well, if solidly and plainly, for the first time in his life, and kept regular hours measured by bed-time and school-time, though this feature of the ordered life did not particularly please him. His clothes had to be durable, capable of being passed on to someone else when outgrown, and frequently had been received in the first place after someone else had outgrown them; which was reasonable enough, but made him early aware that in fact they were not his at all. They told him very particularly that the ninth in the second row of small deal lockers fitted in the day room in 1938 was his, his own, for his own belongings; but when he took them at their word and carved his name on it with a table-knife he still incurred mild, exasperated punishment. A few such disillusionments convinced him that they were all liars, and that the only way to deal with them was to lie faster and better than they. For none of them belonged to him, either; it was like the clothes and the lockers, but much worse, that not one of those querulous, capricious, but on the whole, likeable people was in any way his personal possession.

He went to a local school, like ordinary children, but he went as one member of a crocodile, with a fierce little foster-mother in her teens scurrying alongside; and because mass-living forces order even in things which privately can be done in a cheerfully random fashion, he soon extended his bitter dislike to include all manifestations of order, and he was always the one who loosed hands and ran in the gutter. Then she made him walk hand in hand with her, and held on to him tightly, so that all he could do was push or drag her and himself out of line. She released her hand to box his ears, being tired and at the end of her patience, and he ran into the road. But there was no end there. He was scolded and admonished upon a higher plane, even punished, but the only difference it made was that he showed a mockingly dutiful front before her threatening face thereafter, and played as much hell as possible when she was not looking at him. And the others admired his nerve, and began to enjoy the daily entertainment, and even to copy his tactics.

It was the same in everything, because everything was the same. Yet he liked her. He would have stopped his antics fast enough if he could have walked hand in hand with her from his own choice, and as a mark of her preference.

By the time he was eight years old he had become a headache to everyone inside the Home, and in another two years his influence extended even outside it, to half the officials of the county, including the probation officer. He was a natural rebel, of no sunny and hot-tempered kind, but with a dour persistence and bitter daring which made them say to one another in the moments of worst discouragement: 'That kid will come to a bad end!' He stole, he absconded, he fought, he swore, he acquired and propagated the most imaginative of filthy language, and he defied authority with a ferocity which terrified.

Yet there were curious points about his delinquency. He was avidly copied by weaker vessels, but this flattery signally failed to move him to anything but contempt, and he discouraged it with tongue and arm upon all occasions. He himself never copied anyone consciously, he had a fixed aversion to imitation whether of good qualities or bad, and to hold up an example to him was to make it impossible for him to follow it. The only aim of his being at this time was to be exclusively himself, since no one in the world belonged to him, and therefore there was no one who could be permitted to contribute.

It was also noticeable to an overworked but by no means

blind foster-father that when, in spite of his scorn, his crimes were copied by lesser lights they were almost always meaner in nature, as well as less efficient. They stole occasional pennies from one another, and spent them understandably on sweets; but he stole a symbolic shilling from the office, almost under the matron's nose, and gave away the proceeds to the small fry, which was a less usual reaction. Not that there was anything of the Robin Hood in his make-up. He gave his stolen favours contemptuously, not for love, not for admiration, but rather as if to eat them himself would have choked him. The fact was that he would not be beholden to anyone for anything if he could help it.

'No one has ever done anything for me,' he said, 'nobody! That's all right with me, I can do without them.'

And he tried to, and bore a more inward grudge because, although they would not or could not belong to him, still they would not let him get away. That was the reason for his many attempts to abscond; and even there he did it in a different way. Some older boys when they ran away left emotional notes saying that if they were followed they would do away with themselves; but if Eugene left a message, and he usually did, it was invariably to request them curtly not to jump to any melodramatic conclusions, because he was quite capable of getting along on his own. Other boys, when they tired of the experiment, either came back of themselves or walked into some police station and tearfully requested to be fetched home. Eugene never came back of his own will, never voluntarily gave away his location; he had always to be fetched, frequently kicking viciously.

Yet he was not vicious, and no matter how he bedevilled their overburdened lives, his foster-parents never made the mistake of thinking him so. Whoever bullied the littler ones, or played stupid practical jokes which ended in bruises and danger of broken bones, Eugene never did. In time he even came to avoid lies as much as he could. It was true that these were rather negative virtues; he took no kindly responsibility for the smaller children if he would not torment them, and he disliked having to cover himself by means of lies because they represented in some way a concession to the enemy, an admission of fear of punishment. He had no cynicism yet, only a fierce and tender arrogance which pulled him up short of certain actions because they did not seem to fit in with the person he wanted to be. They offended his sense of his own dignity – they were in bad taste, though the phrase would have been Greek to him.

The probation officer did what he could with him, but he was in his company only occasionally, for limited times, and of what use was that to Eugene? He liked him, because he was young, and not forever jawing; but he had already seen through the myth that any of these people really cared about him in a personal way. He was just one among fifty in this place, and the one of whom the whole lot of them would most gladly be rid. They talked about being in the position of parents to him; that was the bunk, they were paid to do the job, and when a better-paid job offered somewhere else they would take it like a shot. He'd seen it happen already.

So they got nowhere. There was only one person who pierced for a time the shell of cold distrust which separated Eugene from his fellows, and after his going the breach he had made healed very quickly, and made a thicker place in the armour, like all scars. He was a young schoolmaster at the Council school. He taught art, two short periods every week, and taught it more imaginatively than is possible in such conditions except to the very artistic; and he made the discovery that Eugene had colour and line in him, and avoided by instinct the small boy's usual limited unconventionality in looking at the familiar. Eugene really saw, with the fresh impact of a universal newness; and with the irreconcilable determination which vexed most of his elders, he drew what he saw, and not what he thought he was expected to see. Indeed, where he was sure of what he was expected to see he went out of his way to avoid it. It displeased everyone else; why should it suddenly please this man? But it did, and the astonishment offered an opening no one else had ever enjoyed with him. The first connection between Eugene and a fellow human creature was established.

It lasted two years, and was beginning to draw his energies together into the channel they needed, when it was broken. The young man married; that was bad enough, but worse followed. Marriage is an expensive business, and one must consider one's future more seriously when one has a wife, and a baby on the way. The young man looked for a better-paid job, with prospects, found one, and took it gladly. It was not to be wondered at, but for Eugene it set him with all the rest, the ones who talk about parental responsibility one day and dash off the next to make sure of an extra ten shillings a week or more emoluments on the other side of the county. He shut the door on him, left off drawing, and made up his mind not to be taken in like that a second time.

No one else ever managed to do anything with him, though they tried their best. Dimly through the ceaseless flow of the day's routine they did perceive the eddies of other and more obscure currents, in which such unlucky little creatures as Eugene drifted; but there literally was not time to go aside and reach a hand to them; it would only have meant leaving the others to drown.

'He isn't a bad boy,' said the foster-father with conviction. 'I can tell you that. In some ways, as you say, he's the worst of the lot, but you can take it from me that's because of qualities which would just as well mark him out as the best if things had run a bit differently. I'm not saying even in other conditions we might not have failed with him; but in these conditions we never had a chance to succeed.'

So they gave up hope of him, though they never gave up trying.

At fourteen he left school, and went to work in a foundry. He had no theories about what he wanted to do, so they found him the job, and he made no objections. Not having realised even yet the mainspring of his being, they were very much surprised by his complacency. He, for his part, was not concerned in the least with the means of his escape, provided he did escape, and would have embraced any job they cared to offer him, rather than prolong his stay with them by a month. A job meant only one thing, the means of independence. They found him a respectable home as lodging, and he bore with their regular visits to him there as best he could, holding his breath and containing his animosity because they still might, if they would, order him back into the Home. He worked with no great enthusiasm, but without complaint, and found his world enlarged, and suddenly peopled with men who professed no parental interest in him, but treated him like any other boy, and thought nothing of swearing at him or boxing his ears if he offended, without having to invoke a by-law or quote higher authority. He liked them; his footing with them was easy and equal. His landlady also was middle-aged, comfortable without fuss, warm without presumption. He began to take a sudden interest in human creatures, against whom his hand had been set for years; for in contradiction to all his former observations they were various, motley, complicated, full of unexplored potentialities.

The war was just over, and men were coming back browned with the suns of many strange countries, speaking a lingua franca laced with Italian, German, Dutch and Russian words, even smelling differently from the people whom duty or luck had kept at home. Floods of colour and hope broke out on the world in the same years, everything flamed and scintillated and was new. Eugene on his own began to paint.

It happened quite spontaneously, but before long someone noticed it, and encouraged him, not too parentally, to begin work seriously at evening school; and soon, in the hurrying way of things, he was going twice a week to art classes, and once to English, and his ears were full of words and his eyes of colours and characteristics and qualities. He read avidly, he drew and painted incessantly, and all the passion in him, all the energy and restlessness, began to drain to one deep channel, and flow into daylight.

Art is creative. When you are being utterly yourself, just as ruthlessly and singly as ever, by painting an instantaneous vision of other people, you no longer have to express it in more damaging ways – and infinitely less satisfactory – by stealing, and absconding, and flouting authority. What is authority to you, that you should go aside one pace to offend it, any more than you would to appease it?

But a few years change things drastically, and sometimes in the least expected ways. At eighteen, in an England at peace, two things happened to Eugene. The county ceased to have an official responsibility for him, and the country took him over. At eighteen the young are called up into the armed forces. Eugene's brushes went into retirement, and Eugene into uniform, and in due time into the camp near Crocksford spinney, some miles from the portentous shadow of Rose's Folly.

3

In the ultimate bull and boredom, the uselessness and frustration and resentment of Army life during even a dubious peace, an imagination, an eye for colour and form and quality and character, and a passionate desire for individuality and self-expression have no part whatever. All of these things which he possessed for good Eugene had to shelve, and that meant the amputation of about two-thirds of his personality. What remained was not the most presentable part of him, and looked like being of little use to anyone, even himself; but a boy must live with what he has. Only the cunning, astute, bitter and daring enemy of society could help him here; and back he came with a vengeance, the only remaining outlet for all that uneasy energy, the kid who had reacted fiercely against order and form which he felt to be artificial, who had bluffed, and lied, and fought his way through the warp and woof of it once already against the odds. A little more developed now, a little sicker of the whole business, a little less scrupulous about his methods; a profitless conscript, slippery, insolent and not unsuccessful in his passive resistance to the whole enforced pattern of his life.

If it produced anything, anything at all, it would be

different. But it produces nothing. It smooths things out, qualities you had, possibilities you had. It goes on and on every day getting more tedious in its artificial assumption of busyness. People work damned hard thinking up things to give you to do, things that don't need doing, and then thankfully put the next lot to undo 'em again. And all the while the things you could be doing, the things you want to be doing, the things your hands and your heart ache to do, the things the world wants and needs that you should do, are waiting, growing fainter and slighter and dustier – and not getting done. While you cut grass with small sickles to make the job last all morning, because it's no longer allowed to force you to church parade!

If it had not been for the itching of his hands Eugene might not have felt the stupidity of the business quite so much. Those who could relax into the moment did not so badly, for they were not an uncongenial set of boys, on the whole, and there was a certain amount of fun to be wrung out of the passing day. But that worked only if your mind was willing to go to sleep, and even the placid got thoroughly browned off at the first stir of its awakening. And Eugene was not placid. To enjoy as the bare skin enjoys the sun would never in any case have been enough for him, and there was only one kind of energetic enjoyment to be had. It lay in developing to the full the old acid pleasure of outwitting and outfacing authority; and where the penalties were more, and the scruples less, he took a new delight in it. He fought them for every hour of the time they had forced him to give up to them, and felt a little soothed whenever he could wrest back any part of it which was theirs, and put it to other uses, no matter how sterile.

There were no rules in this game, except never to involve any of the other fellows. The odds against him were greater than ever, so lies and sidestepping were fair weapons. Any fatigue you could dodge without doubling somebody else's portion was a point won in the game. Fancy-work like sergeant-baiting and goading of junior officers was for special occasions.

45

When he slipped the leash out on exercise for the first time, and slid himself sidelong into the woods under the lea of the Folly, through the wire on to forbidden ground, that was a triumph. The watch-tower and its quiet pool pleased him, silvering over the exaltation he felt at getting out of that long grind in the sun. He stripped off his clothes and swam and basked the afternoon away undisturbed, painting pictures with his mind from the shadowed view-point over the wide valley. It was easy to skid back from cover into the hot, tired, blasphemous straggle of young men coming back to camp, for the tower commanded a view of the whole stretch of country, and for part of the time of their small martyrdom he had watched them sweating their hearts out. He was so pleased with his manoeuvre that he repeated it, after a reasonable interval lest it should become too obvious.

This time he almost walked into the open by the pool without looking, and only dropped to ground behind the screen of rhododendrons just in time to escape being seen. There was a girl sitting by the pool's tidy rim, only a kid, about sixteen or seventeen, in a grey tweed skirt and a shirt blouse; funny, old-fashioned-looking kid with her yellow hair done up in a bun hard on the back of her head. She'd looked up once, quickly, when the leaves rustled, and he'd got a glimpse of her face, but she lowered it again as soon as he lay still, and then he could see only her profile. Maybe if he waited a while she'd go away. He was in no hurry, he could afford to wait.

He watched her, because she was a human creature, and full of outlines and shades which were new to him, but mostly because he was waiting for her to go away. That, at least, was how it began, but soon he was watching her only because she was beautiful. No one knows precisely what makes a person beautiful, even to one pair of eyes, but the assembled lines of this girl, as she leaned on one wrist steadily looking at her mirrored face in the burnished green water, grew into something he saw as beauty. Spare lines, and faint colours, but the effect was not faint. And why should she, so manifestly tamed, move suddenly and simply as wild animals move, like a silently pouncing cat, and stab out with her finger-tips the image of that faintly-coloured, large-browed, austere bud of a face?

When she went away he found that he would have liked her to stay a little longer; but she walked on into the wood with quick, long steps, and was lost to sight. So he bathed; that was what he'd come for, wasn't it? Not to wonder about some girl he didn't know, but whose face was somehow very distantly, very dreamily familiar, with the kind of familiarity one never manages to trace.

The sun was hot, and the water smooth and cool to his body, and he stayed in it a long time, and then came in to shore sleekly washed in body and mind both, and lay in the turf warming the one and indulging the other with thoughts of the boys route-marching 'at ease', God help them, in the same rays which touched his nakedness so enchantingly. When he was dry, and had done laughing at his success and their dutiful stupidity, he put on his clothes again, somewhat reluctantly, and was just combing his wet brown hair when the bushes rustled again. He swung round open-mouthed with the comb poised in his hand, and there across the water from him was the girl, just parting the rhododendrons deliberately with both hands, and stepping out on to the grass. She held herself a little nervously, but with authority, to which he must always in any manifestation be an enemy. And her face, which gazed at him now directly and unwaveringly, was strangely divided between reluctance and indignation, so that he could not guess what in the world she was going to say.

What she did say, in a small, chill voice a shade higher than either she or he had expected was:

'What are you doing here? Don't you know that you are trespassing? This part of the grounds is private.'

And then he knew who she was.

CHAPTER THREE:

Two Lost Children

1

THE MOMENT she had spoken Rosalba wished that she had let well alone, and gone quietly away. She had nerved herself to wait and challenge him not altogether because it was her manifest duty, but because she knew it was a duty of which she was afraid, and therefore all the more one she must do. She was afraid of a kind of encounter to which her tongue was unused, with a kind of young man as strange to her as an inhabitant of the moon: and the moment she had said the obvious thing she knew she had been right to shrink from it, because nothing could come of it to do either of them justice. He would be insolent and she stiff and stupid, because they were both nervous and both at a disadvantage. How was that possible?

He had risen, slowly, searching her face as he moved with wide-open, considering brown eyes under thick, straight brows, weighing and measuring her. When he answered her the words seemed to have nothing whatever to do with the look, and in no way to disturb it.

'I was bathing,' he said with deliberation, 'and now I'm drying my hair. And the answer to the second question is, yes, thank you, I know.'

Rosalba flushed, and felt ugly in her awareness of it, though the colour which rose to her cheeks mantled like the heart of a tea-rose. And his look did not change, only narrowed and tilted a little as if to dispose a shade more particularly the angle of vision.

'I haven't hurt the pool,' he said, 'the fish will survive.'

'But you are trespassing,' said Rosalba, 'and I should be glad if you would go away, please. This part of the grounds—'

'I know,' he said, tartly smiling, '– is not shown to visitors.'

The allusion was not within her knowledge. 'No, it isn't. I am Rosalba Rose,' she explained, anxious to present her own credentials, because she was scrupulously honest by nature and training. 'I live here.'

'I know,' said Eugene.

'You ought not to be here. If my great-aunt knew—'

'Presently, presently!' said Eugene, deliberately settling the wet thatch of his hair, and a little reluctantly deflecting the intent if not the level of his gaze.

'– and at least look as if you heard me!' she said with indignation, mounting a second and hotter flush upon the rosy receding tide of the first.

'Oh, don't be impatient,' said Eugene, grinning. 'I'll go – I haven't done any damage that I know of, but if you find a few blades of grass broken you can send in the bill to my sergeant. You could get me into a hell of a lot more trouble that way than by just running to your great-aunt, if that's what you want.'

'I don't want to get you into trouble. I merely—'

'I know! You're only acting after your kind, and looking after the family property like a good little Rose!'

'It isn't exactly family property,' said Rosalba punctiliously. 'It belongs to the National Trust, only this part isn't shown to the public.'

'Thanks, but if it's mine I don't need to be shown, and I don't have to get off it, either. Oh, don't worry,' he said wearily, seeing the faint embarrassed anger quicken in her, so ineptly, so incapably. 'Don't worry, I'm going almost any minute now – I've got to, or I'll be missed, and there'll be hell to pay. I'm here instead of on duty, see? You could get me into trouble easy by just getting your old woman to pass on the facts to the right people. And what's more, I shall come here again – when I like. Get her to tell 'em that, too. You and your damned family! Give you my name and number, if you like! Save the sergeant asking a lot of questions! Anything I owe you for the use of the water you can take out that way. If you want interest on it you can tell him I've been here before when I was supposed to be out foot-slogging with the rest. He'll be very interested.'

When she was looked at for long she dwindled; so did he; so do most of us, being human and limited by so many and such distorting considerations. She was only half articulate, he thought, and something of the wild grace he had found in the first glimpse of her, something of the beauty, was already a little shrunken with too near staring. And yet when you shut a candle within horn the flame is not changed, only obscured, and people confronting other people, even those they know, have to some extent shut themselves into a horn lantern. He was sorry he had said half the things he had said, but grateful that he had not said more. And yet that clutching at unfamiliar dignity was itself only another sheet of horn. I wonder, he thought, that we can see each other at all. But whatever had happened to her, she remained visible.

'Great-Aunt Martine would know what to say,' thought Rosalba, 'but I don't. Why am I such a failure at something so simple?' But as soon as the thought took that particular shape she knew it was a mistake, for this was not at all simple. It was the most complex thing in the world, two people without common ground or common language, alien as oil and water, meeting without ill-will but without the possibility of parting unhurt. No one ever wants to hurt another person – does he? Is it possible to want it? And yet from almost every contact of two of these indescribably lonely little planets of people arise shocks, scars, deflections, as unavoidable as they are undesigned.

The moment she stopped thinking it was easier. She said

in quite a different voice, interested and a little shy: 'Why are you looking at me like that?'

'Because you're beautiful,' said Eugene unexpectedly; and if he had said it in another way, conscious of the impact of the words, she would have gone back so far into her shell as to become quite invisible; but he said it vexedly, almost resentfully, as if he didn't like being put off the track of his anger by being forced to give a straight answer to a straight question; and to underline his honesty he suddenly scowled like an ill-tempered child, and said: 'Stick to the point!'

'There's nothing more to be said,' began Rosalba defensively, and then added; 'Except that I – of course I never thought of getting you into trouble. It was only that you had no right to be here.'

'All right, I'm going!' He jammed on his cap at a risky angle over the still glistening hair, and abruptly turned away from her to the downhill path. Rosalba felt suddenly the chill of the aura he had sensed about her, and knew by that shiver that some warmth was withdrawing. The pool did nothing day after day but reflect the sky and the trees. And being a soldier in the environs of Crocksford had never seemed to her to be much fun. People who have never had much fun themselves are not necessarily the ones who want to snatch the last crumbs of it from other people.

'You can come again,' she said quickly. And when he turned in some surprise and stared at her with a young, boy's look instead of the disconcerting one which had made her curious, she went on hesitantly: 'I don't see any harm if you come here to swim sometimes. At least, *I* shan't make any complaint, but you'd have to be careful in case someone else saw you.'

'I'm used to that,' he said with a grin.

She thought, but did not say: 'And yet I sat watching you, and you never knew'; remembering how she had peeped through the bushes at his lean boy's body stretched in the grass, and told herself firmly that she must wait and tackle him, that he was a trespasser and had no right to be there at all. She, who was now begging him to consider the place his own – but carefully, for his own sake. The chill had not receded; she felt it hanging upon his going, only a breath of it yet in her face.

'You're a queer girl,' he said thoughtfully, and turned about and came a step back towards her; there was no hurry yet, he could afford to wait a little while. 'What changed your mind?'

She was silent, having no idea of anything in the least intelligent to say, and being unwilling to cover her uncertainty with chatter. He came closer, and pulling out a long stem of grass stuck it between his teeth, and over the green revolving plume regarded her steadily. Then he said: 'What's it like, being a Rose? Is it worth it? I never talked to anyone like you before.'

'I'm not the right person to tell you,' she said queerly. 'I'm not a proper Rose.'

'You're not?'

'No, I'm a graft that didn't take very well.' You say these things, she reflected, marvelling, only to people you will never see again; and the cold wind in her mind sharpened, and she shivered a little. But suddenly the boy smiled, quite a new, quite a changed smile, timidly eager, anxiously kind, and the shape of his sulky mouth quivered before he spoke, and softened to a wry shape of shyness, blazingly unexpected.

'I'm illegitimate, too,' he said awkwardly. 'It's not your fault.'

Something happened then inside the explosion of shock which went off within Rosalba. Most reactions are so obvious; the ready gasp of indignation rose so promptly, her cheeks flamed so conventionally, and what mattered was something so different, so far removed from any injury to her feelings. What mattered was there with him. It was the first real moment of crisis in her life, and if she had failed to recognise it her life would have been changed; but things fell into place in time, beautifully, with an adult gentleness, and the genuine reaction, the one which was not obvious, the one which was not tethered to her own self-esteem, gave her power to swallow the gasp and the words which were struggling to follow it, to soften the blazing blush with a gradual, sweet and warming smile, and to say with only an understandable stammer:

'It would have been better for me that way, I think. Then I wouldn't even have had to try to be a proper Rose. But I'm only the result of what they call a misalliance. My mother wouldn't have been so much hated, you see, if – if she hadn't married him.'

He blushed darkly red, but it was all right; the horrible hurt of embarrassment had only grazed him; and when she thought in horror of the things she was saying, it was only necessary to repeat firmly to herself: 'You'll never have to see him again, so what does it matter?'

'I made an awful mistake,' he said miserably, 'you're *not*—'

'Yes, I am, only in a different way. It wasn't a mistake, it's quite the same thing.'

It was all very extraordinary. Never had either of them, probably, made a deliberate and desperate gesture of kindness like that before; there had never been anyone in need of it from either of them. And even if the queer little gift he had made her had turned out to be quite the wrong shape, still she was clutching it very firmly, and wouldn't let him take it away again with any apologies. What she had given him in exchange, and dimly he knew the colours of it, was a piece torn out of her family conscience, a thing she had certainly never laid rough hands on until now. But still she was saying to herself over and over: 'You won't have to see him again!' and wondering why it didn't seem to do any good.

'I shall have to go,' said Eugene, suddenly in panic to get away.

'I hope it will be all right. I hope you won't get caught.'

'I shall manage all right,' he said, edging away from her down the slope of grass. There had been all this time a few feet of green water between them; her reflection quivered in it, very gently, touched by a freshening breeze.

'If you want to come again, please do. No one else ever comes here, no one but me. You won't be disturbed.'

'What? – encouraging trespassers?' he said, with the old bold grin and the faint, distinct echo of the old antagonism.

'You won't do any harm. It's different now I know you a little. And I told you, I'm not a proper Rose—'

He was already in the green aisle of the trees, shadowy under pine and spruce darkness, withdrawing backwards by slow steps, and ready to turn and go as soon as the thread of speech between them, already grown so tenuous and delicate, finally snapped. His eyes fixed on her, wide eyes in the shadow.

'You're more like one than any of the others, anyhow!' he said, leaping desperately out of character; and bolting back as abruptly into his accustomed self, span round and scurried down the slope as if all the sergeants in Crocksford were after him.

2

All the day she soothed herself perseveringly but ineffectively: 'You'll never see him again!' and wondered why it didn't allay the racing of her nerves. Martine observed at supper that she was extremely distrait tonight, and Mrs. Fenton, the housekeeper, who was also Martine's maid, and of her generation, hazarded that she had caught a slight chill from too long walking in the woods after the cool of the evening had begun. Warned by these speculations, Rosalba contained her brittle restlessness as well as she could, and waited for the echoes of her own treason to subside within her; but they did not subside.

She went early to her room, acquiescing for her own purposes in the supposition that she might have taken cold. There was a climbing rose under her window, cream flushed with pink, one half-open flower smoothing its cheek against the sill like an affectionate cat. She remembered his anguished compliment, thrown so inexpertly at the last minute: 'You're more like one than any of the others, anyhow!' And he had said she was beautiful, said it in quite a firm way, crossly stating what he saw to be an obvious fact, as it might have been of a glass jug or a landscape. Was she indeed beautiful? Could even a queer individual taste find her so? She peered between her framing hands into the dusk of the mirror, and her own treasons looked back at her through the doubtful, astonished face.

'If I saw him again,' she thought, 'perhaps I could forget the whole stupid business more easily. I was surprised into saying all those things, but they didn't mean to him what they did to me. If I met him again for a few minutes, just casually, I should probably find he'd already stopped thinking about them at all – of course he has, why should he remember them? Then I could forget about it, too.'

That was why she went to the watch-tower next day; but of course he didn't come. Soldiers have a lot of duty time to put in, and even if he happened to be free some part of the day she could hardly expect to hit by chance on the very same hour. And the next day it rained, and the next, and the next after that she began to go to the tower again, and Martine, watching her step quicken at the garden gate of the south lodge, suddenly called her back.

She was smiling, her old eyes narrowed spitefully upon her unsatisfactory kinswoman; before there was anything to suspect, a breath, an accidental word, even a warming of the blood, her senses, quick with jealousy, were fingering forward to where it would come to life, waiting to crush it out.

'Where are you going?' She smoothed and smoothed with her mummified hand at the head of the cat in her lap, and the yellow canopy of the deck-chair jaundiced her face, and dulled her blue-white hair.

Rosalba lied: 'Up to the house.' It came easily, reminding her that she was not a proper Rose. She looked back straightly against the threat of the steel-sharp eyes, and lied with a light, opaque calm and an answering smile. 'Cedarwood is going to rearrange the big case of miniatures in the gallery, and he asked me to help him.'

'You didn't tell me about it.'

'I thought you knew. He always consults you first.' And he had done so on this occasion, but he had not said that he wanted Rosalba's help. This, also, she knew; but best she knew that Great-Aunt Martine's solicitor was expected, and therefore that whatever checks might be made on her truthfulness, the only one she feared would not be made today.

'I borrowed from the library,' said Martine deliberately, 'a manuscript book of Richard Rose's railway journal. I wish you would return it for me.'

'Of course! Is it in your room?' She fetched it, composedly. Every time their eyes met she knew now that they were at war. From this day everything was fair, and anything; lies were not meant to be believed, only to barricade them apart.

She went up the long, long walk to the Folly, and delivered the manuscript book. Cedarwood had his head in the case of miniatures between conducting parties, and hardly looked at her when she gave him the book, or paid any further attention to her as she stood beside him assembling words for what she had to say.

'Cedarwood, will you do something for me?' She had never really looked at him as a human being before, he had been like one of the apocryphal wood figures on the organ, significant but static; but now he was someone who had to decide whether to help her or betray her, and all his looks, all his gestures, had become momentous. When he spread his hand at her in a hushing fashion until he had decided on the best light for Nicholas Rose the Younger, of Bredington, she held her breath.

His beard jerked at her as he turned his head, satisfied. 'Well, now, what am I to do?'

'Not a great thing,' she said, but found it suddenly a very great thing, because she was asking him to do it for no reason, for no reason at all. The boy would not be there; she had nothing so positive, nothing so prosaic, as a rendezvous with him; she didn't even know his name. The barricade of lies was beginning to rise protectively about nothing, about a wreath of mist, about a sigh, like the hedge the villagers built round the cuckoo.

'Oh, no,' she said, 'it's hopeless!'

'Very few things,' said Cedarwood, in his calmly literal style, 'are hopeless. I don't ask any questions. Why should I? What I do, that's something grown in my piece of ground. This grows in yours. I don't ask any questions about what you've planted. It's likely I might be let to see how it looks when it grows, but that's privilege, not right.' All his parables had method about them, though she had sometimes let them slip past her ears and thought him a little mad.

'I wanted to go somewhere else today,' she said, 'and I didn't want Great-Aunt Martine to know. So I told her you had asked me to help with the miniatures. If she asks you about it, will you tell her I did that?'

'Why should she ask me?' he said, unsurprised but thoughtful.

'Because she doesn't trust me.'

'Could she be right there?' he wondered, with a sudden smile.

'In a way, yes. I didn't tell her the truth. In a way, no, because where I'm going is my business, and she won't let it be. You said it was in my garden. Well, you have a right to keep people out of your garden sometimes, haven't you? And if you put up a notice, and they trespass just the same? Nobody *likes* using barbed wire. Why not – couldn't we just say I've turned the signpost round, instead?' She watched him ruminating, and did not fear him, but suddenly she feared that it was all for nothing, that nothing would come of it. 'It isn't as if there was anything to show, even,' she said. 'It didn't grow at all yet. Maybe it never will.'

'Well, you can take good care of it, and see,' he observed placidly.

'Will you tell her I was here with you? All afternoon?'

'How if she follows you herself?'

'She won't,' said Rosalba, 'she has some business to

57

attend to. Will you tell her what I asked you?'

'I won't tell her anything else,' he said, 'at any rate.' And that was enough, coming from him; who could lay better smoke-screens than he? If he chose to think that more honest than the flat lie and the bricked-up stare, that was his business. He wouldn't positively state that the girl had been with him, but he would deploy St. Michael and all angels across Martine's questing, hungry vision in a dazzling procession, blinding her to the small manoeuvrings of mere people.

Rosalba thanked him breathlessly, suddenly full of the confidence she had lacked before, and ran like a hare along the dwindling track from the gate of the courtyard, ran and ran without tiring, as if she knew that the hour of possibility was already slipping past. She ran to the coppice of pine and spruce, and through it, and out into sunlight, the first full sunlight for three days. The pool was bright with it; even the yellowish-grey brickwork so quaintly built into improbable broken columns beyond had a glitter of moist new brilliance about it, as if it had bathed since noon.

He was there, sitting on one of the artistic scatterings of wall, his elbows on his knees, and his gaze fixed critically on something spread out upon the grass between his large boots. When he heard the soft slither of her feet in the needles he looked up quickly, and he was already sure what he would see, for he looked up with an eager smile, half starting from his place, and then stooping again to snatch up the small sheet of paper at which he had been staring. His eyes opened very wide upon her, large brown eyes flecked with suggestions of gold and green like pebbles under sunlit water; his mouth had stopped being sulky, and was wide and young and pleased, like a child's when it is busy opening a birthday parcel, and fairly sure already of what will be found inside.

'I thought you were never coming! I was here yesterday, and the day before, too, but I couldn't stay above a few minutes.'

'It isn't easy for me,' she said, exactly as if the thing had been arranged between them. 'But it rained – you must have got wet—'

'It stopped once, in the afternoon. I nipped up then, but no luck!' They stood close together, looking at each other in an intent, odd way, while she regained her breath. Now that she saw him again, unsummoned but obedient like this, she knew that everything was tremulous with change, now, while they stood there, that henceforth nothing could be relied upon to be what it seemed. She was frightened; almost she would have gone back if she could, but it was already too late. The page was turning, lay down already upon the old, offered an unknown, insecure future without maps. She looked at Eugene with large, dark-blue eyes of panic, and he did not at all understand.

'Look, I brought you something!' He put the square of thick cartridge-paper into her hands, where she regarded it for a moment through a blindness of shock, and saw nothing. 'I'm sorry I had to fold it, but I had to get it in my pocket. I didn't want anybody to see it, and ask such damn-fool questions as they do. I tried to fold the creases out again when I got it here, but they don't come out properly.' The numbness was just beginning to leave her eyes, and lines to appear upon the paper before them. 'It isn't absolutely right,' he said with authority, 'but it's something. I think it's true – only a little speechless— Do you know what I mean?'

Her own face seemed to grow out of the white paper; she knew the lines of it, and each was in its place as she knew it, but they added up to something in the sum which she had never seen before. It was only a pencil sketch, a hard medium with its grey and whiteness and its denial of depth, but the oval face was there rounded and plastic within the spare strokes, gazing at her with measured wonder from large, lucid eyes, the flower astonished at its own unpromising seed. She sensed the lifting of the fine lofty bones under the skin, and the fresh moulding of the mouth lengthened consideringly, thoughtful of all things without, wondering at all things within.

'Do you like it?' asked Eugene directly.

'I'm not like that,' she said. 'You're making a mistake.'

'I don't think so. Why, it's like you, isn't it?'

'Yes— No, only the features. But if you think I'm like that–' She looked up at him helplessly, and suddenly she began to cry, because it had already begun to grow, and still she knew it was hopeless. He looked alarmed and abashed, even a little disgusted, but he grinned, too, and put his arm briskly round her shoulders, and shook her gently.

'Here, damn it, if that's how you feel about it I'll tear it up.' But already she knew enough of him to know that he wouldn't do anything of the kind, and would fight tooth and nail anyone who contemplated as much as marking it. 'If you aren't the limit!' he said. 'I did it from memory, and it's the best thing I did since I came here, and one of the best things I ever did – and you take one look at it and start to cry! What's the matter with it, for heaven's sake?'

'Nothing! It's beautiful! I didn't mean— You see,' she explained carefully, drying her eyes, 'there's too much in it – something you won't find if you're looking here for it. I don't want you to waste your time. I want everything to be honest with us.'

'Then you'd better consider as hard as you're telling me to,' said Eugene. 'We've got to talk, anyhow, you don't know the first thing about me, not even my name.'

'No, I don't. And my name's all you know of me, and that isn't much.'

'How long can you stay?'

'I'm supposed to be helping the custodian, up at the house. I should think I could stay an hour or so.'

'Good, then let's get out of sight, just in case anyone comes. The open side of the tower's all right, and there are plenty of stones to sit on. I've got a lot to tell you,' he said as he turned her towards the fluted brick archway, and led her forward with careful, unaccustomed gentleness in the circle of his thin arm. And so he had, everything he'd been aching to get off his chest for years and years, about the muck that had been made of his early life by Moira and his unknown father and all the other disgusting echoes of fatherhood, and the much he'd gone on making of it for himself since; about the Home that wanted to be a home, and hadn't a chance, about the things which had been his and not his, his with strings on, about the way he'd hated all the people he had wanted to love, because they hadn't time to be loved, much less love him in return. Not that any of it would ever be phrased like that. The tale would be pretty lame, full of bony little facts with no flesh on them, but she had to have it. He'd done pretty well everything it was wrong to do, except get anything on false pretences, and he wasn't going to start now.

But his mind was not like hers, did not probe ahead into the nature of the thing he wanted to get, only moved step by step on a sure-footed instinct, not quavering about considerations which might never arise. He was male, he didn't examine motives. He knew only that this was very important, and that he had to do it right; he hadn't looked very closely what it was. So he was considerably the more surprised of the two when by one consent they halted a moment in the sudden warmth of the archway and looked at each other desperately, and suddenly he said in a low, startled voice: 'I never was this near to anyone like you before!' and more suddenly bent his head the little way it had to go to meet hers, and abruptly kissed her.

3

That was a thing which didn't happen again for some time; it came a little prematurely, that was all, and in a while they almost forgot it again, and even when it happened it started no chord vibrating. Only it made it clear that a phase was ended, and wiped away as irrelevant all considerations of what kind of person he was, or what kind was she. From then on they were of no labelled kinds at all, but two people, each as unique as a solitary crystal of snow, by complete consent sharing their two contrasted lives, in defiance of circumstances which had laid their courses parallel and decreed that they should never meet.

'You could paint here,' said Rosalba, with a sweep of her arm about the empty ground-floor room of the tower. 'Why not? The light's quite good until evening, and if it's fine you could be outdoors, and then it would last even longer. And no one ever comes here but me.'

'I haven't got any brushes, or anything. And the time would always be so limited.' But his eyes had brightened at the thought.

'But it would be something. I've got all the stuff I used at school. It isn't what you need, really, but they liked us to have good materials. I can bring it here; it's never used now. And we could buy more if you need it.'

'With your money?'

'Don't be angry so easily. What I have could buy brushes, it would never buy anything bigger. Don't you know I'm penniless?'

'I know you'll inherit all that's left when the old woman goes,' he said, deflected from what bound to what separated, as easily, as fatally, as she. His face always darkened and closed when he thought of the barriers.

'That's not much now. Don't forget the Folly isn't ours, nor most of the land.'

'There's still two of the lodges – big enough for a block of flats, both of 'em. And how much a year? It keeps plenty of sapphires and diamonds hanging all over her.'

She saw from another level, and said indignantly: 'It's very little, when you consider what we used to have.'

'Oh, I know! You're the new poor! Well, I know more about the old poor. I come from quarters where your few measly pounds a year would buy up the livings of a hundred families. Don't talk to me about your kind of poverty.'

'But who knows,' said Rosalba, drawing back from the borders of anger more readily than he, because he had lived near them all his life, and all her life she had been taught to avoid them, 'who knows if any of it will be left by the time it's supposed to come to me? There may be nothing there to come. And at any rate, we were talking about your painting.'

'You'd still come?' he asked anxiously.

'Of course!'

'Even though I'm not always – what you've been used to?'

'What I've been used to is loneliness. And – I don't know what word to use – can you say falseness? I don't want you to be what I've been used to.'

He groped after her hand, and pressed it briefly. 'You would come? I could paint you. I'd like to try. But you'd be pretty bored.'

'I could read to you,' she said, only half serious.

His eyes kindled. 'It sounds fine. No, honestly! If you'd really like it, I would. I started reading hard, two years ago, but you can't read everything in two years.'

'But you could have belonged to a local library long ago – right from the time you could read. I wonder they didn't start you from the Home.' She always said the word a little hesitantly, as if she thought it might hurt him. 'They ought to have done.'

'Don't blame them for it. Maybe they did try, I can't remember. Anything they wanted me to do, anything they told me to do, I did the other thing. It wasn't all their fault, they never had much chance.'

'And you had none at all,' said Rosalba sadly. 'Grown-ups made a mess of your life right from the start. Oh, Eugene, isn't it damned unfair?'

'Did they do any better with yours?' said Eugene.

4

The sketch he had made of her she took home carefully, and put it in the back of a conventional photograph from her school-days, on the tallboy in her bedroom. She covered it scrupulously from sight; and from that moment she could see, when she looked at the stupid, aristocratic, cool young face in the studio portrait, the other face burning through

63

from behind it, the intelligent, warm, human face Eugene had given her. If he had seen that on first acquaintance, might it not after all be there? If it wasn't already too late! Perhaps what he had seen was less something which she might be than something which she might have been.

Yet after her reason had argued everything back to hopelessness in his absence, the first touch of him upon her senses wiped out the arguments and left a white brightness, to which any quality, any colour might come.

Great-Aunt Martine watched her change; such a flowering she could not fail to see, nor for long to recognise. What remains, then, to be done? How can you stop a bud from opening? She made duties which did not exist, keeping Rosalba in her sight; but the brightness did not diminish. She loosed suddenly, steadily, all the poison of her mind in little, measured drippings which filled the day with cruelty, her tongue a hypodermic pricking quietly, full of withering venom. Rosalba had known little as yet of what resources she had within.

'You have your mother's ability to make goodwill a vice, Rosalba. Like you, she never meant any harm, her vulgarity was entirely natural – a gift at birth. She would appear to have left you the richer by at any rate this one legacy.'

'The Rose family used to have a reputation for beauty. I see that is among the past glories of the house, along with a sense of duty.' And Rosalba thought, I am beautiful; the words streaming coolly from her impervious mind. I am beautiful; he said it, and if it were not true you would not harp on the word now. You are only telling me that Eugene is right. And therefore she smiled radiantly, not knowing that she smiled; and this, too, was seen, and this, too, turned the knife yet again in the immemorial wound so deeply stabbed by the beauty that was gone.

'No doubt,' said Martine, seeing her unscarred, and the smile like sunlight on her mouth, 'you have been the object of admiration for a few obscure young persons in your time. Don't mistake that for a compliment. Even you will find it a little tedious in the end. Even in my days we were not entirely free from the type of girl who enjoyed the standards of beauty of grooms and footmen – and frequently an intellect to match. As far as I know, the Roses were never troubled with that problem. Don't let us reach that stage while I'm alive, please. Your smile, I think, indicates that you have some regard for your face. Did some salesman – or clerk? – I'm not versed in the strata – some clerk on his way round the Folly pay you the rather dingy compliment of staring at you instead of at the pictures?'

Her voice was all the while so still, so tranquil, so amused, that only an accustomed ear could distinguish the current of hate threading it. 'Perhaps you ought not to go so frequently to the Folly while the public are viewing it,' she said thoughtfully, watching ceaselessly the smiling, unmoved face, the entranced, withdrawn face, to see when her knife reached the quick. And it did not reach it; Rosalba was invulnerable.

'As you wish,' she said gently, and smiled still. What was it to her if she never saw the Folly again?

But the quest which had begun with the public visitors to the Folly would not rest there. Great-Aunt Martine would go on looking for the weapon which could kill, since there was a charm on her life against all the ordinary weapons. She would try everything, until she found the vulnerable spot where Eugene was, the touch which could tear the smile from her mouth. When she slipped out to the watch-tower she must never go there directly, but always by devious ways, particularly must she set out by a contrary path, and pass well away from the lodge before she turned, and then turn only in cover. Nor must she too consistently avoid that path, for that, too, would be noticed; but she must take it only when she knew already, and certainly, that Eugene would not be there. It was a long way to the tower, Martine herself could not easily or quickly go there, and surely the stored paint-boxes and brushes, the board and the blocks and all the rest of the treasure there would be safe. She would not depute the exquisite pleasure of discovery to anyone else. But she would question, she would watch, she would wait and probe and spy, without tiring. What Rosalba needed was an ally, someone who could carry messages for her, and cover her tracks if need be; and Rosalba had no friends.

Yet the world did not seem so empty of human contacts now as she had always known it. Something in her own vision was new, that every colour should seem a little brighter than she had ever known it, and every voice a little clearer, and her senses a little sharpened to the sweet of people and things.

The first crisis came when Martine sensed one day her expectation of pleasure, and made deliberate disposal to ruin the day for her. She had learned already to control the gleam of her anticipation, but she could not yet suppress it, and to eyes grown a little clairvoyant with jealousy it was clear that she was leaning forward from earliest morning to contemplate the promise of the afternoon. Martine let her alone until mid-morning, and then put a retaining paw on her like a cat drawing back, almost tenderly, an escaping mouse.

'It's a fine day, Rosalba, and not too hot for me. This afternoon I think I should like a walk. You'll feel free to give me your arm, I suppose? It's very seldom I ask it of you.'

Rosalba said: 'Of course!' with the disappointing assurance of the early desert fathers when prodded unexpectedly by their devils. She marvelled at herself, when she heard so calm a voice emerging from such an outcry of indignation as she had within her. But she had to keep her head turned away for a moment, because she wanted to cry, and she had discovered that even when you think you have it well in hand, that shows badly. 'Where would you like to go?'

The cat pondered, almost audibly purring, but with a thread of anger running through her pleasure still, because the mouse had given no indication of which way it had wanted to run. She weighed possibilities, smiling with her dry old lips, and probing for the spot where the knife could go in.

'It's a very long time since I saw the other side of the estate. It would be pleasant at the abbey on a day like this – or perhaps the home woods would afford more shade. What do you think? The cascade is very pretty, of course—'

She had not put her finger on the place. Rosalba said, without any change of colour: 'Wherever you like. But isn't the cascade rather a long way for you?' She did not try to sound anxious, because she was not sufficiently sure of her voice, but the words were enough. And the cascade was such a probable place, green, deep, romantic, the ideal spot for gallantries, for the meetings of extremely young lovers who have no need to regard the dangers of rheumatism. And perhaps Great-Aunt Martine would take cold there from the ferns and the artistic little dripping grottoes, and die! But Rosalba had not much hope of it, in such an opening summer.

'We'll have Wyatt to drive us to the edge of the woods in the dog-cart, if you fear it will be too far for me,' said the cat, her purr now quite audible. 'I should really like to see the cascade and the bower again. Yes, we'll do that.'

It had been a good choice, thought Rosalba, for it was almost in the opposite direction from the watch-tower, and in woods which huddled cosily between their snug artificial rocks and tamed waters. Therefore if they held to the plan there was no possibility of Eugene being discovered; but she would be happier, all the same, if she could send him some message to explain her non-appearance. He would understand, but the thought of him waiting at the tower and worrying about her was hurtful.

'On second thoughts,' said Martine, pouncing, 'perhaps it *is* rather a long trip for me to make. I believe I shall change my mind, and go to the watch-tower.'

Rosalba did not cry out, nor drop the glass vase she was holding, though she felt as if she had done both. It was a shot at a venture, it could be nothing else. And now she had to be convincing, or all was over before it began, for she was not yet ready to come into the open. She said very carefully: 'It would certainly be an easier walk, I think, but you know best whether you feel able to tackle the other one. Why not try the shorter one first? We have all the summer coming, there'll be time for the cascade later.'

Martine, though she was dissatisfied, held to that. She could go no further; it was impossible to consider going headlong round the miles and miles of profitless Rose territory thrusting path after path in the girl's face, and peering for reactions. To the watch-tower, then, and as soon as lunch was over.

Rosalba wrote a frantic note, and went out into the garden, close by the wicket door and out of sight of the windows of the house, where she would hear the four cleaners coming merrily down the drive to catch the bus back to Crocksford. There was no one else, and she had to find a messenger. She was in a desperate situation now, and must attempt desperate remedies.

The remedy, when it came, did not look so desperate, rather cheerful and matter-of-fact in the middle of this secret turmoil of feeling. Rosalba heard the women come, and left her pretence of weeding to open the door in the wall a few inches, and peep through at them anxiously. Three of them strung across the drive gaily from margin to margin, one coming more leisurely behind, tugging at a stocking which had slipped its moorings. This was the youngest girl, the red-haired one. She had a very alert face, with neat round features and very bright grey eyes, and her hair was always a masterpiece of home hair-dressing, swept high in front and cascading to her shoulders behind in violent baroque curls. She wore baroque make-up, too, but so meticulously applied that the effect was prim, and her gait was the nearest thing Rosalba could imagine to the tripping of dairymaids in eighteenth-century pastorals, with small neat steps and a provocative bounce. Many a young man had got the wrong idea through seeing that gait from behind, only to withdraw abashed when he drew level and had to meet her honest and reproving eye.

She was still behind the others when she came abreast of the door in the garden wall. Rosalba cast one hasty glance back at the house, and then leaned out and called to her softly.

'Please, can I speak to you for a moment?' And when she looked round in astonishment and enquiry: 'I'm sorry, but I don't know your name. I wanted to ask you if you could take a message for me to someone in the town.'

'Sure I could,' said the girl, cheerful but still astonished, for this was as if the tower on top of the Folly had bowed to her. 'What's your trouble?' She could recognise trouble very easily, having lived on familiar terms with it all her life; but for the same reason she treated it in a very cavalier fashion, if not with actual contempt. Rosalba felt a little tongue-tied under her disconcerting bright eyes. She had passed by so often, and never become a person until now, when she was so badly needed; and obscurely some amend was needed, something more than just the pleasant asking and the discreet payment she had intended to make for her favour. She put her shut hand into her pocket, and carefully released there the half-crown she had meant to offer; it wasn't going to be at all that kind of transaction.

'I am in trouble,' she owned, with a surprised little gasp at the ease with which it popped out of her, and feeling instantly better for it. 'I was going to meet someone at the watch-tower this afternoon, and now I have to go there with my – with Mrs. Rose. And I don't want – I want to send a message to my friend, and call off our meeting—'

'I see,' said the red-haired girl helpfully, 'she hasn't got to see him.'

'No, that's it exactly. How did you know,' said Rosalba childishly, 'that it was a "him"?'

That was really too silly to answer, but the grey eyes relented of their critical stare, and warmed to the indulgence competent people show to simpletons. The young lady might have had an expensive education, but good lord, she hadn't got much out of it! Poor kid, she was a mere baby when it came to this sort of thing. Carrying her messages was all very well, but somebody ought to do a bit of vetting, too. Not the old witch, though, that was certain! Pity any young man who

69

had to satisfy her, unless he could prove he belonged to the royal family, and even then she might consider him a bit short in the pedigree.

'What else was it likely to be?' she said reasonably, and was touched by the soft flush which flooded upward through Rosalba's throat and into her earnest face. 'All right, give me your letter, I'll see he gets it.'

And she would, if she said she would, and if she wasn't going to she'd tell you so, bluntly, so that you would know exactly where you stood. It needed only a minute of her conversation to assure you of that. Rosalba handed over her few scribbled lines with a lightening heart, and watched her read gravely the name and address upon the envelope. The formidable grey eyes looked up at her severely.

'The spinney camp? Are you carrying on with a soldier, miss?'

'I suppose I am,' said Rosalba doubtfully, not quite sure what the expression entailed.

'Not that soldiers are any different from anybody else, mind you, but they all look alike, and they all come to parts of the country where they look more alike than ever, because nobody knows 'em. 'Tisn't like some local boy, that you can find out about from other folks – if you haven't known him yourself all your life. I've got nothing against soldiers – but you just want to know what you're getting, that's all.'

Rosalba was a little offended for Eugene's sake, but she acknowledged honestly that if you are asking someone to take an active part in an affair of this kind, however small, that person has a right to examine his responsibility before he undertakes it. She relented, and smiled. 'Eugene's the best kind. You'll see for yourself. But even if he wasn't, this is only to tell him *not* to come. But he *is* the best kind,' she added, suddenly wanting to say it to someone.

'Well, they get the lot, so they get them as well as the worst. Anyhow, I'll see he gets this safe, don't you fret.'

Rosalba knew enough by now to leave the half-crown in her pocket. She was learning very rapidly.

70

'I've got to run,' said the red-haired girl, cutting short her stammered thanks, 'or I shall miss the bus. You go in and keep your face straight, and everything will be O.K.'

'I'm sure it will, now! Please, I still don't know your name?'

'It's Derricks – Flo Derricks.'

'Mine's Rosalba.' She stopped short at that, for the rest would certainly be known. 'Thank you *very* much!'

'That's all right, kid, rely on me. So long!' And this time she did run, for the bus was audibly rounding the corner thirty yards from the lodge gate, but it was safe betting that the others would hold it up until she came.

Rosalba watched her scramble aboard, and the overloaded bus drive on and out of sight; then she went back into the garden, and weeded with a kind of propitiatory devotion until lunch-time. And Flo Derricks tucked the letter into her chipped patent leather handbag, and set off in the direction of the spinney camp.

5

Flo Derricks could put a finger on someone useful in most establishments in Crocksford, having an incurable taste for knowing people, and a power of assessing their qualities which had been gradually developed through a short lifetime of necessity. In the camp under the lee of the home woods, on the edge of the town, there was a young man who was courting her cousin, and had received some help and encouragement from her in the matter when the rest of the family were inclined to disparage his chances. She knew where to find him during normal working hours, for he was a mechanic, and between jobs had a private hide-out in the stores at the gate; and there she ran him to earth, and informed him briskly that she wanted to talk to Private Seale. Observing that she had a letter, the young man offered in sheer goodwill to deliver it for her, but he got no thanks for the suggestion. She intended to see Eugene if he was to be seen. Somebody had to take the responsibility for that kid up at the Folly, and it looked as if it had to be Flo.

'Poor little devil!' said Flo, sitting on a piece of clean sacking on top of an upturned oil-drum, half walled-up into the corner of the store. 'Doesn't know she's born yet! Any bit of a smarty in khaki could be taking her in, and who's to know? No, I've got to have a look at him.' But she said it only to herself, while her cousin's young man was away upon her errand. It was not her habit to give away other people's secrets.

Eugene was doing nothing much; it seemed to him that they spent their days doing nothing much. To leave a fatigue party and walk up to the store hut by the direct way was impossible, but there were various indirect ways not only to any part of the camp, but also outside it, and Eugene knew rather more of these ways than most people. He made his way to the corner where Flo waited for him, and was met by a bright and challenging grey eye which appraised him with a candour for which he did not greatly care. From his boots to his grubby face she summed him up, and appeared to suspend judgment.

'Know me again?' said Eugene.

'Quite well enough!' said Flo, and handed him the letter, which mystified him considerably, for until then he had never seen Rosalba's handwriting. It was young and shaky – or perhaps her agitation had shaken it only on this occasion – and sprawled a little, leaning over perilously to look at its reflection, as she had done by the pool. He looked at it doubtfully, and looked again at the bearer.

'You can open it,' said Flo, 'it's on the level.'

'Is there something the matter?' asked Eugene, caught as Rosalba had been by the competent and knowing air she had about her.

'So-so! But it's all in hand. Don't fret yourself, she's O.K. Go ahead and read it. She wrote it for you, didn't she?'

He did as he was told, while Flo's eyes continued to take him bone from bone; but by the time he had deciphered the few hasty lines within he had grown almost accustomed to the sensation of being dissected, and didn't feel so inclined to make cracks about it. If there was a girl in touch with her

72

and able to help her – if there was even a girl somewhere about her who cared enough to want to help her – he'd better watch his step and not offend her at any price.

Flo said: 'Sorry your afternoon's washed up, but there it is. Anyhow, it's all taken care of.'

'Oh, so you know all about it,' he said, none too pleased.

'If you do, it's because she told me. Seems to me I turned up just at the right minute, for once.'

'Could you take an answer back to her?' he asked.

'Tomorrow morning I could. I go in mornings to char in the Folly.' She added punctiliously: 'Never talked to her until today, mind you – not beyond good morning. Tell you the truth, I used to think she was one of 'em, just like the old woman. The old woman's a bitch, let's face it. But this kid never got thawed until today. Look!' she said, jutting her round but notable chin at him suddenly, 'what are you up to?'

'Up to? What the hell do you mean?'

'You heard! I usually mean what I say, it's simpler. What are you up to with her?'

Eugene's back had become as rigidly upright as outrage could make it. He flamed: 'That's our business!' which was just about what Flo had expected, except that she had rather expected his imagination to stop short at 'my business', and he scored a decided point by the implicit acknowledgement that Rosalba, too, was a person. Then he remembered that this girl was apparently well-disposed toward Rosalba, at any rate, and that this fact gave her an astonishingly precious quality, for she was, apart from himself, the only person who seemed to care a damn for her. He tried to look conciliatory; it was an impossibility, but he managed to look sullenly reasonable, and tried again more carefully: 'I don't know what you're getting at. I only got to know her by accident. I like her, and she likes me. But there isn't any question of being up to anything.'

'You been seeing her pretty regularly, haven't you?'

'Half a dozen times, maybe more. Why shouldn't we?'

'Why not, indeed, if you're on the level? Because she is,

you know. She thinks a lot of you.' Her very direct eyes added clearly: 'Goodness knows why!'

'So do I of her,' he said fiercely.

'All right,' said Flo, 'all right, I'll take your word for it. You don't have to shout.'

'Sorry, but you come here, and start asking all these damned cheeky questions—'

'Somebody has to,' said Flo. She leaned forward earnestly, and tapped the words out severely on his knee. 'Look, kid, I can understand you wanting to fly off the handle, but just think about her for a minute. Oh, she's the educated young lady, all right, knows plenty I've never heard about; but when it comes to looking after herself in the sort of rough-and-tumble most folks get in life, how would she get on? You must know yourself she's as helpless as a baby, anybody could twist her. Well, how would you feel when a girl like that suddenly pops out at you and asks you to help her to get a message to a boy, and then you find out he's a soldier down here – somebody from a sort she ain't used to at all, and her folks would fall down dead if they got wind of? How was I to know what I was doing helping her out? I couldn't have been helping her to grief, and no mistake. Well, I don't do things by halves, that's all. If I thought you were playing her along—'

He said bitterly: 'You have got a nice mind, I must say!'

'Never mind my mind! You keep your eye on the ball, it's your mind what matters here. And what's the use of getting on your high horse, when it wasn't a case of you at all? It was just some chap she'd picked up with, and I'd never set eyes on him before. Besides, don't you think for a minute I'm hinting at just bad intentions. You could be as in earnest as a saint, and still be a fellow about as much good to her as the man in the moon. Or you could be a decent enough lad just quietly enjoying himself and meaning no harm, but that isn't what *she* thinks she's got, I can tell you. Not by the way she looks when she says: Eugene's the best kind!'

His face burned magically bright and young all at once, the inimical stiffness molten out of it in a breath. 'Did she say that?'

'Yes, she did, and you'd better make it good.'

It was Flo who sounded a little cross now, or like a short-tempered schoolmistress forever on the edge of being cross. 'I don't take any hand in things like this in the dark,' she said smartly. 'If it was my own sister, I'd want to see the fellow was all right, wouldn't I? Well, now you can write your note to her, and be quick about it, because I've got a family to feed at twelve o'clock, when school comes out, and I'm getting all behind-hand. I've got a pencil, if you haven't, and there's room on the back of her note – Oh, but you'll want to keep that,' she corrected herself perceptively. 'Here, use my laundry book.'

He liked her for that more than for anything. It made perfect sense to her that he should object to parting with the first scribbled words he had ever had from Rosalba, even to send by that token the first she would ever read from him; and she treated it as a matter of practical conduct, just as solid as the determination to pay no more than the controlled price for onions. But he was by no means sure that she liked him, and it began to sound as though this might be an important consideration.

He wrote his note, only a few bald words of reassurance and comfort, for the lost day and the moment of fear. Suddenly he was face to face with all manner of demons which had to be confronted some day, but had escaped notice in the first warmth and delight of companionship; and only now, when he saw the demons, did he begin to see the real quality of the companionship. He was very much afraid, and he looked it as he handed over the note to be shut up firmly in Flo's patent leather handbag.

'Well, cheer up!' said that young lady briskly, observing the clouded eye. 'You don't have to go into it all today, at any rate. I suppose now you're going to start running like a hare to meet trouble, and lying awake all night worrying *how* to meet it. Don't you do anything of the sort, that's no use to you nor to her. You take things as they come for a bit, that's my advice, and cross your bridges when you reach 'em, not before. So long as you're straight yourself, waiting for other things to straighten won't do any harm.'

'Will I do, then?' he asked, with a flash of impudence, as she was tripping on her high blue heels towards the door.

She turned, and looked at him thoughtfully, and rewarded his inquisitiveness with no more than a discouraging sniff. 'When you've had a few of the sharp corners took off, and your knuckles rapped a time or two, I don't know but you might do.'

6

The demons stayed with Eugene more closely than brothers as he went up the rising path in the pines towards the watch-tower, three days later. They had not left him since he first became aware of them. He knew what he was, or what other people had taken him to be; and it was true that he had told it all, every last, least thing he could remember, good or bad, to Rosalba in his arrogant honesty, and true that she in her loveliness had found nothing there to make her move an inch away from him, but had drawn always nearer when the worst of him came out, and reached for his hand to assure him of her partisan sympathy. And she had a right to choose her own friends, and those chosen – but he knew he was the only one – had no right to writhdraw themselves for a scruple she did not feel. But his mind nagged that the instrument of their entanglement had not really been her choice, that choice did not enter into it. She was a starving creature, and he was the first, the only food that had fallen near her.

Not that he found anything greatly wrong with what he was. He did not think himself perfect, and at eighteen even this was rather superhuman of him; he did not even think himself very admirable if you were considering orthodox virtues. But he thought well of himself in the ways that mattered to him. He was not stupid, he did not accept other people's second-hand judgments, but for what it was worth used his own mind and formed his own opinions; he did not believe in giving in to things or people merely because they were in a position to enforce acceptance of themselves as the established order and the settled authority; he was pretty sure he was going to paint well. For a long time, after his call-up, after the endless dreary waste of time began, he had given up thinking of that, as something smashed; but now he was more sure of it than ever, since he had known Rosalba. He had to have something to offer her, didn't he?

But when these things were all added up, did they amount to the right man for Rosalba? He had never had to think in such terms before, because of course you don't have to start stocktaking your whole life in order to be friends with someone, however different from yourself. But being friends with her was one thing, and now he saw quite another. He believed they were friends, he hoped they were; but that wasn't all.

He knew what she was, too, and it was no good thinking that her innocent and candid acceptance of himself had changed it. She was the last of a blue-blooded and indescribably proud and exclusive line, even if she was the graft that didn't quite take. She was used to a life as alien to him as the hypothetical life upon distant planets. It wasn't the family and the name and the station that frightened him. It was the seventeen formative years she had spent imbibing them. The desire she had to get away from this only life she knew was no measure of the results which might follow from such an escape. How could she know what her feelings would be when she was transplanted? How could he know that in another soil she might not wither away?

He had arrived at this point when he reached the brow of the hill, among the fallen brick stones, and saw her sitting waiting for him in the lee of the tower, coiled up in the grass with her small feet under her. She looked as if she were trying to melt herself into the substance of the wall itself, so slight she was, and so squeezed together, and her dull grey cardigan and tweed skirt against the neutral colours made her almost invisible. He was a little early, which meant that she had been very early, for he knew by looking at her that she had been there some time. She was not looking in his direction, and he had not made enough noise to startle her as he came, because she was very much occupied. She was crying into the back of her arm against the wall, with little hurtful sounds, like an urchin in trouble. When he dropped suddenly into the grass beside her, and gathered her hastily and clumsily into his arms, she turned readily, and pressed her tear-stained face into his khaki shoulder, and went on crying with a new and grateful passion which he was afraid to interrupt. Dismayed and trembling, he held her tightly, and said nothing at all until the flood was spent, and she lay still and relaxed against him, her face still hidden. Little quivering sighs came out of her, but no more sound, and her breathing began to be soft and long, as if she were falling asleep.

He stroked back the soft yellow hair from her damp temples, and with sudden dislike of the hard, disarranged bun in which she wore it, pulled out the comb and pins with which it was secured, and let it swoop down to her shoulders, where it flowed over his hand and arm in a smooth, heavy wave. A piney scent drifted out of it faintly, and dissolved in the air about them.

'What's the matter?' he whispered, 'what's the matter?' Not asking for an answer, only soothing her with his voice as you would a wild thing in your hands when you loosed it out of a trap.

She stirred a little; and put up a hand to wipe away the drifting hair from her face, which she turned up to him pale and smudged. 'I didn't want to do that. I didn't want you to see me. I didn't think it was time yet.' And in a voice more like her own, withdrawing a little in self-consciousness: 'It isn't anything.'

'No,' he said grimly, 'it's everything. Isn't it? The whole way you live, this damned place, that horrible old woman – And it's getting worse, isn't it?' Why, he wondered, had he been wasting time fearing that she might wither in another soil, when she was dying before his eyes in this one? She lay now against his heart, even her face wearily still, looking up

78

beyond him listlessly at the sky. 'Tell me what happened,' he said, with urgency.

'Nothing happened. Nothing does happen. We just walk round each other, talking about nothing, pretending we don't know we hate each other, covering everything up.'

'She knows about us!' he said. 'Doesn't she?'

'Only as you know when there's somebody in the same room with you in the dark.'

'She doesn't know who? She didn't find anything? Or get anything out of anybody? Not that we've got anything to be ashamed of!' he cried furiously, feeling the injustice of this more than all, that they should have to build a wall round a thing so natural and right.

'No, but we have something to be careful of. And I don't want her near it! Eugene, I couldn't bear it if she spoiled this!'

'I don't think she could,' he said defiantly.

'You don't know her! It isn't only herself, you see, it's all the authority she has, centuries of it, all the weight of this place. And you don't know the things she has inside her, the things she can say. And you still don't know what I'm like inside. There are things I can't do. It isn't that I haven't the courage, really it isn't. But when something goes against the whole flow of your life, how *can* you –? All in a moment – How can you adjust yourself like that?'

'No,' he said gently, 'I see it's a lot to ask.'

'It isn't that I can't make up my mind. It isn't that. There aren't any divided loyalties in my mind. Only the everyday part of me, the part of me that has habits – it's got to have time.'

'It shall have time,' he assured her. 'She knows nothing yet, and we can afford to wait. There isn't anyone who could give us away? That girl who came to me – she's the only one?'

'The only one who knows about you – she knows all that matters, but she'll help us, she's kind—'

'There's someone else, then, who knows a little?'

'Only Cedarwood, the man from the Folly – the guide.

79

But it's all right. He knows there's someone; he doesn't know where, or who. He doesn't want to know. He never *wants* anything. We needn't be afraid of him. He's old,' she said simply, 'but he isn't an enemy.'

'Then we've nothing to be afraid of!'

But her face did not change, and with a contracting heart he knew that neither she nor he himself believed it. It was not so simple a thing as that. 'You haven't told me everything! It isn't only what might happen, it's what goes on happening all the time – is that it?' She made no reply, but the reddened lids sank over her eyes until the dark gold lashes lay on her cheeks, and her face quivered a little in its exhausted stillness. His arms tightened about her desolately, sensing already half of the answer. 'Tell me! It's hell, isn't it? Tell me! How can we see what we have to do, unless you tell me everything?'

She told him, as well as she could, but it was doubtful if even then he really understood. He had lived among all kinds of devious motives and violent passions, but he had never been hated as she was hated. And besides, she made less of it than the truth, because it made him so angry and so miserable. She felt him shaking as if with cold, and was ashamed that she had let him see her own distress when the shadow of it so soon and so heavily fell upon him.

'But she's a devil,' he said, stammering, 'just a devil!'

'No, she's only old, and proud, and jealous – jealous for the family, you see, as well as for herself. I'm not satisfactory, I never have been. But she won't let me off anything.'

'You've got to get away,' he said with passionate quietness, and drew a long breath that shook them both with astonishment and dread. It was so simple, and so impossible. 'It's the only way,' he said. 'It can't go on like this. You've got to get away.'

'Away!' said Rosalba, tasting the word slowly and obediently after him. Her eyes opened again upon a faint, delirious hope, but he saw already that they looked beyond to a mountainous doubt and fear. To her it was like saying:

'You must stop breathing!' She knew no other way to live. And even he, though he fought strenuously to convince himself that he was talking sense, saw the dwarfing difficulties draw in about his beautiful idea, confining what he wished to enlarge, building fences of law and convention about what already was barely a live possibility.

'How could I do that?' she asked, suddenly raising herself to face him directly in the flattened grass nest against the wall of the tower. 'I'm seventeen. If I did go away they could bring me back. She's my guardian, I can't get away from her.'

'I didn't mean without letting her know. She doesn't want you, you said so yourself. She hates you. Wouldn't she be glad if you went away and got a job? Wouldn't she agree to that? Couldn't you talk her into it? You'd have to come back here sometimes, I know, but that wouldn't be hell like this is – and you'd have another life in between, and be with different people. Oh, Rosalba, you've got to try it.'

'You don't know her,' was all she said, almost laughing at the inadequacy of his conception of the problem. 'You don't know her at all, any more than you know me.'

'You could do it! Of course you could! Other people have done it.'

'I could work, of course I could, in a fashion. I could dust, and scrub floors, like Flo does; at least I could learn. I could do the things people do without training, without any gifts at all. But you don't understand— How could you possibly understand?' She shook her head hopelessly, and new tears, exasperated tears, squeezed their way between her fiercely compressed lids and trickled down her cheeks.

'It would be better than this!' said Eugene desperately.

'Oh, yes, yes, anything would! It isn't that I wouldn't be glad to do *anything*, no matter how dirty or unpleasant, if only I could really get away from here and earn my own living. But can you imagine if I went to her and said: Great-Aunt Martine, I've applied for a job as a cinema usherette, or – or in a factory – or as a kitchen-maid— Not that I'd know how to be a kitchen-maid, or be any good at it!

But don't you see how impossible it is? Roses have been diplomats occasionally, if they were younger sons. They've even entered the Church, or gone into the army, in a privileged sort of way. But nothing less dignified than that, ever. And the women – the women have never done anything useful in the whole of history, they've only been beautiful and decorative – and only that for a select circle, or perhaps that could have been useful – and had sons. That's all they could ever contemplate, and that's all she would ever allow me to consider, either.'

'But things have changed,' he urged, breathless with despair and his own unwillingness to acknowledge it. 'Even that kind of family has had to make adjustments. Their women go into offices and dress-shops now, and open flower-shops, and things like that. Even that's a way of getting out.'

'Other women, perhaps, but not the Roses. We're poorer than the others, because we hung on longer to the property, and fought off trade after the others gave in. We're the rock in the middle of the status quo. We're not resisting the social changes other people fear nowadays – oh, no, we're still resisting the passing of feudalism – ' She drummed her small clenched fist hard into his shoulder, and sobbed wildly. 'I keep telling you, you don't know us at all.'

He held her tightly by the shoulders, and besought her: 'Don't cry, *please* don't cry!'

'It's only temper now,' she said with a damp and wobbly laugh, and smeared impatiently at her eyes with the back of a hand none too clean. 'What's the use?' she went on more quietly. 'We're only pretending. There isn't any chance that way at all. Dear Eugene, don't think I'm arguing this way because I'm frightened to try it. I am frightened, but that's not all. If someone offered me a really wonderful job, one that would be a credit to her, she still wouldn't let me take it. Not only because of her feudal ideas, but most because she would know why I wanted it, and how badly. She would do anything to prevent me from becoming a person in my own right, to keep me tied to this place and to her. I mustn't be independent, I mustn't be liked or admired – because she was once adored by everybody who saw her, in an artificial sort of way, and made slaves of all of them – and nothing must happen to remind her that that's over.'

'I see!' said Eugene slowly, and turned his face away into her hair.

'And if I went away without her consent, she would fetch me back. She can, legally, and she'd do it.'

'Perhaps she wouldn't,' he said indistinctly. 'Perhaps she would want it hushed up. She'd hate it if there was any publicity, wouldn't she?'

'I should hate it more,' said Rosalba gently. 'Darling, don't!' She was feeling better for her outburst, and immeasurably adult and motherly because of the quivering of his mouth against her neck, through the warm drift of her hair. She freed her arms, very gently, and wound them round him with a wild, careful tenderness. 'Why do we talk like this? We know it can't be done in that way. And even if things were different, and she could be made to agree – even then we should have to face some more facts. I'm not equipped to do any job. I was never taught anything, and I *was* taught – oh, so carefully! – to do nothing, in this particular way. Dear Eugene, it isn't easy for you to see what a difference that makes. I don't *want* to be useless, I just am. But I can't easily change it, or quickly—'

'Isn't there anything you yourself want to do? Most people have dreams about it when they're kids.'

'Oh, those!' she said with a faint sigh and a fainter smile.

'They're just as real as the things people finally do,' said Eugene, rearing his head haughtily in defence of ambition. He looked at her afresh, and smiled; he could do that now, seeing her so nearly calm and so thoroughly grubby. 'Isn't there anything like that with you?'

'Oh, but such hopeless absurdities! How many people ever do anything with them? Once I did think I should have liked to be an actress. Everybody does, at least once, when they get a part in a school play. And besides, it was such fun being another person.'

He could understand that; it had never been much fun to be herself.

'But that's a long time ago, and all over. It was nice, but nobody ever suggested I was any good. I don't suppose I was.' She shook herself impatiently. 'What's the use of thinking about that now? I might as well decide to be a prima donna, without knowing whether I had a note of music in me.'

'But you've got to do something, and you've got to get away,' he said stubbornly.

'I've got to go on here. It isn't any use pretending anything else. It isn't as if I had any money of my own, even – and if I had it wouldn't be mine until I came of age. You see how hopeless it is to think of escaping.'

He saw, but would not see. He shook her between his hands. 'What was that play of yours? Who were you?'

'I tell you it's nothing, not a gleam. You mustn't make it bigger than it was. Don't you think things can hurt you enough as they are? I'm ashamed,' she said with a weary little sob, 'that I made all this fuss. You're wasting your time, I'm only another Rose. Eugene, Eugene, I can't live up to you!'

'Don't talk like that!' said Eugene furiously. 'I don't believe you!'

'You won't believe me!'

'What was it, Rosalba, that play?'

'Oh, what different does it make? It was *Romeo and Juliet*.'

'And you were—?'

'Juliet. I wish you wouldn't bully me. I'm damned tired of talking round and round in circles, when the whole thing is settled for us until I'm twenty-one, and anyhow, what kind of future is there for you? And that's more important, when—'

'It's the same question, your future and mine,' he said, 'and nobody can settle it without us. Were you good, Rosalba? I'm pretty sure you were.'

'They said, promising. Didn't you know, that's what they

always say.' She shut her eyes, wryly remembering a small old excitement, remembering it best by her own failure to recapture any hope from it now, and recited chantingly, mocking her lost enthusiasm:

' "How cam'st thou hither, tell me, and wherefore?
The orchard walls are high and hard to climb,
And the place death, considering who thou art,
If any of my kinsmen find thee here."

'That could have been written for me, couldn't it? And then he says:

' "With love's light wings did I o'er-perch these walls;
For stony limits——" '

' "——cannot keep love out," ' said Eugene.

It was not a strictly accurate quotation, but she did not recognise the slip, for all she fully heard was the tone of his voice so low and aware in her ear.

' "And what love can do that dares love attempt;
Therefore thy kinsmen are not let to me." '

The young, intent voice wavered defiantly to the end of the line, and there broke before a great, realising sigh which shook them both as they leaned clinging together. She opened her eyes upon his face, already so near to her own that almost before she had perceived how newly beautiful it was it had swum out of focus, and his mouth was feeling softly for her mouth, with a blind, frightened, forlorn fumbling which made her tears start again for kindness as they kissed. For that reason the kiss, inexpert as it was, had a bitter, piercing sweetness. She wound her arms about his neck, and held him against her cheek.

'Oh, Eugene, darling, I love you so much!'

CHAPTER FOUR:

Flo

1

FLO DERRICKS lived in Gasworks Row, which was a respectable but dingy little street under the gasometers in the canal quarter of Crocksford. She lived in two rooms at the back of Number 14, one up and one down and use of scullery, which meant also bathroom, for there was no other. The downstairs room had a bed-settee, which accommodated Mr. Derricks at night, since from there it was infinitely easier to rouse him and get him to work – on those spasmodic occasions when he was working – than it would have been had he slept upstairs. It had also an adequate table, covered with clean white marbled oilcloth, enough chairs for everyone to sit round it, a cupboard with the family crockery and linen and cooking utensils, a wireless set, a couple of shelves of books, a threadbare carpet which afforded many perils to uncertain heels after closing time, and a grandmother clock which leaned like the tower of Pisa, and ticked accordingly. A small gas cooker occupied one corner, but had an air of not belonging.

The upstairs room housed Flo, her sister Daisy, aged fourteen, and her brother Sid, aged eight, who greatly resented the arrangement, and lost no opportunity of saying so. For a child of his remorseless energies the room was regrettably small even without two women cluttering it up further. It was all very well telling him that other people in their thousands had to live in conditions as bad or worse, but that cured nothing. At his age he was concerned solely with the plight of the Derricks family.

Flo liked the place no better than he did, but it had a roof. That was about all that could be said for it, and to tell the truth there was one place where even that leaked in heavy rain; but one had to walk softly even to retain that degree of security and comfort. True, they had their name down for a Council house, and would get one when their turn came round; but since there were rather over a thousand applicants on the waiting list, and fresh hopeful young couples trotting to the office almost every day, while exactly fifty-six houses were at present in process of building, and another hundred and fifty in prospect for the next year, one could hardly expect very rapid results from that. They had taken the same steps in the next district, and had their names also on the housing list of Bredington Rural, on the offchance of an earlier vacancy occurring there, but Flo didn't think much of that prospect, either. Young Sid couldn't even remember the time when they'd lived in a house of their own; and even then it had been, of course, rented not owned, for when had Mr. Derricks ever aspired to own his own dwelling? But Daisy could remember it, and harped on it when she felt most grown-up, hankering after a room of her own, where she could plaster the walls with film stars and recline dreamily on her bed to gaze at them when she felt in the mood, without any young brothers making cheap wisecracks, or older sisters crisply ordering her off their joint quilt. Then she reminisced, maddeningly, about the beautiful days in Green Street, which in fact had been so long ago that she remembered the house as ten times more spacious than it had really been, and a good deal more weatherproof.

Mrs. Derricks had died in Green Street in 1942, leaving Sid as a baby of eight months on Flo's hands when Flo was only ten years old herself. She had been a tall, gaunt woman, physically aged beyond her years by hard living and more

87

than her share of work, but spiritually wildly alive, and full of a rather tart and gawky sense of fun which rendered the annoyances of every day into masterpieces of comedy for her. This was lucky, as she had otherwise comparatively little incentive to meet the recurring days; but with this elixir it could fairly be said that she enjoyed her life to the full. Her husband, regarded by some people as a tragedy, she found blessedly comic, and made no secret of it; while he regarded her as afflicted of God in a mild and likeable way, and made fun for her without resentment, though without understanding. And when a neglected cold became pneumonia, and she realised that she was going to die, she was exceedingly surprised and inclined to be resentful, like someone who has run her nose into a threatened foreclosure in which she has optimistically refused to believe. She adjusted herself to this mishap as to all the rest, said it was a blinking caution the way things happened to her, recalled that it had tumbled down with rain on her wedding day, and she'd nearly killed herself laughing at Sam when the curl came out of his moustache, opined philsophically that it's just as well to leave the show while it still amuses you, and so left it without any ill-feeling. It was a fine, sunny day for her funeral, and you could almost hear her saying with her wry chuckle: 'Ah, it would be!'

There was an aunt not too far away in those days, and with her help Flo contrived to raise the baby; but after two more years the aunt also left them, though only for a home in the south of England, where her husband was moving to a new job; and Flo was left undisputed mistress of the household. She had her father's shape, round, bouncing and soft, but a good deal of her mother was hidden inside it, luckily for all of them. It would appear that she had also her mother's luck, for no sooner was the aunt well away from them than one of the early raids of 1944 shook down half of Green Street, the warehouse end, and the tired little house, which had had no repairs put in on it for years, stood up bravely over its tottering foundations for one more week, and then subsided. Luckily they had just warning enough to get out before it fell, and even to get out a few bits of furniture; and the only casualty was Mr. Derricks himself, who in his zeal ventured too close to the wreck too soon, against all orders and for no good reason but inquisitiveness, and received a falling brick upon his head. He was disappointed at the doctor's reception of the wound, and resented the implication that his head had been harder than the brick, though the fact remains that the brick was broken and his skull was not; but the incident became a gold mine to him afterwards, from which he fished up headaches and indispositions at need all the rest of his life.

He was not a lazy man; no one would work harder, indeed more frantically, so long as his interest held; but it held for so invariably brief a time, and bore away his powers of concentration so completely each time in its irresistible ebb, that he had never stuck at anything long enough to do it well. The job which fascinated him was always the one someone else was doing. As children are zealous to dust or get in coal for precisely so long as they are not expected or even desired to do it, so he put his heart into a hundred successive apprenticeships, and learned nothing beyond the labouring stage. They never had more than enough money to scrape a precarious existence on the respectable edge of living, for that reason; but his wife had regarded it as an almost balancing asset that her husband was what she called a cure, or occasionally a scream. According to the standards of some of her friends, her sense of values was a trifle perverted.

Sam Derricks had graces, though, which even outsiders could not fail to see. He was good company, even if chronic penury did eventually turn him into the mildest possible form of sponger. He was amiable, even-tempered, pleasant to have around the house and useful to amuse the children. He amused them, indeed, almost as much as he amused his wife; and only Daisy, after a course of Hollywood films at a susceptible age, found serious fault with the life he provided for her. He told good tales to young Sid at bed-time, better ones to the regulars at the Waterman's Arms just before closing time, but the best ones of all to himself whenever his mind was at liberty to make its periodic and irresistible attack upon circumstances. He never told fairy-tales to Flo, because she knew them all; but she was too good-humoured to say so, and occasionally, when there were new or changed circumstances to be attacked with all the lances of a vainglorious fancy, she made up the appropriate new story for him, and put it into his mouth and the sword into his hand; and counting her bag of dragons at the end of every campaign, courteously let him believe he had really accounted for them all himself.

After the house in Green Street, they had rooms, first by the canal, for want of better, and then here in Gasworks Row. Of the contents of the two rooms only the cupboard, the threadbare carpet, the gas cooker, and the large wardrobe on the landing upstairs were the property of the landlady, but because of these the letting counted as furnished rooms. They paid a pound a week for them, and sometimes after his regular brush with Mrs. Gilpin over young Sid's muddy boots on the lino, or the unidentified finger-marks on the landing wallpaper, Mr. Derricks thought fondly of taking his grievance to the local rent tribunal, and asking them to knock five shillings off the rent. But he had never done it yet, and never would until Flo saw her way to give him the green light. Three months' security of tenure, with a council which would never dream of requisitioning under any circumstances, and in a town where an enforced jungle-full of almost-homeless people waited to knock one another on the head for the sake of one room, let alone two, did not seem to her good enough odds.

It wasn't a particularly pleasant way of living, but they managed not so badly. There was no denying a little more elbow-room would have been welcome to all of them, and Flo could not honestly say that Mrs. Gilpin couldn't have been improved upon as a landlady, but others were worse off. Flo was placid by nature and inclination, even when giving battle; not because she had lived placidly, but because after the life she had lived she was perfectly adjusted to ride to any shock without making a fuss about it.

But when she was tired she had her moments of discouragement, all the same. Mrs. Gilpin was only too ready at all times to get Sid into trouble, which was a needless exertion on her part, for he was quite capable of doing so much for himself; and the war of attrition between them made life no easier. Daisy had an undesirable friend aged sixteen, with a penchant for Americans, and a fixed idea that the best place in the county to spend a Saturday evening was in the shop doorways nearest their camp gates in Bredington; and Mrs. Gilpin had long ears, and an even longer tongue. And father was liable at any moment to tell her so.

But after all, they had always managed, and things might have been worse.

When you looked, for instance, at the hopeless plight of those two kids, the girl at the Folly and her young man, up against just about all the odds in the world – well, thought Flo, it made you thank your stars you weren't in their shoes.

2

The light that love shed on a hitherto familiar world for Rosalba was not rose-coloured, but it had a sharper enchantment, a painful radiance. It fell over things well-known, and people daily seen, at a more abrupt angle, and showed them to her three-dimensional and quivering with reality. Every sound, every sight, however delicate and insignificant, hurt her senses with the astonishment of great pleasure and equally great pain. The very sunlight over the Folly, the wind in the wilderness of chimneys, the pattern of gold foil in the glass-cased manuscripts, all were new. It was as if she had never seen nor heard before, as if her senses had felt at things only through a thick glass wall, and now the barrier had dissolved before one touch of the amazement of love.

It was not comfortable. She was even a little afraid of it,

and throughout the day shrank often from the too sensitive contacts and too vivid colours of her magical world. She awoke with a sort of hunger, an emptiness for Eugene whom she had not yet seen, and for whom the heart of her day waited like a frame. Anything he had touched, anything which had been near him, would set him there in his place and satisfy her. Even the glimpse of some soldier of his unit walking on the gravel maze among the Folly flower-beds would suffice, or a small scribbled note in his hand was riches, and the occasional meeting with him the world's plenty, and enough over for other people to share. One touch of him, and the tensions which troubled her were all relaxed.

And yet this passionate serenity was only the half of truth; daily and hourly in her heart she was aware of the unthinkable dangers and difficulties and despairs which hemmed them in, the pits which waited for their feet, the cold, concerted face of the world deriding the dream of so insane a love. When she read to him parts of *Romeo and Juliet* as he painted doggedly in the shelter of the tower, or more sharply still when she shut her eyes and recited fiercely from Juliet's speeches, it was very clear to her that she spoke for an actual, as well as an imagined love; and she knew by his determined refusal to show any particular interest that it was equally clear to him. They never said it, but the awareness passed between them bitterly, and the wild denial followed hotly after; and had they spoken both it would have been better for them. For the difficulties were real, why pretend otherwise? There were seventeen divided years between them. They made each other mad a dozen times in every meeting. There was nothing restful about the spasmodic course of their companionship; often they quarrelled, and recoiled in the act into their two alien backgrounds, and were astonished and terrified each at the other's rediscovered strangeness.

Yet all the time the conviction of their unity survived, and grew to look ever more permanent and tranquiul, unshaken by the wind of the moment; and in that they rested as in the heart of the whirlwind.

Because she felt things on her own account with a new and

startling intensity, Rosalba's eyes grew round with wonder upon the sensitivities of other people, too. She saw them all, perhaps, through the prismatic glass of Eugene, but she saw more of them than ever before. She felt her way into them with delicate, troubled, tender probings, because there was now so much of her own affection and sympathy and interest that it could not help spilling over into any vessel which came near. Cedarwood had always been a strange and appropriate fitting of the Folly; but behold, Cedarwood was real. The troops of town visitors were people, they loved other people, they were receptive to impressions and responsive to approaches. And there was Flo, who had stretched out a comfortable wing like a hen, and let her in to her warm, unimaginative side; she was real, too, and had a family to worry about, and a heart certainly resilient, but not beyond discouragement. Everyone was alive, and coloured, and potential, and had needs and fears, not, of course, like her own, but in a lesser degree of the same quality. Not everyone could love Eugene, but they managed to feel all of love which could be felt for those others who were not Eugene.

And the borders of her world, which had been always so neat and fixed, suddenly rushed outward to accommodate all these other people whose existence was such wonderful news to her. She was staggered by the stupidities and injustices and complexities which were all at once opened to her vision, and with naïve indignation exclaimed about them, much as princes have been known to cry out that something must be done when confronted with conditions which have existed in the same country with them all their lives. They quarrelled about that, too, and struggled after tolerance with piteous growing pains.

'Anybody'd think it was something new,' said Eugene bitterly, 'for people to have nowhere decent to live, and for other people to own places the size of that dump up there. And plenty of 'em still do! To hear you talk, it's only happening this year that men are busy making guns and bomber planes and all that stuff to kill one another with –

yes, and the best brains on earth being used to work out bigger and better ways of killing, instead of something useful – and others who happen to have the gift of the gab, or to be able to write, are being used to shove out propaganda for this damned silly -ism or that, instead of writing what they really have to say as human beings. You'd think it used to be different! Well, it's always been the same – always! Do you suppose it's ever made any difference what people like you and me thought or wanted? We've always wanted the same things, to live decently, in a friendly sort of way, and not hurt anybody, and have some sort of work to do that we can take an interest and pride in, and have enough money to keep us from worrying about the next day. It's always been the same. You've just never come to life before, that's all. But you needn't start telling me all about it. *I* didn't have any sheltered upbringing.'

'But no one's ever done anything about it,' she said hotly, 'and no one ever seems to feel much about it, not even you, or you couldn't talk like that.'

'Why, what good's it going to do shouting? If I ever see anything I can do, I'll try it. But shout, if it amuses you, shout as loud as you like, and see if anyone takes any notice. Better than you have tried it, and got nowhere.'

'No wonder,' said Rosalba, 'if no one else ever backed them up.'

'Well,' said Eugene more gently, 'somebody's got to be the spark, I suppose, and we can all try. But you get very tired after a bit. You'll get tired, too, and the odds are it won't be either of us who can change anything. Not that way, at any rate.'

'But why do we put up with it?' cried Rosalba passionately, with the heroic optimism of the newly-awakened. 'How is it that all the little people don't rise together, and put their foot down, and say: You've made a mess of our affairs long enough, now we're going to do things our way?'

'Oh, they've tried it sometimes. It's always ended the same way. As soon as they really do that, and get into a position where they think they're in power, a few people a little cleverer and less scrupulous than the rest of them soon realise that a good career can be made out of it. The idea becomes a business all over again, and you're back where you started from.'

'But the majority would be against them—'

'Oh, hell!' he said impatiently. 'Don't you know even yet the majority are dumb and tame and can't be bothered to think for themselves at all? It's easier to be carried. They don't *mind* when the career men take over, they *like* it, they're *relieved*. Then they can go to sleep again, and say: It's all right now. The right people are in charge. The right people never have been in charge yet, they never will be until *everybody* shoulders his responsibility and exacts the last ounce of his rights. But you won't live to see it, and neither will I.'

She sat still for a moment in the grass, the book open in her lap, staring at him with large thoughtful eyes.

'What's the matter now?'

'I was just thinking,' she said, 'that that's what we're always being told already. That's what the old people always say. Do you know what I mean? It's all duty, duty, duty – responsibility, responsibility— You're only using the same words they use.'

'But I mean them,' said Eugene, 'and they don't.'

'Oh, yes, after their fashion I think they do.'

'After their fashion, but it isn't ours. They say, you must learn to think for yourself, you must shoulder your responsibility to the town, to the school, to the state, whatever the body is they're trying to shore up. They say, you must become adult, we must educate you to play your full part in the world. But it all means, really, you must develop all possible powers of doing what we tell you, thinking as we say you ought to think. Listen how they talk about discipline! They don't mean the kind from inside, oh, no, not they! They mean you must be obedient. The first duty of man,' said Eugene, flaming like a sulky fire suddenly bursting into blaze, 'is *not* to be obedient. The first duty of

95

man is to *question*! To weigh, and measure, and select, and reject, and never, never accept anything on anyone else's single authority.'

'But you have to use the experience of older people,' she said, 'or it would all be wasted.' But her eyes shone with the reflected light of divine heresies, and her mouth wore a dazzled smile.

'Of course you have to! Every opinion put together by any human mind out of thought and experience is good evidence. But there's only one instrument you've got to measure and test all these witnesses with, and that's your own mind. And if you don't do it you're failing to shoulder that responsibility they're always talking about. And if you do,' he said violently, 'they'll jolly soon kill you off as too damned dangerous to be let live.'

'I thought you didn't believe in shouting,' said Rosalba, almost in his own manner, and smiled to see him flush.

'But it's true,' he said with careful quietness, and a voice of laborious reason which nevertheless shook with urgency. 'Isn't it true?'

'Yes,' she owned with a sigh, 'it seems to be true. All my life, I've heard about my duty and responsibility to the family, to the name, to my blood. I had to do everything for them – nobody ever asked me to consider whether it was the sort of family I wanted, or a name I was really proud of.'

'Nobody ever does ask you that. Nobody ever asks you if it's the kind of world you want. They just say, you must be prepared to give your life, if necessary, to defend our institutions – our common heritage. What sort of heritage is it? Are the institutions what you could really believe in – is it the sort of world you could really cheerfully die for? No, they don't ask you for your opinion on any of those things. They don't ask you for your *opinion* at all, only for your allegiance. And if you give your opinion without being asked they make significant notes about you in their own minds. From then on you're an unreliable element, or a traitor, or a crank, or a fifth-columnist, or a revolutionary! And it's such filthy *waste*!' he said vehemently, suddenly flinging out his hand towards her with a violence which shook glimmering drops of gold from his brush into the grass. 'The ones who question, the ones who want to be *sure* the end is worth the means, are just the ones who *would* die for something which really satisfied them. It isn't that we're trying to get out of anything – you believe that, don't you? But we need to have a hand in shaping this world we're supposed to give everything to maintain – and they won't let us! They won't any of them let us!'

'I suppose there *is* the vote,' said Rosalba dubiously.

'A choice between two or three men out of thousands, every five years, what's that? And even then they have no hand themselves in half the things that make up living. Parties, what are they? How much voice has the poor little member at the bottom of any organisation, when the very idea of organisation is to make out an orthodox line, and knock everybody on the head who strays away from it?'

She was a little vague yet about all these things, and for that matter probably so was he; and very gently she teased him, because it did not do to be too intensely moved by one's own helplessness. But still her eyes were earnest.

But when they had ranged over the whole field of human frustration, and quarrelled in their wanderings, and paused to draw breath, they were still and always face to face with their own particular lameness, and the wall still showed no way through. Then, even if they did not speak of it, each of them knew that the other was thinking: What hope is there for us? And they would suddenly move together, within touch of hands, or shoulder against shoulder, for reassurance of the solidity of hope. And they would talk with deflected indignation about someone else's problems, which might, to the casual eye, seem almost as great as theirs.

'After all,' said Rosalba, 'there are people much worse off than we are.' And almost she believed it. 'Look at Flo, for instance.'

'Why, what's the matter with Flo? She always seems about as cheerful as a girl can be.'

'Oh, yes, I know, but she doesn't have an easy life, all the same. She looks after her father, and two children at school, and the father isn't always working, and that's why Flo comes scrubbing to the Folly. She has to, they couldn't manage without what she earns. And you know, like me, she hasn't had any training for anything, there was never time, because she's been housekeeper ever since she was about ten years old. And they haven't a home, they live in two rooms with some awful old woman who finds fault with everything the children do.'

'Lots of people are living the same,' said Eugene.

'Yes, I know. She says the town's full of them. And do you know, three or four families could easily live in our lodge, and not even get in one another's way. And I can't do anything about it!'

'Are you sure you'd want to,' asked Eugene, 'if you could?'

She had learned to lie nobly at need, but also to be fiercely honest wherever she might, peering into the corners of her mind before she answered such questions as this. So she said, frowning from the hollow of his shoulder across the falling miles of flax-white grass: 'I don't know. How can I be sure? But I think I should. Of course it's nice to have things, it would be silly to pretend it isn't; but it's lovely to give things, too.'

'If you know that,' he said in a low voice, 'maybe you know, too, how rotten it is when you haven't got anything to give, and you want to – like hell!'

She said reproachfully: 'Oh, Eugene!' and turned up her face to him, cheek against cheek; and Flo went out like a candle, with the rest of the banished world, while they argued again their tormented sharing, and denied furiously that the balance of values quivered on either side by so much as a hair's weight.

3

But Eugene remembered about Flo. She had stood friend to Rosalba, and that was enough for him. He remembered her particularly a week later, when he made one of a fatigue party whisked off by lorries to the far side of the heath, and there set to fetching and carrying for a small army of joiners who were patching up the Warren camp, and surrounding it with a pale fence close enough and high enough to keep out even cats. Every man in the party at once began to ask: 'Who's coming here?' But the labourers didn't know, even the foreman didn't know; and the sergeant, approached more circuitously, professed to be equally ignorant.

The Warren was a large oval depression in the rolling miles of the heath, folded into a crescent-shaped arm of rising woodland which shielded it from the western winds. One of the biggest war-time camps had been left to rot in it ever since the artillery vacated it early in 1946. Every pane of glass was gone; even in this remote spot someone had found pleasure in smashing everything smashable. Ribbons of roof-felting and tarpaulin, camouflaged in faded greens and browns, fluttered desolately against the sickle of pines, and the doorless doorways opened upon floors paved thick with rubble. A long time ago, in 1947, a body of people representing the homeless of both Bredington and Crocksford had made approaches about the possibility of arresting this process of decay, and settling some of the district's wandering families in the hundred and twenty large huts the site could provide when repaired. The camp lay on the border between the two districts, and was therefore a matter for joint negotiation. Crocksford Urban had replied that the camp did not provide the standard of amenities which they could sanction for human habitation, and therefore the scheme was out of the question. Bredington Rural had said that in any case the Army had not relinquished the land, and therefore the question did not arise. The Army had said, through its appropriate

Command, that the matter of surrendering the heath and the artillery range was still under discussion, that there was in consideration a joint Army-R.A.F. plan for a greatly enlarged range which would not only retain all the land now in their possession, but take in most of the remaining grounds of the Folly as well; that, in short, whoever ended up in control of the Warren, it would certainly not be mere civilians, homeless or not. But more years had weathered away the disintegrating huts since then, and precisely nothing had happened until this sudden descent of disinterested workmen and curious soldiers, armed with enough wood, glass, roofing tarpaulin and paint to put the whole place in shape again. And now, it seemed, no one knew for what purpose it was being done. No one, however, supposed that there had been any relenting, on anyone's part, towards the unfortunates on the housing list. More important things than living would be rehearsed here; probably some form of killing.

Eugene made an opportunity to take a walk all round the place and fit into its dilapidated framework the ideas which were already taking shape in his mind. It was perfectly easy to be there day after day, go where you liked, and do no work at all, for so many people were on the site, and involved in so many scattered and wandering jobs, that to put a finger on anyone at any given time was beyond possibility. However, he was willing to work, once the idea had bitten. Even if a house is built expressly for one person, someone else may eventually live in it.

A watchman and a sentry were left on the premises at night to keep each other company, but that was all; and the gate was the only one, and well out in the open side of the site, where daylight or moonlight would keep every movement visible. He was more interested in the rear of the camp, where the pines closed in snugly to the fence, and made approach easy. It was lucky that for some reason, perhaps infected by the atmosphere which hung about the Folly, they'd elected to put up a pale fence instead of wire, making the enclosure look like a kind of intensive deer park.

He took care to be among the party working on that fence when it reached these dark, piny regions; and everything was on his side, the grass about the feet of the thick pales beautifully long and lush, amply covering the interesting fact that six of them, between two of the sunk posts, were not fixed within the twists of wire, but only bound to them with separate strands, easily removable. He would have liked to fix their tops in the same way, to make quite sure of ample tackleway, but there the fraud could be too easily detected, and he thought they would prise aside widely enough to admit even bulky furniture. A pity the place was so remote, but there was a fairly good road owing to the war-time traffic, a hard earth road now half turfed over again, and therefore comparatively silent; and the weather had been dry, so that its passage would be easy and smooth by night.

When he was fairly sure of the practical approach, he went to see Flo Derricks. She had carried more than one message for him by now, and he knew where to find her, but he had never been to the house before, and it was a little daunting to have the door opened upon him violently by Mrs. Gilpin before he could even knock. A disconcertingly sudden and angular person, with scraggy hair knotted back so hard that it dragged her cheeks out of shape, jutted her abrupt chin at him, and cried:

'Will you stop rushing in and out here with your muddy feet? Either play indoors or out, for goodness sake. You're enough – ' She had already realised, a full sentence before this point, that she was not confronting young Sid after all, but the words had been loaded and fired, and could not be arrested. Nor was she in the least embarrassed to discover that she had shot them at a rather older boy than the one for whom they had been intended. 'Well, what do you want?' she demanded. 'When I heard your step I thought it was that dratted kid coming traipsing in again. He's done nothing but tramp in and out, in and out, ever since I polished my lino. You'd think he does it special to annoy. Tell the truth, I believe he does, only I wouldn't say it to Flo. She's a decent enough girl, is Flo, I wouldn't hurt her feelings. Bit high and mighty, mind you, but decent enough – not like that young Daisy – my word, if ever I seen a kid with the makings of a tart— But there, it's been a disturbed world, kids these days haven't had the upbringing they did in my day. Well, who is it you want to see?'

Eugene had just sense enough to ask for Mr. Derricks instead of Flo herself.

'He's at work, for a wonder. But being Saturday, all the rest of the family's at home, worse luck. I wish there was school seven days a week, and that's a fact. Well, will you look there!' She leaned over him suddenly, from the top step of three thrusting her meagre bosom almost into his face, and screamed across the yard: 'Sid! Sid Derricks, you come out of that this minute, do you hear me?' Half the street must have heard her, but in all probability they were used to it, for no one even looked out to see what was young Sid's latest outrage.

Eugene turned just in time to see a small, dishevelled figure take its hand out of the troughing of Mrs. Gilpin's wash-house roof, slither with a horrid scraping of toes down the wall, and drop on hands and feet on the damp, uneven quarries of the yard. Young Sid was red-headed like his sister, and freckled, and grey-eyed, and his instinct was to turn his face towards attack. He picked himself up, and came across the yard towards them sturdily, tugging down his darned brown jersey, and massaging the scarred toes of his shoes against his calves.

'I didn't do it any harm, now then! You can look. And I told you my ball was in there, and you wouldn't let me look! Now I've got it, see!' And he displayed in a very grubby palm a threadbare tennis ball, sodden from the night's light rain.

'I told you to keep off of there, didn't I? Of all the disobedient little devils! And just wait till Flo sees your shoes, that's all. *I* don't know,' she said bitterly, 'what children are coming to these days.' And suddenly launched another yell, this time backwards over her shoulder in the direction of a closed door within: 'Flo!'

Sid drew in rather closely behind Eugene, but made no other move. He was too wise to suppose that Flo's first concern would be with him or the state of his shoes, when there was a strange visitor on the doorstep. Nor did he intend to miss anything for want of keeping his eyes and ears open.

Flo came out wiping her hands from the peeling of potatoes, and looked only faintly surprised at seeing Eugene. Her red hair was tied up in a gay scarf as a concession to Saturday morning, and to hide the curlers. She took it for granted, of course, that he had come to ask some service from her, not to offer one; he could tell it by the ruthless calm with which she assuaged Mrs. Gilpin, got rid of Sid, and shut the inner door upon the pair of them.

'You run off and play, Sid, while it's fine. Go on! Go and call for Bert Johnson, like you said you were going to, and keep from underfoot for just half an hour. Yes, I know you want to come in. I know why, too. Well, we don't need you. Go on, I'll tell you anything you have to know afterwards.' And when he had withdrawn, pouting and dragging his feet, she fought a serene rearguard action after Eugene into her living-room. 'Yes, I know he is, and I've told him, too. But that's the only ball he's got, and I suppose from his point of view he couldn't afford to lose it. I can remember what a ball was worth to me at eight years old. So long as he hasn't done any damage to himself or the troughing, that's the main thing. But I'll talk to him about it – ' She closed the door, leaned against it, and laughed a little breathlessly.

'Do you have to put up with that all the time?' asked Eugene with awe.

'Nearly all the time. It's better that way, you get so hardened to it you don't even notice. But she's not so bad in some ways as you might think. She'll help you in a pinch. For one thing, you can't frighten her, she hasn't got the machinery. You should have seen her in the war! You could leave the kids with her, and be easy. It's only when there's nothing really wrong she's hell to live with.'

'There's a lot of folks like that,' said Eugene.

103

'Most of us, I shouldn't wonder. Mind you,' owned Flo with a sigh, 'I'm not saying I wouldn't like to be somewhere else. I'd give my left hand for a place of our own, and that's a fact; but so would about six hundred other people in this town. Well, now, sit down and tell me all about it, while I get on with the dinner. Dad comes home at one. And better tell it quickly, before Sid comes back. He won't go far, nor be long away, when he knows there's a uniform in the house, and we don't want him stretching his ears after your affairs.'

'Darned sight fonder of a uniform at eight years old, then,' said Eugene with a wry grin, 'than he will be at eighteen.'

'Oh, well, you have to get sense slowly.' She mopped the splashes of water from the oilcloth-covered table with one expert swipe, and clapped the saucepan upon the gas-ring. The grandmother clock in its corner punctured the quietness of the room with loud, lopsided, hiccuping ticks, but magically told almost the exact time.

'It isn't about us this time,' said Eugene, 'it's about you.'

She looked surprised, as if he had said something no one had ever said before, for she was not used to having things carried for her. 'I don't know how you'll feel about it,' he said doubtfully, 'but if you don't like it there's no harm done. You know the Warren camp? Well, it's being put in order for someone to move in.'

Flo turned from the cooker with the matches still in her hand, and gave him a long, sharp, bright look. 'We heard that,' she said, 'from one of the glaziers. Dad knows him. Who's going in there? Do you know?'

'No, I haven't found out yet. I'll tell you fast enough if I can find out.'

'No,' she said, 'we couldn't get to know, either. But the word's gone round, all right. And we're not the only ones who's interested, I can tell you.'

'Well, why don't you do something about it?' said Eugene.

Flo came and leaned on the table, looking at him sternly across it with her determined grey eyes. He stared back

104

brazenly, and smiled. They were getting to know each other fairly well, and there was a lot that didn't have to be said.

'Two reasons,' said Flo deliberately. 'We're waiting to find out who it's meant for. If it's going to be used for ordinary folks much in our position, well and good. Good luck to 'em! And again, in any case, we're waiting till they get it pretty well ready. I don't have to point out to you, Mr. Smart, that if you're going to squat you may as well do it *after* the Army's put the place in shape for you, not before.'

He said with a crow of pleasure: 'So you have been considering it! I thought you couldn't miss it!'

'Miss it? If it hadn't been so far out perhaps people would have been in there before now. But look – we tried every straight way we knew to get permission to move in there. Three years we've been making approaches to this lot and that, and half the Commands in the Army. They even said we could have it, but the site wouldn't be approved on health grounds, on account of the lack of amenities. They did! The Army said that! But now they're doing it up again all nice and new, and for all we don't know yet who's going to have it, you can bet we've got a jolly good idea it won't be us. Well, so I reckon all's fair now. If they're seeing to the amenities, that puts it all right for us to move in. They said it, not me!'

'You're all right, Flo!' said Eugene contentedly. 'I've been wasting my time, you don't need me. But listen, I've made a little contribution, too.' He recounted, with a long forefinger drawing the layout of the camp upon the table, the story of the adaptable and not easily detectable gap in the fence. 'You can bring stuff in fast that way, and with a little care you can have half the night without interruption. And then you can wire 'em up again, and they'll have hard work to find out how you did it, so you can use it again. That's important, because once they know you're there they can try to prevent you from getting in again once you go out for anything. And you mustn't use force – you know that? You mustn't resist us poor devils in the execution of our duty. I can make you another way in by the back, but I may have to prevent you getting in at the front.'

Flo said grimly: 'We've got some expert squatters among us, who know the ropes. There's been a lot of it done all round this town. And even when they threw them out of one camp, they had to find them somewhere else to go.'

'Yes, but look, there's another side to it. Because, you know, all the odds are with them,' said Eugene earnestly.

'I've had the odds against me all my life,' said Flo, not complaining, merely stating the reason for her acceptance of these risks now.

'So have I. You get used to it, don't you? And I don't know,' he owned, 'that it would seem so bad taking on the whole Army and the civil arm, after a spell of Mrs. Gilpin.'

She smiled. She said: 'You're not a bad kid, young Eugene.'

He said: 'Thanks, young Flo! You're not so bad yourself.'

4

Daisy Derricks dressed herself up for Saturday night with the most languorous care, in her best summer coat, the only one which had not been handed down from Flo, and her grown-up hat with a feather, bestowed by Cousin Maud in an unaccustomed fit of generosity, and guaranteed to add at least three years to her age. She added, having first carefully cocked an ear towards the downstairs room where Flo was sewing, and heard the satisfying hum of the borrowed machine proceeding without pause, a great deal of powder and a lavish bow of lipstick in an unsuitable shade of purple. Then she went out to meet her friend Amy on the corner. She went slowly and cautiously down the stairs, shot past the door and across the yard, and resettled her plumage at leisure on her way along the deserted pavement of Gasworks Row. The effect aimed at was something between Margaret Lockwood and Lana Turner. The effect achieved was not so far from the impression gained by Mrs. Gilpin, except for the extreme and pathetic innocence of the young, pleased, expectant eyes. Some day she was going to be very pretty,

106

but nature had been kind to Daisy, and reserved the best for maturity, instead of shooting her bolt too soon, as with many handsome children.

Amy at sixteen was almost as young as Daisy at fourteen, and much sillier. She had a squaling laugh, and a good deal of noticeable fair hair, which curled nicely, and made her look the Anglo-Saxon type to perfection. They were supposed to be going to the pictures. Actually they were going, not for the first time, to the American camp at Bredington. By bus it cost even less, and it amounted to much the same thing. It was true that nothing had actually happened to Daisy yet exactly as it happened in the movies; indeed, nothing had really happened at all. But she had only had her toes in the water yet, and had lost none of her hopefulness.

Saturday night outside the camp gates was a great sight. A mushroom growth of wooden pavilions, cigarette and fruit kiosks, hut cafés, amusement arcades, had sprung up as near as possible to the camp, and everyone who could find a means of living out of hanging on here had already pitched his own camp and spread his stock-in-trade. Soft drinks with hurriedly invented American names were a good line, and every striped hut selling them had some such title as 'Joe's Place'. And here came, on Saturday evenings, buses from all the countryside, crammed with girls. They ranged from experienced campaigners to innocents of Daisy's age, and they vied with one another in the gaiety of their head-scarves, the brilliance of their make-up and the shrillness of their laughter. They stood about in negligent attitudes, and usually in pairs, in the doorways of the shops, about the serving hatches of the coffee-stalls, and in every retired – but not too retired – place, waiting to be picked up. Sometimes they hardly waited. And presently, having achieved some sort of success, they moved off closely entwined with the G.I.'s of their choice to some cinema, or pub, or dance-hall, or wherever else they proposed to disport themselves. But the doorways and not too retired places were always still full.

Whenever girls in the Bredington and Crocksford district strayed from home, it was here, as a matter of course, that their parents or the police looked for them; and here, as a rule, that they found them.

Many of the Americans, as a matter of fact, found this phenomenon as great a vexation as did the parents, and would have liked some rear way out of their quarters; but there was none, and even if there had been, it would not have remained free from the disease for long. But the majority of them appeared to like it.

Amy was not very expert, being too stupid to do even this well; but being with Daisy made her feel quite mature and capable, which was the main reason why she continued to put up with her infantile company. Today she was luckier than usual, and clicked quite early in the evening. He was a large, top-heavy youth with a fleshy face and a wad of imported gum, and he came lounging along with his hands in his pockets and his jaws working rhythmically as a cow's in the meadows, and encountered the tilt of Amy's fair lashes with a glance of contemplative pleasure. Her light hair pleased him. He stopped, propped one shoulder carefully against the wall, and said: 'Hyah, honey?' in a lethargic voice. The only snag was that he was alone. This had never happened before. Daisy nudged her friend, and whispered: 'You promised—'

'It's easy!' Amy whispered back impatiently. 'You've only got to do the same for yourself.' And more ominously she added, in a still quieter whisper: 'Don't you hook on to me!' Then she shook her curls at the foreign ruminant, who turned out, upon closer examination, to be not bad-looking, and even waking up a little.

'Hyah, buddy!' she said.

'Nice evening!' said the young man, his eyes travelling over her. He saw nothing wrong, for he himself was not much older. 'What's your programme, kid?'

'Haven't got one,' said Amy archly, and added, 'yet.'

'Then how about us making one, right now? Say, what do they call you at home – Blondie?' He reached out a deliberate finger, and pulled the nearest curl, which sprang back from his touch with a vigour which proclaimed its genuineness. 'Kinda pretty, that!' he said with warming interest.

'You've got a sauce!' said Amy, bridling, and shaking off the hand which Daisy tried to insinuate into her arm as a reminder of their compact to remain together. 'Nobody's invited you to use your hands, have they?'

'Not yet, baby, not yet! O.K., what d'you say we dance a while first? All evening's a long time, we'll get around to the hands after the feet give out. Aw, c'mon, you don't look the kind to stand out on a fellow. I bet you dance like nobody's business!'

'Not so bad,' allowed Amy brightly, 'or so I'm told.' Having done little else with her spare time for the past two years she did, indeed, dance rather well. The pluck at her sleeve annoyed her. She hissed over her shoulder: 'Oh, don't be such a baby!'

'But you *said*—'

Amy left her with the best will in the world, before the protest had time to reach its end. They had joined arms, decorously yet, according to the rules of the game, and undulated away up the road between countless other pairing couples of their kind, towards the coloured portals of the dance-hall; and Daisy was left standing forlornly in her doorway, alone.

She was, to tell the truth, very much dismayed at the prospect of trying the game alone, but determined not to give in and go tamely home by herself. All the same, everything looked different without Amy, the wandering men more formidable, the gambits of the decorated girls more impossible of imitation. She stood back for a long while, raising her courage, and only pride finally drove her to speak to a man. She was by then so frightened that she hardly looked at the man she addressed; it simply happened that she reached the edge of the precipice and jumped just as this particular man was passing. He stopped and spoke to her in return, sounding faintly startled, for they didn't

109

usually look so desperate about it, or come quite so young. But he was a little drunk, and of a kindly and catholic nature, and they all came alike to him. She went off on his arm feeling a little reassured, and very grown-up and sophisticated.

After he had brought her a drink she felt even more satisfied that she had done the right thing. Now that she was able to look at him, he was not so bad; rather dauntingly old and weather-beaten, perhaps from life in the great outdoors, but he had really only a few grey hairs. But she could not persuade herself that he looked very much like Gary Cooper.

He bought her another drink, and began to paw her. It didn't feel at all as she had expected it to. And he smelled strongly of something nasty; it was whisky, but second-hand it smelled nasty enough to Daisy. She began to be frightened again, much more seriously than before. It wasn't coming out right at all. She didn't know where it had gone wrong, she had copied the pattern as faithfully as possible. By the time he took her away from the pub into the radiant evening in the fields behind the camp she was wishing herself at home, but did not know how to get out of this gracefully. Five minutes of the nearest coppice removed the necessity for worrying about this, for it ceased to be at all important that she should be graceful about it. She simply pulled herself away from his astonished arms, crying wildly, and ran for it.

He wailed after her grievously: 'Hey, baby what's the trouble wit' you? Don't get me wrong! Say, what did I *do* to you, for Pete's sake?' and ran after her a little way in sheer good-natured anxiety to allay her terror; for he was not a bad sort of fellow, and how was he to know the kid had never done this before? But she didn't wait to listen to explanations or protests, but ran as if he had drawn a gun on her, until she fell over a solitary and sad G.I. who was lying in the grass on his back, chewing a long blade of wild barley, and staring at nothing. He was thinking about his girl in the States, and it was only a nuisance to him when another and totally strange girl tripped over him and fell flat on her face.

He said: 'Hey, what's buzzing? Watch your step, sister, I ain't the good earth.' Then, as he perceived that instead of rising she lay where she had fallen, and sobbed into the grass, he lifted his head just sufficiently to take a long look at her. It was not yet even dusk, here in the edge of the open fields, though it was already late enough to be past the bed-time of a kid like this one, he decided. She couldn't be above fourteen. The hat with the feather had fallen off, which accounts for the fact that he was able to judge with such accuracy. When she looked up at him at last he saw that the make-up had become a bit of a mess, too; but of course he could not know what a masterpiece it had been at the beginning of the evening.

Doing the exactly right thing through indolence rather than intelligence, he said to the alarmed cock of her eyes: 'O.K., O.K., I ain't touching you! And, baby, I ain't even interested!'

This was so palpably true that she began to cry as vigorously as before, but for reasons of disillusionment this time. He was disgusted; all he wanted was a little peace to forget that England existed except as something to lie on under the rim of the trees, and a nice scent from the ground, and here when he avoided troubles they came tumbling over him. He sat up resignedly, and looked her over with an extremely unenthusiastic eye; he was not fond of kids when they got past ten years, especially if they happened to be feminine, but he didn't like to see anyone being as miserable as this if it could be helped. Besides, she was making a noise. It was pretty evident to him that she had somehow got into the wrong basket. Perhaps he had seen more of tarts than Mrs. Gilpin, for to him Daisy did not look at all like one, only like a small girl doing her best to look like a tart, which was quite a different thing.

'That's all right with me, kid,' he said, not unkindly. 'Get it off your mind. What happened? Meet a bear, or something? These woods sure are dangerous.'

Daisy gathered herself into a forlorn little huddle in the grass, and sniffled: 'It was a man – he – he frightened me! I didn't *like* him—'

'You don't say!' said the young man with polite interest. 'Where did you find this guy?'

She told him, in spasmodic gulps, the whole story; there

111

was not much of it, and even by this method it did not take long. He listened respectfully – he had to if he was to hear more than a strangled word here and there – and at the end of it he said reasonably: 'Well, what can you expect, if you come here looking like what guys like him are looking for? Anyways, looking like you thought you was it! Don't ask me to blame that feller, honey, you sure asked for it!'

'I *didn't*!' sobbed Daisy. 'I *never*! I didn't know it was like that. The books and the pictures never say nothing about it being like that—'

'Say, you don't want to go bothering about the way it is in the books and pictures,' protested the sage. 'That's to look at, see, like Mother Goose. Anyways, even if you could read all about it in books, baby, that ain't no one easy lesson you'd be taking. There's books tell you all about how to swim, but you don't have to read 'em and then go dive in the river. That's sense, ain't it?'

She allowed meekly that it was.

'And another thing,' he said sternly, 'you don't want to go around with the sort of friend who walks out on you that way, see? You can see for yourself, sure, she's no good.'

Daisy, gulping and scrubbing at her eyes, was understood to admit that she never wanted to see Amy again; and further, that Flo had always *said* she was no good.

'Flo sounds a right sensible girl,' he said warmly. 'You go by what she tells you from this on. Say, who is Flo, anyways?'

'She's my sister. She looks after us.'

'She does? What's with your mother, baby?'

'I h-haven't got one. She's dead.'

'No mother!' he said to the dipping beech-branches over him. 'The ones I meet, they have to have no mother! Jeez! Don't it get you?' And to Daisy, who heard this uncomprehending: 'O.K., Marlene, clean your face up a bit, and let's get out of here. You're going home.'

'I don't want!' she wailed, the lateness of the hour and the ominous nature of her welcome suddenly borne in upon her at the suggestion. 'I'm scared.'

'You heard! Your ears ain't cloch! What's there to be scared of, for goodness sake? You was pretty scared when you made your crash-landing a while back. Think of that, and I guess that sister of yours won't seem so fierce. Anyways, baby, you ain't staying on my hands. Here, wipe your face clean, and tell us where you live.'

She obeyed with the greatest humility.

'O.K., I'll put you on a bus, and you're going to go straight home – or else! See?'

She saw. She said in a voice still tame and shaken with fright, but quite new to his ears: 'I do think you're wonderful!'

'Hey, wait a minute!' said the young man ominously, stopping in his tracks. 'Don't you start them tricks with me, or I'll slap your ears down good.'

'I'm not starting any tricks,' said Daisy obstinately. 'I just said I think you're wonderful, that's all.'

'Well, can that stuff! I don't go for it from little girls who'd ought to been in bed hours ago, see?'

More faintly, but with reinforced conviction, Daisy said through tears: 'I'm going right home like you've told me, and I did listen to everything you said, and I'm not trying anything. But you *are* wonderful.'

'Jeez!' said the young man, very large and formidable beside her in the twilight of the trees, hustling her along with a hand at her elbow in an undignified and exasperated fashion, 'the breaks I get! It sure does shake you!'

Since the only thing now to be done with Daisy was to get rid of her as speedily and safely as possible, he had run some of the remaining breath out of her tired little body, to no bad end, by the time he got her back to the bus stop. This end of Bredington was getting into its Saturday-night stride, in a flare of early garish lights and a strident parrot-house noise of giggles and screams and loudspeaker music. Every doorway was occupied by at least one necking couple, and such few people as were in the bus queues upon their respectable and unavoidable occasions wore the inevitable resultant faces of uneasiness and distaste, the faces of people

113

preparing to write letters to the local press signed 'Disgusted' and 'Worried Parent' and 'Old-fashioned'. Daisy tremulously indicated the queue which served Crocksford, and the young man looked it over without much lifting of his now settled gloom. Daisy looked him over with no less attention and much more satisfaction. If you looked at him from one angle – the worm's eye angle proper to her present position in his large left hand – he didn't look so very unlike Gary Cooper. She had now a somewhat better idea of how Daisy Derricks ought to behave to that worthy if ever she met him; and the sort of handling it entailed, if not in the highest romantic movie style, filled her with a comfortable, safe and thankful feeling to which she clung with all her tired senses. No more cheap make-up for Daisy, no more trying to be big when these all-wise eyes could see her age at a glance, no more distasteful friends, no more loitering in shop doorways. She was long past the picking-up stage, grown out of it in one small shock and one marvellous recovery. Daisy was deep in love.

The shock, however, was not yet put by. No one could live through so much of her education, through so many emotions and experiences, in one evening, without being quite exhausted; and Daisy was trembling. The young man looked dubiously along the bus queue, and saw only homing lads and girls of a type less than useless to her, and censorious middle-aged faces which, he realised, were judging him to be the occasion of her present dilapidated state; and at the end, finally, two who didn't belong. A boy and a girl, holding hands, but very quietly, looking straight before them, looking a little remote, a little afraid, but very happy; she with a large portfolio tucked under her arm, he carrying her small green leather attaché case. This boy was a soldier, too, but a native one, and he wasn't in any case to see the girls in the doorways; why should he, with that one beside him holding his hand? Only kids, the boy ordinary enough, plain, brown and fiery-looking, the girl a real little beauty. Queer couple! She was what they'd call here a lady. Dressed as drab as the road, but in stuff that cost plenty, and moved like a racing filly. And Jeez, was she in love! It flew off her like sparks off a catherine wheel on the Fourth of July.

Well, maybe it was hardly fair to wish a strayed kitten like this one on to their hands, when there wasn't a thing they wanted but each other; but they didn't look to him as if they had to keep saying as much every other minute, and anyhow, he liked the look of them. And there was nobody else. It had to be somebody decent. He lugged Daisy unceremoniously over to where they stood, and asked a little sheepishly:

'Pardon me, folks, but do you go as far as Crocksford by this bus?'

They said they did; smiling nicely, a little startled, as if he had awakened them by the question, but meeting his appealing look with the ready comprehension of four large, candid eyes prepared to love the world if it would approach them as directly as this.

'Would you mind seeing this kid gets off there all safe and sound?' He looked down, not without a gloomy grin, at the wreckage of Daisy's grande toilette. 'She ain't come to no harm, but I guess her folks don't know nothing about this jaunt. She started a little young, that's all. Didn't know what it took. She won't be no trouble to you.' He felt the trembling small hand pressing his sleeve, and saw the lowered lids blinking above a deep, dreadful blush, and felt depressed, but weakened into kindness. 'She ain't a bad kid,' he said in a voice confidentially low, 'and she ain't going to do this no more. That right, honey?'

The bent head nodded speechlessly.

The girl loosed her hand from the boy's, and drew Daisy with them into the queue. Her face, which was pale and bright as an angel's, flushed a little, warmly, and her smile was shy but willing. 'Of course!' she said. 'She'll be all right with us.'

'Yeah, she's fine! Only got a scare, and that ain't been a bad thing, the way it turned out.'

Daisy said nothing at all, even when the kind young lady

115

called her a poor child; and the boy was so content to watch the girl being motherly, so sweetly, so clumsily, with such a divine desire to give away her happiness to everything on earth, that he could not resent the occasion of the gesture. Daisy's unwilling but thorough escort saw his mission ended, and made no bones about being glad; but even when he had thanked them, and left them there, and was on his way back to camp, he could not lose his depression. It could easily have been worse; and he viewed this reflection not as comfort but as a threat. The whole set-up *was* a lot worse. What an evening! And the devil's own noise about the camp even when he reached it, and his own head aching. What a world! What a goddamned world!

It was very much like other Saturday nights around closing-time, but it looked twice as bad to him. He hated having to exert himself; and what right had unknown infants to come blundering through his closely-planned dreams of Lou, and knock them endways? Much worse, when he walked into his hut and groped for his bed in the half-light there was someone in it, or at least on it, rolled up in one of his blankets. A girl, not all that old, straw-fair, three parts drunk, and dead sure of a welcome. She unrolled the blanket when he touched her, and flashed black-rimmed eyes at him, and murmured:

'Hyah, Caesar! Get a load o' Cleopatra!'

Well, so he could have a little fun, after all. He was dead tired behaving nicely, and a guy can choose his own sort of fun, can't he? He picked up the girl by anything that came handy, hauled her outside to the low wire fence, and threw her over it into the waste dump. He liked the way her enchanted gurgles changed to squeals of incredulous abuse halfway out, when it dawned on her he was different; that made him feel better. He liked the way she landed; hard; about twenty seconds she didn't have any breath to swear. He didn't care if she broke everything she had, but he knew by the stream of language which followed that she hadn't broken a thing, unless it was the last remaining inhibition.

He went back into the hut as soon as it stopped making

116

him feel better, but he couldn't fancy his blankets. He went and slept in a leave bed for the night; and before he was halfway to sleep the good effect of that little bit of exercise had all worn off. He felt like nothing.

'The hell with women!' he said. 'The hell with England, and women – little tarts and big tarts!'

'What about the other kind?' asked someone sleepily from the other end of the hut.

'What other kind?' he said. And just before he fell asleep he gave tongue again, less distinctly but with equal vigour. 'The hell with military aid!' he said. 'Boy, do I feel unco-operative!'

5

Sid came home only half an hour after the time at which he had been told to report himself, and was put to bed; and as Flo was in the provident habit of allowing an extra half-hour when issuing her edict, that was all according to plan. But young Daisy did not turn up promptly after the first-house cinema crowds came swarming across the end of Gasworks Row, and her sister, who from long acquaintance had a nose for trouble, began to suspect its approach. She never had an easy mind when the kid was out with that Amy; she knew well enough that Amy was a fast little dimwit, but had hoped that with only a little remote control Daisy would presently discover as much for herself, for it was a principle of the Derricks family to move off in the opposite direction from that in which they were pushed, and who should know it better than Flo? The experiment in patience, however, looked like becoming a shade dangerous, and she would have to take the other risk and put her foot down. In the meantime, they might be only giggling and gossiping in some entry on the way home, or buying chips if they had any money left.

But the pubs closed and the fish-and-chip shops closed, and Daisy did not come. Mr. Derricks came home, radiantly sober but satisfied, from the Waterman's Arms, his round blue-grey eyes awed by his own tall stories, and was jolted badly to find a grim older daughter waiting for him, and no younger one. He said it was a facer, and waited for Flo to tell him what to do about it; and Flo told him to wait a little while longer.

It was the right advice, obviously, for about a quarter of an hour later came a very light tap upon the window, and when Flo ran to draw back the curtain, there was Eugene Seale's face outside, very serious and a little sulky, and in his arm, looking extremely tired and quite swollen with crying, was Daisy. Flo nodded wildly, and flew to the door to let them in, lifting the latch noiselessly and fingering her lips at them as soon as they entered, so that they came on tiptoe, and reached the inner room unobserved. Mr. Derricks, in the relief of seeing Daisy intact and in what Flo appeared to consider good hands, recovered sufficient confidence to feel a father's part heavy upon him, and was about to go up like a rocket, when Flo hissed furiously at him to be quiet, and gestured towards the room across the minute hall, where Mrs. Gilpin was undoubtedly ready to stretch her ears at the first raised voice. Everyone responded in superhuman fashion to the need for quietness and normality, and the interview went almost in whispers.

Flo said: 'My, that was really smart of you, Eugene! The window, I mean! One tap on that street door, and she's out like a jack-in-the-box. My God, if she'd seen our Daisy looking like this!' Daisy began to cry again, but very feebly and without noise. Flo's knees gave way under her suddenly, and she sat down trembling in a chair beside the table. 'It isn't that I'm really thinking of this bloody respectability more than of her, not really it isn't,' she said towards Eugene, herself near to tears. 'But you don't know what it's like living here.'

'I can guess a bit, though,' said Eugene. 'Besides, it's her it would be worst for in the long run, if the talk started. But I'm pretty sure she's all right. Really! She says she is, and the fellow that brought her to the bus stop said it, too. Said she'd come to no harm. Said she wasn't a bad kid, and she wasn't going to do anything like that any more. She promised him she wouldn't. She was taking notice, I can tell you. Honest, I think you needn't worry. And don't row her tonight. I wouldn't! She's had about enough, and anyhow, she'll only howl if you begin on her now, she's so tired. Tomorrow you can give her hell, and at least she'll hear what you say.'

'Where did you get her?' said Flo, her calming eyes running over Daisy's draggled face and hair and coat in a self-reassuring way, and marking in passing the fact that the feather in the very unsuitable hat bequeathed by Cousin Maud was broken, and drooped at half-mast over one eye. And a good job, too, it had given her more than enough ideas in its brief heyday.

'Bredington. I was coming back from there – with – ' He saw the quick, humorous lift of her eyebrow, and knew that he need not say with whom, though it was the first time he had ever been with Rosalba in any place in the world but the watch-tower on the heath. 'We went to a dealer's there this afternoon,' he said, 'to try and sell a picture, and then we stayed all the evening in the park. We were waiting in the queue for the last bus when along comes this American G.I. with Daisy in tow, and asks us if we go to Crocksford, and if we'll see her safely into the town, at least. He said she'd had a bit of a fright, but was O.K. And you know, I think she is.'

'What was he like?' asked Flo.

'Straight, I'm pretty sure. And on the way home she talked to Rosalba quite a lot, and Rosalba wanted to come all the way with her, but you know how it is, she mustn't be late, or there'll be questions asked, and everything has to be just the same as it's always been, or it's the end of the world. So she went straight home, and I came with Daisy.'

He thought of Rosalba's face, so astonished, so tender, stooped over Daisy's disordered hair as the child cried into her shoulder all the way back in the bus, quietly and wearily. No one had ever leaned on Rosalba and cried before, no one had ever clung to her arm and said she was ever so nice, no one had sobbed small, personal, ridiculous sorrows into her ear, and taken pleasure in her inexpert attempts at comfort; and he had seen her opening like a flower, like the beautiful chilled rose she was, in the melting warmth of Daisy's trust. But he had been so busy watching Rosalba that he had heard nothing of Daisy's story, and tomorrow she would have to tell it again for herself, with no such uncritical audience, either.

'It was that Amy, I suppose,' said Mr. Derricks resignedly, for he liked her no better than Flo did, but that was because Flo had communicated her own uneasiness to him.

'Yes,' whispered Daisy.

'It's about time you stopped seeing that little madam,' he said bitterly. 'You'll never get anything but trouble from going about with her.'

'I've told her that already,' said Flo, 'a hundred times if I've told her once, but – ' She shrugged her round, soft shoulders; she was past the worst, and relaxing into a sense of relief. The practical energy to get some good out of this very narrow shave would come later. She looked the miserable little figure up and down, and said with a sigh: 'Well, you look a nice object, I must say, Daisy Derricks!'

'You needn't worry,' said Daisy, still in her creaking whisper, for she was quite voiceless with so much crying, 'I'm not going to see her any more.'

'We'll see how long you stick to it,' said Flo, unimpressed.

'I'm not! You'll see! She's *no good*!' said Daisy, as if she had found out so much for herself.

'My goodness, look who's talking! Oh, go on,' she said, suddenly ill-tempered. 'Get upstairs, out of my sight! Go and sleep off your gin and lime, or whatever it was – don't think I can't smell it! Go on, this minute! I'll talk to you tomorrow.'

Daisy drooped towards the door forlornly, dragging her feet. 'Well, anyhow,' she said, for her own comfort, 'I've met just about the most wonderful man in the world.'

The shot was not without its effect on Flo, but she merely

replied sharply: 'Then I'll tell you tomorrow what he probably thinks of *you*! Now do as you're told, and go to bed.' And Daisy, crumpled once more into childishness, went.

She went quietly, but they heard the other door open. It was not her fault, it was not even Mrs. Gilpin's fault, but the cussedness of things decreed that they should pass there in the yard-wide hall, in perversely the best light there was in the house. There was a pause while they all held their breath and then Daisy's feet, creditably steady, going up the stairs, and Mrs. Gilpin, bright of eye in the doorway, gazing at them all with pleasurable excitement. She had come for quite another reason, but what she very naturally asked first was: 'What's the matter with your Daisy? She doesn't half look out of sorts! And 'tisn't like you to let her up so late, Flo, I must say.'

They all thought fast, but Flo was in charge here, and they left the initial lie to her, and made ready to embroider it at need. Time had been when Mr. Derricks would have leaped first, with marvellous ingenuity and disastrous effect, offering some epic fantasy to which no one could possibly live up for long. But he had learned to rely on Flo for the more solid and hardwearing effects.

'She went into Bredington for me,' said Flo, 'and missed her bus back, or she'd have been back an hour ago. And there was the usual Saturday night rumpus going on there – scandalous, I call it, people having to stand and wait for their buses right by that dance-hall. There's always a fight, or something. People don't like it. I'm glad Mr. Seale was there to take care of her.'

'There was a bit of bottle-throwing,' elaborated Eugene. 'She got knocked off her feet, with the queue trying to get out of the way. She isn't hurt, but you could see she was properly upset, poor kid.'

Mrs. Gilpin didn't believe a word of it; she couldn't say it in so many words, but the air reeked of it. But before the inquest on Daisy could proceed further, Flo said pointedly: 'Did you want me for something?'

121

'Oh, I didn't want to disturb you at this late hour of night I'm sure! Only I heard a bit of news – it's going all round the town, I don't know if you've heard it already – about the Warren camp. You know they're doing it up again, after all this time? Well, Joe Waltham's wife told me that she heard from her husband who's coming there. And *he* heard it quiet-like, through keeping his ears open on the job.' She paused for effect; there was no need, for already Flo's eyes were fixed and staring upon her face. 'You'll never credit the nerve of it! Americans, my dear! Some of the ground crews from Bredington are being moved up here to be near the range.'

Flo made the exclamations which were required of her, but she made them automatically. Her eyes remained filmed and placid until the door had closed again upon Mrs. Gilpin, and even then for another moment, until she was sure that the door of the other room had also closed upon that well-informed lady. Then they flashed sudden cool, ferocious resolution. She sat knotting and unknotting her hands, and waited a full half-minute before she spoke.

'Americans!' she said. 'After we've waited three years, and asked, and asked, they bring in American bomber crews! *Bomber* crews! Americans!' she said. 'That does it! Now we've got to go through with it, or die trying. Over my dead body,' she said, 'they'll get into the Warren!' And she looked up at Eugene with bright, practical, alert eyes. 'Where did you say that gap in the fence was?'

6

The project had never been real until then. Not even Flo could carry sixty wavering families into a deal single-handed, and she had never really believed that the thing would happen; but the news of the imminent arrival of Americans went round like wildfire, and screwed a great many faint courages to the sticking point. Whoever was actually to blame for the state of affairs at Bredington – and they knew enough to be sure that other garrison towns shared the same maddening problem – in the popular mind the whole thing centred round the word American. Individually they could be decent enough chaps; but the cumulative effect of their installation at Bredington had been catastrophic, and nobody, nobody at all except the teen-age girls who would then have no bus fares to pay on Saturdays, wanted them any nearer Crocksford. The district had tried hard to digest them, but there were economic reasons for its killing failure. Houses were not the only things which were short; beer was short, cigarettes were short, labour was short, land was short; and the helpless aliens, immeasurably better provided with leisure, amenities and money than the natives, remained sprawled over too great a share of all these things, an immovable lump in the long-suffering throat of England, innocently and injuredly unable to understand why they could be got neither up nor down.

So it was every man's hand against them when the news went round. Some of the tradespeople thought of the influx of money, and wavered; but even they had daughters, and the pull was not all one way. Those who had nothing material to gain did not even hesitate. Lorries and small vans were quietly borrowed and lent, numerous ponies lost a night's rest in the cause, neighbours sewed, contributed, helped to load, promised support in the expected local warfare to come. Not all would keep their promises when the pinch came, but many would, if only because they themselves were safely out of the forefront of the battle.

Only one person in the Derricks household suffered divided loyalties. It had not occurred to Daisy that she would ever see her depressed knight-errant again; but in spite of her disillusionment with the amatory habits of certain of his countrymen, and her resultant recoil into extreme circumspection in the matter of approaching them, the fact remained that he was American, too. Sometimes, in the excitement of looking forward to a new home without the old cat Gilpin, she felt a twinge of conscience at the thought that she would be keeping him and his fellows out.

All the same, he had told her to do what Flo said, because Flo was obviously a sensible girl; and it was highly desirable that she should leave the vicinity of Gasworks Row, because she knew that Mrs. Gilpin was saying things about her. To everyone! The shock of having to care about gossip was new to Daisy, and hurt her exceedingly, and Flo's strictures had not been without effect. Certainly she had time enough in which to grow up, and certainly the process was already beginning.

But love was the main motive of all that Daisy did. Love from afar, the comfortable, unvulnerable kind which takes no count of pigtails; short dresses and strap shoes, because they are never seen. So she need never dress up, she need not regret the broken feather in Cousin Maud's hat, she need not even tidy her hair or wash her face; she could think herself into his presence beautiful, grown-up and accomplished, without lifting a finger to be any of these things. As for trying to captivate another man, American, English or what you will, that, of course, was unthinkable. There *was* only one man.

So Daisy was a reformed character for more reasons than a salutary fright. To be sure, she was also pretty useless, as all her free time had to be spent in some romantic solitude, such as the bedroom, regarding some convenient blank space into which she could imagine fondly the gradually improving features of the most wonderful man in the world. The evening sky, whitely blue outside the window, did very well for this purpose; even the mottled wallpaper would do at a pinch, or the blue-grey deeps of her own eyes reflected in the mirror; but she preferred a large canvas, because he had been a large young man, and was steadily growing larger. Absorbed into his delectable countenance, she let her hands lie idle upon any work people tried to give her towards the great plot; and this was a pity, for to do her justice she was a very handy little monkey at her best. But at least she took down all the pictures of Tyrone Power, Errol Flynn, Stewart Granger and Michael Wilding, and burned them; she left Gary Cooper for a time, until the most wonderful man in the world became so far ahead of him that even he ceased to have any significance, and went into the fire.

Flo let her alone, since this was obviously a love of the highest moral influence, and she owed the original some thanks already. He was safe from annoyance, and no one else had anything to lose. In the meantime, her own hands were full. Mr. Derricks was one of the leaders of the movement; that was quite easy for her. Every time they held a committee meeting she would go over the ground, consider the possibilities, and make suggestions, thus: 'Don't you think, Dad, it's the drinking water we've got to look after first? Now if someone's put to see to it immediately that the flow's on, and the tank there full, we shan't have to worry for a few days.'

And Mr. Derricks, beautifully brushed and combed and shaven and muffled as always for a crisis, would bide his time in the meeting to lean forward and give utterance: 'Now, yo' chaps, there's one thing vital. First thing first, I say. Wheer'm we going to be if they cut off the water, eh? Yo' tell me that! Now, look here, this is my plan—'

All the plans worked out by Flo, all the hints she got from Eugene, evolved through the channel of Mr. Derricks' innocent eloquence, and he grew inches taller with pleasure in his own prowess. Flo liked to see people enjoying themselves. She gave him the sketch map Eugene had drawn for her, in which three gaps were indicated now, the two auxiliaries only for individual passage, and not on any account to be used until a state of siege set in, and then with the greatest care. What could be more demoralising than to be aware that the apparently fast-immured citizens are walking in and out through your lines much as they please, and to be unable to find out how? This Mr. Derricks did not fail to point out with a flourish to the committee, who took the point as readily as he had done when Flo pointed it out to him. He was entirely happy; and he was a nice little man to have about the house even when he was depressed, and in happiness he was delightful.

It was necessary to enrol Sid, too, into active service, in order to impress upon him sufficiently the need for keeping his mouth shut. To keep the plot from him until the night of its accomplishment was quite impossible; but he was already well versed in spy stuff, and in the role of messenger could imagine himself Dick Barton to the life, and torture would not have dragged from him the least of Eugene's secrets.

The day chosen for the invasion was the last day of June. They would have liked a moonless night for the attempt, but it had to be made, in good conditions or bad, at the precise time when the repairs had reached their most advanced point of safety, and the advent of the Americans could not be regarded as impossible for more than one day longer. There was a moon, but there were also fitful clouds which made the whole expanse of the heath a mottle of shadows, shifting like water across other long, soft shadows which were the slight, undulating hollows of the ground. Across that quivering striped wallpaper landscape no sentry was going to stand and stare all night, or he would fall asleep on his feet from the dazzle of it. Besides, who was going to crop up in such a godforsaken place, on this night out of all the nights? Eugene, judging from his own observations, had suggested that both the sentry and the watchman would be inside the gatehouse, taking occasional alternate peeps out at the closed gate, which after all was what the sentry was supposed to be guarding. It turned out much in the pattern he had indicated.

For the sake of silence they used the pony-carts and floats for the first advance, as the night-bound procession set off up the high heath road of thin, splayed turf; but the crescent of hanging pinewood acted for them, and effectively cut off sound from the gatehouse with its sickle of higher ground, and the wind was unexpectedly high, and blowing to them full across the oval of the Warren, making a stormy music among the pines to eclipse even the noise of lorries. It could not have been better, thought Eugene, feeling the wind with his hand through the window of his own hut in the spinney, and exulting in the direction and force of it. And Rosalba gazed out from her bedroom window above the roses at the south lodge, and made curious, confused little prayers to her own heart for Flo; because it wasn't fair, it wasn't sane, that people who wanted to live ordinary, decent, hardworking lives should be denied the space for that life so that other people, who probably wanted precisely the same thing, could be forced to practise means of killing. It was no longer enough to be told: 'This part of what you call your rights is forfeit to the common good,' when you had once begun to ask: 'What do *I* believe would be for the common good?' Because not one person in a million would be likely to suggest bomber squadrons – not even after much nudging and a little prompting from authority. Certainly not those callow, bored, lonely, restless young exiles at Bredington, she thought, shivering at the memory of so much wasted muscle and mind and time. Half-past ten! In two hours more Flo ought to be inside the fence.

And in two hours more Flo was. They had no trouble on the way up, for most of the transport lorries were off the site by now, and everything was at the finishing-touches stage. They had to bring the carts crawling up to the fence by a handway of Eugene's blazing, slashes of luminous paint making the night weird under the pines. He hadn't dared to mark the fence itself, but Flo knew where to find the six movable pales, and they fanned away, when released, widely enough to admit tables, chairs and cupboards with inches to spare. Not that anyone had anything very massive to bring! Two chains of people could handle small stuff together. Everything was put inside the fence, as quietly as the job could be done; and then every family could sidle along the aisles of huts, and choose their place, and begin the business of installing their effects. The lorries could not come so near, but must halt on the far edge of the pines; and from there they manhandled and carted in relays the rest of their possessions. Every family of the sixty-two which had chosen to take part in the operation had a member fixed and firm inside its hut before the sentry and the watchman knew there was anyone there at all. They had made sure that the water tank was full, and the water on; they had a man watching the gatehouse, and Sid in the grass beside him, waiting to run with a message as soon as there was any sign of an alarm.

Now, with so many of them already in, and so much already done, they had a means of getting the rest of the stuff in; all round that wide perimeter the smaller urgencies could be tossed from hand to hand, wherever the unenviable enemy were not. Flo, hurriedly throwing together bedding in the stuffy darkness of her chosen hut, really felt sorry for those two in the gatehouse; but how could they be held responsible for failing to keep out about a hundred and eighty people?

Inside the camp, in that remoter part of it which they had naturally elected to inhabit, there was a dark, frantic, but almost silent confusion. As ink licks into blotting paper it had begun at the gap, and seeped gradually nearer and nearer to the gatehouse; but there were still huts in between. Sid lay beside his partner, wide mouth open with excitement, large eyes hungrily fixed on the gleam of light which indicated the enemy. He did not regard the odds as a hundred and eighty to two on, but as himself, a sort of lone star ranger, against the whole of the army; and he wanted action. The noises from behind, painfully smothered until every nerve and muscle ached with going carefully, and every finger-tip was raw with feeling a gingerly way along rough weatherboard walls, seemed to him to lap nearer and nearer to his eyrie, like small recurrent waves, and presently to have gone over his head and just touched the wall of the gatehouse.

And then Mrs. Forster's eldest boy, who was fifteen, but notoriously unhandy, dropped a brass kettle of the heroic proportions appropriate to a family of eight; even at that, this might not have mattered very much, if he had not dropped it over the top of the fence from a cart's height, and into a corrugated zinc tub, which thereupon gave vent to an enormous hollow clang suggestive of the crack of doom.

Inside the gatehouse the watchman dropped his cigarette

and missed the double-top he was aiming for. An instant of shattering silence followed the last reverberations of the extraordinary noise, while they gaped at each other in almost superstitious dread.

'My God!' said the very young and very reluctant soldier in a whisper. 'What was that?'

'You tell me! But it wasn't no pine-cone dropping, my lad!' The watchman reached for his cloth cap. 'Come on! If you ask me, we've got a bit of trouble aboard.'

'Rot! There hasn't been a sound till now. What could be going on, up here at the back of beyond?' But he also adjusted his cap, and clattered out after his companion. And he'd thought he was on an easy job! But if anybody was playing tricks, they'd be for it!

The moon was hidden just then, half the face of the sky covered by a great cloud; and the high wind plucked at the tattered edges of it, and frayed them in long ribbons of black across the starry faces over the pinewood, where the branches threshed stormily with a ceaseless, monotonous sound. In the blown half-darkness fragmentary mocking echoes of the prodigious gong-stroke he had heard seemed to steal out at the bewildered soldier from round the corners of huts, and out of the tunnel-like corridors between them, and to linger in the hollows of doors and windows. He stood in the open ground within the gate, and looked all round, and could see nothing but the lawful brown-and-whiteness of the wooden huts, and the glossy new faces of roofing, and the sheen of fresh paint, and hear only the single, excited muttering of a stormy night, but that was a sound in which any number of others could sink themselves and be hidden. He had a feeling that the place was full of people, and the shadows full of eyes; and uncomfortably he felt sure that all the eyes were laughing.

'I'll go down this road to the left,' said the watchman. 'You take the right. That row came from somewhere over the back.'

The two main arteries copied in a softer arc the shape of the perimeter, and met at the rear, throwing off lesser capillaries on both sides as they went. The soldier took his at a loping run, and as he went he certainly became aware of a frantic activity ahead, compounded of small sounds of things being moved, dumped, tossed from hand to hand, and even, he thought, minute muffled gigglings and shushings which infuriated him beyond measure. He looked down every alley as he passed, but the flat crossing shadows made a real darkness there instead of the half-light of the open heath, and he could imagine all manner of movements going on within it. He was determined not to go aside except for something he knew to be real.

Suddenly somebody whistled behind him, the deliberate wolf-whistle of the hunting American beholding the passing of a likely girl. He swung round in his tracks, just in time to see a small dark figure bolt away down one of the runways; and after him he went, in his indignation forgetting or rejecting as irrelevant the consideration that the complexities of this place favoured the quarry every time. Sid kept him at it for more than five minutes, popping back at him by unexpected ways and yoo-hooing in his ear round corners, until the soldier had him pinned in a long, straight alley, and in the heat of the chase forgot his awe of the night, and yelled after him at fullest voice: 'Stop! You little devil, stop!'

Someone else gave tongue almost in the same moment, from away at the back of the camp: 'O.K., Sid, ready!'

And Sid stopped; he stopped so abruptly that the pursuing private, who had had singularly little confidence in the force of his own authority and was still running full-tilt, fell headlong over him and bloodied his nose against the unpleasant gravel and cinder of the track. Sid went down with him, but in the light fashion in which small boys usually fall, and clear of his weight, and had only a grazed knee to show for it, while the soldier was winded. Sid waited for him to recover and felt a little aggrieved when his first act on regaining his breath was to shoot out a large hand and seize his quarry vengefully by the collar, exactly as if he had still been running away.

'Got you, my lad!' he said. It struck Sid as in some way,

without being exactly a lie, yet a gross misrepresentation of the facts. But he had been told not to argue when caught. He said unkindly: 'So what?' Echoes of the Americans had reached these present quarters ahead of the reality. He twitched his shoulder resentfully. 'All right, you needn't pull. I'm not *trying* to get away.'

His captor nevertheless held on tightly, and marched him as fast as he could go towards where the voice had called, and where the shadows rustled in that darkly suggestive fashion. There were people there, dozens of them, not trying to hide now, just waiting. The watchman was there just before him, he could hear his voice raised in expostulation: 'What's going on here? Do you folks reckon you can get away with this? There's going to be hell to pay in the morning!' He passed dark, shadowy warmths which were plump women, standing quite still in the doorways of huts, their breath a small, soft breeze, infinitely soft, as he passed. Little shadows moved curiously after him, and were almost silently called back to their mothers. Lumpy shadows standing around in the trampled grass and on the gravel way, the tumbled effects of many households; angular shadows of table and mangle and chair, soft padded shadows of bundled bedding, rolled-up curtains, rugs; tea-chests showing pale in the darkness with their blond plywood, full of china and kitchen utensils. And in between these, people turning now to receive him; peacefully, because he came so late. He stumbled over one of the rolls of rugs, and somebody said helpfully:

'Hold on a minute, let's have a light.' And the next moment there was a light, a wan thread of it first on one side from a large electric lantern on the sill of a window, then on the other a glow from one of the huts, where someone had lit an oil-lamp.

The soldier strode into the crossroads of the two gleams, very young and rattled and angry, dragging Sid by the collar in one hand, and mopping at his nose with the back of the other one. He felt lost and at a disadvantage, and accordingly he stamped a little, and shouted.

131

'What's going on here? What do you all think you're doing here? Do you know you're trespassing on Army property? You're all wasting your time, you'll only have to clear out again, and all your precious trouble for nothing. You'd better pack up and get off back where you came from, while the going's good, if you've any sense.' And when they made no haste either to go or to respond in any way he shouted still more loudly: 'You can all get into bad trouble for this. You could easily end up in gaol!'

He looked round at them fiercely, but they were all smiling, quite broadly but quite gently. All kinds of people, men, women, children, all with their sleeves rolled up and their hands full. And in the middle of the light, blinking a little, a nice-looking girl in a chintz overall, with red hair blown on end by the wind, and bright alert eyes, who looked at his smeared face and childishly mopping hand with concern and a sudden flushed annoyance, and said with sharp reproach:

'Sid, I *told* you not to do anything to him.'

'I never hurt him,' shrilled Sid, injured. 'I never touched him! He fell down.'

'I'm ever so sorry!' said Flo, still flushed with vexation. 'Honestly, we didn't mean for you to get hurt.' She advanced upon him with an authority there was no gainsaying, detached his grasp from Sid's collar by some means of which he could afterwards recall nothing, and before he knew where he was had him turning his face to the light for her to see how bad the damage was. 'I didn't want anything like this to happen, not for the world! But don't take on, we're not going to make any trouble for you, nor let anyone else if we can help it. Nobody can say it was your fault. How can they? What could anyone have done, in your position? Why, there's over a hundred and eighty of us!' She made him sit down on top of a tea-chest, and lean back on her arm. 'There, now, keep your head back for a few minutes, and the bleeding will stop.' Something metallically cold – it felt like the flat, wide blade of a palette knife – was deftly inserted into the back of his collar.

132

He made an effort to remain angry, but it was against his will and the drift of events. Out of the corner of his eye he could just see the watchman accepting a cup of tea from a bounteously fat woman in a flowered frock of dazzling pattern. He felt cheated; he would not admit to himself that the engagement was over so easily.

'Do you know,' he demanded indistinctly, from the hollow of Flo's arm, 'that you've got no right here, any of you? This is Army property. You'll only get thrown out on your ear, the lot of you.'

'Well, not tonight, anyhow,' said Flo soothingly. 'There's a lot of us, you see, and you'd have to use force, and it would take a long time. So I shouldn't worry about that, if I were you. Just wait a bit until your nose stops bleeding, and clean yourself up, and have a cup of tea; and then you'd better go and phone, perhaps, hadn't you? Just to cover yourself – it won't make any difference to us.'

'You don't know what you're biting off,' he said weakly. 'You're going to find it more than you can chew.'

'Well, maybe, but we'll see. Anyhow, there's nothing you can do now, is there, unless it's to tell your bosses what's happened. So you may as well have some tea, and go about it nice and friendly. *We* shan't hinder you, you know – we know we mustn't. And now that you've found out, there's no point in our going on with our work in the dark, is there? We shall get on a lot better with the lamps on, and the electric's in already. Isn't that grand? I was a bit worried if there'd be enough fittings, but my goodness, they had just everything here.'

'Home from home!' said Mr. Derricks, looking out of the further shadows at him for a moment with his arms full of cushions, mats and bedding; and grinned, and winked, and disappeared again. All round him lights were going up in the huts, and busy people were bustling about, hefting furniture, grunting round awkward corners, rounding up the children to beds already made up for them. He thought of the morrow and his heart sank. The thing had already a horridly permanent look. And yet how could he have prevented it?

And how the devil, for that matter, had it ever happened?

'I don't understand,' he said in muffled tones, through the handkerchief he was holding to his nose, 'how you got in at all.'

'Ah!' said Flo. 'Well, that's all right; we didn't want you to understand it.'

'You certainly didn't come through the gate.'

'No, we certainly didn't.'

'Well, then, how?'

'We flew over the fence,' said Sid, perched upon a chest of drawers close by, fascinated by the sight of martial blood.

'You'll fly back again,' said the soldier, stung, 'when they hear about this down in Crocksford. With a flea in your ear, my lad!'

'Now, then,' said Flo sharply, like the mother of quarrelsome sons, 'no need to carry on like that. We're here, and it isn't your fault. We may just as well behave properly about it, there's nothing to gain by acting like enemies. So come along, now, and I'll give you some hot water to wash your face, and then you can go on with your telephoning, and your investigations.' She led him towards her new home, which already had cretonne curtains at the windows, and a brand new mat inside the door. 'We shan't get in your way,' she said reassuringly. 'We shall be busy.'

7

The news had gone round by morning. Like a malignant germ it visited Company H.Q., District H.Q., the local offices of Bredington Rural District Council and Crocksford Urban District Council, and all the members of those two august bodies, and set up everywhere a sad irritation and sickening, like an epidemic. Everybody made great haste to ask everybody else what he intended to do about it, before the same inconvenient question could be put to him; for this had happened before, and the responsibility was by no means popular, and some part of it would fall on everybody.

The Army had the ground and the property; right, the Army could see about getting possession of it. But the load of the sixty-two families, now without room of any kind in the town and district except the ones they occupied in the Warren, would promptly fall back upon one or other of the local authorities. People have to live somewhere. One family at a time can be told to fend for itself, quietly and privately, but sixty-two make quite a noise, and their utterances are liable to be taken up by others indignant over their plight, making an extremely uncomfortable situation for local councillors who cannot, as a matter of fact, create houses out of thought, and therefore prefer not to be reminded of the lack of them. Secretly the two local bodies hoped the Army would lose its campaign, not because they did not sympathise with its object, but because if it was achieved they would be left holding the baby. But they had to show willing, at least, in the fight to get the squatters out of the camp, because authority must back up authority. They assured Major Cox of their extreme desire to co-operate in any way they could, and left the means to him. The first morning ran away very quickly in the establishment of communications, and the exchange of irritated compliments, while three more families slipped quietly into the Warren camp by a back door which still had not been discovered.

Everybody damned the sentry and the watchman, who were retired from the scene with ignominy as soon as they had let in – by the front door – the contractor, the Major, and a half-dozen harried attendant junior officers and N.C.O.'s. The fact was that when the Major became abusive on the spot he soon found himself being barracked by a gallery of indignant women, who rather liked the boy, and had even asked advice from the watchman over the fixing of locks and rigging of electric fixtures before morning. One cannot keep one's dignity with angry young mothers crying: 'Shame!' all round one, and: 'Leave the boy alone, it wasn't his fault!' and: 'Think you could have done any better, mister?' And having made the fatal mistake of trying it, Major Cox was forever prevented from doing justice to the occasion even in private, because of the small reminiscent smile which kept twitching at the boy's lips as he listened. So nothing came of that. As for the contractor, his displeasure with the watchman was merely part of his stock-in-trade; he disliked seeing lawless people get their own way, but it was by no means certain that in the end they would, and in the meantime, provided he was paid he had no grave complaint to make.

But the Army minded very much. They minded, individually and collectively, as a cat minds which sees a mouse drinking its milk. It began not very seriously, not very bitterly, because they expected an easy victory, this being one of the childish articles of faith with them which no number of disillusionments seemed able to shake. But it was quite against the rules for these people to fight back, and that they should fight back successfully, and even with style and dash, was something which could not be forgiven. In a few days it was war.

Major Cox made a speech to the squatters, such of them as stopped their morning's work to listen. He advised them to think matters over, and go back home. He could not understand why this raised a great shout of laughter. He told them honestly that they were entering on a struggle which they could not win; and some among them had even at this stage not the slightest doubt that he was right, but they were the ones who had already weighed that consideration and warned their fellows. He told them a few of the things which could be done to them to drive them out, and some of his hints proved useful later; and finally he said that he would remain in the gatehouse office for an hour, and advised them to send a deputation to him within that time, and strike an agreement to move out, on the undertaking that every help would be given with Army transport, and there would be no recriminations. Upon which someone piped up with the pertinent question: 'And where do you suggest we go?'

Major Cox was neither a magician nor a humorist; he said he didn't know, but it was up to the local authorities to find them somewhere to live. Without any malice towards councils no worse than most, the squatters could not help laughing once again at this. It was a daunting experience talking to them, good-tempered as they were; it was like trying to play an organ with all the stops wrongly labelled.

However, to satisfy him and leave no doubt of where they stood, they sent a small committee to meet him before the hour was out. To them, as responsible men, he said the more abstruse and sacred things about the sacrifices private people must make in the cause of defending our way of life. The stops were still wrong. A lean man with a collier's cough merely asked him:

'Mister, did you ever try our way of life?'

Then they told him what, in any case, their wives had ordered them to tell him, that they were here, and so long as a toe-hold remained to them they would stay here. And from then the war was on.

They had asked that the children of school age should be allowed to proceed freely back and forth to Crocksford, and their re-entry should not be impeded; and the same favour was asked for the men, who naturally wished to go to their work. In return they offered the orderly and friendly behaviour of everyone in the camp, and co-operation in the unlikely event of other accommodation being found. It was all they could offer, and at least it kept the atmosphere reasonable and decent between them. The Army, characteristically, said neither yes nor no, but talked round the subject and declined to commit itself to any standard of conduct. And though the older children, on this first day, got back from school before the real engagement began, and no one interfered with them, by the time the men came home from work a large detachment of troops from Crocksford had arrived and thrown a cordon all round the pale fence. They had still underestimated, however, and under cover of darkness, after some camouflage parleyings and some artificial indignation, the men slipped in through the first of Eugene's emergency gaps, wired it up again neatly, and went to continue the business of settling in. The Sergeant-Major who was now in charge of operations, an old

137

regular of stubborn habits and uncertain temper, had intended to let them languish in the woods half the night and then send and admit them on his own terms. His messenger failed to find them, and reported accordingly. The Sergent-Major sent to their wives, and found the men of the house very much at home. He was exceedingly surprised and even more annoyed. His blood was up. He said that from then on anyone who left would have to get in by the same way, and swore that by the next day he would find out how the hell they did it.

So the children did not go to school, the men did not go to work. The secret ways were in danger, and in any case could not be over-used. And the day was weary with emissaries from this body and that paying endless visits, making endless speeches, exhorting them to listen to reason and get out while the going was good. They explained patiently that they could not even if they wished, and they did not wish. Their boats, which had never been seaworthy in any case, were already burned, new eager people in the hated rooms they had occupied. They had literally nowhere to go. And besides, they liked it here. It wasn't too far for the kids to go to school when a sensible bargain could be struck, and the sanitary arrangements had been made in lavish style for the expected Americans, and the electricity, praise God, could not be cut off without blacking out the nearer quarter of Crocksford. Water and supplies were their most vulnerable points, for the water could be cut off, since it served no one but the camp, and on Crocksford Urban District Council's tenuous goodwill depended their future supply. Daily they saw to it that the store tank remained full; but once the water was cut off from the reservoir they could reckon with only about three days grace.

But the weapon was not used yet. Sergeant-Major Thompson contented himself with going over the fence pale by pale, and inevitably the main gap was discovered, and rapidly fastened beyond hope of further use, with enough barbed wire to intimidate a real enemy; one of the lesser gaps evaded notice by some negligence, and was twice used

138

for secret shopping expeditions, but on the second occasion the return of the party was observed, and the affair ended in a race for the gap, undignified on both sides. The last and fattest of the shopping ladies, panting along in the rear, had the satisfaction of swinging a half-sack of potatoes with a beautifully accidental ferocity, and laying a sergeant flat with the weight of it in the wind; which gave her time to get herself and the sack laboriously through the fence before he could recover enough breath to intercept either. Sid, who had watched the whole thing from the gap, dancing and squealing with partisan fervour, thereupon clamped the pales shut, and fondly imagined that another point had been won. Perhaps it had, but the result was that meshes of barbed wire closed that exit, too, within an hour afterwards. And now it was really a state of siege at the Warren.

The Army sat and waited, and as the inhabitants did exactly the same, there were a few comparatively tranquil days. They were disturbed only by five or six reporters from the local and national press, two school attendance officers, a mysterious War Ministry man of determinedly nondescript and civilian appearance, to whom the Sergeant-Major and even Major Cox deferred sulkily, and the postman, who found the long walk up to the camp well rewarded by the entertainment when he got there, and took back copious bulletins to the town. The local press negotiated, as did all the other non-official visitors, from outside the pales, like holiday-makers at a new and peculiar zoo. They were not concerned with taking the part of either protagonist; they were chiefly interested in outdoing one another in the size, headlining, and sensational quality of the printed page, but they had the effect of whipping up public sympathy on one side, all the same. Furious letters began to fill the correspondence columns, abusing the Army, the Council officials, the councillors. People seized, as they always do, on unbelievably minor points, not even relevant to the main issue, and went off after them full cry, bowling over in the process amazed and well-intentioned public servants who had nothing whatever to do with the matter in hand. And while the Sanitary Inspector of Bredington Rural District and other remote casualties sat and wondered what had hit them, the main contestants, unscarred, sat watching each other in the Warren like two rival cats with lashing tails, waiting for the next move, and concentratedly unaware of the chaos raging all round them.

Tempers were high by then. For three days no one had left the enclosure, supplies of food were thinning, and still the stubborn wretches would not move. The Sergeant-Major had even gone so far as to approach them, instead of waiting for them to crawl to him, as he had sworn, and they had told him what he could do with his terms of surrender. From then on they were not his own kind to him, but some alien species, because he had leaned hard on them and they had not broken; if he had had a free hand he would have thrown them out by force, men, women and children. He had not a free hand, and knew the force of both law and public opinion well enough to restrain himself. But without exaggeration he hated them.

'He said: 'I'll get these b—'s out or die trying!' People did not defy the Army, that was all; not twice, at any rate. It was his job to make them sorry they had even tried it once.

He persuaded Major Cox to get the water turned off. From then on it was a race between the dwindling supply in the tank and the resultant outcry among the good people of Crocksford, who raised a rumpus which threatened to overthrow public order. The outcry won, the water was turned on again, and the besieged breathed freely after the worst crisis yet. Appeals went out for groceries, vegetables, food and cleaning materials and all the necessities of life, and anyone who had nothing better to do would take a walk up to the camp to collect the latest news, and catch flung notes and money over the heads of scowling patrols, who could not interfere. Then they would go back into town to do the shopping involved, and bring back the goods to the beleaguered garrison. There were various ways of getting it in to them. Some things could safely be thrown. Bags could be hoisted over on the end of line-props, or boys could hand them down from the boughs of the pines, which overhung the fence in several places. One or two of the young soldiers, incapable of feeling the Sergeant-Major's sick devotion to the Army, and therefore feeling none of his personal resentment, would even slip things in at leisure when none of the dutiful were looking. There was even some fraternisation with the enemy. It was evident that the squatters were in no imminent danger of being starved out.

'If you ask me, sir,' said Sergeant-Major Thompson, 'we'll do no good here without a court order. Only way's to dump all their stuff outside by force, and them after it.'

'You won't easily get an order,' said Major Cox, who knew his district. 'Find me a magistrate who isn't also a local councillor; and every local councillor thinks first, if we throw these people out *we've* got to house 'em. We don't want to pin these locals into a corner if we can help it. There must be some sort of nuisance value we still possess.'

There was, and they exploited it; they had hardly begun to draw on their real resources by then. The next day they moved into the camp a detachment of troops from Crocksford, and settled two of them into each hut with the squatters.

Eugene was among them. As soon as they were ordered up there he guessed what was in the wind, and when they were briefed at some length on their job of making life unbearable for those b—'s in the Warren until they gave up and crawled off with their tails between their legs, he held his tongue only with great difficulty. It was too much to have to make one in the breaking of something he had helped to make possible.

No one was very enthusiastic. When they were told off in pairs on their way through the camp, and had to knock on hut doors and push past astonished and abusive housewives with their kit, they were considerably the more embarrassed group of the two. It was not a pleasant encounter for anybody. Voices shrilled, and fists were raised, but by superhuman efforts every woman among them kept her temper, and no one was actually hit. Sergeant-Major

141

Thompson got no grounds for action, though he was waiting for them with watering mouth.

Eugene, penned defensively into a corner of a hut with an equally uneasy partner beside him and a large, angry woman before him, fended off her rage as well as he could with short, appeasing sentences whenever she paused for breath, but was neither heard nor heeded. He sat on his kit-bag, and sighed, letting the storm blow over him.

'Whippersnappers like you,' she said, shrilling, 'to come here poking yourselves into the houses of respectable people! A nice way of carrying on! But you can tell that Sergeant-Major of yours, my lad—'

'He isn't mine, thank God!' said Eugene, shuddering.

'– You can tell him, if he hopes to get us out like this he's barking up the wrong tree. If I'd been going ten times over, now I wouldn't budge an inch. I'll show him whether he can come his nasty little Nazi ways here, and you can tell him that!'

'You tell him,' said Eugene gloomily. 'He can't get *you* put in the glasshouse.'

'And do you kid your young selves you're going to make up your beds here, and spend the nights in with us?' she demanded, gradually grasping the full implications of the situation.

'Now look,' said the second victim, spreading his hands, 'we've got no more choice about it than you have. We just get told off for the job. We can't do anything about it. If we refused, that's mutiny. It's all right for you, so long as you don't actually manhandle anyone you can do just as you like, but *we* can just about breathe for ourselves, and then you've said it.'

'Then you *are* staying here?' squeaked the lady, the heavy iron saucepan quivering in her large hand. 'Well, if that isn't the end! My husband did six years service for this here country. Wounded, he was, twice, and over a year in a prison camp, and what's he come home to? This! Another prison camp it looks like being. That's the sort of reward a fellow can expect, it seems – ' Eugene really disliked the look of that saucepan; it was full of boiling water, and for a horrid moment he thought she was going to forget herself, and throw it.

'We can't help ourselves,' he said, 'any more than you can, so don't take it out on us. We shan't get in your way any more than we can help, so for God's sake help us to keep *out* of it.'

But what really saved him from at least getting his ears boxed was the fact that at that moment the spirit stove on which she was cooking fired with a small compact report like a muffled gunshot, and spiralled upward in bluish flames, one of its less pleasant occasional habits. Eugene, unspeakably relieved to have some active way of breaking up the moment, pounced on it with such zeal that he had it quenched, tamed and behaving reasonably in far less time than the operation usually took.

'There you are!' he said, slanting an impudent grin up at her from the floor, when all was over, and enlarging the smoky blackness of one cheek with a quick pass of the back of his hand, 'you see, we're going to be downright useful.'

And once she had subsided, they did not get on so badly. Everything was makeshift, the screen of blankets fencing off their corner of the room, the careful courtesy with which they sidled in and out, avoiding too frequent and too close contact; but it could be made to work for a short time. On this principle, probably, most of the shock troops settled in, though some were of Sergeant-Major Thompson's mind, and regarded their weight as something to be thrown, and not coyly withdrawn into a corner. At best, the situation within the huts was one of embarrassment and continual strain; at worst, it was a little, confined hell of friction, stretching the nerves to breaking-point. But still the Warren squatters squatted resolutely, and refused to be driven out.

8

The small rumour of war, gathering tides of public

indignation, and partisan currents, and seething round whirlpools of controversy, washed up to the south lodge of the Folly, and made an uneasy, summoning music in Rosalba's ears. She heard it, perhaps, louder than the reality, because it was the first such trumpet which had ever seemed to echo beyond the edge of Rose land, and the very turrets of the Folly trembled in its vibrations. The absence of Flo from the daily procession of cleaners passing the lodge gates ached like the void left by a brother away at the wars. Rosalba, fevered with treasonous loyalties, burned to draw a sword with the rest, against the established, against the forces which have, and possess, and sit sprawled over society, leisurely hitting over the head anyone who dares to question the rightness of things as they are.

She had to keep silence when Martine struck the ferrule of her ivory-headed stick against the ground, and marvelled what rottenness ate at the heart of England, that such sick disorders should be possible so near to her domain; and when she hoped, a little disdainfully, that the Army authorities would stand their ground, and make no concessions, starve them out if need be; implying, in her large impervious scorn of change, that even the Army was by no means what it used to be or ought to be, but that one must still accept it as the lame modern version of one of the props of living. But even her anger and disgust were insulting, leaving out of account as they did the possibility of any serious threat. If the turrets shook, if the horn sounded, she felt nothing and heard nothing. Her security was rock.

All the more Rosalba longed to add her weight to the struggle. She was afraid it was piteously light, but at least one could try. She took the biggest basket she could find, and some money, and slipped out of the lodge garden by the wicket gate, and went down to Crocksford. If other people, with very little to spare from the feeding of their own families, could carry gifts of food to the besieged squatters as the local paper said they were doing, then so could she.

In the bus she sat looking incredibly young and solemn and excited, the faint rose in her cheeks deepened to a rich unaccustomed colour and radiance, her eyes blazingly blue. She had never in her life done anything like this before. It might be only a matter of filling a basket with groceries, but it was the first grand gesture, as momentous for her as the first unfurling of the lily banner for Joan of Arc; and on such an occasion you may well be a little frightened. In even small wars many people get killed, and even more injured; however sure you feel of your burning rightness, you may well hesitate a little at the plunge; and especially when you are virtually a traitor to everything you have ever known or been taught. Thinking for yourself, feeling for yourself, is the first duty of man, she told herself firmly; it comes before any inherited loyalties. But she felt all the eyes of generations, centuries of Roses, boring bitterly into her treasonous mind, and heard the family voice, a louder trumpet than her own, stormily denouncing her. For a moment, as they entered Crocksford by the long, drab street to the parish church, she even wished herself back at the lodge, and the expedition abandoned; but the moment passed, and excitement became exaltation, lifting her above consideration of consequences.

She did not go to the shop where Martine's housekeeper dealt, because she would be known there, and if to evade curiosity too insistently was needless complication, to court it was folly. She bought off-the-ration tinned goods wherever she could find them among the other shops, because tinned things could be either used or kept, as occasion demanded; and the top of the basket she filled up with fresh vegetables and fruit, with an improbably ripe and heavenly-smelling melon perched precariously on top of all. This was perhaps an extravagant flourish, but Rosalba was now riding high on a wave of rebellious joy, and flourishes came natural to her.

The walk up to the Warren made her hot and tired, but did nothing to quench her spirits. A few cheerful people coming back from similar errands met and recognised her for one of themselves, though not one of them knew her for Miss Rose. What they recognised was the basket full of gifts and the light in her eye; and on the strength of these they were so sure of her that they called out greetings and fragments of news.

'As good as a picnic up there today,' they said. 'That old Sergeant-Major Thompson's getting proper frantic – real spiteful he is, just because he can't get his own way. Watch out for him!'

'I will!' said Rosalba, flushed and starry with pleasure at this magical admission into the circle without even initiation; and she went on with a lighter step, swinging her passport to humanity so gaily that the melon almost fell off, and had to be steadied back into position with her free hand.

There were several people scattered around the rim of the pinewoods when she got there, spaced out in ones and twos, and holding shouted conversations through the pales of the fence with the garrison within. A large cabbage went sailing over the barrier, and was hilariously fielded on the other side. A small boy crawled along a branch of an overhanging pine, and let down a bulging string bag upon the end of a cord already providently fitted with an iron hook. At regular intervals along the fence were spaced bored and embarrassed soldiers, fending off those who came right up to the pales, and even intercepting, in a shamefaced fashion, such thrown goods as misfired and fell within their reach. They looked extremely sulky about the whole thing, for the most part, but one or two were angry and flustered, and had begun to take some vengeful pleasure in their part. Those who had not reached this stage, and were still hating it, had occasionally to assume the same manner; and by the suddenness with which they did so the invaders knew when Sergeant-Major Thompson was near, and withdrew accordingly to the shelter of the pines, intent on giving him no handle at all for abuse or violence, either of which, it was plain, he was in condition to enjoy.

Rosalba stood in the shade of the trees, almost under the small boy in the pine, and looked at the enemy with awe, for he was certainly a formidable figure. To her he appeared old, though in fact he was barely forty, and physically

146

considerably younger still. He was big, and lantern-jawed, with almost no shaping to the back of his neck and head, and flat temples curling with greying hair, and a complexion the colour of good Midland brick. He came swinging along with great cat-strides, light as a feather on his feet, but looking as if he could make the ground shake if he wanted to. He stopped to be vitriolically rude to a young soldier who had just let a basket be lowered by prop behind his back, and though half a dozen female voices began jibing viciously at him from behind the pales he suffered from none of Major Cox's disabilities, and cursed them again heartily in tones they could not match. Rosalba shrank; she was not used to hearing such words addressed to anyone, and felt considerable dismay at the thought of incurring them herself; but she was indignant, too, and her resolution mounted. She waited until he was gone, and then went up to the fence, midway between two of the soldiers, so that éach of them could consider her to be the business of the other. She peeped through the pales, and examined the camp with curiosity.

It did not seem to her the sort of place one would willingly live in if there was anywhere else to be had. The huts were clean and newly painted, spaced closely about their cinder and gravel paths and half-bald grass; and the sun over them now in the high afternoon gave them a brightness they would not otherwise have had. But they were so close, and so inevitably the same, squat and harsh in one another's pockets. How bad, then, must be the conditions from which these people had flown so thankfully even to this. True, the pines were there, rich and sweet, and the miles of deep springy turf would be grand for the children if only they could hang on until things became settled. Little lines of washing, brilliant with the small coloured garments of children, flapped in a fresh breeze from hut to hut. Many people were moving about within, soldiers and civilians busy on a hundred small jobs, or simply standing talking to their friends through the fence. More cabbages were coming over the pales, and the women were catching them, cheered on by the soldiers now that the Sergeant-Major was out of earshot.

Rosalba called out to the nearest person, but before she could get as far as asking for Flo a young girl came darting out of one of the doorways, took a sharp glance at her, all unfamiliar and striped behind the disguising pales, and then hailed her jubilantly:

'It *is* you! I said I knew that voice! Oh, miss! Oh, it's that odd a life here, you wouldn't believe! Oh, wait'll I tell Flo you're here!'

And after Daisy out came tumbling Flo herself, with a face of blankest astonishment, for of all the people she had least expected to see as a partisan in this contest, only Martine Rose herself was less probable than Rosalba. And indeed the first glimpse of her was as strange as a meeting at the bottom of the sea. She had put the basket down, close in the turf against her feet, and was clinging to the bars like a little pale prisoner; and above the gripping hands her face was only three bright strips of face, lit with twin segments of eyes bright and wide and deep blue as gentians with excitement. This once, and so fragmentarily seen, Rosalba looked at once as brave as a young lioness and as vulnerable as a baby.

'Well, I'm damned!' said Flo.

'Oh, why? Didn't you expect to see me?' said Rosalba, as if she had fully expected to be there, whereas she was quite as astonished as Flo, and the contemplation of someone else's astonishment merely renewed her own.

'Well, I thought it would be impossible. It isn't a matter of being willing. But my goodness, if it should ever get round that you've been here, your life won't be worth living!'

'It doesn't matter,' said Rosalba, her strangely bright eyes dancing. 'I don't care! It isn't all that nice now. And I wanted to bring something, too. Why shouldn't I?'

'Well,' said Flo thoughtfully, 'I could say, it isn't your fight. Bless you, my dear, we're not doing so bad here, folks are very good to us. But *you've* got someone else to think about as well as yourself, you know, and it doesn't do to take too many chances.'

148

'Yes, but I wanted to be very good to you, too,' said Rosalba, childishly pouting. 'Oh, Flo, don't tell me to go away, please! I did want to know how you were getting on, and to bring you these things myself. Sending them wouldn't have been the same, and anyhow, it's safer to bring them myself.'

'All right, then, and you're a real pal. But you mustn't stay long, in case anybody knows you. Much use it would be to me,' said Flo with stern tenderness, 'if you went and messed up your own chances just for this.'

'Oh, Flo! And you know you don't think we've got any chances, really!'

'Yes, I do!' said Flo, flushing fiercely.

'I don't think you do. But I sold another picture for him – a little water-colour of the pool. He doesn't know yet, I haven't seen him. It isn't much money,' she said honestly, 'but it's a beginning, and that dealer in Bredington likes him, I could feel that he does. And it will get easier – we've only just started—'

'Oh, miss,' said Daisy in a rich whisper, leaning close to the barrier, 'he's *here*!'

'Eugene? But how? What's he doing here?'

'They've got the job,' explained Flo simply, 'of being such a nuisance to us that we shall pack up and get out – even if we have to camp on the heath. But don't you worry, it isn't working out that way.'

'But – *Eugene*! It's monstrous!' said Rosalba, her bright cheeks flaming deeper, and her blue eyes growing intense as sapphires with indignation. 'Don't they *all* hate it? It – it's indecent!'

She did not mean the domestic difficulties involved, but Flo had had such things on her mind so long that they came first to her thoughts now. She said comfortably: 'Oh, he's all right, don't you worry. It's not so bad as it sounds. The couple he's with, they're old enough to be his parents, he's all right with them. And she isn't a bad sort, even if she does nag over things a bit. Nobody's budged yet. We just made a partition of sorts in each hut, and they keep their side of it,

149

and we keep ours. Makes quarters a bit cramped, like, but we're managing. And I did hear they're going out tomorrow. I don't know if it's right.'

'I hope so!' said Rosalba, still flashing deep blue rage. 'I think it's just abominable to give all these hateful jobs to soldiers – the only people who can't go on strike even if they *are* asked to do something against their principles. Flo, where is he? Is he here? Could he come? Only for a moment, I promise I'll go then.'

Daisy said: 'I'll go and find him,' and flew to make her word good.

'He'll tell you to go home and be sensible,' said Flo, with a teasing smile.

'I bet you he won't! He knows better,' she said, 'what I need. He'll be *glad*!' And suddenly aware how ridiculous she was, but now how splendid, she laughed and pressed one small hand towards Flo through the bars. 'Flo, don't be angry! I didn't know about him! I came for *you*! And now I can't talk or think about anything but him, after all. Please, tell me quickly if there's anything I can do, anything you want that I can get for you. Or if there's anyone one could go and *see* about all this. I should be glad if I could help.'

'I could do with some soap,' owned Flo, humouring her, 'but I've used all the family coupons until next week. You don't know how dirty you can get, and your things, too, when you're doing some extra cleaning in a place like this.'

'I can get some for you,' said Rosalba eagerly. 'Toilet soap or household soap? Or soap flakes and powder?'

'Soap powder I'm shortest of. And all the rest you can do for us is, don't worry yourself. We're all right, we're doing everything anyone can do, so you mustn't fret yourself on our account.'

'I won't,' promised Rosalba docilely, appeased with soap powder since she could not hope for swords.

'Here's Eugene!' said Flo, and he came like an arrow for the fence, and set his hands alongside hers, and smiled at her between exasperation and delight, but nearer to delight. Caution did not matter very much here, where every soul on one side of the pales was anonymous to people on the other side unless they happened to be as well acquainted with the lines of his face as with a lover's. Friends talked with almost as much privacy as in some fantastic solitude, three yards from their fellow-creatures on the same errand. Only when they moved away from the striping, veiling pales did they become recognisable to others.

'I didn't expect to see you here,' he said, letting his fingers lie over hers.

'Nor did I you! Flo told me about it. Oh, Eugene, isn't it wicked?'

He made an ugly face. 'Well, it isn't fun, exactly. But they say the Americans are coming – we've only been keeping the place warm for them.'

'They've got to do the same? To settle in with these people here and try to drive them out? Oh, it isn't credible that they could do such a thing! It's so beastly for everybody!'

'That doesn't worry the people who make the bullets; as usual they don't do the firing. But that's only the beginning yet, and nobody's even talking about retreat here. They're all right! I can tell you, these people are all right, Rosalba! And you're grand!' he said, his voice dropping to a whisper, his cheek near to hers, only the flat, rough pales holding them apart. 'I knew you were, even before, but now I must tell you. Now – this minute! Darling!' It was only the softest breath, this last, hardly speech at all.

'I'm glad I came,' she said, scarcely louder. 'I was almost scared – *quite* scared! Now I'm awfully glad! Eugene, I sold the water-colour. He gave me four guineas for it. It isn't much, but he said he could find a buyer for it easily. He said it was *good*, Eugene.'

'It wasn't very,' said Eugene. 'If it had been as good as I wanted, he wouldn't have offered four guineas for it. But I didn't *try* to make it so it would sell.'

'And I asked him about some more local sketches. There'll be visitors now for about two months. He said bring him anything of the same kind.'

'There won't be anything of the same kind if I can help it. Nothing so lousy! But there may even be some decent ones he can use. Oh, Rosalba—'

'I brought some things for Flo,' she said, looking down at the basket at her feet. 'I shall ask that boy in the tree to let it down inside for me. I didn't know what to get. Do you think these are all right?'

Flo had withdrawn quite unnoticed, and was cleaning the windows of her hut a little way from them. 'She'll love 'em,' said Eugene, 'all the more because you brought 'em.'

She gave him a bright and flashing smile. 'No, she was inclined to tell me I ought not to have come. Because of word getting round to Great-Aunt Martine, you see. She said *you* would tell me to go home and be sensible, too.'

'You'll wait a long time to hear that from me.'

'I know! I told her so.'

'But no need to take risks we don't have to,' he said, moving so far against his nature as to admit for her a caution he would never have entertained for himself. 'Better not stay too long.'

'No, I'll go now, as soon as I've sent these things over. I can, now! I'm satisfied, now! And seeing you, too – that was something I didn't expect.'

He gave her hand a last warm pressure as she withdrew; and when she became visible as a whole girl, instead of three elusive strips of girl, he was dazzled to see how young and fresh and alive she looked, shining with excitement and resolve as she walked backwards from him a few steps, and stumbled against a tussock of grass, and gave a skipping jump back to save herself, laughing like a child at a party. But it wasn't a party! It was a piece of doubtful and anxious living, for her as for them; and his heart suddenly ached with love for her.

'Saturday? If we're out of here I'm free in the evening.'

'Saturday, usual time! If you don't come, I'll understand!'

Then she ran, hugging the basket, back to the pine tree and the busy and useful child, who was having the time of his life, and working probably harder than he would ever voluntarily work again in his life. He accepted her basket with awe and delight though it was heavy for him, hauled it up by his hook from her arms, and leaned to swing it out over the fence. Rosalba stood back under the tree, watching his progress with a rather frightened face, between the wobbling child and the wobbling melon in a constant start.

'Be careful! Please be careful!'

'Garn!' said the small boy cheerfully, edging his way along the bough on his stomach. ''Ad 'alf a 'underdweight of taters on the end of this, I 'ave – and got 'em over safe, too.'

'You wouldn't credit it, miss,' said the nearest interested bystander, folding ample arms over her comfortable bosom as she watched his progress, 'but he has, too. Never seen that lad so good for so long in my life. Don't know what we'll do to satisfy him when this jaunt's over, and that's a fact. Our row hasn't had so much peace in years. You wouldn't know the place.'

'I'm so afraid he'll fall,' owned Rosalba, gazing skyward. 'Do you think he's quite safe?'

'Safe? Jimmy? Don't you fret, he was brought up in trees. Safe as houses!'

A small gallery followed every operation with sympathy, and willed the goods safely over the fence. They had matter for concentration here owing to the behaviour of the melon, which constantly rolled ponderously to the edge of its balance, hung there a breathless instant, and rolled as majestically back to its base. So intent were they upon its progress that they did not mark the return of Sergeant-Major Thompson, in close pursuit of a second small boy, who had not sufficient start to be entirely out of reach of the enemy's cane, though so far he had avoided the hand that reached for his collar. The origin of this hunt they never discovered; it could have been one of a hundred small disasters with thrown things, or merely a piece of cheekiness at an ill-judged distance; but the field broke on them suddenly from nowhere in a series of leaps and yells, fell over a root, recovered itself smartly, and swept across Rosalba's vision as the basket swung overhead. There the

Sergeant-Major neatly abandoned a chase never very seriously undertaken. His control of his big body was very fine to watch, if one did not detest him too much to take pleasure in it. He halted on one long stride, swung easily to rest, switched the cane, and stood grinning after the fleeing child, breathing as easily as if he had not run a step.

It was at this moment that the melon perversely rolled not merely to the edge of its balance, but slowly, slowly, over it, and with beautiful deliberation fell. Everyone saw it except the Sergeant-Major, who was standing under it; but no one uttered a sound, except the boy in the tree above, and he only in sheer delight.

'Bombs gone!' he yelled, and followed the warning with a long-drawn descending wail to indicate the trajectory of his block-buster.

Sergeant-Major Thompson reacted in the worst possible way; at the sudden shriek above his head he started and stared upward. The melon hit him with all its lush, ripe weight on the left cheek and temple, split on his big nose, and burst, a bomb beautiful beyond the dreams of ten-year-old film fans accustomed to making do with imagination. It laid him on the grass like a felled ox, and kept him there a full half-minute speechless, with only his first curious, squashed cry for epitaph. The basket, swinging above, debated following up the success with a shower of carrots, but considering them an anticlimax, gravely righted itself, dangled drunkenly over the pales, and descended. Then the dutiful boy above could laugh as he wanted to, with every bit of his body and mind, hugging the bough on which he lay, and sobbing and shrieking joy at the sky, and the birds as they passed him. Nothing so wonderful had ever happened to him before, and this had been a gift from heaven, without any endeavour on his part, a reward to the startlingly good. He considered that at this rate it was really worthwhile being good permanently.

Laughter was safe, for everyone was laughing. A great shout went up from both sides of the fence, though those without had the best view, and those within the safest position. People forgot everything else in order to be able to laugh properly; the basket reposed unemptied in the grass under Flo's hands, the child in the tree neglected his best opportunity to escape, and those who had been in the act of leaving the scene came back to enjoy the spectacle of Sergeant-Major Thompson slowly sitting up on the ground, shaking his head from side to side, and wondering what had hit him. The melon, grossly distorted, with burst sides, lay like a half-deflated caseball beside him in the grass; and Rosalba, regretfully, acknowledged it as a casualty of the engagement. Once let the enemy turn his back, and some of the children would rescue what was rescuable; but its true splendour was already over.

Rosalba did not know what to make of herself. Was it really like her to laugh immoderately at the spectacle of someone being hit over the head? Even if he was rather an objectionable person? And particularly, she reflected with shame, when she was the occasion of the accident. He had really something to complain about now, and he was just drawing a long breath and clambering, with awful deliberation, to his feet. From the colour of Midland red brick his face had darkened ominously to the best Staffordshire blue. His eyes rolled over the ranks of his tormentors, and fastened upon the boy in the tree. In the terrifyingly quiet tones of a naturally noisy man pushed momentarily off-balance, he instructed him to come down. The very pitch of his voice was enough to put the order past obedience; only the tone-deaf and shortsighted would have been likely to comply. Jimmy, aware of a lamb already dead, resolved on the sheep, too.

'Not in these trousers!' he said, hugging the crotch of the tree for dear life. 'Wipe your face!' he said reprovingly. 'You ought to be ashamed of yourself, stealing people's melons.'

The Sergeant-Major's precarious quietness broke then in a great bellow of rage. He mopped his sticky face and cursed them all up hill and down dale, in a clipped, regular Army fashion which expressed his whole soul. He promised them repercussions from this day, every man jack of them, the

criminals and the accessories; and in particular he promised
Jimmy that at whatever hour he did decide to leave his tree,
someone would be waiting for him at the bottom.

Eugene, between laughing and swearing inside the fence,
shook the pales in exasperated hands, and wished Rosalba
would have the sense to go; but he knew she wouldn't. He
knew she wouldn't leave the scene until the music stopped,
in case someone else had to face a few bars of it. He knew
she was crazy, and lovely, and gallant, and terrified, and that
he must keep his mouth shut and not give the show away to
the whole world that she belonged to him, and he to her; but
he didn't know how he was going to do it.

'She's going to!' he said in a helpless groan into Flo's ear.
'I *knew* she would! As if he can't look after himself, without
her making any scenes!'

'Maybe she can, too,' said Flo, patting him with a soothing
hand.

'Like hell she can! A baby couldn't be more helpless!'

'Don't be so nesh for her,' said Flo with salutary calm. 'If
you *want* her to grow up, that is. Folks don't die of being
sworn at.'

And Rosalba did not die. She waited for the
Sergeant-Major to draw breath, and moved a little towards
him, her frightened blue eyes very big in her pale and rather
annoyed face. Not even verbal rough-and-tumbles were
much in her line, and besides, she was at a disadvantage
because this odious person really had a grievance; but it was
quite impossible to go away and leave things like this.

'I'm very sorry that you've been hurt,' she said, 'but it was
quite an accident. I brought the things in the basket, and this
boy was merely helping me. It wasn't his fault at all. But I do
apologise for the blow you've had, really. If you would let
supplies be handed in in a normal way, you see, this kind of
thing wouldn't happen.'

'And who the hell, madam,' said Sergeant-Major
Thompson, eyeing her up and down in astonishment at her
impudence, 'who the hell might you be, to come here telling
me what ought to be done around here? Do you know that if

we liked to push things to the limit every one of these precious friends of yours could be put out on the heath overnight, with all his sticks of furniture? They can thank their lucky stars, and so can you, that we're a long-suffering lot, and haven't gone the limit – yet. You're sorry! That's mighty kind of you! Then what the devil are you doing here encouraging people to break the law? And breaking it yourself?'

'I didn't think it was against the law,' said Rosalba, sticking out her chin, 'to give things to people, if we want to. And I still don't think it is. At any rate, will you please be so just as to leave this boy alone, and deal with me? I've told you it wasn't his fault at all, and I think you show a very bad example to these soldiers who are in your charge, when you behave as you are doing. I can understand your feeling angry, of course. It wasn't a nice thing to happen. But it was an accident. If anyone caused it, *I* did.' She added punctiliously, and with a small, unhappy flush: 'I'm really very sorry we laughed, too. It wasn't very nice of us. But you know, you did rather invite it, you were being so unpleasant about everything.'

For a moment words failed him. Then, his tongue recovering power and impetus together, he flashed out at her with as bitter a piece of invective as he had ever achieved even to an awkward squad of recruits, less blasphemous, but just as cutting. He told her to precisely what low form of animal life squatters belonged, and how antisocial it was to encourage them with gifts and backing; and gave her distinctly to understand that he considered her to be of a class whose natural place was with the resisters of disorder, not with its formenters, and that she ought to be ashamed of herself for turning traitor; and, which she understood already from all that she had seen, that if she persisted she could expect no more quarter than they would get. From outrage and chagrin the expression of her large, attentive eyes changed to incredulous distaste. At the end of it, when she should have been either in tears or too angry to speak, she said with tremulous dislike:

157

'Thank you, I'm quite aware that the battalions are on the other side. We're not all accustomed to choose our causes by that standard, you know. I appreciate your advice, but I intend to go on being the keeper of my own conscience.'

'Then you'll damn well take the consequences!' he said. And suddenly, in the act of turning away, he plunged back again to take another long, searching look at her. Eugene, kicking the pales in his anxiety, said clairvoyantly: 'He's guessed! Oh, why the dickens does she have to talk like a book when she's annoyed?'

'You're from the Folly, aren't you?' said the Sergeant-Major in a sharp and quiet voice. 'I've seen you there. Aren't you Miss Rose?'

'My name doesn't matter at the moment, I think,' said Rosalba.

'It might,' said the Sergeant-Major, 'to someone else if not to you.' But he did not persist. A formidable calm had descended upon him, and wrapped in it as in a cloud he turned on his heel and stalked away. Ten yards on he halted with equal abruptness, and looked back. The damned girl had flown to the fence, and had someone by the hand through it; she was smiling at him in a blind way which meant only one thing, and somewhere not far behind the blue eyes, in spite of the smile, were the tears she had felt no desire to shed until now. She was speaking, quickly and low, too low to be heard, and apparently only a few hurried, cajoling words, interjected into the equally quiet speech of the fellow inside.

It was a pity that he couldn't see who it was; a khaki shoulder was all he could distinguish between the wide pales, and at this stage he could not turn back to get a better view. Nevertheless, Sergeant-Major Thompson walked on not entirely dissatisfied. It was a soldier she had come to see, not merely somebody among the squatters themselves; and by the look of her when she joined hands with him, this was an affair of no slight growth. Somebody might be very interested in that, very interested. The little bitch would laugh on the other side of her face yet before he was finished with her.

158

9

The Americans came next day. No one had been willing to believe, until then, that they would really come; it was felt that as strangers in the country, or guests if you preferred that description, they would not readily lend themselves to this war of attrition which was going on at the Warren, but would wait until the ground was clear or the project abandoned. But on top of the news that the education authority intended taking proceedings against all those who were keeping children from school, irrespective of the fact that they could not send them without having them barred from the enclosure on their return, or at the least used as bargaining power, came the very rumble of the American transports driving circumspectly up the dirt road, and the first sight of them drawing in to the gates.

Children ran with the word, and everyone came out and stood to see, grouped in small solid phalanxes, silent, watching. A new phase was opening; they trained their sharpened intelligences upon the invaders, weighing with narrowed eyes the probabilities of their behaviour. You would not have recognised these motionless and voiceless but quiveringly alert people for the same ones who had sent up so frank a bellow of laughter yesterday at the downfall of Sergeant-Major Thompson. That had been pure pleasure; this, but for the brief pleasing observation that the melon had given him a veritable black eye, was strictly business.

Large, bulky, awkward young men jumped down from the lorries as they pulled in, and began to manhandle their kit inside the gates. They looked and sounded rather subdued; only an occasional voice was lifted as they worked, and when they entered they avoided looking at the silent groups which watched them so steadily. On the whole, they looked considerably more depressed than the squatters. Flo found herself feeling sorry for them; she knew how she would feel if made to go and take up residence in the teeth of neighbourly decency, like this, and she suspected that some of these boys were feeling even worse, the miles which separated them from their own homes doubling the weight of their discomfort.

'Oh, God,' she prayed with her usual stern logic, 'let me have somebody I can dislike, so that I shall be able to fight properly.'

And then she wondered, equally sensibly, if perhaps they were not putting up the very same prayer. So wouldn't it be even better if they could rather like one another, so that some compromise could be struck? The men had not worked all the week, betting on the possibility of an early agreement, and unwilling to take any risks in the meantime; but no work means no money, and pretty soon at this rate they were going to have to appeal more urgently to the generosity of outsiders. Flo didn't like the idea at all. And the children were missing school, and their parents being threatened with summonses for keeping them away. That was one move in the campaign of annoyance, of course, but the problem could not be shelved much longer; the summonses, if they took effect soon, would not be answered, and that would mean worse trouble; and fines could not possibly be met. So they had every reason to examine their new tenants with extreme care, and weigh up the chances of a working agreement with them.

'I don't know but it might be easier to come to terms with these,' said Flo in her father's ear, 'once Thompson and his lot are away. After all, for all he's an old rip, he has had the Command's reputation on his conscience, so to speak – hospitality to our dear allies, and all that. Our dear allies might not feel so bad about it. They might be glad to get the kids off the place during the day, too,' she added, entertaining half-seriously the idea of banding the kids together into a gang of such nuisance value as to hasten the decision.

Sid pricked up his ears at that, looking up at her with a horrid doubt. 'You mean we'd have to go back to school?'

'That's just what I do mean.'

The concession was one which Sid, at any rate, patently

did not desire to invite. He had been relying on two or three weeks more of stalemate, and then the blessedly legal August holidays. But he said optimistically: 'I bet they've got their orders. I bet they won't give way.'

'We could try, anyhow,' said Flo briskly. 'If they don't want you off the place for a few hours a day, I do!'

'Maybe we could get an agreement,' said Mr. Derricks, wistfully. 'I certainly would like to taste beer again. This place hasn't been the same since we emptied the last bottle, and even that was poor stuff. It'd be even worth going back to work to be able to call in in the evening, blowed if it wouldn't. Here,' he said, as if the bright idea had just dawned upon him, 'I think I'll go and have a talk with old Joe about this – see if we can't get our plans made.'

Flo was not really building much hope on it. These young men might hate the situation as much as did their involuntary hosts, but what could they do about it? Until the men who made the bullets had to do the firing it would not be enough for the rank and file to bear each other no ill-will.

'We'd better be in the hut,' decided Flo, 'when they come, so as to look after our rights. We don't know what sort they're going to be, after all, nor what orders they've got.' And back they went accordingly, she and Daisy, leaving Sid to stare his fill.

Flo looked round the hut, and suddenly marvelled how it had grown at least halfway towards a home. Two accommodating lodgers they'd had, who had kept to a modest corner, and helped to rig everything up nicely for her; and now they were packing their kit again and preparing to get out as soon as their opposite numbers showed up. The new curtains looked gay and brave, and the freshly painted wooden walls were light and pleasant to look at. In an ecstasy of beginning-afresh Mr. Derricks had shored up the little grandmother clock in its corner until it stood straight as a guardsman, with the result that it was now wildly out in its rendering of the time. A cunning arrangement of curtain and screen separated their end of the room into two at night, and made room enough for Sid and

161

his father to share one side of it without getting in each other's way; and Mr. Derricks had even begun on a permanent plywood screen from the various tea-chests they had used to convey goods in the great move, and was now held up only for lack of wood. And two soldiers at the other end were infinitely preferable to Mrs. Gilpin across the passage.

'I wonder what they'll be like,' said Daisy, cupping her chin in her palms and wandering away into her ready dream. Excitement of immediate events had somewhat dimmed the brilliance of her vision of the most wonderful man in the world, but instincts of loyalty stirred now that his countrymen were coming, and coming in the face of so much prefabricated dislike.

'Nothing like Gary Cooper,' said Flo unsympathetically. 'Here, come on and let's get the place straight before they come, in case there's any awkwardness after. We don't want to be behindhand.'

They tidied the already tidy, jealously, and dusted the already glossy. When the expected hand finally banged at the door, and thereupon thrust it unceremoniously open, Flo had already cleaned and polished half the doubt and depression out of her system, and was able to turn to meet them with the dignity of a hostess, even if they did not intend to be considered as guests. Daisy drew close to her side, and with a late but rewarded instinct patted the natural wave over her temple accurately into position, in case it should be somebody nice.

But the first one was short and stubby, with a chest like a prizefighter, and legs like a cowpuncher; not the kind of cowpuncher with which Daisy was familiar from films, either. He hoisted his kit over the doorsill, looked round him widely, and rolled a wad of gum from one cheek to the other. His cap was on the back of his head, and he left it there while he looked the two girls over without apparent enthusiasm or revulsion.

'Hullo, folks!' he said, and over his shoulder to the second man coming behind: 'This is it, Budge, boy! This is where we live.'

The second young man came into the doorway and filled it. He had a lot of dark hair which went all ways, and a face full of hollows which aged him, side by side with innocent smoothnesses which kept him preternaturally young. He moved with an indolent slowness, and even seen in the shadow as his bulk cut off the light from the doorway, he looked unexpressibly sad, as if the world had done very hardly by him; and ominously aware of his injuries, as if he might at any moment turn round and take out every one of them in one grand outburst, something incalculable, something cosmic. He looked into the hut reproachfully with his lustrous, wounded, put-upon eyes, and said sorrowfully:

'You'll pardon us, ma'am, but that's right, we live here! Say, I hope you ain't one of those dames who throw things. I just seen the saddest thing – ' He shook his head. 'Maybe we should'a thrown in our caps, the first thing. Hell, she's got red hair, too!' he said, and sighed. His left shoulder came naturally to rest against the doorpost, and there settled snugly.

Daisy drew a long breath, and receded into an ecstasy never equalled before in the loftiest days of her dream-life, before she even began to grow up. She murmured out of it into Flo's ear, in fading accents of delight: 'It's him! Flo, it's him!' And her voice, small as it was, carried to the young man's ears and struck an ominous chord, causing him to look at her again and more exactly; upon completing which examination he heaved a long and protesting sigh, and remarked to the centre of the ceiling in tones of the most abysmal dejection:

'Marlene! Jeez, the breaks I get!'

CHAPTER FIVE

Budge

1

BUDGE FETTERBRAND was twenty-nine years old, and as children wander through the world of fantastic misadventure and persecution in a dream, he was astray among inexplicable circumstances with his eyes wide open. This sickness, like most, is worst if you contract it in maturity.

All he wanted was to be let live, with his feet up as often and as long as possible, but he wasn't insistent even on that. A nice little place, a job he could hold down, preferably with one hand, enough pay to keep a nice little wife quiet, a bit of incalculable fun sometimes – what more could anyone ask? And what less could anyone take, and be satisfied? And people's troubles, told off to come here, go there, do this and lay off that, as if he belonged by rights to anyone in the world but himself. And he didn't know what in the world to do about it.

Budge was used to being up against it, but what he wasn't used to was the change in the nature of the 'it' he was up against. In his experience it had usually been something he could, when necessary, bash over the head and lay out cold; that he could understand, that he was competent to manage. He'd been getting himself along by his own weight and the judicious use of various trips, blunt instruments, retreats, and the simple exercise of his own good legs, ever since he was a kid. The land of the free had not treated Budge to any penthouses, cars or orchids, but he had developed a faculty for getting along with it; and now, when he felt more injured than ever before, and knew himself more threatened, there was positively nothing he could bash. Whatever 'it' was, was not far out of his reach. This he held to be the unkindest cut of all, and it puzzled him incessantly.

He'd always had to scrap for everything, a newspaper round in Chicago at ten years old, his job when he left school, and later every one of the small artifices by which he managed to supplement his earnings. In his experience of the American way of life, of which he was fondly proud, you had to be tough to survive, and Budge had always been a bit tougher than that, and survived with a margin in hand over his rivals. He was not a self-assertive fellow when left alone, but he did take justifiable pleasure in always being one up on anyone who sought to be one up on him; and since the whole of society as he knew it was engaged in trying to be one up on its neighbours, his life had had a certain monotony.

Naturally indolent, the ideal of laziness, of relaxation without the necessity of forestalling those out to forestall, remained before him like a mirage. He was going to reach it one day. He was going to settle down behind fussy gauze curtains, and put his feet up; and his mother was going to come and live with him and Lou, and quit her job in the laundry, and be a lady of leisure.

Law was something which didn't worry Budge; he'd been back and forth over the fringes of it too often, and knew the kinks in it too well to make any mistakes now. Twice he'd tripped over nominal offences, but what was a few days in a fellow's record? And they'd never managed to pin anything else on him since then. In a civilisation continually reaching for things in competition, all he'd done was over-reach a little and upset his own balance. That could happen to anybody. It even happened to big shots sometimes. But when he settled down Budge was going to forswear even these formal risks; he was going to stake out his little claim, and mark it clearly, and bash only those who infringed its frontiers; and those he was going to bash once for all.

He wasn't clear why he'd wanted to join up in 1943; it was just one of those things. Maybe he'd been a little high at the time, or maybe Lou had been having one of her periodic attacks of romantic attachment to uniforms. He couldn't remember. But he joined up, and in early 1944 he'd come to England, a queer, little sort of country where the fields were the size of pocket-handkerchiefs, and the people spoke English, but didn't speak it good. And from there he'd soon gone on into France, which was even queerer, being at the time full of small, violent men with guns but without uniforms, and just about shot to pieces wherever he saw it. He didn't get the French at all, but they fascinated him; he went through their country like a small boy going through an aquarium, with his nose pressed to the glass, and his eyes as big as organ-stops. Then there was Germany, which not unnaturally was full of Germans. Here his early training came in handy, because he had had to learn to recognise, at a very tender age, the particular kind of amiability in others which meant that he was being got at; and the appropriate response came quite promptly and readily to his fists. But this was a kind of annoyance which depressed him quickly, and he was glad when he got out. He never had to do much fighting, but what came his way he did with the shattering thoroughness of one whose whole life had been conducted perforce on the same principle as warfare, what might be called the 'him or me' principle, and who therefore had little need of adjustment.

When he got back to America, in 1946, he figured the Army Air Force might be a good career, at that, now that the war was over; he knew lots of jobs in which fellows had to work a lot harder, and this way he could keep a wife, and settle down on American soil with the status of a war veteran and a serving man, and none of the worries of civilian life. Lou could still walk out with a uniform, too; that would please her. So he signed on again. That was his worst mistake.

He signed on again to be a happy peace-time soldier, and

before they had everything even planned for the wedding, let alone fixed, he was ordered back to Britain. Foreign service all over again! And why? They all explained to him, the Government, the Press, his officers, they all told him at once, in fearful chorus, why it was required of him to leave his girl and his carefully selected life on his own soil, and be shipped away again to the queer little country with the coal fires and the silent, many-eyed pubs; but after they had all talked their heads off, he still felt that they protested a lot too much, and that once again he was somehow being got at. Nobody is that voluble without having something to cover up. And that was the first time he really came up against something he couldn't bash, something that wasn't there at all, except in its effects. And it was then that his expressive countenance began to wear that look of sadness and suspicion, and that boding hint of reprisals working obscurely up in the limited but decisive intellect behind, which marked him out in the years he spent in England.

He hadn't been long enough in England the first trip to have a very detailed picture of it in his mind, and he had scarcely stood still long enough to feel its reaction to himself. He felt it now as one who stands in a cold draught, and is not permitted to move. At Bredington camp he was many miles from home, and Lou left behind on the opposite side of the world; that would have been burden enough even in the best conditions possible, but that was by no means all. Something was very wrong with Bredington. After he had been there a few weeks he reminded himself that the British people are supposed to be a shade slow in making friends, but after several months he could no longer get out of it that way. He was lonely, he wanted company. He went in pubs and offered drinks enough to float the transport that brought him over, but the offers were seldom taken up. He went into dance-halls of the reputable town kind, and asked pleasant-looking girls to dance with him, and either they made the excuse of being already engaged, or else they danced with him once, very correctly and quietly, and then were always unaccountably out of sight when he looked for them again. Nobody was actively rude or unkind. People served him pleasantly in shops, answered his approaches in buses and trains without coldness, but remained elusive; if there was no coldness there was no warmth either.

It was the same with all the other fellows. They were not admitted into the general conversation in pubs; if they started a line of their own someone would respond politely, but it was always a separate circle, never the main one, and frequently the man who had felt bound to help them out would move over unobtrusively to another corner as soon as he decently could. And the girls – the nice ones, the ones any fellow would like to be seen with – they were just about as hard to get as ice-cream in hell. Private family circles? – they remained private. The Americans were oil here on very deep water, and that was all.

Company of a sort, of course, they could have without asking, just so long as they had plenty of money and cigarettes and candy. Company of a sort! The sort that came in buses and hung about the gates shrieking in doorways, and went and got tight with the disillusioned on pay nights. Mostly floozies or infants; and a lot of the infants were rapidly turning into floozies. What sort of comment was that on England? Sometimes in his injury he was disposed to forget that that kind exists everywhere, and to multiply their actual numbers out of all truth; but in his saner moments he realised that what it really meant was that Bredington camp was draining off that type of girl from a very large area, not merely from the town itself. And what sort of comment was that on America?

The chip on his shoulder grew and grew. What was the matter with Americans, anyhow? Had they got the plague, or something? Budge liked to be liked; he expected to be liked; he was hurt and incredulous that anyone could dislike him. But when he read the letters in the local papers he could hardly convince himself that he was really wanted here. What the residents said about him was that he was demoralising their daughters, occupying their houses, cornering their builders and carpenters and materials, monopolising their inns and cinemas, and making their streets uninhabitable. Like him? They hated his guts! And what had he done to them, for God's sake?

But if they didn't want him, he didn't want to be here. He didn't want any part of their unfriendly country, their short-supply goods, or their less palatable women. Budge had been brought up respectable, and he liked himself that way. So if they didn't want him, as was obvious, and he didn't want to be there, which he personally guaranteed to be the truth, what was he doing there at all? Someone had slipped a very fast one over him. Someone had slipped the same one over thousands like him, and over thousands of Englishmen, too; and here they all were together, in a tailspin from which they would be heartily lucky to get out alive.

If he had the guy here in front of him! The guy or the group of guys! But you cannot bash an idea, or an institution, or a method of living, or a mistaken article of policy. They can bash you, they can push you around all they like, but when you hit back, you hit the air. Maybe once in a hundred years, for some lucky little guy with a grievance, they show themselves rashly in some tangible form, and then comes the pay-off. But Budge no longer believed in his luck; it wouldn't happen to him. But if ever, by any blessed, incredible chance, it did – Oh, boy!

Blundering through this alien world, looking for somebody to whom he could show Lou's photograph, someone who would appreciate it and him, this repulsed, aggrieved, well-intentioned child went where one more push directed him, and found himself in the Warren camp, standing in the doorway of a hut, gazing without much hope at the Derricks family.

2

The first thing he did, and that almost involuntarily, was make friends with Sid. Sid was without prejudices; he associated Americans with candy and chewing-gum, but even without these attractions he was willing to consider them as human beings, and take them as they came. And this one came large and mild, with a pair of useful hands for a kite or a catapult, and in the course of a few conversations turned out to know all about aircraft, or so nearly all that Sid was not likely to require a better guide. That was enough to go on with.

As for Daisy, she behaved like an angel. He had half-expected to see her get herself up the first evening with all the war-paint she'd worn on their first meeting, but she remained pigtailed, demure and shiningly clean. Her approaches were different now, domestic to a degree, bent to show him, in this unexpected heaven, how she had minded his words and acted on them. Never had Daisy been so attentive to Flo's orders, never so helpful and eager to learn, as while Budge was sitting on his cot within earshot at the other end of the room. When they made tea she brought him a cup, and hard biscuits of her own baking with it, and took care to inform him who was the cook; the way to a man's heart, she remembered, is through his stomach. When Staff Sonderson was also in the hut she made no advances, being a little shy of his looks; but as soon as he was safely out of the way some small offering or service was bound to materialise, with Daisy insinuatingly behind it. Well, as long as she kept up that standard Budge could unbend, and treat her much as he would have treated a little sister who thought a lot of him. Anyway, it was nice to have one or two people around who were willing to talk to him.

About Flo he wasn't sure, and Flo wasn't sure yet about him. He'd tried jollying her along, and she would play, all right, up to a point, but he felt that he was on probation. And after all, that was natural, wasn't it, when they were here as ostensible enemies? Still, she didn't freeze him up; she was a reasonable girl, she listened, honestly, fixing him with her clear grey eyes, not committing herself yet, ready to declare war on him or sign a truce, as occasion directed.

He made a bad break over the old man. The first evening, after they'd come to an agreement by which the squatters could leave the camp and return without hindrance, pending the outcome of further discussions, as the politicians say, Mr. Derricks abandoned his tea early, and began to put his boots on. There was a flaming light in his eye which roused Budge to ask where he was going, and on being told that his destination was the Waterman's Arms, in Crocksford, whether he could go with him. Sonderson was already out, out on the loose. Sonderson didn't have a girl in America, only a wife, he could shake his feet without any twinges of consciences, and the usual product in the shop doorways was what he liked. His entertainment came easy. But the Waterman's Arms in the company of a regular sounded like paradise to Budge.

Mr. Derricks on his first evening of freedom for over a week would have taken the devil himself along, he felt so large-hearted. And it worked; the friend of Sam Derricks was every man's friend. Budge threw his money about too rashly, and made it difficult for men to repay his treats, but they forebore from turning their shoulders on him for Sam's sake. He enjoyed himself; so did Mr. Derricks. The result of it was that they came home after closing time through a heavy rain, Budge a little drunk, and Mr. Derricks rather more than a little, holding each other up and swearing friendship for life.

Flo's eye on them as they came at the door undid the good effect. Sonderson wasn't in yet, and she had the whole hut for her strictures, but she cut it sternly short. Mr. Derricks, too far gone to feel the cold very strongly tonight, got himself unsteadily to bed at once. Flo took Budge by the arm, and sat him down on his cot without anger but without relenting, and said: 'Look here, we've got to understand each other. If you want to get on well with me, let me tell you, that isn't the way.'

But she didn't just draw the curtains close against him, and go away in a cold silence of disapproval. Not she! She bawled him out decently, like a good kid, in a very quiet but very firm voice, so that the conversation shouldn't carry through to the sleeping children. She didn't just draw herself

171

away and abandon him when he offended her; she gave him a chance. She told him what he'd done wrong, and not to do it any more; and she told him, if not in so many words, what she'd do to him if he did do it any more, and that if he was a good boy, and didn't, she'd forget all about it this time. He understood that way of carrying on; he knew where he was with her.

'Aw, but look, honey,' he said pleadingly. 'I only wanted to give him a good time. I didn't figure on either of us getting high, it just kinda happened. I only wanted to have him enjoy himself.'

'I know you did,' said Flo. 'That's why I'm talking to you this way. You meant to be nice to him. Well, it wasn't so nice, see? My father would have gone down there by himself, and had a lovely evening on maybe two drinks, without hurting anybody or being in debt to anybody. He can't afford to pay off at your rate, see? He earns maybe two-thirds of what you do, even when he's working, and this last week, with things as they are, he hasn't earned anything. Well, he likes beer, and he likes obliging people, and he'll go on drinking with you as long as you care to ask him, but it isn't really good for him. Here we all like to pay our way, you see. It doesn't really make folks like him happy – not inside of them, it doesn't – when somebody like you keeps on doing the paying. I know you meant it kind, but it's kinder to stop at his limit.'

'But, Jeez, kid, I got so much money—' he began.

'I know you have,' said Flo quietly. 'That's the trouble. You got too much to be accepted among people who can't match you. It's cleverest not to flash it around, lad, if you *want* to be accepted. Besides, I don't want my father turned into a sponger, and made miserable, nor I don't want him coming home tight, and you be a good boy, and mind it, see?'

'Yeah!' he said meekly. 'I get it.'

He sat there in his wet clothes, looking forlorn and young, not quite drunk, not quite capable of taking care of himself, only profoundly pondering this difficult and unwelcome guidance. He looked permanent, as if he had been there motionless for centuries contemplating the sorrows of life, and would be there for centuries more. She touched him rallyingly on the shoulder.

'Come on, now, you'll take cold if you sit in them wet things. After all that beer, can you drink hot cocoa? I'll make some for a nightcap – keep that cold off you.'

The lugubrious face brightened a little. He said: 'Yeah, ma'am, that sure would be O.K.' And when she went to make it, he hurried to obey her, almost as anxious to satisfy her as in childhood he had been to keep his mother's tongue from nagging. She passed the steaming mug to him through the curtain, and told him to go straight to bed with it, and she would collect it in the morning. And he did as he was told, faintly surprised to find it so pleasant being ordered about.

'Looks like I got me a kinda boss,' he said to his pillow drowsily, just before he fell asleep.

After that he went very softly for a day or so, and did an inordinate amount of thinking. It made his head ache, because he wasn't used to it, but it produced some result. While Sonderson was out in the evenings running round the town, Budge sat indoors, or played with the children in the pinewoods by the camp, and kept a weather eye open for any little things he could do for Flo. Buying his way in, that was it. When the catch of one window stuck, and she couldn't open it, there he was suddenly at her elbow, edging himself in like a large dog uncertain of his welcome, smiling foolishly, with his big hands ready to compel things to go the way she wanted. It was always: 'Say, ma'am, I could fix that for you!' And most drastically and successfully of all did he fix the camp loudspeaker equipment, on the evening of the third day, after it had blared orders or news or military music all day and nearly driven everyone out of their minds. This was one of the weapons of offence adopted of policy by the authorities, and so nearly effective that suddenly even Flo threw down her sewing, and squeaked that she couldn't bear the damned row any longer. Budge, who was sitting on the doorstep dangling his hands, and doing nothing but twirl a grass between his teeth, pricked up his ready ears, and presently got up and drifted away, wearing the expression of strain which indicated that he was thinking. Five minutes after his going the loudspeakers chattered, crackled and fell violently silent.

It dawned on Flo that there was a connection between the two happenings, even before he came sidling back looking so guileless and so contented that it was plain he had satisfied some profound desire. She let him settle down again and wedge his shoulder against the weatherboarding, and then she asked interestedly:

'What did you do to it?'

'Me? Why, ma'am, I never done a thing!'

He added thoughtfully: 'Looks like they got some trouble. We sure got some incompetent mechanics in our outfit.'

'And some competent ones,' remarked Flo. 'But I'll bet they'll soon have it mended again.'

'Don't let that worry you none. I know twenty-five more ways that transmitter can go wrong.'

Suddenly she put down her sewing and began to laugh helplessly, leaning her head upon her hands on the table. He turned and smiled at her a little uncertainly. 'What's eating you? It ain't that funny!'

'I was just thinking what a rum one you are,' she admitted, recovering. 'Your job's to get us out of here. Everybody else is doing it just as hard as he can. Your lot think up all sorts of ways of annoying us, and quite apart from that ghastly row they were kicking up with the radio, I'm sure all you fellows have got orders to make yourselves as awkward indoors as you can. Anyhow, most of 'em are doing it, all right. Isn't it the truth?'

'Yeah,' acknowledged Budge, 'they sure are relying on us to make you feel kinda not wanted.'

'Well, and we're fighting back with anything we've got – cooking smells, lines of steamy washing in the huts, babies— My goodness, some of the babies in this camp have gone to war before they can walk. Our folks bang about among the

174

pans just as deliberately as yours turn the loudspeakers up to their loudest. Mrs. Jones, next door, she goes out and leaves the two boys there to look after her three kids – and right hellbats they are! Mrs. Fryer washes out all her baby things in the evening, deliberate; she could easy do it in the day, but it wouldn't annoy her lodgers then. Everybody in this camp is just behaving one way, except you. I don't say any of us are really like that when we're left alone, but we're acting about as friendly as wild cats now. And here you go, stopping the draught from the loose window for me, fixing the stove, helping to hang curtains, thinking up all sorts of gadgets to make the place nicer. What is it makes you different?'

'You've treated me all right, too, you know,' said Budge, but looking extremely gratified.

'I never had reason to do any other. You haven't done anything to me, and you can't help being pitched into this business, you got no choice. I don't *like* being nasty, but don't you make any mistake, if you'd acted the way some of 'em have, you'd have got it back with interest. Why,' she said, marvelling, 'anybody'd think you liked living the way we are, and were afraid of the day when it might finish.'

Budge said deprecatingly: 'Well, you see, I guess that's about the size of it!' He got up from the doorstep with what was, for him, an expressively sudden movement, and came and sat opposite to her at the table, leaning forward upon his folded arms. 'Look, honey,' he said earnestly, 'I been wanting to talk to you about this ever since we came. I never got round to it with anybody before, somehow. What is it with us? Have we got the fever, or something? Your folk have got simply no use for us. Just "Good morning" and "Good evening", that's all any of 'em got to say, except the ones that come after what they can get. Well, I ain't judging on them – I guess you got no more of 'em to the million than most countries, if you got as many! It's the others that bother me. What have we done to 'em, for heaven's sake? Look, *I* didn't want to come here. All I wanted was to settle down, back home, get me a solid job, and get married. This

175

is where I ended up, but that ain't no choice of mine. I'm a companionable sort of guy,' he said plaintively, 'I like plenty of folks round me, like it was at home and among friends. Hell, baby, you don't know how lonely these parts can be when you got nobody to talk to, and home's a few thousand miles away.'

Flo had left off even pretending to sew, and was gazing back at him across the narrow space of the table with wide, sympathetic eyes, concentrating upon him with flattering intensity.

'That way,' she said gently, 'anywhere would be lonely. It's nothing new to us, really. Most families found out about that in the war. But I see your point. Sometimes we do sort of forget that's the way you feel now. Only, you see, there's something to be said on our side, too.'

'I know we ain't exactly angels,' he said hastily. 'I ain't saying we go out of our way to make ourselves popular—'

'Well – you know what's it's like in Bredington since you came. Not all folks say about it is true – more than enough is, though. You see, foreign armies are never exactly loved – you don't know, of course, you've never had any since the War of Independence, but the world's got a long way to go yet, and it could happen. It *ought* to make a lot of difference, perhaps, what brings 'em into the country, but try living among 'em, and you find out it makes precious little. You can have them as friends and helpers, or as occupying forces, but to the man who sees 'em throwing about in one evening what he gets to make do for a family all the week – and the mother of forward kids like our Daisy, who sees 'em turning into camp-followers – and the boys who lose their girls to 'em because of a uniform and a bit of extra money or a few pairs of nylons – do you suppose the label makes any difference? And could you tell by their line of talk which they are? Folks don't live in labels, you see, nor in headlines, either. They live in a day-to-day sort of world where the little things, the personal things, count a sight more than what the politicians say. England is a picture into which your lot just don't fit. However you tried to adapt yourselves you still wouldn't fit. It's partly the money – it's a good deal the money. Lots of people round here earn just over four pounds a week, and pay through the nose for everything they get. Even your privates get five pound clear, and a heap of things arranged for them free or cheap. Then there's things like this camp. Three years ago we asked for it, and we were law-abiding, and didn't just walk in, we asked and went on asking. They said it didn't come up to requirements, and so we couldn't have it. Three years this place rotted, and then they started doing it up – for you. They couldn't do that for us, oh, no! But for you there was the labour, there was the material, there was priority for the work, and money to cover it. See what I mean?'

'Sure do! But, hell, honey – pardon me! – *we* can't help that if we wanted to.'

'I didn't say you could *help* any of it,' she admitted, smiling rather wryly. 'Oh, no, all you could alter is your own habits and behaviour a bit, but that wouldn't change things so much as you might hope. Not if you all grew as silent and well-behaved as judges. You'd still be something that stuck in our throat. No, it isn't your fault, any more than it's ours. It's just something wrong outside us that's got us all tangled up in a mess we didn't make and can't undo. At least,' she added thoughtfully, 'we haven't found a way yet.'

'Yeah,' said Budge, frowning horribly over the effort at understanding, 'yeah, I see! Yeah, I get it, all right! If I was in your shoes I guess that's how I'd be feeling. You ain't blaming me for any of it, though, are you? Well, then, look – how if we aim to make it a bit smoother than it looks, instead of a bit tougher? Staff, he won't worry us none, he ain't got but three interests – there's no spite in him. If *we* make things comfortable between us, that's a help?'

'I believe you do like being here,' she said, smiling.

'You never saw inside the camp at Bredington. This is heaven after it. Why, if you stay here, and the kids, and your old man, I even got me a sort of home life! Sure I like being here! *Sure* I like it!'

'But it can't really last like this, you know,' she said

gravely, 'something's got to give way.'

'Well, let's you and me string it out as long as we can, anyways. You keep your folks up to the game, I'll take care of little things like loudspeakers. I got a way with them things. Plenty other things I can fix, too.'

Flo laughed, a lovely sound that seemed to be shaken like a chime of bells out of her baroque curls of bronze and gold. She shot out at him across the table a small, roughened, needle-pricked hand. 'Shake! You're in!'

'Aw, Jeez!' said Budge, so overcome that unaccountably he blushed, all round the large, wide grin of delight which illuminated his face. He tugged at his breast-pocket, and hauled out his wallet, fingering through his papers frantically until he found what he wanted. 'Look! That's my girl! Name of Louise – I call her Lou. Ain't she a honey? Boy, do I miss that baby!'

Flo looked at the picture of an extremely pretty blonde, brightly smiling from under a Veronica Lake haircut; exactly like any other extremely pretty American blonde, so that she could have been a publicity still for almost any starlet known to Hollywood. She admired her duly, touched far more by Budge's fond and shining pride than by the lady herself. It needed very few words from her now, for Budge was launched; a haze was in his eyes, and his smile looked very far away.

'Lou and me, we planned to get married. We got our eyes on a little place, too, nicest you ever saw. Then they send me here— But wait'll I get home again – just wait'll I get home—'

3

Everything hung in suspension again, as if both sides held their breath. The camp was ominously quiet, waiting for the next outbreak, and the Derricks family, on the principle that every thread of gossamer helps to hold fast, went on hanging pictures, fitting up a full-width curtail rail across their hut, trimming their shelves with clean white kitchen-paper, screwing in hooks for the cups, fixing up a plate-rack by the minute sink, and generally making everything look so permanent and domestic that no one should have the heart or the courage to dislodge them. It was a reciprocal arrangement; Flo darned Budge's socks, Budge rigged up the plate-rack. It worked very well; she got a devoted handyman out of it, he got a background which delighted him, was mothered, spoiled, scolded and managed at every turn, for Flo was used to dealing only with children, or with Sam who was practically a child, and she extended the scope of her activities to include the new member of the family without considering any change of tactics.

'I'll catch hell,' Budge would say complacently, 'if I'm late home and wake the kid.' And to a doubtful invitation: 'Aw, no, I can't show up in a place like that. If my family heard about it I'd be in trouble.' This made him ridiculously happy, and even aroused some envy among his fellows, which served to underline the happiness.

It was a fine sight to see the whole family going out together in the bright summer weather which had settled on the countryside. Now that re-entry was permitted, it was possible to go off on week-end picnics into the folds of the heath, and sit and eat cucumber sandwiches in a windbreak of high broom, within sight of Richard Rose's macabre masterpiece. On these occasions it was Budge who rounded up Sid, and jollied him into washing his face and combing his hair, while Flo was cutting the sandwiches and packing the bag, and filling a thermos with tea, and a large bottle with scalded milk. If Budge thought face-washing a good thing, Sid was willing to believe that there might be some sense in it, even though he had not discovered it yet; and his appearance usually pleasantly surprised Flo by the time Budge had done ribbing him about the bits he missed the first time. As for Daisy, provided Budge did not forget to tease her just a little more than anyone else, all was well with her. His presence on these trips had also made her take a careful pride in her appearance; and having taken the hint successfully, Budge was never tired of emphasising how much better a girl looked without make-up, and in nice, simple clothes suited to her age. Luckily Daisy had never seen the glossy Hollywood-starlet snapshot of Lou.

Away over the crest of the heath they would go, Flo with one basket, Budge solemnly beside her with the other; her father on her other hand, carrying the small, cheap box camera with which he would compose unbelievably complicated and difficult groups after tea. Daisy on Budge's left, beautifully demure and scrubbed and ribboned, with braided hair; and Sid cantering round them all, walking backwards, falling over tussocks of grass and recovering with an elastic resilience, hugging Budge's field-glasses as if they were the treasure of the Indies. No one else was ever allowed to carry them, not even their owner, though they were so large that Sid could just quaveringly maintain them in position while he looked through them, which promptly upon arrival at their picnicking place he did, in all directions.

They had a favourite spot, for families are conservative societies, and like to go back again and again to places they have proved, rather than to experiment with new. It was on top of one swell of the sea of grasses, where a knoll of thick short turf settled at its head into a shallow crater, providing pleasant places shaped ready for the back. Here they would spread their cloth and have tea, and after it, and when Mr. Derricks' film was quite used up, sit and watch the evening come down. Mr. Derricks smoked for a time, and soon went to sleep, gently in his niche of grass; and the others, when Sid had exhausted himself with racing about the nearer stretches of the heath, flying his kite, or playing with whatever happened to be in season, sat all together and talked. They talked about many things; Sid about what he was going to do when he left school, Daisy about how wonderful it must be to live in America, and Budge about all the places he had seen and the people he had marvelled at, but most about his home, and his mother, and his girl, and the fabled day when he would be back there with all of them. Daisy did not mind so much a girl who was her rival only at a

180

distance of thousands of miles, but grew thoughtful when he spoke of returning to her.

Flo didn't talk very much, she was better at listening except when her opinion or advice was required upon something definite. She liked to see everybody living peacefully like this, but she knew there was a certain artificiality about it. He could shut the door on the rest of the world, perhaps, but she couldn't; and therefore it was better not to look even so far ahead as the next day.

From here they could see the Folly plainly, asprawl upon its shallow headland, crested and battlemasted and stuck with towers, with twisted chimneys clambering alongside, and shot-windows narrowed against the sunset; nineteenth-century Gothic, shameless and awe-inspiring, vast among a scattering of enormous gardens. Budge studied it often and long through the field-glasses, learning by heart the very colours of its brickwork, and the mottle of its wilderness of windows.

'We've got nothing in the States like that,' he said positively. 'Not that I ever heard of.'

'All the better for you,' said Flo. 'It's a real horror.'

'Looks like one of those places in the fairy-tales,' he went on artlessly, 'like it ought to have an ogre. And maybe a captive princess.'

'It's got both,' said Flo, 'or something so like 'em I should think they'd do for the parts. Sometime we can go up there. They show it to people certain hours of the day.'

'Gee, I'd like to see the inside of it. Have you ever been?'

'Have I been!' said Flo scornfully. 'I used to work there, and I'm going back again, too, now we can get out and in O.K. But it's a pretty awful dump. Talk about marble halls! Gives you the shivers. So big only giants could live in it comfortable, and so draughty you'd think even they'd get pneumonia. But I'll take you – there's plenty to see.'

'Does nobody live in it now?' he asked, training his glasses upon the vast front door, which leaned out over gargantuan descending swirls of stone staircase, and was canopied with a writhing of Titans.

'Not a soul!' she laughed. 'Matter of fact, they couldn't get a caretaker to live inside it, it always got on their nerves so. The old chap who looks after it now, he lives in the east lodge, way off over the other side there, and the lady, she moved to the big lodge, the south one, when the National Trust took over the house. Yes, it's national property now – tries to keep itself on what the visitors bring in, but I wouldn't mind betting it doesn't. No, there's nobody there at night, ever, except the ghosts, but it's nice enough in the gardens on a sunny afternoon. We could go up on Saturday, if you like.'

'Sure would like! Go on!' he said, prompting, 'tell us more about it. Whose house was it, before the state took over?'

'It's a family called Rose. Mean to say you been at Bredington all this time, and never heard about the Roses?'

'Guess I never asked before,' said Budge apologetically.

'Well, these Roses, they've been here since the year dot, so they say. There used to be a very old house there once, but one of the family, last century, got very keen on railways, and made a lot of money. First Rose for a long time who was noted for doing that. And he had such big ideas he pulled down the old house, and built this one. Well, that was all right, but the ones who came after him soon lost all the money again, and it takes a lot to keep up a place like that. So they gave it to the nation. Funny thing, you know,' she said wrinkling her nose, 'they hadn't any of 'em got a hundredth part of the energy this one who loved railways had, and they all lived on his reputation as well as his cash for years afterwards, and made out he was a great man because everybody else said so – but they're ashamed of him really, all the same, because he went into trade of a sort. Trade's beneath 'em, but it makes it more respectable when it's very successful, like his was.'

'I guess so! And what's happened now with the family!'

'There's only two Roses left now. One of them is an old lady – *very* old,' said Flo, looking at eighty years from the infinite distance of eighteen, 'and very left behind. She'd be a sad sort of person, maybe, if she wasn't such a bitch. But she is; no two ways about it, that's what she is. She wants things to stand still round her, nobody to have but who had before, nobody to have a say but those who always have had one, especially her, nobody to be looked up to, or admired, or made much of, only her. And you can take it from me, it hasn't been much fun for that niece of hers, a young thing growing up there. Why, if there hadn't a boy turned up in time, with the right ways with him, that girl would have been getting ready for just such another old age. Only,' said Flo honestly, 'I don't know that she's much better off now, really. She'd like to get out of it all right, now, but it isn't done like that. Y'know,' she said, wrinkling her smooth brow under the blown red hair, 'it's funny about that place. The house is almost new, when you come to think about it, and came out of something new. It's only a hundred years or so we've had railways. And the fellow that did all this, he ought to have made a sort of new start for the family with it, and got them out of that sort of living in tombs, and holding off the future. But somehow it didn't come off. What he stuck up there on the hill only turned out a bigger tombstone than ever, and the life they lived in it got deader than ever – more walled-up, if you see what I mean, and shut in with only the family bones – until it's no wonder they all died off. *She* knows it's done for,' said Flo, emphatically nodding in the direction of the distant storm of chimneys and stare of windows, to indicate the old woman sitting there in her sterile state, spitting defiance at a live and moving world. 'Only she thinks it'll last her time. Shore it up with her hands, she would, to see that out, and after that, to hell with the lot of us!'

'Sounds a real sweet old lady,' said Budge.

'Maybe you'll see her if we go up there. She can't keep off. It's still hers, she's always around.'

'What about the young one? Did she take the germ bad?'

'She met this boy in time. Only, you see, unless something happens pretty quick there isn't a hope for them. The old lady's still boss; and he's nobody's kid, brought up in an orphans' home. What a hope! Mind you,' said Flo, suddenly

183

turning upon him with a strenuous ferocity, for the contemplation of Rosalba's problem always depressed and angered her, simply because there was nothing immediate to be done about it, 'mind you, I'm telling you all this in strict confidence. I don't talk about it to anybody else, naturally; only I like you, and besides, you've seen 'em – these two kids.'

'I have? When have I seen 'em?'

She told him. Daisy was off after Sid and his kite, about two hundred yards away and out of earshot or thought, so there was no need for subtlety. Budge's eyes peered back at that half-forgotten evening, and drew again upon the clean surface of his memory the picture of two very young people, ten years younger than himself, holding hands in a bus queue, and shining silently and resplendently with love. Something about them had touched the sentimental side of his heart even then, and found and fingered it again now, tenderly. So that was the princess! Pale and bright with angelic happiness, how vulnerable, how pathetic! And the saturnine, clever-faced boy, glowing to every look of hers, loving her so that the air around them was wrung.

'Oh,' he said, '*them* two!'

He thought for a long time. He was comfortable, and relaxed, and grateful, and his heart was ready to be melted. And here were the obscure forces which moved people about the chequer-board of this mismanaged world, the capricious bunglers of his own destiny, at work upon the lives of people here no less surely. He didn't recognise the look of them, nor the voice, nor the bulk, because he had never seen, nor heard, nor measured them; but he knew the touch all right.

'Jeez!' he said, 'I sure would like to do something for them two. Just all the more if they're friends of yours, too.'

'Not much you can do,' said Flo with a sigh, 'unless you could put a bomb under the whole blasted place, and blow it sky-high.' She shook herself, putting off the momentary shadow of sadness, and gave him a rallying smile. 'You might, at that,' she said, 'on the top of your form. I wouldn't be surprised at anything you did, and that's a fact.'

CHAPTER SIX

Four Lost Children

1

MARTINE CAME down the great staircase in a rustle of grey-blue taffeta, her thin, translucent claw of a hand outspread upon the broad balustrade, where it lay and drifted like a leaf capriciously balanced there by the wind, insubstantial and light as breath. Over the blue-white tower of her hair a film of gauze lay, lifting softly in every stirring of the air. And in this haze of greyness and mist her eyes, in the dried, fleshless, mask-like face, glittered like pale and piercing jewels, only a little bluer than ice, and no warmer at all.

She looked down the staircase before her, past the foreshortened portraits of Rose and Rose and Rose, still and sterile on the black panelling of the wall; and above her in the gallery her own picture stared out as stilly, young, beautiful, but over, a past creature as surely as the darkened and damaged ladies in the Van Eyck head-dresses below. Time had been when Martine could halt before it, and feel her blood lift and dance to the knowledge of beauty; but the tired beat of her heart when she looked at it now was like a tolling bell.

Time had been. She had seen this hall below her, paved black and white and grey, filled from end to end with dancing couples, the young, the noble, the famous from five counties flocking to its doors on the high nights of Christmas, the hunt balls, the glittering winter evenings ringing with frost, when the sky over the Folly dazzled with stars. She had seen the chandeliers blazing, coruscating with points of light, and the swirl of colours under them like a garden of flowers, waiting only, waiting always for her own whiteness, the lily, the magnolia, the white rose. All that had been here burned through her blood in a confused, narrow and virulent pain when she saw the trippers come, the alien people with their loud, cheerful voices, their frank, curious eyes, probing along the galleries where the bright ones were gone before them, the tall ones, the proud ones, the ones that flourished when she was young.

She remembered, when she saw the children scattering handfuls of gravel for their amusement on the great wide pathways outside the door, the crisp, thin autumn mornings when the heels of the horses rang there, the mornings of rarefied gold in the old time, when she mounted and rode, and the cream of the county followed her, followed because she could not be outridden. She remembered the singing wind of her own flying, in a morning which was still, and her beautiful, easy hands, and the stretched, lovely creature under her arching to the touch and the persuasion of them as a bow to the crooked fingers. The children of the strangers, atomies of spray cast up from the encroaching sea of another humanity, played now over their gravelled ways. Uncouth young men in shapeless garments of a muddy brown, big-booted and clumsy and rawly new, perched on the mounting-blocks with stubs of cigarette between their stained blunt fingers. Where was beauty now? Where was the flame of the spirit which had illuminated this hall of this hideous house, and made every affronting turret splendid? Where were the high days now, and the transcendent evenings, and the exultant nights? Where was the house gone, the true house into which she had been born? For even the echoes were changed here. Into one old heart in one shrivelled and shrunken body, under a death's-head for memorial, came all the past for refuge. There was nowhere else for sound or vision to hide, that touched no living ear but hers, and kindled for no other eyes. There were no more Roses. The girl was a haberdasher's daughter, without blood. What need had she of that imperial face?

The conducted party grouped in the hall looked at her as she came slowly down the stairs, and took their eyes and their minds from Cedarwood's Old Testament face. Martine never looked directly at them, but always through them, because it seemed to her, except in moments of cruel realisation, that they were not substantial as she was, and never became fully visible. Cedarwood she could see, because he was always there, and had respect to the past even though he had not shared it, and was himself a symbol of its passing. And to him she could speak and listen, because he, too, had heard the sea lipping at the cliffs of her crumbling island, and recognised the slither and fall of infinitesimal inches of the kingdom into that alien ocean of new time. He did not, as she did, measure the remnant of his own life against the time which was left, and take comfort in believing it shorter. For him hands angelic and terrible opened and shut these sluice-gates of inexorable change, and man and the life of man were grass; because he was without desires. This Martine could never understand; this she despised. But he heard the tune of the ages turning, and knew the dangers which were not immaterial to her; and sometimes she had seen his eyes upon her measuringly, without passion, as one assessing a champion who attempts the crossing of the sea afoot, or the holding back of the sun in its course.

In the voice of cream which came so strangely out of her bitter lips, she asked him: 'Have you seen Miss Rose this morning?'

'I think,' said Cedarwood, 'she's somewhere in the garden. In the arbour at the end of the yew walk, now that the sun's there, very likely.'

Martine thanked him, and passed, going slowly with her weight upon the ivory-headed cane. Her eyes swept over the group of people who followed him, and swept them all away out of her path. She drew in her skirt with her other hand from passing too near the staring children. She did not know that she did this; it came instinctively to her.

She went out through the patterned beds of opening roses, to look for Rosalba in the garden.

'That's the old girl herself?' asked Budge in a child's very loud and sibilant whisper, when the tapping of the stick had died away beyond the enormous archway of the door.

'Ssshh!' said Flo, frowning furiously. 'Folks'll hear you! Yes, that's Mrs. Rose. Now you've seen 'em both.'

'Not real, is she?' said Budge interestedly, turning frankly to stare after her as the wraith-like drift of her gauze scarf floated from view.

'She's this real, that she holds the purse-strings, and she's the boss. When you're seventeen you can't do as you like, somebody else has the last say on everything. And that's her!'

'But that's terrible! That poor kid – why, she ain't got an icicle's chance in hell with a witch like that.'

Flo said: 'Ssshh!' again, for his voice in indignation was liable to rise to an overtone and rather more, before he even knew he had ceased to whisper confidingly. 'Come on!' she said. 'Up the stairs, or we shall get left behind.'

Budge followed docilely, smoothing the tree-wide balustrade with an admiring palm as he went, and stopping to admire the carved grotesques which decorated the uprights, every one different from its fellows. 'Some money sure went into this joint. Get a load of these dawgs!'

'Lions,' said Flo automatically.

'O.K., lions, then! But I seen dawgs look a bit that way, I never seen lions.' His mind went back aggravatedly to Martine, in one leap from the curious predilections of Richard Rose. 'She sure looks like somebody, though, you got to hand it to her, she sure is a dowager duchess.'

'This family was too proud ever to have any duchesses. Go up one from the duchesses, and back a long way from where most of 'em start their pedigree, and then you've got what she is.'

'Jeez!' he said, impressed. 'That makes 'em real old, don't it?'

'That's the trouble!' said Flo. 'Too old! There's no room for anything new here, and no room for anybody young. Except, of course,' she added bitterly, 'for the old to live on.'

'We got to get her out of this,' said Budge, stopping dead on the threshold of the gallery, and thumping the blazoned panelling with his large and hefty fist. His face had set into the startled and mulish obstinacy which characterised the moments of his profoundest explorations into the iniquity of things.

'Who, Mrs. Rose?'

'The kid, of course! You bet we got to see this thing through. We got to see her all right.'

'I'd like to know how!' said Flo. 'And anyhow,' she added truthfully, 'we've got troubles enough of our own, and don't even know how to put them right, let alone someone else's.'

'They're the same troubles,' he said, inspired, but could not for the life of him have said how he made out this unity of misuse.

'Well, maybe! But that doesn't bring us any nearer knowing what to do about it – not how to get her out of this place and settle her in a sensible job among human beings – nor how to fix up so that we can keep the Warren, or have somewhere else decent to live – nor how to get you back home, and let you marry Lou and settle down. So what's the good? Come on,' said Flo good-humouredly, taking him by the arm, with a rallying shake because the mention of Lou had caused him to grow abruptly melancholy for his own sake. 'Come on, let's finish looking the ground over, and then you can decide where to plant your dynamite. Come on, when we're done with the conducted tour you can tell me how we're going to change everything, and by gosh, if it will make you any happier I'll believe every word you say.' She squeezed his arm gently. 'You're not a bad chap, you know, Budge Fetterbrand. Sometimes I could almost be a bit jealous of that Lou of yours.'

It was in moments like this that the image of Lou, for some unaccountable reason, trembled a little in his mind, and lost the clarity of its lines, like water shaken by the fall of a leaf. He didn't know why it was, but he couldn't recall the exact colour of her eyes like he used to do. A deep and subtle disquiet, too subtle by far for his analysis, preserved a darker undercurrent beneath his domestic contentment in the Warren camp. All he really knew was, he was sick with wanting her, and she got further and further away all the time, till he could hardly see her at all. And he wanted, how he wanted, just to go home!

2

The commonplace of Rosalba's relationship with Martine now was a kind of veiled savagery. It hurt to come near it, as sharp and acrid colours hurt Eugene, whose senses had become half her senses; and yet to avoid the old woman was only to hold off from actuality moments which were continually implicit in the occasional meeting of their eyes, or their entering into the same room together. It was only the difference between a curse expressed and a curse unexpressed; for the act came before the expression, the act was in the intent, constant, fixed and inflexible.

In a way, perhaps Martine was mad; not clinically mad, but nevertheless not sane. Almost Rosalba pitied her, for since her own enlargement into Eugene's undisciplined breadth of heart she was so spacious that she had room in her for pity. But one defends oneself against the mad, even while one pities them; and one defends one's own against the mad, and the ache stops short there. For Eugene Rosalba would have killed Martine, if there had been need; for herself she could only shrink from her, steel herself against her shafts, and wait. And waiting is hard when you are waiting for nothing but the cessation of a pain.

Eugene had once said, and with the same impatience, almost exactly what Budge had said, that they had all the same trouble, that Martine was typical of the adversary, the power that used and confined the young. And Rosalba had said: 'Martine isn't typical of anything! Almost no one ever is, you know.' And he had understood her, and been brought up short against something she had learned and he had not.

Martine never sent for her, always waited and waylaid; and for that reason she was astonished and jarred unpleasantly when she came in from her long walk over the heath, and was met by the housekeeper in the hall with a request that she would go to Martine's room. Mrs. Fenton – she was really unmarried, but the title was a relic of the Folly hierarchy in her young days – had seen the withering of Martine from before her husband's death; and a poor, bloodless thing he had been beside that vital creature, his cousin and wife. Mrs. Fenton was of the old order, knew her place, which was only below Martine herself, had an iron grip on it, and despised whatever Martine saw fit to despise. She was a tall woman, and broad-boned, shrivelled as if in imitation of her mistress, but younger by fifteen years, and in a brown, swarthy way, even handsome. She took pleasure, Rosalba thought, in delivering a message which was meant to imply censure and to make the recipient burn at the implication, burn visibly.

'Has she been looking for me?' she asked.

'Yes, Miss Rosalba, she thought you were in the garden.'

'I went for a walk, further afield. It was so nice. Very well, I'll go to her at once.'

Whenever she went near her great-aunt now, she spread out the arms of her spirit defiantly, protectively, round the glowing thought of Eugene, that no drop of Martine's acid might fall upon it and corrode it. Often he had begged her to tell the whole story, to make a bid for independence openly, or, better still, to bring him to Martine and let him put the case himself. She smiled, bitterly, sweetly, at the thought. As if she would ever willingly let them come within touch or breath of each other, to destroy with the shrivelling experience of their hate and dismay the one illusion in which

191

she still desperately hoped! Never! Never! She would tell all the bitterest, blackest lies, use all the deepest, unworthiest deceits, rather than unloose on the image, the innocent poignant image he had of their love and its adversities, this corrosive truth which her own image of it sustained every day. Perhaps it was because he believed more firmly in their unity that he was prepared, yes, and even able, to risk so much more. Perhaps it was not that she understood more – only that she believed less, and could the more easily lose their iridescent bubble of a love. But she dared not face that thought. She believed! Surely she believed!

She tapped on Martine's door, and let herself in silently, moving with a terrible grace and carefulness in the presence of something she feared fastidiously. Across the rococo writing-desk, framed in the redoubling glitter of the silver mirrors, the ruin of great beauty looked up through Martine's eyes, and Rosalba felt the acid of that inescapable loathing sear her face. It was like having vitriol thrown at her; she never became sufficiently used to it to overcome the moment of recoil.

'Close the door,' said Martine.

She closed it, and stood waiting, unsmiling, yet not far from a small dark smile. 'I wonder,' she thought, 'if my eyes hurt her as hers do me?' And almost she believed that they did, for Martine trembled when she met them, and her stare grew harder, stonier, more brilliant, flashed from mirror to mirror in a play of poniards. The silence was always meant to make her speak first, but now she never gave in to it. Words from her, when they encountered in this way, were spare and few.

'Where did you go this morning?' asked Martine.

'For a walk. Mrs. Fenton says you were looking for me. I'm sorry!'

'Where did you go?' asked the voice so much lower, so much softer than Martine's voice. She was stooped a little, flattening herself behind the desk as a cat flattens its ears in the stillness of great anger.

'Over the heath.'

'Alone?'

'Of course alone!'

'Did you go to the Warren?'

'No,' said Rosalba, faintly surprised.

'Liar!' said Martine, in a half-swallowed gulp, reaching forward with her strange, walking claws of hands across the shaken little desk until she gripped its edge. 'Liar!' she shrieked in a sudden, thin, distant stab of sound, like a hat-pin reaching out after Rosalba's eyes.

'I didn't go to the Warren,' said Rosalba, with weary simplicity, and waited, with her arms locked round the thought of Eugene, whose very origins had been clean, whose disordered little world had been honest after its fashion. She thought of him begging to be allowed to tackle this interview on her behalf, and smiled, really smiled at the thought, with so much inexplicable beauty and tenderness and indulgence that she gained years before Martine's eyes. 'Even to please you,' she said, almost with sincerity, 'I can't alter where I've been. But I can't make you believe me, either, if you don't wish to.'

'Come here!' said Martine, her voice again level and deep; and when she was obeyed she took Rosalba's wrist in one dry, rustling palm, and dragged her into the full light from the window and the mirrors, reflected upon her from all angles, a silver light, touching her pale face gently everywhere, without shadows, so that she seemed to be lit from within.

'Dare you tell me you haven't been to the Warren, among the rest of the rag-tag and bobtail of the town? If not today, other days! Carrying groceries to your friends from the gutters of Crocksford? Dare you deny it? Lending my name to people who are fomenting their little seditions here under our very eyes? Have you forgotten already that distasteful scene? Only a week ago! Yes, it took a week to get back to me. But there are people who have a sense of duty, if you have none, and feel some regard for tradition, if you feel none. Well, are you dumb? Were you there?' The hand, light as a dead leaf, shook her sharply; she felt its

193

strengthlessness and yielded to it, for fear it should break into a withered dust.

'Yes, I went there. I haven't forgotten it. I'm not ashamed of it. I wanted to go again, but I could only send.' She let her pendent hand be drawn across the desk, shut in both of Martine's own. She was afraid of killing what she would willingly have had dead. Sergeant-Major Thompson had pondered his little vengeance a long time before he took it. And how had he acted? Through his officers? Probably that was the way. 'No business of mine, sir, but the girl's only seventeen, and – well, I think it might be well if the old lady was told what's going on. Avoid something worse, maybe!' And perhaps he even meant it in that way. Who was she to look for the worst of motives everywhere? And the Army wanted no trouble which could be avoided, and she represented an item which could easily be avoided, among many which could not. They might well think it a good deed to pass back the responsibility for her to her guardian, and be rid of one awkward complication.

'Let's not rage at each other,' she said. 'What good does it do? I went there because I sympathise with those people, and I wanted to help them to stand the siege.'

'Law-breakers,' said Martine thickly, 'out of the lowest dregs. The scum of a new society which, God knows, is not worth much at best. Drifters from one cheap opportunist adventure to another, looking for a life without labour, and making as much trouble and disturbance for the rest of the world as they can find material to build. The little discreditables of chaos! Is that where you've taken my name?'

'It's my name, too,' said Rosalba.

'You're not fit to have it. You thought you'd kept it from me, didn't you – that little adventure? Not only the contact with such disreputables—'

'You're wrong,' said Rosalba. 'They're ordinary hardworking people, who went there in desperation, because they had nowhere else to live. Do you think people fly to Army huts from *pleasant* places?'

'—But the other affair, too. Did you think that wasn't observed? Your hand in his through the fence— A public holiday for the townspeople, wasn't it? A Rose in abject love, running down into the Warren to take hands with her private soldier through a pale fence before galleries of eyes! A *Rose!* Are you out of your mind? Do the women of my house behave in that way now, like the camp-followers who trail out of the ditches after an army on the move? Is it for that I've trained you, and taught you what is due? Was that in your mother's blood, as well as ribbons and buttons and safety-pins? It was never in ours until now!'

Rosalba shut her eyes, not to see the ruin of loveliness become hideous. Hate like that flays; she felt her every nerve uncovered, and shrank to the furthest reach of the mummified hands, her blue-veined lids firm to her cheeks, her nostrils starting and her lips drawn long and taut in incredulous distaste. Shock came first, and the immediate despair only after; one sudden stab of realisation, and where was Eugene now? It was all over, even in the pain and alarm of having him known. She had been right to hide him, but she had not hidden him well enough.

'Did you think I was blind?' hissed Martine. 'Did you think I could not see behind that sick, cheap joy of yours, to know there was some man buried there? Did you think I had not known for a month and more that you were meeting this – this creature of yours behind my back? But to be warned of it like this! – to see you on a level with your peers, to be told to keep you in hand, like some shop-girl gone amok among the camps! – You could be silent enough and demure enough to me, but now you shall speak! Who is he?' she croaked, tightening her frenzied hands upon Rosalba's arm. '*Who is he?*'

The wits become numbed when one withdraws into one's own midmost being from sensations too ugly and pointless to be faced, and it took many seconds for Rosalba to understand what was being said. She opened her eyes, blue and dazed, staring at the old woman's face. It was not so bad as she had thought. Sergeant-Major Thompson had seen

195

much, but not everything. Eugene stirred again inside her heart, fretful against imprisonment. Now she could think again, gather again the threads of living, for the enlarging circles of Martine's detestation had not yet touched him. A shade of colour, faint but clear, came back to her cheeks. She drew herself a little taller, and breathed deeply, and said in a quiet voice:

'Listen to me! There is no need for us to threaten each other. I am not what you think me – if it's possible you believe what you're saying. I expect you're not quite what I think you, either. But we're a long way apart! Isn't it better, since we have to be together, that we should have some sort of peace from each other? I don't wish to hurt you—'

'Peace!' said Martine, loudly and scornfully. 'What do you suppose your domestic peace is to me? I brought you here as my own blood, and you use your entertainment as some stray she-cat might do that I'd picked up from the ditch, and talk to me of peace between us! Answer me, who is this soldier? *I will know!*'

'From me you never will!' said Rosalba fiercely.

'You admit he exists, do you? What, haven't you got more lies to tell me?'

'I'm seventeen,' said Rosalba. 'Why shouldn't I know people? Why shouldn't I have friends of my own?'

'And lovers, too, eh? And lovers? Like the rest of your kind?'

'This is indecent! When you say lovers you make it sound obscene, but it isn't – it isn't! And people will love each other in spite of you,' cried Rosalba.

'And still live on my bounty? Is that what you think?'

'Your *bounty!*' Suddenly she began to laugh, and snatching her hands away from Martine's hold, shut her hot face between them, and tried in horror to press the horrid, hysterical sound back into her mind, whence it welled too strongly to be suppressed. Even Martine started away from her at this, and stood staring as if she had seen a dragon in the goldfish pool. 'Great-Aunt Martine,' said Rosalba, gulping back aching sobs of anger and laughter and despair, 'let me go away! All we do is torment each other. Let me go somewhere else, and work for my living! I don't want anybody's bounty. Let me go and get a job, and stop driving us both mad!'

'Let you go! In my house you revert to type, and then ask me to let you go and find more license elsewhere! Still with my name? Can I even trust you out of my sight?'

'You must know, unless you're really mad, that I've done nothing to be ashamed of. You accuse me of such abominable things because you hate me. Not because you believe it, only because you'd like to believe it! You'd like me to be what you say I am, so that you could have a real reason for hating me.' Rosalba took her hands away from her face, slowly, and stared at them in astonishment because they were shaking so. Her voice, too, had run upward from its true pitch, and sounded harsh and frightening in her ears. She wanted to get away, now, before they destroyed each other veritably, but Martine was between her and the door, Martine leaning and quaking on her ivory-headed stick, with her great gaunt head reared, and her gem-hard eyes smooth with satisfaction even while they were white with hatred. 'Better let me go,' said Rosalba, 'for your own sake! Not to have to see me! Wouldn't it be worth years of life to you? Not to be reminded every day that you're old, old, old! – old, and dried, and done with being beautiful – done with it a long time ago! Not to know all over again every time you see me that I'm loved, and that nobody ever loved *you!* – Nobody, do you hear me? Not even when you were lovely and famous – never! Only your face, and the kudos they got from being near you, and the pleasure of being fashionable. Nobody ever loved *you!* Not even your husband! He was afraid of you – maybe he hated you, too.'

She pulled herself up with a shock of revulsion because the voice suddenly reminded her of Martine's voice; she turned, and walked blindly towards the door, intent only on escaping from this person who was not herself. But Martine set a shrunken twig-like arm across her path before she could reach it.

'Stop one moment more! This is not new to me. You show me nothing about yourself I don't already know. But whatever you are, you're still a Rose. You'll stay here – do you hear? Here, where I can watch you – here, where everything you do will come home to me sooner or later. Do you hear me? You live on me, and you shall live as I wish. Every penny that keeps you is mine. For all I care you could go back to the gutter, where you belong – but *not with my name!* If you try to leave here, I'll drag you back, scandal or no scandal. While I live I'll not let you go aside from the path I made for you – worthless as you are!'

'Even you will die!' said Rosalba.

'But late for my comfort!' said Martine hoarsely. 'Very late!' The breath rattled in her old throat, rustling like the wind in dry leaves. She drew back her hand; it was an old hand, but surely the shapeliness had not left it. She looked over Rosalba's shoulder into the quiver of silver mirrors, at the reared hair, blue-white, still beautiful, the cheeks which had refined their curves away to something spiritual and delicate beyond the reach of youth. 'I am still straight,' she thought, 'I carry myself as I always did, like a queen.' But still she looked again, and the lines of her figure shook before her like water under rain. 'Now go!' she said in an almost voiceless whisper. 'Go – go – go away – out of my sight!'

Rosalba felt her way carefully out of the room, and went and shut herself in her own. She lay upon her bed, trembling wildly, the taste of her own words bitter as gall in her mouth. She lay staring at the picture of herself with the other picture, Eugene's picture, shut behind it. She thought he had happened too late. She thought he had seen something which could have been herself, truly, but which had tired already of waiting on the doorstep, and gone sorrowfully away.

Inside the watch-tower, when the rain came drifting from the south-west, thin scuds of it groped their way in by the shot-windows, and made glistening narrow pathways across the beaten earth floor. Then Eugene left of working, because only in the wet patches was the light sufficient for his purposes indoors. He came and sat on the stone bench in the dry corner, where a green-grey darkness hung even on summer noons, and there Rosalba came, too, driven soon from the archway which was her stage, and her small privileged audience followed her to the shelter of the dark. There they sat all together, almost invisible in their grey corner of a green world, listening to the indescribable sound of soft summer rain upon leaves and standing water, a drowsy, slender music, monotonous and sad; and if they talked at all, it was in green, soft, subdued voices, following hesitantly the same chimed monotony.

This day for a long time they did not speak. Then Eugene asked: 'Did you hear any more about the rumours?'

'Nothing new,' said Flo. 'Budge has been keeping his ears open, but he didn't get hold of anything definite.'

'Not a cent's worth,' said Budge sadly.

'I wish we did know the worst. It's like living on the edge of a volcano. I thought I didn't mind it,' she said wryly, 'but it gets you down after a while.'

The rumours had cropped up everywhere. Rosalba had heard them in the shops of Crocksford, Eugene among the local units in training, Flo on her own doorstep, where they had suddenly erupted among the squatters in an outburst of uneasiness and gloom. An enormous new bombing-range was to be made for live practice. Well, that was only too credible where so much open heath persisted. Even the first range of the wooded uplands with this same watch-tower, said some versions, would be included. And soon, very soon, the first night exercises were to be held, and to clear the way for them the Warren was to be emptied of all its mixed and conflicting inhabitants. That could also be true; those who knew the ways of the Army best said it sounded the most probable thing in the world. Only nobody *knew*.

Where did these frightening suggestions come from, that they seemed to distil in the steam of every kettle that boiled in the camp, to blow in the smoke of every stove, and drift in at the ill-fitting cookhouse windows with the rain? No one knew how they began; no one ever knows.

Rosalba hugged her knees, and rocked a little, sadly. This drowned world had also its influence, soothed one away from hopefulness as a running stream does from wakefulness. 'What will happen to you,' she asked anxiously, 'if it's really true? If they are going to make such an enormous range, then no one can possibly live in the Warren at all. It's right in the middle of it.'

'That,' said Eugene patiently, 'would be the clinching argument.'

'Yes, but it's so senseless. I suppose it becomes quite legal to throw people's things out, and them, too, if it's declared unsafe for them to stay – that makes that quite all right. But then, Budge, your people have got to give it up, too. It wouldn't be any safer for them. So what on earth is there to gain? They just repaired and painted this whole camp, spent a lot of money, so that you could use it. It isn't possible they'd throw all that away, surely? One would have to be crazy!'

Eugene laughed, not his pleasantest laugh. 'Much you know about the Army! Cutting their nose off to spite their face is no new thing for them, they do it all the time. If that's the only way they can think of to get the squatters out of the Warren, they'll do it like a shot – if they have to pull all those beautiful new roofs off over their heads to make 'em move. Having the use of the camp themselves has become a very minor issue compared with chucking Flo and company out.'

'But it does no one any good,' she protested, frowning over his absurdity.

'Now you're being irrelevant. The Army doesn't exist to do anyone any *good*.'

'I sure feel bad about this,' said Budge.

'Don't be daft! 'Tisn't your fault! Even if you didn't come into it at all,' said Flo astutely, 'the Army would still take jolly good care to have the last word when it's up against mere civilians.'

'But they would have to find you somewhere else to go,' persisted Rosalba.

'No, I don't think they would – not if it's done that way. They just dump us out, and leave it to the local Councils to find a place for us. All the Army's responsible for, as far as I can see, is putting us out of the danger area.'

They sat for a moment in silence, anxiously contemplating the uncertainties which hemmed them in every way.

'I wonder if it's true,' they said unanswerably.

'What will you do?' asked Rosalba fearfully. 'Will you fight?'

'I don't know.' Flo sounded for once a little tired; you cannot keep up this kind of warfare for ever, and feel no reaction. 'The men talk about resisting – just barricading ourselves in the huts, and refusing to move. But I don't know. Only thing that would happen then, they'd get us committed for contempt, or some other legal dodge, and we'd be sent to prison. Protests are all very well when they stand to gain *something* for *somebody*. I like a reasonable chance, though, especially because of the kids. We've got a lot of kids with us. If the men and women get themselves so far in the wrong that they go to gaol, what happens to the kids? We've got no homes, looks like we'd have no families, then, either. I don't know. Seems to me if they put us out there's nothing to do but go. You can't argue with bombs.'

'You could send another deputation to the C.O.,' said Eugene, very dubiously.

Flo laughed. 'We did. He said we shouldn't listen to rumours, he hadn't got any information about what was planned, and so he couldn't take any attitude about it.'

'That's the old flannel!' agreed Eugene bitterly. 'I'll bet there *is* something in it, then. When these chaps start knowing nothing about anything, there's dead sure to be something in the wind. Oh, hell!' he said, 'what's the use, until we know something definite?'

'What's the use, even then?' said Flo. 'We've about had it. Back to Bredington for you, Budge, my boy!' She nudged him with her elbow, for he was sinking again into his profound melancholy, which expressed itself with palpable silences. 'Come on, cheer up, one day you'll be going home, even if it does take a long time to get around to it.'

Budge chewed pregnantly on a grass, and heaved out of the depths of him the most shattering of sighs. 'We could maybe raise a mutiny,' he said, but without much hope.

'I doubt it! Most of your buddies don't think so highly of the Warren as you do.'

'No,' he agreed, 'they ain't been adopted like me. But I sure will hate to break up that little home now. You should see it! We got a new set of book-shelves – made 'em from a packing-case. It acts kinda rough, of course, but we planed it down, and fixed the shelves, and stained it, and it looks fine. Even Staff, he helped to stain it. We were getting the place real nice. And now – aw, the hell with it!' he said, and the spark sank out of his eyes again, and his shoulders slumped. 'Home!' he said. 'That's the nearest I been to home in this goddamned country. I should have known it was too good to last.'

'So should I,' said Flo, with a wry smile.

'Aw, honey, hark at me talk, when it's worse for you! If I could think up some way to help you hang on there – gosh, I'd feel better about this whole thing.'

'Never mind!' said Flo consolingly. 'You worry about yourself, lad, we shall get out of this somehow.' She put her arm round his shoulders and gave him a jockeying shake; he was like a big kid to her, with his one-way mind and his blonde cutie. She would miss him; it did not occur to her that he might miss her even more, for wasn't he safely preoccupied with Lou? 'You keep your eyes fixed on any little chance of getting back home,' she advised him gently. 'Get a germ, or something – one that hangs around and looks important, but doesn't do anything – one that makes 'em send you back to America. Or couldn't you just get involved with some bigwig's daughter – just enough to make you an awkward person to have around the place? Or—' Her imagination failed; she laughed, and shook him again.

'Or you could get roaring tight and smash up Crocksford,' suggested Eugene, 'or shoot your C.O. – you needn't kill him, only damage him a bit. Only I suppose that would mean a gaol sentence, as well – and dismissal from the service—'

'Brother,' said Budge with fervour, 'dismissal from this service might be worth a gaol sentence, at that – if it was served in the U.S.A. Might be worth a C.O., too – anyways I never did like that guy.'

'Now look what you've done!' said Flo reproachfully. 'You want to be careful what you put in this chap's head. Most folks talk, but *he* goes and does it.'

The wind sang, wailing high; the green rain dyed by the trees eddied in its changing currents, crept in at the shot-windows and drifted, cool and light and sweet against their faces. Rosalba in the dark greenness felt for Eugene's hand, and found it; it was cold, cold as her own. 'I hope it will stop soon,' she said, 'I ought to go back.' She sounded afraid; her voice had the extreme and careful composure of fear, even its lightness.

'What's the use!' soliloquised Budge gloomily. 'Here I am, Budge Fetterbrand, guy who fixes things back home. Guy who fixed plenty other wide boys in his time. Can't fix anything for his girl and himself, can't fix a thing for his friends. Only a set of book-shelves, and how long you figure we got them, even? Can't fix so Flo and the kids and her old man shall have a decent place to stay, can't fix so Rosalba gets loose from her ancestors, can't get one goddamned shot in so's everybody goes home and acts sensible, and gets on with growing things and making things. Everybody playing ducks and drakes all across the goddamned world with live bombs and goddamned dead ideas, shoving us around like we was chequers! And there ain't a mortal thing this fixer can do about it! Oh, boy,' he said gloatingly to his immortal soul, deep, deep inside him, 'wait'll I get my hands on one little chance – just one! Oh, boy, have I got a grudge to get rid of!'

'I *must* go!' said Rosalba, in a soft, hurried voice, edging restively along the stone bench, but keeping fast hold of Eugene's hand, in the obscurity between their bodies where no one could see. Sometimes she was so quiet, he thought, in these later days, that she could almost be forgotten, or taken for a part of the evening, like the soft coolness of the air, or the little umbrellas of rain continually opening and shutting over the surface of the pool. Sometimes he could feel her listening, her head reared at every sound heard or imagined outside their beleaguered fortress, her eyes always looking inward instead of out, but wary, and on the watch for danger. She started at a touch, and paled at a sudden movement. But she said there was nothing more wrong with her than usual, and even smiled at him as she said it; and though he knew she was not telling the truth, he could not utter what he knew.

'It's still raining,' he said, 'you'll get wet. Wait a bit longer.'

'No, really I must go. I shall run. I shall be quite all right.'

No one said Martine's name; no one ever did. But they were all aware of the shadow which went with Rosalba wherever she walked, and even Budge understood, in his fashion, that her fear was not of any positive consequences, but rather something magical, like the fairy-tale fear of a pointed forefinger which could turn flesh to stone. If she must go she must go, like the enchanted princess at midnight, to keep a spell unbroken.

She buttoned up her coat close to her throat, and looked out at the rain. 'I think it isn't so bad. I do hope, Flo, that this scare will blow over. I'm awfully worried, after all you've done.'

'Him, too!' insisted Flo, clapping Budge on the shoulder. 'Wish you could see that new bookcase of his, it's a treat.'

'I wish I could. Good-bye, Budge! Until Saturday!'

'You bet! We'll be here. So long, Rosy!'

'I'm coming with you to the edge of the wood,' said Eugene.

'No, really, I shall be quicker if I run – and you'll get wet, too.'

'Then I'll get wet,' he said, and shut her firmly into the circle of his arm as they dived out into the slant, sweet rain. But under the trees, under the black-green pines, the soft fall scarcely touched them; only here and there, where water had gathered and made a channel through the branches in some thinner place, heavy drips fell into the thick silt of needles under their feet, with a slow, ponderous falling which made a counter-rhythm to the touchingly gentle music above. A deep, moist twilight received them; they walked ever more slowly, for to the edge of the wood it was not far.

'Will they really?' asked Rosalba. 'Make a bombing range, I mean?'

'I don't know. I think they will. We keep getting these stories, and I'm afraid they're true.'

'Poor Flo!' she said almost inaudibly.

'Well, but we don't know yet, all the same. You're shivering,' he said, feeling the tremor of her body. 'Are you cold?'

'No, just someone walking over my grave.' She looked up along the aisles of the pines, a dark green dusk arched over them very high and still. 'It's quiet here, isn't it? Eugene—' she said, and stopped, her small voice drawn away into the silence.

'Mm?'

'Do you suppose anything will come of any of it? Really?'

'Any of it? What do you mean by that? Just because Flo's affair hasn't all gone right—'

'It isn't only Flo,' she said, 'it's us, too. It's all of us. Thousands of us – millions, I expect. People trying to make some sort of stand. Does it ever come to anything, Eugene? I'd like to know it sometimes did.'

'Of course it does!' he said doggedly. 'Often! What's got into you, to talk like this?'

'Nothing. But I doubt if it comes out right very often,' she said simply.

'Because there are difficulties, you think like this! Did you expect it to be easy?'

He always sounded angry, indeed, in an anguished way was angry, when her voice fell into this drugged calm of reason; and then she wanted to placate him, to reassure him that all was as he desired it to be with her courage and resolution. She smiled a little now, looking forward into the grey late evening daylight at the end of the wood. He felt the sadness of her smile, and its lassitude, shutting his throat upon all the words he wanted. She turned breast to breast with him. 'You must go back now, Eugene.'

'*Did* you expect it to be easy?' he persisted, unable to express any other anxiety.

'I don't think I ever expected it even to be possible, really,' she said. She put her arms round his neck, quickly, drew his head down to her, and kissed him. 'Now I'm going to run,' she said. 'Good-night, my darling!' And she ran, out of his arms and away over the tussocky path through the slender, slantwise rain, her outlines growing steadily more shadowy and colourless until they melted into water and air. Even her running, fleet as it was, had somehow lost the tension of belief.

4

The expected news that the Warren camp was to be emptied and abandoned lingered for a few more maddening days, and even then fell almost unnoticed upon Eugene; for it was forestalled by a matter of hours by another piece of news which affected him even more nearly. The fourth battalion of the county regiment, which considered him among its more dubious assets, was ordered abroad; to the East, but as yet no one knew exactly where. The current rumour, probably with the usual deadly accuracy of ill omens, said Malaya.

It was quite safe; the powers that be were becoming extremely wary about such matters as length of training, and had checked up that every man involved had had his twelve weeks. No one wanted angry M.P.'s, backed by even angrier mothers, beating up public opinion to whip the boys off shipboard at the last moment. That was bad for the reputations of ministers and officers, as well as for public confidence. No one was likely to raise even the most feeble of protests against this draft. A fortnight's grace was all they had, before leaving for the southern depot from which they would eventually embark; and a few days leave for every man would be granted before the move south.

The news hit Eugene out of the blue, for of all the things he had considered, this was not one. He had always known it could happen, as everyone knows lightning-stroke can happen, but the thought of it had never been able to reach him since all the nearer dangers which moved invisibly about Rosalba had taken possession of his mind. Some sort of success with her had been a possibility, the achievement of a kind of emancipation for her, the establishment about her of an atmosphere in which he could move and breathe without remaining for ever an alien; and failure had always been a possibility, too, discovery, anger, banishment, or the retreat of her overburdened mind into its own element, abandoning him. But there had been no outer perils for him, none that were not threats first and directly to their mutual love, none that were not sprung out of it. This sudden blow over the heart came treacherously, and for a moment stunned him. To have his time with her, and struggle, and fail to hold her, that was one thing; but to be thus calmly forced away from the fight before it was decided, this was quite another. And his first thought was that this stroke was fatal; past question, past combat, a death-blow.

He went and sat on his cot, with his face turned away from the few others who were moving about there, and clutched his chin, and thought frantically: this is the finish, it's all over. Behind him William's polished gently at his boots, and whistled 'People will say we're in love', grossly out of tune. Two more were arguing, down at the end of the hut, about the probabilities of death in Malaya. One had seen the jungle already; the other, who had not, was the one who naturally knew all about it. Sergeant Manson, who was a discouraged regular, and almost human, came and thumped Eugene on the back, and sat down beside him.

'What're you looking so thoughtful about? It isn't that bad!'

'I don't know that I'd be singing any songs of joy about it,' said Eugene darkly, 'even if I hadn't got anything on my mind here. But I have, and now it looks as if the Army's written finish to that. Why the hell can't they leave us alone?'

'Nobody ever gets let alone for long,' said the sergeant, rather surprisingly. 'If it isn't the Army, it's somebody worse. You'd much better give up girding about it, and make the best of a bad job. That's what you'll be doing most of your life, unless you're luckier than most of us.'

Eugene gave him a long, considering look, and wondered if he was somehow being got at. 'Why aren't you singing the same song as the rest of the old brigade, anyhow?' he said unkindly. 'I thought all you fellows thought this was what God made us for.'

'When you hear me say that,' observed the sergeant, 'let me know.' He proffered a crumpled packet of cigarettes, and a lighter after them. 'I'll be ready for Colney Hatch that day,' he said.

'I didn't know you felt that way. And if that *is* the way you feel, why do you stay in?'

'Because I left it too late to get out. I joined up in the hungry days, rather than be on the dole for good. Long-term! Then we had a war. And here I am, too old to start fresh on any job in a none too easy world, too timid to take the plunge – so I stay around the only place I know where I go for somebody, even this much of a somebody. Where the money's safe, and the food safer than most places. And where I know the language.'

'My God!' said Eugene. 'I hope I never get to that stage.'

'You never know what you'll come to,' said the sergeant equably. He looked at him for a long minute through the smoke of the cigarette, and said quietly: 'I've been keeping an eye on you, in a non-professional sort of way, for some time. Began to think you were getting reconciled. Why don't you just make the best of it? It's only eighteen months, not a life sentence.'

Eugene said nothing; as he saw it, it was precisely a life-sentence, for it was depriving him, life-long, of Rosalba. A few months might be all the time involved, but they were the months on which all the rest pivoted. He sank deeper between his masking hands and exhaled smoke furiously.

'You haven't played hell for weeks,' said Sergeant Manson simply. 'I'm not asking why, I just notice the fact. Quite a reformed character – even Thompson's noticed it. Not that you love us any better than you used to . . . I'm not kidding myself on that score, believe me. Just you began doing things well because no other way was good enough to satisfy you. Or something. You know the facts better than anybody.'

If Eugene did, which was questionable, he kept his mouth tightly shut upon them.

'I thought you'd come to the conclusion it wasn't worth breaking your head against a mere eighteen months. No more it is, lad. Why don't you make up your mind to it? You could get on very nicely with the Army for that time, even if you do hate the sight of it. If you put your mind to it you could get promotion.'

'I've got other uses for my mind,' said Eugene bitterly, 'and for my hands, too.'

'So I gathered, but for your service time, my boy, you can say good-bye to 'em!'

But Eugene had other good-byes to say. That was the hell of it. From one banishment into this narrow, sterile, unproductive world of khaki he had escaped into Rosalba; from a second, forced back even from her, he doubted if he would escape. He didn't know how he was going to tell her; he dreaded the instinctive recoil, the relaxing of the tension which held her erect, the placidity of despair which is so much more frightening and immovable than its rages. As he went up the fold of the hill towards the watch-tower next day he groped about in his mind for the right words to let himself down lightly, as well as her, and could find no formula. Never had he rehearsed any contact with a living soul until now; but the approach immediate and direct was no longer safe. He had discovered, as she had already to her pain, the fragility of love, which a badly-chosen word, a breath of spite, an unimaginative phrase or a single distasteful memory could threaten, could perhaps even destroy. They did not yet know so much of its strength and resilience as they knew of its delicacy.

Rosalba was there before him. He heard her voice raised to the watery sun which sought to break and dispel the clouds over the heath, and for a moment he stopped outside, at check, without calling to her, to hear the ring of her speech when she was being someone else. She was being two people now, two more star-crossed lovers. The lady first, a high-spirited lady to match her lord:

‘ “Out, you mad-headed ape!
A weasel hath not such a deal of spleen
As you are toss’d with. In faith
I’ll know your business, Harry, that I will.
I fear my brother Mortimer doth stir
About his title, and hath sent for you
To line his enterprise; but, if you go—” ’

And then Hotspur, the sudden, deeper, rallying, teasing interrupter:

‘ “So far afoot, I shall be weary, love.” ’

And Kate again, imperious, hot-tempered, flying to scold and threaten him for under-rating her, and ready to throw even the perfection of their understanding love at his head if he treated her as a mere woman:

‘ “Come, come, you paraquito, answer me
Directly unto this question that I ask:
In faith, I’ll break thy little finger, Harry,
An if thou wilt not tell me all things true.” ’

210

Eugene moved to the rim of the archway, where he could look in on her. His heart warmed with the vigour of her voice; such a Kate could not give in even to distance, surely. And her movements now, the passionate, preoccupied gestures of Hotspur leaning forward to adventures, and yet plucked back into spirited tenderness by the imagined, angry small hand upon his sleeve, had a breadth and vehemence she never achieved in her own person. If the mettle of heroism was to be sought so, she could not fill her mouth with finer words, nor her mind with more headlong clarities than these two.

' "Away,
Away, you trifler! Love! I love thee not,
I care not for thee, Kate; this is no world
To play with mammets and to tilt with lips:
We must have bloody noses, and crack'd crowns,
And pass them current, too. God's me, my horse!
What say's thou, Kate? What would'st thou have with
     me?" '

And his wife, for once striking a note all of gravity, and even for a moment of doubt:

' "Do you not love me? Do you not, indeed?
Well, do not, then; for since you love me not
I will not love myself. Do you not love me?
Nay, tell me if you speak in jest or no." '

She played the scene out, and he did not venture into her sight; but when she flashed back from the very act of mounting to make fullest amends in one sudden embrace and three lines of marvellous understatement of love:

' "Whither I go, thither shall you go, too;
Today will I set forth, tomorrow you.
Will this content you, Kate?" '

211

she suddenly turned towards where he was standing, and cried:

'Eugene!'

The sudden descent of her voice into smallness and doubt and anxiety troubled him beyond measure, and he sprang out of hiding and went to her quickly, stumbling in the grass in his haste.

'Yes, it's me. Who did you think it could be? Of course it's me!'

'I don't know! I knew it was you, really. I knew it all the time I was speaking. Only suddenly I was frightened – don't know why. It's silly, I know. I think my nerves are a little frayed. Oh, Eugene,' she said with unaccountable fervour, locking her hands about his arm as they moved towards the crest of the slope together, 'it's nice to see you again.'

'After four days!' he said gently.

'I know, but it seems longer.'

They sat among the imitation rocks, looking out over the falling miles of grass, washed now with soft rains, and palely, brightly green. She let her hand lie in his, between them on the ridiculous brick rock. Her profile was pure and still against the darkness of the pine trees, but sometimes now it seemed to him not only a little more alive to sensation, a little more vivid and generous, than when he had first met her, but also noticeably paler and more translucent and troubled, as if the spirits love had let in had done little yet but tear her. She sighed, and let her head slip down to his shoulder, and all he could see of her face was the white, wide lunette of forehead, and the long, fair lashes, deep gold curtaining her eyes.

'Don't you want to work?' she asked, stirring a little against him.

'No, I don't feel like it, just now. What was that you were playing when I came up?'

'It was Harry Percy and his wife, in *Henry IV*. He was going south to meet the rest of the conspirators against the King, Owen Glendower and Mortimer and all of them, and she wanted to be in all his secrets because – well, just

212

because she was really a match for him, and he'd always treated her like a man – I mean, with as much respect as a man. Did you like it?'

'Yes,' he said simply. No matter how moved he was, he could never praise extravagantly, so she was used to monosyllables. The great thing was that he would not even have said 'Yes' without the full weight of its meaning behind it.

'I always liked them. They loved each other so much more than most of the couples in Shakespeare, and made so much less fuss about it. And they quarrelled a little, and teased each other, and behaved like human beings.'

He wasn't ready to talk, he didn't know how to begin; he would have been glad if she could have gone on playing for him, soothing with her untamed, untutored, balletic movements the painful chaos of his mind. But the weight of her head upon his shoulder felt settled and weary. She wasn't really in the mood, either; she had only flown to these dead and gone lovers for company until he came.

'You're all right?' he asked in a low voice. 'Nothing's happened – at home?'

The head was shaken sufficiently to nuzzle his sleeve a little. But the answer would have been no if the whole fabric of the south lodge had been shaken with it. 'No, I'm all right. There's nothing new.'

'Rosalba, please tell me if she – if things get worse for you! You will, won't you?'

'There's nothing new,' she repeated, but even more softly, and folded her hand over his.

'We've known each other a long time now,' he said, fumbling. His mouth was dry, and the voice that came didn't sound natural to him, but she made no move. 'Do you still feel the same as you used to about it? There's been a little time, now, time enough to consider. I can't tell you what it's meant to me, having you, I couldn't if I went on trying all my life. I told you about my mother, and the way I've lived – and the Home, and what sort of hopeless, useless kid I was—'

213

She raised her head, then, and began to look at him closely, and said in protest: 'Oh, Eugene, how can you talk to me like this? You were *never* hopeless or useless, I won't let you say it.'

'Yes, I did my best to be; even if it wasn't quite my fault, it wasn't anyone else's, either. People were pretty good – as good as things would let them be. I know they were, now. I didn't know it then, but I do now. Only nothing makes up for having no one of your own. You can do without things, if you have somebody of your own. Even when I found out about painting, it was almost good enough. It kept me busy, and made me stop wanting to take it out of the world because I didn't have a family like other people, or even one person to keep on being fonder of me than of anyone else, no matter what I did. I could have been anything bad by now if it hadn't been for liking to draw.' He was trembling a little with his extreme truthfulness, remembering that antago- nistic darkness very clearly. 'I *hated* people, until then. All the good things they did for me were because of themselves, because of their consciences, not because of *me*. And of course kids are selfish, of course they are! They haven't felt anything but themselves yet. So I went all out to make people behave naturally to me. I knew they didn't really care a hoot about me – how could they? There were more than fifty of us – nobody wants a fiftieth of somebody else's heart, not when he's seven or eight years old. So I did everything to make them act as if they didn't care. I made them nag at me, and report me, and cut down my privileges, and dock my pocket money, and shut me up, and cane me – they hated that, but they didn't have any choice, and I didn't care. I kept my end up! But it isn't *nice*,' he said, old smarts suddenly breaking tenderly into the level of his voice, and making it quake, 'it isn't *nice* living like that, Rosalba!'

Rosalba scrambled to her knees on the brick rocks, and put her arm round his shoulders, and hugged him reproachfully. 'Don't talk about it now, Eugene, darling, don't think about it – it's all over a long time ago!'

'Only I want you to understand. I'm being a damned silly

214

baby again now, really, only a different way. Making a case for myself, asking for what I wouldn't ask for them. Only I want you to know what you've been to me. What you are! It was fine even beginning to like people through pencils and brushes, because of what I found in them, and not what I wanted them to find in me. And making things, that was fine, too. It took all the energy I had. But it wasn't the whole answer. And then I thought I'd even lost that, you see, when I had to join up. Back into the old lump-living, only far worse, with nothing sensible to do, and time wasting so fast it made me mad. You don't produce anything, you don't do anything, and yet they fill up even the odd ends of your time with useless jobs for the next chap to undo again, just to make sure you don't find something sensible to do yourself, in your own way. That was nearly the finish of me. If I hadn't found you, it would have been the finish. I don't believe paint could have got me out of it again, not after a year and a half of this. It was uphill work even the first time, because, you see, that dead-end kid I tried to be was very nearly all there was of me by then.'

She kept her place, holding him gently against her heart, and smiled down at him with the indulgent and maternal smile which made her most beautiful and most absurd. Let him talk as foolishly as he wished, if it helped him; let him even malign himself, that she might have the pleasure of scolding him afterwards. 'You're silly,' she said, 'and sweet. In a minute I shall have to shake you!'

'No, but listen, you must listen! Oh, Rosalba, don't take me on trust! I'm trying to tell you! It's you, now, everything's you. I'm different because only the best I can do is good enough for someone who loves you. I'm different because I can afford to be good. I've got everything in the world, why shouldn't I be good? Things I could have done cheerfully six months ago I can't do now because – because they're just not good enough for somebody you love. Rosalba, you do love me, don't you?'

'More than anything in the world,' she said tenderly, 'even when you're so stupid.'

'I feel safe because of that. You see, I'm asking for something for myself, as usual. If you stopped making me feel safe everything could very soon go to hell again. Rosalba, you won't go away from me, will you? No matter how bad things may be?'

She took him by the shoulders, and looked at him fixedly. 'What are you trying to tell me, Eugene? There's something the matter. What is it?' Her voice was urgent and afraid.

'We're going overseas,' he said.

'Oh, *no!* Oh, Eugene!'

'We go south next week. And from there somewhere out East. We don't know yet where it will be.' All his strung nerves relaxed with an almost audible groan, because at least it was said, whether well or ill.

'When did you hear?' she asked in a numbed whisper.

'Yesterday. I couldn't send word. Oh, Rosalba, listen to me! It can't make any difference to us, can it? Because we shan't see each other, is that going to separate us? I've told you, almost everything I am depends on you.'

'Do you think,' she said, 'that I shall ever be anything without you, either? Oh, Eugene, my darling, why did this have to happen now? Oh, God, what are we going to do?'

Eugene drew her down to him again, for she was trembling and pale; drew her down into the hollow of his arm, and held her tightly, feeling her quivering embrace relax a little in the certainty of his touch. He had been right to be afraid, for she clung to him with a passion which made him aware that she was in terror already of being withdrawn; against her will, against her judgment, by the plucking of habit and pressure of daily compulsion, drawn away and away from him once this hold was broken. Over them the struggling sun shone out suddenly, and thrust the clouds aside vigorously, warming their twining arms and cold cheeks with the first positive ray. Rosalba lifted her soft mouth suddenly, and kissed his cheek with a desperate solemnity.

'Whatever happens, I love you with all my heart, I always shall, always!'

'What should happen, except that we have to wait a little? Nothing's changed, except that we can't meet for a while. What could be changed, just because we have to separate for a mere year or two?'

'But I need you so much!' she said.

'So do I need you! I told you! Well, I have you, and you have me.'

But his need of her could be satisfied across distances, she thought, while hers of him was immediate, urgent, a matter of every day, the need of the magic, renewing touch which could make her constant and brave. 'I'll try!' she whispered desperately, 'I will try! I want to be worth trusting, I want it more than anything in the world. Only I don't know how much I can stand. I'm frightened of letting you down! I don't want to, but I'm frightened! When you've gone—' Her voice failed in dismay at the very words.

'When I'm gone, I'll write to you – every day, if I can. And you'll write to me often, too. It will be like meeting again. Don't be afraid of it – oh, darling, don't be afraid!'

'Do you know what life would be like,' she asked with a bitter little laugh, 'with your letters arriving all the ime under Great-Aunt Martine's eye?'

'Then I'll send them through Flo. She'll let you have them faithfully – and you can talk to her—'

'Yes,' she said eagerly, 'yes, we could do it like that. Yes, of course, somehow we'll manage it. I won't let you down, I swear I won't! Oh, Eugene, don't think too badly of me for being frightened. You don't know what it's like for me. When you're here, when I can see you regularly, I could face anything for you. But when you're gone – and everything else goes on— One gets so tired, and it could be so easy to slip back into the old way—'

'It could for me, too,' he said huskily. 'Rosalba, I'm scared, too! If you let go of me now—'

'I won't! Never, Eugene!'

But there was something in her voice, something in the fever of her vehemence, which kept him from asking her to promise it. He wanted so painfully to be reassured, to be comforted, that he was afraid to look too closely.

'How long have we got? When must you go?'

'Next week, on the Friday we leave. Everybody'll get forty-eight hours off, but we shall have embarkation leave later, after the move. I could come back then, we could have a few days together.'

'Yes, yes,' she agreed eagerly, clutching at every straw he held out to her, just as he was clinging desperately to all she could offer, 'we could see each other again then. It would be a very little rehearsal, wouldn't it? We'll make plans for every day. Somehow I'll manage it, no matter what happens afterwards.'

Between their two thundering hearts, so young and so desperate, other ghosts rose unexpectedly. Things they had almost forgotten in this extremity were extreme to others, and all their world one pathetic little desperation struggling against the odds. There was Flo, so much more, when they could remember it, than an adjunct of their own affairs; there was Budge, who in his fashion shared this very pain of theirs, and had been so generous in caring about the cares of his friends.

'They begin night practice bombing on Thursday evening,' said Eugene miserably, 'before the main exercises start. I expect you heard.'

'Yes. Poor Flo! It all seems so useless.'

'Have you seen her?' he asked. 'What are they going to do?'

'What can they do? They've asked for the Major to receive a deputation, and of course he will, but nothing will happen, nothing ever does. They're going to see if the Council will do anything, too, but really we know they won't. We know they can't!'

'Then they'll have to decide whether to refuse to go, and have the roofs stripped over them, or just give up, and move out.'

'In either case it means they must go. All the difference it makes is whether they go to prison, or to the old casual wards in the workhouse. One or two might find rooms again,

218

some will go back and squeeze in with their relatives, like they did before; but that's the only accommodation there is to offer to the others. Oh, Eugene,' she said, turning her face into his shoulder with a small, tired laugh, 'it seems as if everything's gone to pieces, doesn't it? And now you and I— Everything was against us. We didn't know, any of us, what we were tackling, or perhaps we should never have begun it.'

'Yes, we should,' said Eugene, hugging her jealously. 'It was worth anything – *anything*—'

'How many days have we? When shall you come again?'

He told them over in his mind, and shrank with dismay at the sight of their littleness. 'I shall be free all day Tuesday and Wednesday, that's my forty-eight. I could stay here, and we could meet both days, couldn't we? Couldn't you make some excuse to be out all day – oh, Rosalba, couldn't you? Then we could go right away for a few hours, and forget this place even exists. Couldn't you manage it this once?'

'Tuesday I might,' she said, kindling. 'Her lawyer comes to lunch on Tuesday, and stays most of the afternoon. She'll ask questions afterwards, but I don't care! Yes, if it's fine on Tuesday let's do that. But I daren't try to take the whole of Wednesday, too.'

'Tuesday, then! Shall I come here for you, or shall we meet at the bus station in Crocksford? There are always so many people, no one will notice us among them.'

'Yes, there, please there – in the morning? At ten o'clock. Is it too early?'

'And Wednesday evening, here,' he said. 'It will be the last. You will come, Rosalba?'

'Of course!' she said, and wound her arm round his neck and held him to her cheek, for pity and love of his suddenly tremulous face. 'Oh, darling, darling, don't be afraid! It came so suddenly, I wasn't ready, I hadn't had time to think. I'll never give you up. How could I? It would be like giving up the light of the sun, and motion, and breath—'

But still they were afraid.

5

After the order to evacuate the Warren had fallen upon the camp out of its long-sagging cloud of rumours, on the first day of the school holidays, the quiet there changed to intense activity. Long since a committee of three had been chosen to act as advocates for the squatters in this desperate case, and the whole of one day they spent dragging their neglected cause from office to office and back to the Army, achieving only a single day's delay in the execution of the sentence. There was no appeal. They had to go.

The three men came home tired half to death, and were met by the whole population of the camp; but before they could say a word their faces had told everything, and people were drifting off to their huts in the silence of despair, one or two to debate the questionable uses of further resistance, one or two even to put them into practice, but most to begin the sad labour of pulling to pieces the homes they had made out of next to nothing. Early in the morning, even this same evening perhaps, all the men and half the wives would be out hunting for somewhere to go, anywhere rather than the casual wards of the institutions of Crocksford and Bredington, which was all the local authorities could offer them.

Mr. Derricks came creeping into his hut a beaten man, and sat down tenderly to take off his boots, which had been hurting him for the last three of many miles. Daisy, tearful and silent, brought his slippers. Even in this extremity she remembered that the beloved eye of Budge was upon her, and acted the domestic angel with as good a grace as she could find in her.

'Me feet are killing me,' said Mr. Derricks, and sat back in his chair with closed eyes. 'And all for nothing,' he said, 'of course! They're all very sorry for us. Thank you, we says, that'll keep the rain off a treat!'

'What did Cox have to say?' asked Flo, standing grimly in the middle of the hut with her hands on her hips.

'Much what you'd expect. Said our first duty was defence measures, and we must all be prepared to sacrifice for it. Reckoned this here night exercise for the bombers was a vital necessity – as if they hadn't suddenly rushed out all the troops for miles and miles around to throw up fences and wire and notices, and have the ground laid ready for Thursday night! Bloody sudden necessity! So I asks him how he makes out that bombers are a means of *de*fence. And old Joe says if they don't find living quarters for us soon, and so something about the cost of living, there'll be nothing to defend except the Army, and the members of Parliament, and the folks with a thousand a year and up. And I says well, that'll finish off the class war for you, anyhow. But we didn't let off steam at him until we knowed we'd get nothing out of him. Same with the others. All we can expect from them is a bed in the workhouses. Said we ought not to regard it as any disgrace, it was simply intended now as emergency accommodation for just such a case as this, until we could find permanent quarters. Anybody might have to make use of it. Well, daresay that's true enough, but it's the still the workhouse to most folks.'

'Well, so we've had it,' said Flo. 'Well, I suppose we can't complain. We knew we were up against the odds when we started, and we reckoned it was worth it. Only the gamble didn't come off. So we got to pay up, and look big.' Her face was quite fixed and calm; Budge had been watching her all day with a wariness entirely inappropriate, as if he was expecting an outburst resultant on some misdeed of his own. 'We said at the beginning, they always win in the end; what have we got to kick about now they have won?'

'Well,' said Mr. Derricks, 'we're advising everybody now not to get into worse trouble. If we go quiet they may be more ready to help us to some other camp; there's others to be found, if not so good as this. But if anybody chooses to go the whole hog, and resist the order, he does it off his own bat. *If* he does, we'll all stick together in doing what we can for him, short of chucking our own families in, too. But we advise sticking on the right side of the law, because that's been our policy all along, and it was understood before we started. That's the official line. But there's nothing to stop us from going across it, girl, if you want it.'

'I don't,' said Flo. 'I know when I'm beat. Because you lose a battle, it doesn't say you've lost the war. But there's at least two things to stop us putting ourselves outside the law.' She cast a significant glance at two very subdued children, who sat side by side on the edge of Sid's bed, wrangling in low tones and with little spirit.

'In that case,' said her father, 'put the kettle on, and I'll have a cup o' tea, and then I'd better be off again and see if I can find some rooms somewhere in the town. You never know your luck! We might be the ones that drop on our feet.'

'The kettle is on, it'll boil in a minute. Daisy,' she said over her shoulder, 'make some tea for us, that's a good girl. Now, then, Dad, you've done enough tramping for one day. If you like, you can stop here and start packing up the little things, and I'll go and see what I can find.'

'I'll come along with you, honey,' said Budge at once.

'You wouldn't be any help, lad, on this job. No, you stay and help to pack, and keep an eye on the kids for me.'

Mr. Derricks gazed round the room with a pessimistic eye, and seriously considered whether it would not be preferable, after all, to leave the packing to Flo and walk down into Crocksford again to tramp the streets in search of lodgings; but his feet hurt him, and Flo wore a look which he did not like to cross. So it was she who put on her coat after tea, and set off for the town. She looked much as usual, quite brisk and cheerful and lively, tripping out of the camp on her high blue heels with that provocative gait which raised the wolf-whistles from every corner; and to Budge, whose depressed countenance affronted her, she said on parting, none too kindly: 'For goodness sake don't look as if you were on your way to your own funeral! It's only ours!' And then, relenting at his hurt glance: 'Don't mind me, you big dope! It won't be the death of us, even if we do have to go in a 'rest centre'. Now you go and see how much you can get done while I'm away; and if those two kids aren't in bed when I come, if it's after ten o'clock – both of 'em, mind, no favourites!—They'll catch hell, and so will you!' And having, by this means, warmed his heart unreasonably, she patted his cheek suddenly and lightly, and tripped away down the earth roadway, past the sickle of pines.

She was late coming back. Mindful of her threats, which even in jest were as sacred as her promises, Budge took care to chivvy Sid to bed at nine, which Mr. Derricks on his own would never have managed; and Daisy, more diplomatically teased towards her pillow at ten, was by then so tired from much hard work in his company that she was not sorry to go, sorry as she was to leave him. She stood a moment to look round the room they had partially wrecked, and smudged her grubby, hot face with the back of her hand, smearing the first tears through the dust to leave muddy trails after her fingers.

'Aw, c'mon, baby!' said Budget gently. 'Don't you let it get you down.' And when her face promptly crumpled, after the way of women the moment sympathy is offered, he held out solid, safe arms to her, and she flung herself into them and cried like a six-year-old, without restraint, all her young ladyhood thrown headlong. After that she felt better, and washed her face, and suffered herself to be jockeyed into laughing a little on the rebound. Budget despatched her behind the curtain to her bed with a kiss on the forehead and a slap behind; if Sid had delivered a slap of half such weight she would have resented it as an assault, but from Budge she accepted it with complacency. At fourteen, after all, women are comparatively easy to manage. It's later on the grade gets tough. And she was a nice kid, and a honey to look at. He was going to miss her. He was going to miss them all, Flo most of all. He had known it was too good to last, but maybe it had already lasted too long.

Flo came back at eleven o'clock. He heard her carefully quiet step at the door, and turned almost guiltily away from the packing-case over which he was bending. Mr. Derricks, who had been resting his feet, and his eyes, too, in the armchair, sprang up in time to look busy. She came in softly; she looked very tired, and it was quite plain, even before she shook her head in answer to their questioning glances, that she was empty-handed. Sid was already asleep, and it was as well to pretend that they thought Daisy was, too, therefore they spoke in almost silent whispers, and sparse, symbolic words.

'No luck?'

'No.'

She hung up her coat and took off her shoes, and began to help Budge at the packing-case.

'Try Ma Gilpin, too?'

'Yes – at the finish. She's let 'em.'

So there was nothing, not even that precarious corner of respectability; no room anywhere for the Derricks family, except in the old casual wards.

'I'll go again tomorrow, early,' said Mr. Derricks sturdily.

'O.K., you never know.'

But her tone, even in a whisper, indicated that she did know, and was only unwilling to damp any spark of hope he might still possess.

'Gee, honey, I'm sore!' whispered Budge.

'You'll be sorer still if you drop that jug,' she said, with a still warming flash of her old smile. 'Here, hand it over!' And she took it from his hand and bestowed it carefully; and then, meeting his unaccountably mournful eyes full, summoned the real smile in all its glory, stood on the tips of her toes, seized him round the neck, and pulled his head down to her own. She kissed him frankly and heartily, and then as decisively pushed him away from her. 'You're a big lug! Go to bed!'

At that moment Staff Sonderson, innocently drunk, came rolling along the walk between the huts, his steadying hand thudding along the wall, his soulful voice raised in a chorus of unbelievable sadness and slowness. Budge flew to throttle him down to silence and bestow him without incident, and the moment was lost or saved. But for that, no one knows what might have happened.

6

A column of Army transports moved them out next day. About half of the families had managed to squeeze themselves back into cramped spaces with already overcrowded relatives in town, and these moved out first, in a tangle of tears, squabbles, scuffling children and sweating troops. None of this group felt it worth locking the doors of their huts and defying the order. Two childless couples among the others did, and remained there until harassed and shamefaced young soldiers, bitterly cursing under their breath, were detailed off to start stripping the roofs over them, and breaking the windows for more speed. One of them was a carpenter by trade. He wrenched away at the top of his ladder, almost in tears, and no one had the heart to revile him. But when the roof was well holed the inhabitants came out, the wife swollen with crying. No one went to prison. It could have been only a lost protest. Too many people were in plights equal or worse, for this to rouse much feeling outside one small circle of England.

The Americans remained until everyone else was out of the camp, for the Army was determined not to let in new squatters on the heels of the ejected. Squads of men were told off to do some quick injuries to the huts not now occupied by American soldiers, to ensure that they should be uninhabitable. The stripping of roof timbers went on, with less haste, so that at least the wood could be used again.

'But it won't,' said the depressed carpenter simply, to the nearest group of his fellow-creatures. 'They'll *mean* to use it again, all right, but bless you, they'll just stack it somewhere and forget it. Only time they'll think about it again is when some chap who's got bloody sick of seeing it rot pinches a bit for his own uses. Then they'll run him in and fine him – unless he happens to be in uniform himself, in which case he'll know better how to set about it. Expert training's everything!'

Flo sat on the most substantial bale of her family's motley

225

belongings, and watched the lorries loading up. She had finished the packing that morning, cut large packages of sandwiches for midday, made a quick estimate of the weather, and decided, accurately, that it was going to be fine. She was grateful for that. This day at least could be alleviated by treating it as a kind of demented picnic. Tea out of a vacuum flask always brightened Sid's young life by its associations, and sunshine was half the battle. She had trotted round most of her neighbours to see if they needed help, and lent it where she could; and now there was nothing to be done but sit and wait.

'The only good thing about not having much,' she said to Budge, when he came along to sit beside her, 'is that you don't have such a load to move at a time like this.'

'Where's Sid?' asked Budge.

'All over the camp. Sid likes to see boards ripped off. He's probably helping. Why not? If they want it done, he may as well enjoy himself.'

'I shall never understand this goddamned country,' said Budge hopelessly.

'I told you not to use that word!' she said.

'O.K., this darned country!'

'Did you understand your own?'

He thought a moment, and said: 'I guess not! I guess I never noticed how crazy things were there, but right here it comes fresh. I guess the place is so small you can't help noticing. Flo, honey, I sure hate to see this happen to you!'

'Shut up!' said Flo with sudden fury. 'I'm behaving well, aren't I? Well, then, keep quiet about it!'

He was getting sense. After a minute of unresentful silence she said: 'Sorry, Budge! You're a nice lad, I'm a cat! Just don't keep reminding me, that's all. Not unless you want me crying down your neck in floods.'

Budge did not. Daisy was as much as he could manage in that line. 'Anyways,' he said glumly, 'it's me I'm thinking about. Watch out I don't start weeping down your neck, instead.'

That was better, for she laughed; but even laughter was a

226

little precarious. He found it best to go away for a while, and leave her alone; and going forward to assist with some heavy loading just inside the gate, where a few sympathisers and onlookers from the town were coming in to help their friends, or merely to stare, he ran full tilt into a hurrying Rosalba.

'Oh, Budge,' she said, breathless after running all down the heath where no paths were, 'I'm glad you're still here. I was afraid I wouldn't see you to say good-bye.'

'I ain't going that far away!' he protested. 'Only back to Bredington. You'll be seeing me around the place some more.'

'Oh, yes, I hope so! But you didn't come to the tower on Saturday, as we arranged – I know you couldn't, of course, we'd heard about all your troubles here. And it won't be so easy for us all to meet when you're back in Bredington. And now Eugene—' She broke off resolutely, for she had not come to talk to these two already dejected creatures about Eugene. 'How is Flo?' she asked anxiously.

'Well, like you'd expect. She's been fine, tough as they come, but she don't feel so good, really. You come and talk to her, it'll do her good to see you.'

He drew her out of the track of the lorries, which had cut up the semi-circle of turf inside the gate into intricate patterns of interlacing ellipses. Grunting men were piling someone's bed-settee on to the back of a van, while its anxious owner hopped alongside like a cat on hot-bricks, and gave frenzied directions which were not heeded. A feverish bustle, confused as the eddies of flood water, filled the hemisphere of the pale fence, which unenthusiastic soldiers were beginning to pull down. Some of the newly-painted window-frames were already out, half the roofs already peeled rawly clean of their felting. Over all the impartial sun beamed radiantly.

'They're very determined, aren't they,' said Rosalba, pausing to look round ruefully on this chaos of destruction, 'that no one shall have a second chance to walk in here.'

'Sure are! I reckon they can't afford to let anybody else have the last word. Matter of prestige, I guess!'

They walked side by side, with subdued voices and quiet

steps, down the aisle between the brown huts, where the children were unconcernedly kicking a ball about, a home-made stocking ball finished off with coloured wools, somebody's mother's handiwork. Budge went aside a pace to kick it back into the game when it strayed towards him, but in a desultory fashion which made Rosalba suddenly look at him with a sympathetic smile, and take his arm.

'I'm awfully sorry, about you, too. Flo told me about how you want to go home and settle down – I hope you don't mind? But it *will* happen, it must happen, some day. Perhaps sooner than you think. Nobody *knows!*'

'Yeah, maybe!' said Budge sadly. He pulled up, and suddenly fished out of his wallet and presented to her eyes the blonde Lou, with her bang of fair hair obscuring one eye, and the other one roguishly smiling, and all her white teeth displayed brilliantly in a dental cream smile. 'That's my girl, Louise. She's waiting for me back home. Can you wonder I'm all steamed up being pushed around here?'

'She's lovely,' said Rosalba. 'Oh, Budge, really lovely! Even if you have to wait a little, I think you're a lucky man.'

When she was praised he could always see her a little more clearly; and then she came alive from the fixed charm of the photograph, and again he could imagine her walking, and talking, and kissing him warmly. Then his uneasiness was a little allayed, and he brightened, and realising once again that she really was extremely pretty, himself warmed to praising her. Then he stopped wondering if that blonde hair was not a little tedious and pale, that smile a shade artificial. A small photograph, after all, can hardly carry around the world the whole content of a live girl.

So he was grateful to Rosalba for the words, and for her dazzled look, and her smile, and the deep gloom receded a little from his eyes. 'Yeah,' he said eagerly, 'she *is* a honey, ain't she?'

'When you go home and get married to her, Budge, you'll soon forget all this stupid waste of time here. It seems terrible, now, but then it won't be so important. You'll see! You'll soon forget all about England, and Crocksford, and us.'

228

'Gee, no, not everything, I hope! This last bit's been kinda nice, since I got me some friends. Only,' he said, furrowing his large brow in painful and depressing thoughts, 'seems like we're all in trouble just about as deep as we can go.' He replaced Lou carefully in his wallet, and tucked her away against his heart, reassured that she was indeed all he had thought her.

'Yes,' said Rosalba, 'I'm afraid we are. Will you be involved in these air exercises, Budge? You're in a bomber crew, aren't you?'

'Yeah, I'll be right in it – the first night. Around midnight you can lean out of your window and wave to me, I'll be just about overhead. Bomb-aiming! Is that any profession for a sane man? A handful of little Pathfinders, and some nice flares on the heath to represent their target markers, and then I come in with bombs. Bombs! Jeez!' He recovered himself out of a crushing sigh to ask: 'What about Eugene? I guess they'll find them some damn-fool thing to do, too?'

'No,' she said with downcast eyes. 'Eugene's lot are going south next day. They're going overseas.'

That stopped him in his tracks for a moment. But what was there to be said to her, any more than to Flo? No right words ever visited him; perhaps none existed. All he could say was: 'Gee, that's tough! Honey, I'm real sorry!' And in another moment: 'How long's he going for?'

'I don't know. He's got just over a year left to serve – I don't know where he's going, either. He doesn't know himself yet.'

No, there was nothing to be said. They went on in a heavier silence to where Flo sat enthroned on her mounds of baggage, close to the door of her hut. When there was no point in action, Flo could sit still; she was quite sure she would need all her energy later, nor did she need to work off her rage and despair by tiring herself out with useless activities now. She had perhaps come nearer to the limit of her endurance than usual, but she had a few paces in hand yet.

She jumped up, however, at the sight of Rosalba, and flew

229

to meet her with a fervour which said much. 'Oh, Flo, darling!' said Rosalba, hugging her fiercely. 'Are you all right? I wanted to come before, but I couldn't get away, and now I'm too late to be any use. You didn't – did you – find—?'

'No, we couldn't find any lodgings, not yet. But you never know,' said Flo sturdily. 'We're bound for the old "rest centre", same as plenty more, but we shan't stay there any longer than we can help. Anyhow,' she said, 'it's nice to see you, even if it is too late to show you the old home.' A sweep of her hand indicated all that was left of it. 'We're sitting on it. That's it! There's Budge's bookcase – poor old Budge! He was as proud as a peacock of that. Hope it stands the journey! And there's his plate-rack, that's a nice piece, too. Cheer up, lad, we'll find another home for it or die trying. Then you can come to tea, and wash up the dishes, so's to use it again.'

Rosalba whispered in her ear, very doubtfully: 'Flo, do you need some money? Please, I'd like – you needn't use it unless you want it, but I want you to have it, in case.' But the few tightly-rolled notes she tried to insinuate into Flo's hand were gently put back again, and her fingers firmly closed over them.

'You're a sweet kid, but there's no need at all. We're O.K. Thanks for the thought, and bless you for a darling, but no! Don't you worry about us, we shall be all right. 'Tisn't the end of the world.'

'But – look, will you promise to ask me, if you do need anything?'

Flo looked more alive already for her coming. Her smile was a real smile, and the embrace of her strong young arm sudden about Rosalba's thin waist was warm and positive. 'Sooner you than anyone, give you my word! But we don't need anything, not a thing – only a place to live! And you haven't got that in your pocket for us – not even you.'

'In our east lodge,' siad Rosalba wistfully, 'where Cedarwood lives, there's room for three or four families, easily – without even getting in one another's way. In the one where we live there's even more, only I'd be sorry for anyone who had to share it with us. But isn't it hell that I can't do anything about it? She'd never hear of it, never in the world! And it could be done so easily! It wouldn't need so very much alteration, and wouldn't cost much, either.'

'It won't happen while she's alive,' said Flo definitely, 'so don't waste time thinking about it.'

'I could ask her,' said Rosalba. Her face paled to marble stillness at the thought. She asked for nothing now, spoke not one word in the presence of Martine if she could help it, and when she must enter the same room with her, kept as much space as possible between them. She would need to be desperate, indeed, to make such an approach as this. But for Flo, she could perhaps be more enduring than for herself; and now there was almost nothing to lose. 'I could at least try,' she said.

'Don't you do anything of the sort. It would be breath clean wasted, and it wouldn't do you any good, either. So put it out of your mind, and just you look after your own interests, and quit worrying about mine. I'll be satisfied, anyhow, if you keep your own end up there. And Eugene's worth it,' she said, giving Rosalba's waist a gentle pressure. 'You concentrate on him.'

'Eugene's going overseas,' said Rosalba. She had not meant even to mention it, but it filled her mind so that at a touch it slipped out of her lips.

'He is? My God! When?'

'They have to leave here for some centre in the south on Friday morning.'

Flo sat back against the bookcase with a long, resigned sigh, and looked at Budge, who was as fixedly regarding her.

'Well,' she said, 'that's about the finish!'

'Yeah,' agreed Budge, 'looks like we're all damned together. Nobody ain't getting away with nothing around here.'

The sympathy which has to be circulated from hand to hand in shared disasters may as well never be expressed. Silence settled on them again like a heavy cloud, from which

Mr. Derricks startled them at last with word that the lorries were now ready for them. Flo got up slowly, and drew Rosalba aside with her to give them space. A small army of shirt-sleeved soldiers and perspiring neighbours descended upon the mound of bedding, the packing-cases, the few bits of furniture; and the collection disintegrated very rapidly, and proceeded aboard the covered Army lorry backed up between the huts. Daisy appeared wanly from one direction, detaching herself from two or three friends of her own age; Sid from the other, rosy-faced and by no means downcast, clutching his kite, with which he trusted no man but himself. And within a few minutes Sid was in the cab of the lorry with the driver and his mate, and inspecting at close quarters the marvels of the engine.

'Every little helps,' said Flo. 'It's a good thing somebody's easy satisfied.'

'Ready for you, honey,' said Budge. He said no word more, because now, at the last moment, her face had begun to quiver and crumple alarmingly. Instead, he made Daisy happy by hoisting her into the lorry with his own large hands, and kissed her resoundingly in mid-air into the bargain. 'Be a good girl, and mind what Flo tells you.'

'You'll come and see us, won't you?' said Daisy, clinging to his hand until he appeased her with his promise.

'Sure, honey, I know where to find you, and I'll be around. You take it easy, you'll be seeing me.'

'If you're still able to come up to the Folly, as usual,' said Rosalba, 'we can see each other regularly, Flo. Oh, darling—' She clung to her, and kissed her, and suddenly the tears were coming fast. 'Oh, darling, I'm so terribly sorry! Oh, don't! Oh, Flo, dear, you're making me cry, too!'

'Don't you let go of Eugene,' whispered Flo into her cheek, 'just because he'll be a long way off. Don't you, Rosalba – you'll be a fool if you do.'

'No, I don't mean to, I mustn't. But never mind that now, we'll talk about it some other time. And things will be better for you, I'm sure they will! *Something* will turn up!'

'When I'm pushing up the grass, very likely,' said Flo

strenuously, and groped after her handkerchief. 'There, it's all right! It just didn't come off, that's all! We always knew it was a gamble. Good-bye Rosalba!' She turned to Budge, who was standing gloomily regarding the space of scoured cinders between his boots. 'So long, Budge! Take care of yourself!'

'Yeah!' he said, with the depressed ghost of a smile. 'I'll be fine.' He lifted her after Daisy; she was no weight, she went up like a two-year-old. 'So long, honey! Keep your chin up!'

But Flo, making for herself a small seat beside her father on the roll of bedding, was crying bitterly. Flo, the pillar of the house they did not possess, was bowed at last, if only for a season; they felt the enormous significance of her tears as they waved sadly after the lorry, as it bumped ponderously along the rutted track, and turned slowly out of the gates. And there they were left, Rosalba and Budge standing forlornly in the scuffled grass among the wreckage and the walking casualties, with ribbons of felt fluttering overhead in a gay, heartless breeze, and window-frames stacked against the walls; circled by a disintegrating fence, hearing in the withdrawing echoes of the lorry convoy on the earth road the tired footsteps of an army in retreat.

The unequal struggle for the Warren had ended as everyone had expected it to end, of course. There was no surprise among this cold medley of feelings with which they were left.

'Well,' said Budge glumsly, 'looks like that's the end of it. Looks like its pretty well the end of most things!'

CHAPTER SEVEN

Judgment Eve

1

ON TUESDAY morning Rosalba met Eugene at the bus station in Crocksford, and they went out to a riverside village some miles away, and there spent their day. The sun shone on them faithfully, and they walked, and rowed, and sat in the cool turf by the waterside, and in the cool of the evening tramped through the woods to take another bus home from another village. They had never been together for so long a time before; and some charm of good sense was on them, so that they did not quarrel at all.

But the next day, the last day, was very near; and as they went up the darkened lane which led to the south lodge, close under the tall holly hedge on the rim of the grassy bank, it drew closer to them, walking alongside within touch of them however tightly they held to each other's hands. Never before had they walked the lanes like real lovers, intertwined, two bodies drawn into one, and the whole of the world drawn down into them. Never, perhaps, would they do so again.

A hundred yards from the gate, deep out of sight in the holly shade, they said good-night.

'Come early tomorrow,' said Eugene. 'Come at six.'

'I'll try, but it isn't so easy for me. But I will try.'

'It's the last time,' he said. The ghost of tomorrow stood

234

closer, pressing between them though they stood breast to breast.

'I will come! Somehow I'll manage it!' Her heart ached with the thought of all the other days to come, so many and so empty. She tried to think of his letters filling the emptiness, but somehow no miracle happened. 'Please, Rosalba – I want another sketch of you. Only for myself, not for anyone else to see, ever. I want something I can carry with me – as small as that. Will you let me make it, tomorrow night?'

'Of course!' she said, and her arms went softly about his neck.

'Be very beautiful! It has to last me such a long time!'

'I should like to be unforgettable,' she said in a whisper. And they kissed very gently, as if they had all the time in the world. Today had been a day of possession, with leisure for love; but there would be no more like it.

'Good-night, darling!'

She slipped out of his arms, and went away into the darkness upon the grass verge, so softly that he could not hear her feet touch ground.

Whenever she left him, and returned to the stillness, and propriety, and scorn of the south lodge, she foretasted what was to come. Feeling the influence of her own background fold her in again, as if she had escaped for a brief while from some picture-frame in the gallery at the Folly, she knew how it would be after tomorrow night, when she could look forward to no more meetings, no touch of him to renew the charm which kept her brave. And always she was afraid.

If only she could really get away, if only she could be with normal people, stand on her own feet, with no chains about them! If only she could begin to do something worth doing, learn to be an actress after all, perhaps, or even train as a nurse, or look after people's children, anything to be out among those who worked for their living and dwelt in a developing world, interested in something more than maintaining a small personal domain undamaged to the death. Then letters could bring him to her three-dimensional, warm and securely beloved, for in that atmosphere he could live.

But what hope was there of that? She was seventeen, penniless, shut up in her glass globe until some force from outside smashed it. And that would not happen. It happens in fairy-stories, not in life. The globe was very strong, of thick crystal, she thought, or rose quartz, not of glass at all. Rose quartz! The outside world had been trying to find a power strong enough to break it for a very long time. But Martine still felt safe.

Nevertheless, the thought of Eugene filled her heart with a desperation of courage. She would try, with all the valour that was in her. And first she would go to Martine, and ask her at least to consider turning the east lodge into flats. The east lodge – the little one in the pinewoods – even in that there was room enough for three or four families, in this south lodge there was still more space, though perhaps its arrangement was a little less adaptable. The remaining two lodges had been pulled down long since, when the first remote edges of the enormous estates began to be eaten gradually away.

Between tea and the light dinner which she always ate in her own room, Martine usually slept, or at least lay down in the curtained dimness of her room and rested. Rosalba made her attempt over tea, with every restraint and delicacy she could assemble to the task; and at the very first words she felt her heart turn in her as if she had braved tigresses. It was hate she was afraid of, and the revelation that she could hate, too, that she had the same blood in her veins, and in hot moments could feel towards Martine almost as Martine felt towards her. Of that heat within her she was painfully, wincingly afraid.

'Have you acted so closely in accordance with my wishes,' said Martine, 'that you think you can ask what you like of me?'

'I'm not asking it for myself,' said Rosalba with extreme submission. 'I ask you only to consider it as a help towards housing these people who have nowhere to live.'

'So that you may choose the tenants?'

'Not even that, of course you would take anyone you

236

pleased. It's only that the space is there, and isn't being used.'

'The last thing I'm likely to consider,' said Martine coldly, 'is opening my remaining property to these people who, to judge by their recent behaviour, are the sweepings of Crocksford. Your infatuation with them I find unaccountable, but your tastes are not mine. Even if I was prepared to have the lodge used as you suggest, it would certainly not be by any of them.'

'It would be something to have it used at all,' said Rosalba, unimaginably patient in spite of the flurry of her heart. 'I mentioned them chiefly because they have nowhere to go.'

'But I understand that accommodation has been found for them.'

'Oh, yes, but one couldn't possibly live there for long. It's meant to be used only in emergencies. In the old institution wards – the husbands and wives have to separate, and – and they all regard it as the workhouse still.'

'I'm scarcely concerned with the workings of their minds,' said Martine with a face of distaste. 'It's the legitimate place for such a crisis, and all the authorities have to offer.'

'The authorities would be very grateful if anyone could help them with something better.'

'You over-estimate their interest in these people,' said Martine, 'or at least you over-estimate mine.'

There Rosalba stopped, for there was no point in persisting. Nothing good would come of it, as well to let it lie.

She took care to remain where Martine could see her, seated with a book, and looking as permanent as possible when her wings were already poising for flight, until Martine went to her own room, and the curtains were drawn, and the house quiet. Then she went softly up the stairs, past her own door, up to the attics where the exiled treasures were, the riches and spoils of the past for which the south lodge had no adequate setting. Chests and chests of albums, pictures, books, small collectors' pieces, clothes. A long mirror on the dusty wall showed her her own slender figure, coming in furtively like a frightened thief. She saw her white, long-sleeved blouse and severe grey skirt, and their drabness offended her. It was not as if the blouse had any originality of cut, or the skirt the fashionable fullness. They were beautifully made, but had not, she thought, been worth making. Who would remember her by these? Who could look at them daily in exile, and not tire? She was confirmed in her foolishness, in her madness, for she knew that she was acting madly. No matter, it was the last time. The sun shone, the light was brilliant, and Martine lay behind drawn curtains, and would not so much as look out from the window until dinner. The way to the watch-tower was long, but lonely; she could go by the garden-room door and the wicket gate, and be unnoticed; by the first coppice, the edge of the gardens, and the long, black yew walk veiling her on either side. No one would be there. The Folly closed its doors at five. Cedarwood went home in the other direction. No one would be there to see.

Sometimes in her childhood – what childhood there had been for her – she had longed to take out the glorious dresses from these chests, the gowns of Martine's youth, the gowns she had made sacred by her triumphs at concert and ball, and from which she could never bear to be parted. What child would not wish to dress herself up in them and preen before this mirror? But it had never been permitted. She had never been allowed even to handle them, past stroking gently, under supervision, the folded silks and laces and brocades which Martine nursed on her greedy arms and barely suffered within reach of the small fingers. Now she opened the largest chest, and the sweetness of lavender rose in a great cloud, and covered her. Careful tissues wrapped everything from sight, and separated the exquisite folds. Nothing of the goddess had ever been thrown away, nothing ever given away, unless perhaps even she had had her failures, and discarded the memory of them to let the rest shine flawless.

Unforgettable! So she would be! She was still young,

Rosalba, her beauty not locked up in tissue paper in a chest in the attic, but alive and clothing her body. She would be beautiful for him this once, and if he never saw her again, if she failed him, at least he would not forget her, nor remember her, if she did not fail him, by the grey skirt and white blouse. She lifted out dresses, surrounding herself with silk and sweetness, refreshing her eyes with delicate colours, a little drunk very soon with excitement.

The white ball dress of 1890 slipped a fold of its skirt out of the wrappings as she lifted it, shedding white net and silver lace over her hand and wrist in a waft of perfume. She unfolded it and held it up to the mirror, where it shimmered like moonlight, a tightly boned bodice, a foam of lace low round the shoulders and breast, and a slim waterfall of tiered white skirt. She knew it for the gown in which Martine had sat for her portrait, but that did not matter one way or the other; for the moment Martine had gone out like a candle, and was forgotten. The folds of the lace had yellowed a little here and there, from long lying packed away, but one would have to look closely to see the dull patches. And the appearance of her own face, seen over the resplendent thing in the long mirror, excited her strangely. She laid the dress down very carefully, and began to tear off her skirt and blouse. Shoes? Her sandals were the lightest and gayest she had, and would have to do. She let her clothes lie where they fell, trampled over them, and reverently climbed into the white dress.

Evidently Martine had been much of her size, though a little more gracefully rounded, at least when this gown was made. The young shoulders emerging naked from the foam were a little angular, but beautifully poised and straight, and the inadequacy of the gentle breasts was supplied by the generosity of lace. She looked at herself in the mirror, and drew breath upon astonishment, so tall, so regal she looked, not even colourless now in her blazing clear whiteness, with the blood mantling wildly in lips and cheeks, and her eyes like sapphires. She kicked the grey skirt impatiently out of her way, and swept nearer to the mirror, pulling the pins out of her hair with long, imperious sweeps of her thin hands. Soft pale gold flowed down over her arms; she held it up in great swathes, piling it high upon her head, but she had no comb, and not enough pins, and the coils slipped out of place. She turned, and let herself out of the room, and went softly down to her own mirror, and the many curved combs with which she had at various times tried to master the art of putting up her hair.

At every glance in the mirror she started at her beauty. Who would have believed that she could look like this? Now, with the winged gold mounted from her temples, and the length of her hair coiled on top of her head, making her taller by inches to the sight, she was splendid, and feeling power in her, moved splendidly. She was aware of it, and delighted in it, the turn of the shoulders and toss of the head, the sudden, swooping hands, the slight wrists and long, thin, strangely elegant arms. Eugene had asked her to be beautiful. Was she not obedient? She knew that she excelled.

The house was quiet; all that change of body and heart had occupied only fifteen minutes. She picked up her snowy skirts, and went down very gently to the garden-room, her ears pricked for Mrs. Fenton's tread, her eyes enormous with watchfulness; but she met no one. Out through the garden like a flash of light, and then the wicket closing behind her in the wall, and the friendly trees so near, so near.

She ran, up through the wood, leaving the wide path which might be frequented for the wild ways which she knew well, where no one would come. Straight for the watch-tower, by the edge of the Dutch garden, and then by the long, straight, magical double blackness of the yew walk, with the arbour at the end, she set her course and held it; and when she came near the tower, within sight of the gleam of the pool and the soaring, spurious masonry of the battlements high above the pine-tops, she smoothed her slender, cascading skirt, and slowed to a walk, to draw breath before she came into Eugene's sight.

He was sitting in the sunny turf close to the wall, where he could watch all the possible paths by which she might come; and when he saw her he rose very slowly, and stood quite still, staring at her, until she stood within reach of his hands, until she reached up and kissed his astonished lips, and said childishly:

'Don't you know me?'

2

The sun shone, and Eugene worked. She sat with the cascade of her lace skirts about her, her head erect under the pale gold coronal, her shoulders superbly reared out of the froth of net, looking grave and inappropriate and sombrely beautiful, like an Undine come out of the lake; a little lonely in this curious upper world of castles and forests and men. She felt the weight of her beauty bearing her down, and she felt, too, the slither of unarrestable moments going by her on their way into time past. That was what made her eyes so large and solemn with wonder and regret.

The sun declined a little, and the shadows of pine and of masonry grew long and jagged, stabbing the grass. Eugene's hand lagged, hovering above the image of her face; hardly bigger than a miniature, something to be carried in a wallet frame, under safe covering from finger-marks and dust. The copied eyes questioned him sadly, apprehensively, exactly as hers did whenever he met them. Time running through his fingers in a rapid stream caused the outlines he had shaped to quiver. She seemed to be about to speak, or about to weep, and whenever he looked at her so, this evening would come to life again inside his mind; the black setting of the pines, with the faint blue sky and the bright gold sun causing them to glow still more ebony-black, and under the phoney castle wall the moony and starry glimmer of this magical being, proudly lifted the cold alabaster whiteness of shoulders and throat and face out of the filigree whiteness of sea-foam; and in this imperious pallor the sudden hectic

241

roses of her cheeks bright with fever, and her soft, hesitant, down-drawn mouth, and her great, young, dismayed, piteous eyes. The bewitched princess, the child shut in the stone, the fairy caught in a snare! A comfortable picture to keep against his heart!

'Is it finished?' she asked. 'Can I move?'

'Yes, finished – as finished as it ever would be.'

'I want to come to you,' she said. 'Can I move now?'

'Yes, come!' He laid the block aside, and his brush, and went and lifted her by the hands, and the fragility of her flesh as he touched her seemed beyond the fragility of the fabrics that covered it, as if she might melt into air. 'Come and sit on the bench outside, the sun's still on it. You won't be cold?'

'No, it's quite warm.' Indeed she could not have felt cold or heat tonight, her sensitivities had all become absorbed into more urgent matters.

He spread his battle-dress blouse over the stone for her to sit on, and settled her there as gravely as if she had been some queen, and he an ambitious creature who reverenced queens.

'What about your brushes, and everything? Don't you want to clear everything away now?'

'Later will do for that,' he said. 'We haven't so much time that we can afford to lose any. I'll clean up and stow everything as usual, and then you—'

'I shall have to take them all away,' she said, 'some time when Great-Aunt Martine is asleep, or something. They're quite bulky now, we've brought so much stuff here.'

'Yes,' he said. 'It was fine while it lasted. If it hadn't been for you it could never have happened.'

Her lips, which in repose looked so tender and afraid, curved to a delicious faint smile as she began remembering. 'If you hadn't come here swimming that day—! Oh, Eugene, have I changed as much as I feel I have? You didn't like me, that day.'

'I loved you! Then or as soon as I left you, I don't know which. Now sit there a minute,' he said, touching her coiled hair with fascinated fingers, 'and I'll show you your portrait.'

'Please!' she said submissively, and folded her hands

decorously until he brought it; she was matching every movement, every inclination of her head, to the gown she wore, as instinctively as she breathed. She was playing for him as she had never played before, to be remembered, to be remembered poignant in beauty as now, unflawed, remembered by one perfect performance; but she did not know that she was doing it, or the performance would not have been perfect.

Eugene put the little portrait into her hands, and leaned over her with an arm about her naked shoulders as she sat for a long time looking at it in silence; so long that he asked, a little anxiously, even a little indignantly, for he knew his worth: 'Don't you like it? What's the matter with it?'

'It's very beautiful,' she said, and the words were not conventional; she sounded soothed and satisfied. She sat holding it, and her eyes softened to a placated, dusky blueness. 'But she looks frightened,' she added next, as if speaking of a stranger, and a slight, anxious frown furrowed her brow for a moment.

'Because you do look frightened,' said Eugene, and laid his lips very gently against her temple, at the edge of the lifted wing of gold hair.

'I suppose it's because I am frightened.' She put up a hand, and touched his cheek, then smoothed away the billows of skirt to make room for him beside her. 'We haven't much time. You said it yourself, so come and sit down now, before it's all gone.'

Eugene laid the block carefully aside in a niche of the brick rocks, and sat down obediently. He was almost afraid to touch her, so delicate she was, but he stroked the flounces of silver lace with a wondering finger-tip, timidly curious. 'I never was so near to anything quite like this before. Nearest I ever saw such a dress was in the films.'

'And I never wore one before,' she said. 'I was never even allowed to do more than just touch them. They're hers, of course – she keeps them all in caskets, laid up in spices – all her triumphs. I wanted a triumph, too.' She leaned nearer to him, because he was almost afraid to come to her. 'I wanted

243

to see you look – like you did look, when I came. I wanted to look nice for you.'

'You looked like a snowflake. But why are you frightened, Rosalba? What are you frightened of?'

'Myself,' she said, staring across the folded, sunset country below her, where the shadows lay long and shallow in every undulation of the turf. 'I'm afraid of – not being able to live up to you.'

He said reproachfully, but with starting terror, too: 'We've had all this before! You promised me—'

'I didn't! I never made any promises, I wish I dared to make promises. What good are they, Eugene, really? How do we know what we can bear to do? How do we know what we're strong enough to do? All we know is what we want and mean to do, that's all. How can I promise you anything? I don't know what's in me to promise.'

'I know,' he said jealously, 'that I'd die rather than give you up!'

'Ah,' said Rosalba, with a wrung smile, 'that might be even rather easy. I could almost promise you what my answer would be to that, if it was a simple choice. What I don't know is how it's going to be with me when you're on the other side of the world, and there's no one to keep reminding me. You'll go away, but this place goes on, my days with *her* go on, all the habits and routines you managed to interrupt a little, they go on, too. I shall get the old standards dinned into me, dinned into me day after day. I shall see nobody *she* doesn't approve. Even Flo won't be there. It's too far for her to come from the rest centre, she has to find some job in town. I shall hear no opinions but *hers*, no thoughts but hers. Look, Eugene, I was born and brought up in that way, I have to reverse everything I ever was taught to go against it. Even with you here, I've had to hang on to my courage with tooth and claws to go with you as far as I've gone. How do you think I'm going to manage without you?'

Her hand lay in his, light and slack, but trembling. She fel as if she had untied some cord which bound them, and cas

244

him adrift; and yet she was only warning him, only begging him not to expect too much. Suddenly she knew she had never really believed in it, never from the moment it began. All she had done was shut her eyes to the truth, and cling to it with the strength of desperation while it lasted, to have while she could, since she might never have again.

'Are you trying to tell me,' he asked very carefully, 'that you don't want to go on?' And somehow he kept himself from closing his hand upon that cold small hand, and his arm about her, arguments he despised, but which his whole body ached to use; arguments he must resist now, because after tonight they could never be used with her.

'I'm trying to tell you I don't believe I shall be able to go on. I don't believe I'm strong enough. I don't believe I'm brave enough! Oh, Eugene, my darling,' she said, steadily but frantically gazing out across the sunset land, 'it was a mistake ever to let it begin. I ought to have known I was no use to you, I ought to have made it easier for you to see it, too—'

'You've thought better of it,' he said. 'You *do* want to call it off! Well, it was asking a lot of you, to give up all you're used to, just for me.'

'*No!* It isn't like that!' she said in a small wail of pain. 'What do you suppose I should be giving up, except everything I hate and dread? If I *could* give them up, all that life, all those beastly ancestors, everything I've had round me since I came here – if I could throw them all away this minute and come with you, don't you suppose I'd do it like a shot?'

'How am I to know that?' he said. 'All I'm asking of you now is that you should go on waiting for me.'

'And go on fighting – by myself. And I'm not refusing, Eugene, I'm not asking you to let me off anything. I shall try. I shall do as well as I can. I'm only begging you not to build too high on me. I'm so frightened of hurting you worse. How much strain do you suppose I can stand, and for how long?'

'I *know* you're strong,' said Eugene, 'and I *know* you're

brave. And I know if you let go of me I shall go to the devil. I'm not going through this over and over again, and all for nothing! I shall write to you, regularly, and you'll answer, won't you?'

'Yes, I shall answer – at any rate, as long as I can—'

'But why not? What should make it so hard for you? I can't understand you.'

'No,' she agreed, 'you can't understand. How should you? We've tried very hard, all of us,' she said, 'to put up a fight, but what have we achieved? And do you think it gets any easier? When you're tired, and alone, and every time you even look out of the window and see this—' Her hand gestured fiercely back from them to where the tamed wilderness, the arrogant trivialities, the old, old, immemorial self-assertions of the Rose family lay basking in the declining sun. 'This! – just to remind you that everything goes on just the same, no matter what you do!'

He began to protest, but his own voice sounded frightened to him, and indeed the walls stood stoutly where they had stood before, for all of his blown trumpets. In his eyes, even while he scolded, she saw that he felt the ground shaky under his feet, and touched the borders of her despair. Her tears started at the thought, and then he could no longer keep his tormented young body out of the argument, but shut his arms round her with a great sob, and went on stammering his passionate beliefs into her ear, while her tears fell scaldingly against his neck and shoulder. And suddenly it was late, late and almost dusk, and even here, even with her, he had achieved nothing.

'If only *something* would go right for us,' she whispered, a lost breath against his throat, half sobbed away into silence, 'if we'd made even one little crack in their walls – if they'd had to give in to Flo!— But we go on breaking our heads against it, and you see it stands as strong as ever.'

'It won't always! Rosalba, you can't give in – why, we've scarcely begun!'

'I don't want to give in – I don't want to! But what's the use, when you see it makes no difference?'

'But it will! Some day it will!' he insisted wildly.

'I don't believe it will. The old men have got their hands on everything just as tightly as they ever had. People try to make protests, but they don't even notice. Not even one little crack in the wall, Eugene – not even one!'

She wound her arm round his neck and held him tightly to her. 'Only, remember, I love you, always, always, as long as I live. Even if it's to be all for nothing, I love you!'

'If you do, you've got to believe, and go on believing. If you do, you *can't* give up.'

The beginning of dusk came, the true dusk, mysteriously translucent after the departure of the sun. She felt the chill of its passing, and raised her head suddenly, saw that the night was swooping upon them out of the pines. All pale things began to glow with their own innate light now that the light of the sun, the light of colour, had withdrawn itself from the world.

'I must go,' she said, starting up enormous-eyed out of his arms, with the tears standing on her cheeks.

'Not until you tell me you do believe!'

To her it seemed that all was over; the stillness and acquiescence of the twilight confirmed it. Every protest was stilled, every shaft broken, and every heart, too, and the course of the world fixed and unalterable for evil. But what was the use of telling him so, when he was Eugene, more stubborn than life itself, and had been fighting all his young days against the odds, a battle which was forever losing but never lost? What did he know about the nature of despair? He scarcely even knew its name.

'I believe in you,' she said, 'I always shall. I'll try to live up to you.' But her voice sounded too easy, too soft.

He went with her to the edge of the trees. She had become a white crescent moon under the pines.

'Now you must go back. I'm very late, and I must go quickly.' She lifted her face to him with the same spiritless gentleness, the tears still on her cheeks. 'Good-bye, Eugene!'

He kissed her. It was perhaps the last time, but what more

was there to do or say? His arms went round her passionately, his cheek against her cheek, his mouth whispering, stammering almost wordlessly into her neck, kissing, stroking, trying to convey by touch what he could not make her understand by speech, the sacredness and splendour of the duty one has to fight for one's faith, for one's love, as long as the body has breath. 'Good-bye, Rosalba! Oh, Rosalba, darling, don't let me down – don't let go of me—' He could make no stronger appeal, for he felt her thin arms straining him to her in a sudden agony of love, breaking that drugged calm of hers, before she kissed him through a storm of wild weeping, and broke from his arms, and ran.

She ran with her skirts gathered in her hands, glimmering across the open heath, smaller and smaller like a brilliant moth fluttering, until she reached the trees beyond, and disappeared from his sight.

3

Martine stood in the open doorway of Rosalba's room, and looked in upon a small, hurried chaos of shed hairpins and discarded brush and comb upon the dressing-table. The mirror swung a little in the breeze which streamed through the room from the open window. The tiny drawer under it hung half-open, too, left so after some ornament had been snatched out of it in haste. Rosalba's sensible shoes lay upon the rug, one overturned upon its side. And Rosalba was not in the house; she was gone to her lover, gone to her wretched little soldier like the furtive thing she was.

The curtain, flung by the wind as the door opened, had swept down from the top of the tall-boy a framed photograph, and now it lay upon the carpet with its back split open, and the contents spilling out at Martine's feet. The smooth young face, with all the character tailored scrupulously out of it in the studio, stared up at her glazed and faded by the cross-light stroking the glass. She put the ferrule of her stick accurately in the centre of it, and leaned her weight upon the ivory handle with deliberate slowness until the glass shivered and starred, lightnings running from the middle into every corner, slivers of silver starting out of the frame. The face crumpled and folded upon itself, distorted into astonished ugliness, and stricken with ruled wrinkles, as if she had aged in an instant. Martine smiled, and drew sweet breath.

What was to be done with her, when daily her presence became worse offence? What was to be done with the poor remnant of the property, which she would neglect and waste, which she did not value, the land she wanted to leave, the memories which meant nothing to her? How could the past be protected from the present, when there was no one left, no one to continue the Rose name, and only one creature left with the old blood in her veins, and she was a gnat, a nothing? If she had her way, she would bring more gnats, more nothings, to live in the lodges which at least had served the family in its high tide, and known their steps, and kept their state. She would give them a free hand to turn loose their snivelling, soiled children among the freaks of Richard Rose's vast imagination, and let them hang out washing on the box hedges and across the shaven lawns. Nothing in her, no sensitivity, no racial memory, would feel the land aching, or know how the stones remembered and the trees mourned.

As long as she lived, Martine would care for them; she at least valued and worshipped the tradition which it was fashionable now to decry. But after her? What would become of the Folly then, the stupendous folly of old greatness, the last monstrous joke of a race whose very frolics had been titanic?

Ever since tea, ever since the terrible vision had visited her of Crocksford children scuffling and bawling among the gardens, and their mothers gossiping over the landings of the east lodge, Martine had lain in her dimmed room, thinking, ever more clearly, that Rosalba must never inherit what was left. Even when she no longer lived, Martine could at least

249

ensure that. The alternative was no joy to her. Cousin Robert, distant in the south, was more alien to her almost than the girl, but even if he had not the name, he was of a responsible age, and knew how to keep what was his. He would be Rosalba's guardian, and probably would allow her to do very much as she liked with what was hers, and with her own life; but never, never would he let her take liberties with what was his. He loved possessions not as Martine did, because of what was owing to them, but because of the lustre they added to his own name and standing, and for sheer lust of having. He, too, was a tradesman, not a Rose; but there were none left but tradesmen, and the girl must not inherit. What strange influences had she not already brought in, what hurt had she not already done to the holy places?

Restlessness had brought Martine out to look for her after her solitary dinner was over. By the quietness, by the gentleness of the house, she had somehow known that Rosalba was not in it. Now it was already dusk, and still she had not come in. Somewhere she was with that faceless soldiers of hers, dangling centuries of a tradition she did not understand as a present into his grubby young hand. To be rid of her was not enough, to have the fragments of the past guarded from her was not enough, when Martine thought of that meeting.

She drew the smashed photograph nearer to her with the point of her stick, and bent and picked it up delicately by the edge of the frame, shedding flakes of glass in a silver shower to the carpet. The pierced face dangled aside and slipped to the floor. There was something more, hidden beneath it, a pencil sketch of the same face, and yet by no means the same; wildly alive was this face, with candid eyes and softly hesitant lips, a little startled, a little afraid, passionately aware of the unsafeness of the world, of pains and difficulties and joys not yet sampled, and daunting upon too sudden discovery. Martine shook it free from the frame, and let the fragments fall from her hands. Out of this stranger, the mysterious private soldier, the artist of this portrait, all this mischief of rebellion and rottenness had come; she saw it in

250

the certainty of the pencil strokes, so spare and fierce and resentful of tameness. The same hand had drawn its way into Rosalba's mind, into her life; there was no mistaking the signature.

In the lower left-hand corner of the paper there was a tiny sketch, only a few lines lightly drafted in to fill a few minutes of waiting, perhaps for Rosalba herself at some assignation. There was no mistaking this, either, an oval of pool hinted at, a surge of tower scarcely more than dreamed, angular shading of pines. Martine knew the watch-tower. Beneath it now, almost in its shadow, ran the new fence which marked the boundary of the bombing-range, and below that the miles on miles of heath where the War Office notice-boards frowned people away, their paint new and aggressive in yellow and black. There, then, after all, was their meeting-place! There, for all their lies and evasions, they were to be found now!

Over the crumpled portrait she looked into the mirror, at her own face strangely pleased, anticipating the discovery, her bright cold eyes shining, her withered mouth suddenly moved to smiling. Old! Not yet old beyond admiration, that reared blue-white head, the ethereal face, still hauntingly the wan ghost of the face which had once flamed like the sun among the hearts of men. Never loved! She, who had put out the lesser stars as you blow out a candle! Never loved! She had been a legend, she was a legend still. No, she had not sat in the retired places of the woods making love-play with grooms and the boobies of Crocksford, if that was to be loved. She touched her cheeks, stroking them, turning her head from side to side to let the light caress her; and the gleam of her eyes grew brilliant with triumphant hatred, and colour came to her withered cheeks, the fierce colour of anger.

She threw down the sketch, and walked over it to the door, and so down the long stairway, going lightly, forgetting her need of a stick. All the evening the slow, beating ache with which she was growing familiar had pounded in her head, but triumph and anger had driven it away now. She had imagined herself actually growing ill, she who had never known illness, and Mrs. Fenton had begged her to see a heart specialist after that last attack of pain; but now she knew that she was strong and invulnerable. She could walk to the watch-tower unaided, and she wanted no witness to what she had to say, and what she might choose to do. She could have walked to the last corner of the Folly grounds to find Rosalba in the arms of her lover, her trivial little lover, and have the sweet savour of their furtive, frightened faces like incense burning before her all the rest of her life, to see them grope apart, and start from her, and try to smooth their disordered clothes with trembling, young, unpractised hands, to hear them bluster, and cringe, and cry, for they were too inexperienced to stand upright at such a disadvantage.

Martine went strongly through the garden, and into the wood. The nearest way was in the open; people creeping to an assignment do not go by the open way. Her mind flew ahead of her, selecting, judging; by the edge of the garden, by the yew walk, skulking in shadow, so would Rosalba go. By the same way went Martine, steadily, firmly, and did not tire.

It was deeply dusk, but not yet dark. The tall trees shut in to earth a profound night, but wherever the sky looked in through their branches light came, glimmering out of every stone and every grain of gravel, the soft, colourless, innate light of dusk in which even the brightest reds grow grey. The flowers hung motionless in a warm stillness, and the stars were all but invisible overhead, pin-pricks of silver in the remote iris-purple of the sky. Magical silence stirred under Martine's feet, hushing their steps to the faintest whispering of gravel; there was no other sound.

She came to the end of the yew walk, and the twin blackness and the pale path between ran forward from her far into the dusk. For the first time her pace faltered, and for a moment she did not know why. Then the gleam which had caught her eyes at the far end of the tunnel of dark moved and came nearer to her, a dissolving light, a drift of luminous thistle-down travelling where there was no wind left now to carry it, not even a breath, not even a sigh. Something, she did not think of it as someone, came to meet her, pace for pace, slowly, steadily, as if at the end of that long, straight way there was a mirror, and out of it some creature was stepping, mating movement to her movement. But when she stopped the glimmering thing did not stop, it came onward, and more rapidly, afloat, she thought, above the ground, and moving with more of flight than of walking. It took its face out of veiling hands, and saw her, and reared its head suddenly, and stared at her with a white, flamelike, imperious countenance; and even the face glimmered like a dazzle of silver and pearl, starry with tears.

The years trembled over Martine's head in a sudden flying fall, as the leaves come down when summer is over. She could not go on; she hung trembling upon her quivering cane, bowed a little into her shoulders now, staring with fixed and recognising eyes, for she knew this being. She knew the snowdrift whiteness, the silver sheen of the gown, the lightness of it blown where no wind was, the supple splendours of naked shoulders and swelling breasts under the foam of lace; or she had known all these when the hand could touch them, and they had texture and weight. The long throat, erect and arrogant, the graceful, thin arms outspread with reckless haste, long-fingered, fastidious hands all white, white as pearl, wringing blood out of her memory.

Of what use was it to assure herself that the hand could pass through that flesh and feel nothing, that the imagination stirred too far had its wraiths, its spectres of the living? Air itself is with power when the savage driving of the time can force it into such formidable shapes. And the white, wand-straight creature came on in her drift of light until she had the very features, the known features, great blanched brow and glimmering eyes standing dark with unregarded tears, pale gold hair piled high upon that young, imperious head, lips parted upon passionate breath. She stared full upon Martine, a pale thing blazing with grief and anger and

253

despair; her lips moved in speech to Martine, but said no word which ever was heard. If she had voice, that, too, would be recognised; and already the heart had encountered more than it could bear and live, the old, scornful heart which admitted no infirmity.

She knew that she must get away, and quickly. Who can bear to meet herself in the way? And if the flesh and shadow come together, how far away is madness then? Martine crumpled and bowed before the blown gossamer form, for what is there left to pretend when you have come face to face by night with your own body in its pride, your young, arrogant, cruelly lovely body sweeping down upon you to destroy the last illusion, to hold up to your face the last mirror of all mirrors? To tell you it is time, and more than time, for the ruin and parody of beauty to lie down and be covered from sight.

The ferrule of the cane scraped in the gravel as she turned gropingly upon it, and bowing down her head as if she cowered from a blow, began to hurry crabwise away, going brokenly, lamely, scuttling, shambling between the black yew walls, running from the apparition of her dead youth. She was old, old, old, and the first trumpet had sounded.

She went with shut ears and shut heart, and did not look back. She thought that a young voice cried out after her, not loudly, but in astonishment and fear, but she would not hear it, she covered her ears and battered away the sound, for she did not wish yet to recognise the lamentation of her own spirit over the death of her body. There would be a time for that. There would be a long, long time for that, time and to spare.

4

Rosalba came in by the door of the garden-room, not as she had gone out by it, but gravely and without concealment. She was only about four hours older, but within her life had suddenly begun to reassemble its materials, and to consider what could be made from them. She had stopped crying, and in the last cool walk through the woods, taken at leisure because to hurry was to catch up with events before she was ready to deal with them, the stains of her tears had faded from her cheeks, and left her smooth and pale. She was not even afraid now, but had reached a still place beyond that necessity. She did not look ahead, she did not look back. But she did not think that this state was quite despair. When you despair you do not wait for anything, you do not hold your breath, there can no longer be anything to startle you, nor do you strain your ears for every sound; but Rosalba did hold her breath, her senses were stretched for the first whisper, she was ready to be startled and not to start.

She did not at all understand what had happened to Great-Aunt Martine, but it was not after that mystery her mind went pursuing. It was not a time for thought, only for waiting; things were happening which must be encountered as they came, and as best might be. Like the pause before eternity began, a halt in the pulse of the world, a moment while the great unquiet heart did not beat, and the whole business of living hung suspended at the crest of the wheel's turn.

She went to look for Mrs. Fenton. She was so much at home within her own forgotten body now that the strangeness of her attire could be disregarded, indeed she had no awareness of it left, and felt nothing but impatience when the housekeeper stared at her with lifted, hostile eyebrows, as if she had been an unwelcome ghost.

'Miss Rosalba, are you out of your senses? Whatever possessed you to dress yourself up like this? You must put it away quickly, before Mrs. Rose knows you've had it out. She'd never forgive you if she knew!'

'Where is Great-Aunt Martine?' asked Rosalba shortly, disregarding the whole of this.

'In her room, Miss Rosalba – I've just left her there.'

'Is she quite well? Did she behave at all strangely?'

'She seemed very upset about something, but she

wouldn't talk about it, she says she's perfectly well. I'm sure I don't know what should suddenly possess her to go out wandering about in the dusk, like this, but she wants to be left alone, and it's true she seems to be quite all right.'

'Please go up and tell her,' said Rosalba, 'that I've come in and would like to talk to her.'

'It's no use, Miss Rosalba, she wants to be left alone, and I don't think you should disturb her tonight.'

She was used to saying things like that and having them accepted, but this time her fiat was not accepted. 'Go and ask her, at least,' said Rosalba. 'It will be better for her if she does see me tonight.'

'Like that?' said Mrs. Fenton, looking significantly at the white ball dress.

'Certainly like this!' said Rosalba.

But the housekeeper came down again in a few minutes to say that the door was locked, and Martine, in full possession of her normal qualities of voice, at least, refused to open it or submit to being disturbed any further tonight. Rosalba wondered if she was not making much out of nothing, but she could not leave it there. It was not in her to pretend any love for Martine, or any concern, which she did not feel, but one has certain responsibilities to one's own conscience, and must keep them coldly where warmth has been made impossible. She gathered the white folds of her skirt in her hands, and went slowly up the stairs. Still she listened, still she held her breath, waiting for what should come.

She tapped upon the door of Martine's room, and the familiar voice, strong and deliberate, asked from within: 'What now? Am I never to be left alone?'

'It's me, Rosalba! Let me in for just a moment, please!'

There was an instant of silence, and then the voice said, upon a lower, almost a wary note: 'What do you want at this hour? I'm tired.'

'I'll keep you only a minute or two.'

'You can have nothing to say to me. Go away!'

'You must listen to me,' said Rosalba, close to the panels of the door, so that she might speak softly. 'It was I whom you met just now in the yew walk. You wouldn't wait for me when I called after you. I'm afraid I startled you. But it's only your white ball dress. I put it on tonight, and I'm wearing it now. Won't you open the door and see for yourself?'

In the hush she imagined with intensity the glitter of silver and light inside the room, for a thread of gold showed under the door; a hard, bright pallor, and in the heart of it Martine, sitting up in the great draped bed, a pair of ice-blue eyes sparkling out of a mound of fine woollen lace and silk, with one shrivelled claw extended upon the bedside table to the light switch, and hesitant upon it. This creature also was listening, was waiting.

'I really didn't mean to startle you,' said Rosalba, 'I never thought of meeting you.'

'Go to bed!' said the low, rustling voice. 'I have no wish to see you being ridiculous. And you did not startle me.'

'But—'

'I have asked you to go away. There will be time in the morning for anything you can have to say to me.'

'At least you understand what I've said? It was I whom you saw.'

'Whom else should I suppose it to be?'

'I don't know. I suppose there is no one else,' admitted Rosalba.

'Then please go to bed, and let me sleep.'

'Very well, Great-Aunt Martine! If you're sure you understand! Good-night!'

No answering voice wished her good-night; no heart had wished her one from within this room for at least a year, probably longer. She was well aware of it now. And now she had told everything, in however few words, and why should she go on holding her breath and waiting? But the air still hung motionless, the turn of the wheel still delayed. She felt the oppression of thunder closing in as she turned to her own room.

No wind stirred the curtains now, everything was still, and the clouds moving across the expanse of stars, and piling up

257

in imperial purple in the western sky, seemed to move of their own power rather than to be moved. As she crossed the room she felt glass splintering under her feet, and looking down, saw the pierced and trampled copies of her own face, the real one and the doll, staring up at her fearfully. She gathered them up without surprise, and tidily went and fetched brush and pan, and cleared away the splinters and powdering of glass. She collected her blouse and skirt from the floor of the attic where she had left them, and folded up into its tissue paper the white dress. Then she went and sat in her room, too wide awake to sleep or hope for sleep, waiting for the storm to break.

It was all over, her heart broken, Eugene gone from her, love folded up and laid away with the white dress. But she waited; but she listened.

CHAPTER EIGHT

Judgment Day

1

BUDGE FETTERBRAND went out and got as high as a lark on Wednesday night, just to see if it made him feel any better. It never made him incapable of steering his own course, he was too used to it, even if he hadn't done it very often since he left his wildest pre-Lou years behind. He took Staff Sonderson with him for company; in the camp at Bredington there was no one for whom Staff had to be kept quiet late at night, and if any of the boys wanted him quiet they could throttle him for themselves.

They went out and painted the nearer end of Bredington, in a comparatively mild way, a bright shade of pink, but it wasn't a success. There was a slight awkwardness with two British airmen who were just about as drunk and much less used to it, but it was broken up without fulfilment, and they went back to camp no less sad than they left it. It was hot in the huts, and still the storm did not come. Budge lay miserable in the darkness, thinking about Lou, and wishing English beer had more kick. The United States felt a million miles away.

On Thursday morning he had a thick head, perhaps from the beer, perhaps from the thundery air; either way, they told him in no uncertain terms, he was hell to live with. He felt like hell, too. Maybe he was out of practice. Maybe he was just tuning up for one thundering row with the world. And the day was spent preparing for an imaginary row with a hypothetical enemy, when he had plenty of quarrel with things real enough and a darned sight too real, and couldn't find out how to get his hands on them.

He hadn't seen Flo since they left the Warren, she for the dubious comforts of the old casual wards, he for the known boredoms and frustrations of Bredington. Once he'd met Daisy in the street, but for only a few minutes, and she'd looked so downhearted about things that he hadn't cared to ask her too many questions. Daisy had been surprisingly well brought up, considering the circumstances, and always said thank you, they were getting on all right, when she really meant things were hell; but if he probed too deeply, being the person he was, she was liable to come clean, and go into voluble details, too. So when he was assured, if he had needed assurance, that his redhead was living against rather higher odds than ever before in her young life – which was saying a good deal! – he clamped down on that subject and asked about Rosalba instead.

Daisy shook her head sadly: 'I don't know how she' getting on now. Flo don't go there no more, it's too far from our side of town. She's going in mornings cleaning some offices now – that's earlier, and close to us, but it isn't nice and it isn't much money. Eugene goes away tomorrow,' she added mournfully, putting her finger plumb upon the focus of the matter.

'Yeah,' said Budge, 'I know.'

'It's awful sad,' said Daisy.

'Yeah, honey, it sure is hell.'

But what was there to do about it? Here he sat, nursing hi thriving grudge and his ineffective hangover, and scolding a every unfortunate who dared to raise his voice in song o even speak above a whisper, as helpless a creature as if h had never been given hands, or muscles, or even rudimentary brain. Flo and her family were herded into kind of communal living not even the most socially-minde could want to see, sleeping in segregated wards because th accommodation was not enough for anything better, handing their ration books to an administration as downhearted about the business as they were themselves, and eating what was given them as a result, their few belongings stacked up somewhere to rot, their efforts and energies all wasted, and everything to do again. Eugene – nice little chap with another chip on his shoulder, but not all on his own account – Eugene was bound south and overseas, to trail around in just such a foreign-service limbo as this for a ridiculous, useless year or so and then be sent home; or, worse, to fester into fever or make a target for some elusive patriot's rusty old out-of-date rifle in the jungles of Malaya – guy he'd never set eyes on, and had no quarrel with. The time a guy could spend abroad in eighteen months service wasn't even worth the transport costs back and forth, no, not even to those who thought the cause a good one; but it was enough, more than enough, to dislocate a fellow's life, separate him from his girl once for all, and send him tradeless, shiftless and disillusioned to the devil.

And the girl, Rosalba, that nice kid up there at that Citizen Kane house, what was to become of her? Without Eugene she wouldn't last long. All her upbringing was against her, what chance had she got without a stake big enough to rouse her to extremes? And if the stake drifted away to Malaya or the Middle East, out of sight, could she go on putting up a fight for it? She'd try, but all the things pulling her the other way would pull harder, and it was long odds that in the end she'd give way, recoil into her chrysalis, and be done with the warmer part of the world for good. All that starry look she had when they were together that illuminated the air about her with reflected joy, that would be lost, and not only to Eugene Seale.

And if it came to that, Budge Fetterbrand wasn't doing too well himself! They were all of them in a pretty hopeless mess, and he as deep in it as anyone, wanting to help them, wanting his girl again, wanting to go home. Every day more bitterly, every day more fiercely and lugubriously and indignantly, he wanted to go home.

He thought about it when the first flights began at dusk and the first flares pin-pointed the distant targets in the mile of heathland. Out there on the runways of the airfield it was always bleak, even in summer evenings with little wind; and in the first shadowless twilight green and grey of grass and tarmac soon faded into one colour, and all that distinguished them upon the ground was the sheen which one had and the other lacked. Across the untinted flatness planes flashed whitely, and the ridged roofs of buildings fringed it on all sides, and the domed control towers made huge shining grey eyes staring at the sky. Like great, rigid, ungraceful birds went the bombers, ponderously leaving the ground and portentously returning to it, as self-important as men, and as vulnerable. But in the sky they had even some severe mechanical beauty, wheeling in measured silver patterns against the pearly greyness. The explosions of their fire deliveries punctured the quietness of the declining night over the heath, and the new range was well and truly christened. In the town people began to look out from their windows and crack cold, caustic jokes about peace. Peace, it's wonderful!

This noise would go on, at intervals, until about three o'clock in the morning; but the many folds of grounds across the heath would shut up many of the impacts from Bredington ears, and even some from Crocksford. Certainly, however, there would be enough left to cause the usual spate of sarcastic letters, indignant letters, embittered letters in the papers; and the powers that were would take exactly as much notice of these and all other protests as they always took, which was precisely none.

There was some cloud, enough to be interesting; and here, where only a flatness and uniformity of grey ran away on all sides upon the ground, that turmoil of movement above had more colour and excitement by far than the pygmy activity below. Angry deep purples still tinted the west, but the threat of thunder was past for the moment, the air thin and clear and cool. Budge stared at the sky while he smoked his final cigarette before the first run; he preferred it. It was the same sort of sky he could see sometimes at home, and it had, apart from the occasional darting plane, no human creature in it, which for the moment was benefit. His pilot came along and drove a knee into the small of his back, and asked:

'What's eating you? Haven't heard a cheep out of you all evening.'

'Nothing to say, I guess.'

'You're all burned up about something, aren't you?' said the pilot, examining him with sympathy.

'Sure am!' said Budge.

'Why don't you get it out of your system some way?'

'I tried that last night,' said Budge simply. 'Wasn't any good! Too many cops, one kind or another. I don't seem to be able to get going none over here. Guess I'd need that atom bomb to get it really out of my system.'

'Is it that bad?'

'Sure is!'

'And you ain't parting with it?'

'Hell, what's the use? Here we are, let's get on with it. Only way I know out of this is clean through it,' he said darkly. 'Come on, let's get going!'

From above things looked for a time rather better. Once they were aloft, gazing down over twilit England, there was more colour and shape and texture to everything, the fields gained a quaint quilted comeliness, so miniature, so smooth, that you felt you could pick up a handful of them, and they would feel like bits of velvet cut out for patchwork. There was more light, too, and the molten activity of clouds pressed nearer without darkening the world, a soft woollen tumult. There below, the two towns fell away from them, one on the left hand, one on the right, two shapeless sprawls of dull red and black rapidly shrinking together and acquiring shape, two large lax hands clenching smoothly into purposeful fists; and between them the great fawn-coloured space of rolling grass, and the hollows of trees, and the bottle-green pinewoods, folded hillock and long furrowed valley which from the ground were almost imperceptible shapings of soil, spinney and copse and hard road of gravel and chalk, marked white across the tawny face of the wilderness. They straightened out across the sky, flattening into their first run, and heeled over the vast, multi-chimneyed bulk of the Folly.

Unmistakable by any light, there it lay, neatly laid out in a patterned expanse of gardens and woods, but lifted above them upon its low rocky outcrop. From the ground it was awesome, from the air and by twilight it was fantastic, acres upon acres of tiled roofs turning, turning slowly, like a mannequin displaying some outrageous creation. All its enormities, the several colours, the scallopings and casual apings of history, the crested battlement and crenellated towers, and the untidy jumble of leads and gutterings between, showed up as brilliantly as by day, making shadows for themselves where there should have been no shadows, by the very violence of their shapes. When you thought you were at the edge of it, it shot out more assiduous fingers, fastening them acquisitively upon more folds of green England. As if it were holding every blade of that ground, every leaf it bore, down under its stone finger-ends.

These ancient monuments! These big things that lie on the little things like gravestones, leisurely squeezing them to death!

At speed now, and dropping over the great deepening darkness of the range, with its pin-points of flares, and the sky alive with machines and men, all keeping their due place, all doing what was expected of them. As tame as tame mice in a cage, like he used to keep when he was a kid. Running on ruled rails, oiled, responsive, doing as they were told. There were no protests in the world any more. Nobody made big bangs with holy places, nobody lit beacons, or blew holes through traditions, or questioned the rightness and necessity of what the big shots said was right and necessary. Father knows best! Does he hell! All the centuries and centuries we've been relying on father to know best, and the messes he's led us into – and the number of

264

times, the unending number, that the poor little saps who mustn't question his judgment have doubled to and got him out of trouble at the last gasp, with their blood and their bones and their patient, forbearing, gullible little lives. And still taken his word for it, once he got his breath back, that this time it would be different! And still trusted him!

'O.K., Budge, boy?'

'O.K., chief!'

'Right, pin 'em! Here we go!'

'Easy!' said Budget contemptuously, and flicked a glance down at the small pin-pricks of the flares.

'Bomb doors open!'

It was clockwork to him, he could do it blindfold; something in the fingers as much as in the eyes, they prickled when the moment was right. Trouble tonight was that they kept on prickling. The brave bangs below in the wilderness did nothing to comfort him. The rocking of the air, and the flashes, and the physical excitement which shook the night upon impact, were familiar. And what had the tormented soil down there done to him, that he should blow holes in it in shaven places, and pock-mark its face with pits of ugly clay?

Nobody was in the Folly at night, after visiting hours ended. Flo had said so. Nobody was there but the ghosts. Well, we could do with a few less of those, the ground wants clearing of a lot of ghosts, one way and another.

The dusk deepened about the artificial birds now flying homeward. People in Crocksford were looking up at their wing-lights with inured eyes, for the most part too used to them by now to have any pleasure in them, or feel much irritation. Some of the children thought they'd always been there, remembering no time when they had not made these tiny green and red sparks in the night sky.

They touched down, and came out into the air to watch others going by the same way.

'Too simple,' said the wireless operator. 'Better after tomorrow night, when the real stuff begins and we can get further afield. These practice runs kill me.'

'Better with some opposition,' said the navigator. 'Get some o' that later on, too. Still, that range isn't bad. More space down there than I figured. How was it, Budge?'

'Spot on!' said Budge. 'I'm betting you!'

'I'm not taking you.'

'Yeah, that's it!' said Budge sadly. 'Nobody ever takes me up on certainties.'

'Take you on the next run, if you like!' offered the pilot, for it would be dark by then, and really dark, in the midnight of these open, manless places. On the ground their darkness is never complete, never so Stygian as the darkness of cities when their house-lights are quenched; but from the air it is enough.

'Done!' said Budge. 'Lay you a week's pay on it!'

It grew dark almost imperceptibly; one moment the lambent light still lifted distances to view, the next they were gone, and the world had shrunk to an airfield's space, and its inhabitants to a dozen handfuls of men creeping in and out of the bowels of bombers, like the Greeks out of the wooden horse.

The second run was by darkness indeed, for the clouds had spread over the sky and taken away much of the innate light which lingered after nightfall. But he knew the ground below him by sheer touch now, every yard of it; it wasn't for nothing he'd lived up there for a little while. He knew the beginning of the turn which was not yet quite over the Folly, and already his finger-ends prickled. He could even see, or persuade himself that he could see, certain vast shapings of darkness leaning upon one another, the gargantuan cocksure figure of the enemy suddenly grown and overgrown personal, visible, shrunk for one minute into this pile of masonry, for even into so colossal a vain thing his enemy had to compress itself from infinity. For Rosalba there could be a morning without a Folly – no pinnacle for the family to stand on any more, to make itself so almighty tall! A bonfire for all the grievances of all the pushed-around and put-upon, a torch to light up their revenge, a grand gesture of warning on behalf of all the other worms who haven't turned yet, so they'll be able to see their way round when they've had enough at last!

'Oh, boy!' he said aloud, 'it could be good!'

'Eh?' shouted the pilot.

'I said it could be good!'

'What could?'

'This could!' said Budge, and his itching fingers tightened, his heart soared and sang. He knew the exact moment by his palm, he knew he was spot on his target, as he let the load go.

'With love,' shouted Budge, 'from all at home!'

The night split apart under them, in an explosion of light and sound, and an expanding cloud of dust reached upward with a faintly undulating motion, straining impalpable fingers to pull them down, but its arm was too short by far, and only the rising wind of blast rocked them a little and set the air quivering and pulsating round them. The pilot had let out a yell of sheer surprise, but Budge's yell was louder. He had seen, in the heart of the flash, the largest town quake and buckle together slowly, in infinite astonishment, and that was enough for him, without the rumble and roar of its falling. Who could have done it better? Right under the base of the tower, where it soared from the main roof of the great hall! Right where the useless tons of its masonry descending could bring down half the lower levels of the house with them, and sign his work! They wanted competent bombing, didn't they? Now let them stand by and watch the work of a master!

'Oh, boy!' he shouted. 'Oh, boy, was that spot on, or was it?'

They were all shouting, asking him if he was crazy, craning to see the first tongues of fire go out skyward, ominously, delicately, from his lit beacon. Sure he was crazy! Sure he was! Every non-conforming guy is crazy, according to the guys who do conform. They were a decent set of fellows, they were trying to figure out already a way to say he didn't know what he was doing at the time. Yelling at one another that it was an accident, a brainstorm, a mistake,

267

and that they'd all better be in the same tale by the time they touched down. As if he was going to let anybody stay in error about the way it had happened! As well not have done it at all as let its voice be quieted!

'Sure I'm crazy!' he said, laughing at their horrified faces. 'War nerves, that's what got me! I ain't responsible! Aw, why don't you guys take another look down there? Did a crazy guy hit that joint plumb over in one? Yeah, battle fatigue, that's my trouble!'

'You're out of your mind, man,' yelled the wireless operator. 'What got into you to do a thing like that!'

'I had a week's pay on it with the chief,' said Budge. 'Boy, you sure owe me that money! Did I hit my target! Oh, boy, did I?'

He looked below, and the night was alight and alive. The wind had freshened with full dusk and the coming of coolness, and drew now with energetic breath at the compact, quivering heart of fire on the high place of the Rose family idolatry. Fingers of flame lengthened along the tide of it, silhouetting the broken edge of the main tower, outlining the grotesque turrets with scarlet and gold. For the first and last time in its life, Rose's Folly was beautiful; and all about the edges of the town people rose, and called out other people, and ran to clear viewpoints, and stood there at gaze, holding their breath and living through their eyes, to see the pyre of centuries burn out, and the beacon and alarm of new centuries take fire from its ashes.

2

Cedarwood heard the earth struck and shaken for the latest of many times, but knew by the direction of the sound, and its volume, that this impact was different. He got up and looked out from his window, and saw a great soft rose of fire, with a nimbus of angry purple-black cloud about it, opening into gradual perfection of blossom upon the curved black crest of the upland.

He knew to a hand's breadth, almost, behind which exact segment of that rolling skyline reared the towers of the Folly. The light of their burning came over the hills to him in scarlet and gold, hectic and splendid. He stood dazzled at the window for a long minute, and then pulled on his clothes and ran down through the half-empty, echoing spaces of the east lodge, and out on to the heath, to the highest place on this rim of the estate. A steady, full wind tugged at him, tugged at the long streamers of distant, rose-coloured light and drew them out into ribbons, into hairs, standing tall and wavering into the sky, and when he reached the crest, and looked forward to the higher crest where the house should have been, the familiar shape of it was all changed and fallen, a shatter of masonry like a battered skull, from which stood up a head of long, flaming hair, bright red hair erected in horror or exultation. He saw ten centuries burning in the funeral pyre of the Rose family, all their deeds, all their thoughts, all the pomp and circumstance of their long, inflexible, tenacious history suddenly struck into fine ash and adrift in that tempest of heat and destruction.

Cedarwood remembered comets and signs in the heavens, and knew the quality of the last years of things, when one cycle has turned ponderously to its close, and another as sombrely begins the upward turn which may last who knows how long? His senses wondered, observing the marvels of light and darkness, of suddenness and deliberation and change; but his mind did not marvel, it merely accepted and recorded, aligning itself with the motion of grace without need of understanding. When the hour is, it is time; and until it is time, the hour cannot strike. And the hour had struck, and the dutiful hand reached for the tocsin. For what the watchman sounds he knows neither gratitude nor regret. The laying of a finger upon shut lips may be the end of an epoch a million years long, or the touching of fire to straw may turn the small wheel of only an hour; but the signs are there to be read faithfully, and sent out upon the air; and if some understand them, and some fail to understand, that also is in God's hand, and the palm of time, which is limitless, has room for all the complex, flawless purposes of God.

For him the death of Rose's Folly did not proceed from the indulged impulse of an aggrieved G.I. in a passing bomber, but out of a calculated progression of circumstances arranged by the fingers of providence, out of a mind to whose intents obscure unthinking gestures of defiance come as handily as plague, drought, or war. He was content that Rose's Folly should burn so bonnily in the rising wind on its beacon hill, and call the countryside to heel. Budge had had no more hand in it than the mechanism which opened the bomb doors; and that he should sit in the guard room window admiring what he conceived to be his handiwork, and warming himself at its glow, was only another evidence of the vanity of man, which is endless.

Cedarwood did not call the fire brigade; that was logical if the time had come for the Folly to burn to the ground. But he began to trot along the ridge of the heath and down through the plantations to the south lodge, to sound the alarm there if the crack of doom had not already been heard and heeded. Folds of land laid quietly side by side like resting fingers upon a book intervened, and the night was full of dull explosions; and a prophet must prophesy, or of what use is he?

In the garden, motionless, standing only a few yards from the open door of the house, he saw the thin pale figure of Rosalba, and the quaking light which was reflected upon her from the cloudy sky showed him her face immobile as marble, but with eyes enormous and aware in it, not yet excited, not yet exultant, only hesitant upon the last stillness of a held breath, before the following, perceiving cry. She stood with her thick boy's dressing-gown clutched together in tight hands over her little immature breasts, staring up at the pulsing waves of light which passed in soundless, passionate tide across the sky's face. Her pale hair, shining like primrose petals in the darkness, was loose about her shoulders, and swung and drifted about in the wind, across her face, over the dilated eyes, in a silken curtain. She leaned forward a little, and he could feel the intensity with which every nerve in her was drawn taut. It was impossible to be sure whether she had been there for centuries, or whether she had only this minute thrown open the door and run out, to pause here upon tiptoe and stare until her sleep-confused mind could grasp the tenor of the time. For the young are improvident, and do not listen, and it needs more than one summons to make them hasten or perceive the need of haste.

He said to her: 'It's come!' and made to pass on into the house, but she put out her hand and caught him by the arm. Her lips were parted in expectation, but in incredulity, too.

'What is it? *Is* it the Folly?'

'Go up to the crest and see!' She saw his face clearly now in the strange, quivering light thrown back from the sky, his hair erected and redly streaming, his cheek-bones above the crimsoned beard burning into small bright glowing fires, the whites of his eyes glazed with gold. When he lifted his hand and gestured towards the surge of the heath she almost expected lightnings to go forth out of his finger-ends. 'Who's to know,' he said, 'the length of the time? I heard the midnight strike, and after it this bolt fell, and in one blow half of that great place fell after it. Go and look!'

'It's impossible!' she said. 'Why should it happen like that? Why should it happen now, tonight?'

'Because the hour was right for it, and it had no longer to live. Ask your own heart these questions, and not me,' he said, and turned with hand outspread to the doorway, where Mrs. Fenton stood dumbly wringing her hands and wryly weeping, with fierce contortions of her face and twitchings of her shoulders, jangled to pieces with all her faculties dangling in the fall of her world. 'Where is Mrs. Rose? Does she know what's happened? Have you told her?'

'No,' said Rosalba, and: 'No!' said Mrs. Fenton, shuddering. 'How can I tell her such news? Why, it's her life's gone if the Folly's gone! It's the end of everything for her. How am I to tell her such a thing as this?'

'She hasn't been out of her room all day,' said Rosalba,

with a quick, unheeding lightness, only half of her mind on what she said, the rest flying before her to the rise of the hills, to warm its hands at the blaze. 'She doesn't want to talk to me, about this or anything. I've tried twice since morning, and she won't let me in.'

'Is she ill?' asked Cedarwood, sensing the toppling of more towers than the towers of brick and stone.

'I don't think so. She says not, at any rate. She eats, and reads, and writes letters. The cat can go in, only I can't.' But her voice was high and confident, lifting into excitement; the unrealities of the day were behind her.

'All those lovely things,' sobbed Mrs. Fenton, 'all those records of the family, centuries of them, and all lost, all lost! All the portraits, all the books and parchments – how can I go to her and tell her they're all gone? I haven't dared go near the room since it happened. I called to her as I came along the corridor. She said she was all right, and had heard the crash, but oh, Mr. Cedarwood, we'd no idea then what it was! How am I to break it to her? What am I to say to her?'

He passed her in the doorway, and went up the stairs, by a way he knew well, not even reaching for the lights as he went. No line of pallor hemmed the foot of Martine's door, and no movement stirred within the room. He stood and listened for a moment with his hand raised against the panels of the door, and then he knocked, loudly, firmly, as became the messenger of providence.

'Mrs. Rose! Do you hear me, Mrs. Rose?'

In the long quietness there was only a small rustling sound, her sleeve of silk on the arm of a chair, her skirts drawn along the floor as she turned her head to listen, and hesitated to put her voice to the necessity of replying. It was much trouble for little worth; there was nothing he could have to tell her, much she could have told him if she had wished. What did he know, for all his angels and demons, of the death of the Roses? Then, in order that he might go away and leave her alone, she answered in a slow and heavy voice, all the voice she had left:

'I hear you. What do you want here?'

272

'You heard the explosion? The Folly's hit and burning. It will burn to the ground,' he said with certainty, 'the time is come for its place to be vacant.'

The rustling silence lasted again for a long minute. Then she said: 'Go and tell the people who own it. The Folly is no house of mine.'

'It was the only house you had,' he said, 'the only abiding-place. More than the walls and the roof have come down with it.'

'Why do you come to me,' she said in a loud cry, 'with your lightning strokes out of the Apocalypse? Do you think there is anything to be said to me? Fool, I sit and watch it burn!'

He waited, but she said nothing more; the startled echoes of her utterance ebbed very quickly, and were lost into the corners of the darkness, withering as his senses pursued them. Within the room silks sighed again as she straightened, face to the window.

No sound followed him as he went down the stairs. Only a more than ordinary stillness settled again upon the house, its heart in that room with her, sitting in the darkness, watching the sky flower with destruction. She had drawn a heavy chair to the window, and sat with her skirts spread about her in state, and in the midst of their inverted silken bell her old body grew lax and cold, all the tensions slackening out of it. On the horizon the bonfire of the past burned steadily, lighting the chilling lines of her mask of a face.

And there went into ashes the only house she had, the only abiding-place. More than walls and roof was come down with it.

3

Rosalba dressed herself quickly, and ran through the garden. When she looked back at the windows of the lodge she could see the rosy light gleaming weirdly upon the old woman's face, motionless there behind the glass like a wax figure in a case. But it meant nothing to her, it might have been some doll discarded at the end of her childhood; the glitter in the sky, the quivering air, the night's fantasies alone were real.

She turned her back on the lodge, and ran, up the long slope of the heath and through the wood, where the shuddering scarlet light fell down through the black branches in dazzling handfuls, so that the ground before her feet was paved with fire. When she reached the crest and came out into the open, panting and out of breath, waves of rosy light went pulsing over her, light as bright as day. All the sky, all the surging seas of grasses, quaked with radiance, the earth seemed molten and trembling. She stood a moment to regain her breath and to stare, held motionless by the prodigy before her.

Where the Folly had been the low table of stone now blossomed monstrously with new and unimaginable roses. The woods about it lightened and shook, and in their framework, as the wind alternately raged and repented, sometimes the broken edges of the walls stood up blackly, and sometimes hid among the flowering flames. The main tower with its conical hat was gone, snapped off at roof-level in a jagged edge of brickwork, two of the turrets smashed beneath it in its fall, only the low shell left, and that a brazier full of fire. Out of it flames stood up tall and slender and brave, streaming diagonally down-wind, giving the night a heart of intensity. The activity of men was already about the foot of the rosebush, for she could see small figures lit and running in the bleached grass, and upon the leeward side the garden trees were folded in a haze of smoke and steam from the attentions of firemen. But they must know already, past doubt, that all they could do was spare the trees, and watch the Folly burn. The faint rains which had visited it of late weeks had hardly cooled its enormous forehead, and the whole of its interior was panelled thick with seasoned wood. It would burn like a torch, like a bowl of magical fire. To the ground, falling turret by turret, wall by wall, sagging into a heap.

Rosalba went nearer, staring with dazzled eyes forward into the glare, and feeling her mind caught upward into the rising wind, the hot wind leaping out of the pyre. She could feel already the surge of that great draught, whirling skyward and tearing out of her heart all the doubts and fears and weaknesses which had harboured there, making her clean and empty and bright within, like a house newly swept and dusted and warmed for a homecoming. The heat came in gusts from the fire, and beat over her face. She leaned to it eagerly, in a bright, void excitement. Everything was changing, everything was changed. She knew that men do not break their bloody foreheads altogether in vain. For there before her eyes, disintegrating in showers of sparks and whorls of smoke, went the first outpost. There went the fortress which was to last out her time, in a moment, in the twinkling of an eye; and so would go all the other ramparts of the old warring world.

She went through the gardens and drew near to the turmoil round the house. Fire-engines had come very quickly, there were five of them spaced about the hot and sodden ground of the rose gardens and the lawns. Hoses were snaking about the gravel, men were playing them upon walls and trees from the ends of long ladders in mid-air. The nearest pool was sucked down to half its depth, and sulked blackly in mud and slime. Officers from the Army camps and the American airfield were there, talking agitatedly together, anxiously following Cedarwood as he moved about and about the prodigy with his hair and beard redly streaming, and his eyes flames. People had risen from their beds and walked across the heath to see, they were slipping out of every coppice as Rosalba watched, silently, wonderingly, greedily, and forming up in solemn ranks just out of range of heat and activity. They stood there quite still, with wide eyes and intent faces, like worshippers, drawing back a pace or two in beautiful unison when the wind caught back its breath and blew the flames nearer to them, but never taking their eyes from the resplendent blaze. They looked neither sorry nor glad; they looked as Cedarwood looked, receptive, acquiescent and fascinated. Nothing must be missed; but did they know what they were witnessing?

Miles away they saw the beacon. In the towns, in the small farmhouses scattered among the fields, in the unexcitable villages, they stirred out of their sleep to see their walls quaking with the reflected light, and drew back their curtains upon the fiery dawn which Budge Fetterbrand had made. In the close dormitories of the rest centre on the far side of Crocksford they got up to the windows and stared, and wondered. In the Spinney camp they could read by the light of it, and sleep was impossible.

Eugene went out to the edge of the wire, and felt the heart being drawn out of him with desire to go and discover what was happening; but he could not go. And even tomorrow there was no way up to the heath for him. The train left at ten, and he must go without more word of her, without knowledge, with only this false flicker of wonder and hope tormenting him, and silence and darkness shutting it in all round until it cooled and died like the rest. He held by the wire, and narrowed his eyes to stare into the ferocious brightness, and tried not to feel the betraying hope, for miracles do not happen. Not to the Eugene Seales of his world, at any rate! And yet it burned still, there on the skyline, magnificent and unexpected, the one thing not allowed for. And he could not help hoping, and hope tore him abominably all night long, and sleep did not come at all. If only there had been something he could do, instead of agonising there against the wire like an animal in a cage. If only he could have gone to find her! He must not hope. It would be all the worse for him tomorrow, if he did, when the time ticked by toward departure without further word or sign, and the train pulled out and steamed solemnly by under the shadow of that ruin, leaving it still unexplained, unrelated to past or future, like a broken promise. He must not hope. But he was eighteen, and he had to hope, he didn't know how to shut it out. He thought of her white and gleaming and cold with despair on that last evening together, and he could not believe that this omen in the night mean nothing, he could not believe that God was making fun of him.

Rosalba waited all night among the watchers in the gardens. In the clean void within her, from which doubt had been blown headlong away, positive hopes were taking shape, and they had all Eugene's face. She smiled into the dazzle of the fire, brilliantly and tenderly, remembering the coldness of his cheek against hers, and the rough, hard texture of his khaki sleeve upon her bare arms. At ten o'clock the train would go, carrying him southward away from her. It was strange how the world had shrunk in only a few hours, for now its width did not seem to her enough to blur his face at all. He could go to the ends of the earth now, and still be near to her, since the weak were not so weak as they had seemed, nor the strong so strong. Separation was terrible, yes, distance was anguish, and a year an age and an age wasted; but all together these things were not defeat, as only yesterday they had seemed to be.

By dawn the fire had burned into a darker glow, blackened with water, forsaken by a falling wind, grown hungry and tired from its own vehemence. After the red artificial day the true grey day came almost unnoticed, diminishing the prodigy, and the ruinous splendour became unveiled ugliness, a sodden, angular shape, squat and crippled, wretchedly containing sullen acres of embers. Rosalba turned homeward, past the pathetic small stacks of salvage, armour and books and cases of manuscripts, which alone remained of the accumulation of centuries, past the emptied pool with its trickle of dirty water painfully threading a basin of greenish-black mud, past the trampled and flattened rose-gardens, and down the sweet open heath. The light paled and whitened over her, and the day opened like a magnolia flower, still blanched and waxen until the sun's coming. Rosalba marched downhill unwearied, her steps springing in the deep turf, her hands reaching out after the occasional young bushes of broom which fringed her path, and drawing the cool shoots silkily through their fingers. Her face was soiled with smoke, damp smuts dulled the sheen of her hair; she was singing, loudly and clearly, snatches of any song which came to mind.

The death's-head face was no longer visible at Martine's window. For hours Rosalba had forgotten about her, and even now she remembered only with the surface of her mind, and went on singing as she opened the gate and let herself into the garden. The sight of a familiar car drawn in upon the gravel drive silenced her, and she considered its significance with sharpening awareness as she went into the house.

Mrs. Fenton was just coming down the staircase, heavy-footed, grim of face but calm; a light of satisfied excitement shone through the severe formal grief of her face, as people look greedy and pleased at funerals. Behind her came the doctor who attended Martine on the rare occasions when she could be persuaded that pain had a cause, and eighty years was past the prime of physical achievement. He wore a slight professional frown, and was saying in the perfunctorily lowered tones of a busy man courteously adapting himself to someone else's mood:

'It was certain to happen sooner or later. I've been telling her for at least a year that her heart would give out on her if she went on treating it as she did. Any shock could have stopped it these last six months.'

'And such a shock!' said Mrs. Fenton, shaking her head. 'Everything gone but the two lodges, in one stroke, as you might say, like this. And the poor young lady—'

They saw her then, and the rhythm of their descent was jostled out of time. The poor young lady was standing in the hall, looking up at them with great, shining, sapphire-blue eyes, her lips parted and glossy upon alert, contented breath. Her long gold hair was down on her shoulders, and tangled into soft, confused curls by the night wind; her face was very dirty; she had a branch of flowering broom in her hand, and held it sloped against her shoulder like a rifle, or like the palm which Peace carries in newspaper cartoons. Her colour was high, her presence crisply cool as the chilly air of dawn; she looked up at them, and seemed arrested in

278

the middle of a dance. They looked at her a little helplessly, each waiting for the other to speak first, and there was a queer, brief silence.

'Something's happened,' said Rosalba directly. 'What is it?'

They came slowly down the last few treads of the stairs to her, and hesitated how to phrase it.

'I'm afraid this will be a shock to you, Miss Rose,' began the doctor. 'Your great-aunt—'

'She's ill?' said Rosalba, frowning a little over his slowness, and looking from face to face with large, questioning but unalarmed eyes.

'A night such as you've just had here,' he said, 'is no small shock to an eighty-year-old. Her heart was in a bad state already. She seems to have sat up at the window watching the fire, instead of trying to rest. It was altogether too much to ask of such worn machinery.'

'I went to her,' said Mrs. Fenton, twitching at her handkerchief with nervous fingers, 'but she sent me away. You know how she hated to be crossed – I was afraid of agitating her if I insisted. But I took it upon myself to send for Doctor Royle, because I was afraid of the consequences. And right I was!' she said tremulously. 'When I looked in again she was sitting at the writing-desk, and lying over it as if she'd fainted. Writing to Mr. Pearson, she was, to make an appointment about some alterations to her will.' Tears of excitement started in her eyes. 'The poor lady, whatever it was she had on her mind, we'll never hear it from her lips now.'

'I wish,' said Rosalba, 'you would tell me what's really happened. Are you trying to say that Great-Aunt Martine is—' She hesitated upon the word because it was so unfamiliar, and she had never before made its acquaintance so closely as this.

'She was dead when I got here,' said the doctor. 'I'm very sorry!'

Rosalba stood gazing at them with an intent, considering frown, only the lightest shadow of astonishment dimming

279

her brightness. She put down the branch of broom very carefully upon the table, and began to bite her lips thoughtfully upon these vast new responsibilities which opened up suddenly behind the void where the old woman had been. All kinds of things to be done, and she had to do them; the solicitors would help, of course, and Cousin Robert would have to be sent for. She pondered, trying to remember what are the duties which fall upon a household after a death. She wanted to do all that was required of her, punctiliously, to discharge the last cold penny of her debt to Martine, living or dead.

'Oh,' she said slowly, 'I see! I suppose you've already told Mr. Pearson? He ought to take charge of all the papers. Oh, dear,' she said, her frown deepening, 'I'm not very good at this. There are so many things to be thought about. I'll write to Cousin Robert at once. That's the first thing, at any rate.'

The doctor said: 'Don't worry now! There's no need. Mrs. Fenton and Mr. Pearson between them will take care of everything. Better have a rest, and let things slide for a few hours – you've had a sleepless night, too, you know.'

'Oh, good gracious, *I'm* all right!' she said in surprise.

She knew that she ought to feel something; not sorrow, for that was impossible, but at least some sort of shock at the abrupt removal of the half of her life. But the truth was that it would have been infinitely more astonishing if Martine had been still alive. The world had turned about in the night, and it was natural that she should be gone with the things which were gone; in the world this morning, now that Rosalba examined it, there was no corner at all into which Martine fitted. One might as well expect the darkness to stay over the earth after the sun had risen.

4

Rosalba sat in the Crocksford bus, which was late, and looked at her watch every other minute, to make sure that she had still time left to reach the station by ten o'clock. She had bathed and changed and brushed her hair, had written to Cousin Robert, spoken on the telephone to Mr. Pearson, swallowed the sketch of a breakfast, and rushed out of the south lodge to the bus stop. Several indispensable people were running about busily within the house, and no doubt Mrs. Fenton thought it heartless and wicked of her to rush away from the activity to a rendezvous of which Martine would passionately have disapproved. But Mrs. Fenton was shrunken into insignificance now with the spine taken out of her by the loss of her mistress, for without Martine there turned out to be little left of her.

Rosalba's mind quested like a bewildered but interested pup through the tangled undergrowth of her new state. Cousin Robert would be her guardian now, and that was satisfactory, for Cousin Robert was easy, and within reason would certainly let her do as she liked with what was hers. If it had been his, that would have been a different thing, but he wouldn't care very much if Rosalba chose to turn the east lodge into four flats, and fill them with exuberant families from Crocksford. Provided he was not there to be annoyed by shouting children and flapping washing, and a few broken panes occasionally in the cold frames, and the industrious excavations of pet dogs, he would allow her to endure it without much protest. She was sure she could manage him.

Already her head was seething with plans. There would be very little money, but what did she care for that? If there was enough to start her in some honest job, that was all she needed or wanted. Mr. Pearson would shake his head over the changes and deplore the passing of the old days, for he was old, too, and fond of keeping what he had, like most of them; but the architect who had come once to plan some alterations at the Folly was young, and would be on the side of the homeless. Rosalba knew where to find him, and was sure he would help her. Flo should have a home, Flo and all her family. And until it was ready they should come to the south lodge and share it with Rosalba; as soon as Martine's funeral was over, and everything settled, she would bring them there, into the empty rooms, to fill them with voices,

281

brave voices, cheerful voices, young voices. No ghost and no evil memory would survive a day of Sid's Indian yells, no shadow of old beauty turned to horror would live long in the same house with Flo's lovely normality. The wall was breached, and the triumphing army was flooding in.

When Eugene's train was gone, she thought, she would go straight to the rest centre, and find Flo, and tell her. People can put up with bad times calmly enough when better ones are at least in sight.

Poor Mrs. Fenton would perhaps find the prospect more than she could bear; but as she had taken one shape from Martine, so she might yet take another shape from the newcomers; and if she could not reconcile herself, perhaps something could be found for her, some quiet place with somebody old, where she would be at home in an atmosphere she understood and preferred. It would need thought; every move would need thought, as every human creature deserves to be considered respectfully in the schemes which involve him.

When the salvage was completed at the Folly, and the official enquiry into the unaccountable accident had run its course, she would know more of her possessions and her responsibilities. She wondered only a little about the cause of the fire, though she knew that a bomb had started it, and she supposed that some unfortunate had been to blame for the fact that it had strangely fallen there, instead of miles out in the heath. Perhaps something could be done even for him, since many of the treasures lost in the show-cases would have come to her had they survived. National property and Rose loans had lain cheek by jowl there, and been molten into a mud of metal and leather and rubble together. What rigours might have been launched against the culprit by Martine she could at least withhold, and what weight she had she could lend in his defence. She owed him more, much more, than she was ever likely to be able to repay. A crazy world, she thought helplessly, where any creature could be forced into the incredible position of being grateful for destruction; but even if the results were not so easily visible, this unknown G.I. had created more than he had destroyed. At least she must ask about him, visit him if they would let her, help him if she could. She felt brave and full of counsel; she wanted to help all the world.

The sun beamed on the road before her as the bus drew into Crocksford. At the first halt she must get out.

'Station, please!' she said to the conductor as he slithered up the gangway whistling, his pencil dangling behind one ear.

'O.K., miss!' He leaned over her and tinged the bell.

'You're late this morning,' she said, peering anxiously at her watch for the hundredth time.

'Don't you worry, miss, he'll wait for you!' said the conductor, appraising her radiance with a saucy grin.

'He can't,' said Rosalba, smiling back at him a shade ruefully, 'he's going by the special train at ten o'clock.'

'Overseas, eh?' Everybody in Crocksford knew all about it. The conductor raised sympathetic eyebrows as he moved forward to let her alight. 'Never you mind, miss. They'll soon be back. Eighteen months ain't such a long time.' And he leaned out after her to call cheerfully: 'Tell him to keep his chin up!'

Rosalba acknowledged the advice with a smile and a wave of her hand as the bus rolled away. Down this little street, by a short cut through the market alley, and across the Lion yard. Only ten minutes to go before train time. A short farewell, but short farewells are best. All the same, she began to run, headlong as a boy, her sandals sliding on the cobbles of the inn yard. The long fawn fences of the station came into sight, the nineteenth-century pagoda buildings, curly-crested and blonde and soiled. She pushed a penny breathlessly into the platform-ticket machine, and caught at the nearest porter's arm to ask from which platform the special train would leave. Then she was slipping along to the bridge between gently undulating groups of people, and there was the long drab train, and the hundreds of young men in khaki loitering until the last minute outside its carriages with their friends and relations. They all looked so much alike that for a moment she despaired of finding the one for whom she was searching; and the worst of it was that he would not be watching for her, since here she was totally unexpected. She went questing down the length of the train, looking from face to face, from window to window, and at last she found him.

He was already in the train, leaning in the open window with his arms folded and his eyes moodily cast down. The thick, straight brown brows were drawn closely together in a painful frown, and his mouth, she saw, was drooping in a quite unaccustomed softness and sadness; but when she tugged herself through the close knots of his companions towards him, and cried out: 'Eugene!' as wildly as a lark rising, he looked up sharply with an incredulous face. His eyes grew childishly round and glad, bright as sunlit brook water. He wrenched open the carriage door and came tumbling into her arms.

THE HEAVEN TREE TRILOGY

Edith Pargeter

Volume 1 THE HEAVEN TREE

England in the reign of King John – a time of beauty and squalor, of swift treachery and unswerving loyalty. Against this violent, exciting background the story of Harry Talvace, master mason, unfolds. Harry and his foster-brother Adam flee to Paris, where Harry's genius for carving draws him into friendship with Ralf Isambard, lord of Parfois, and the incomparably beautiful Madonna Benedetta, a Venetian courtesan.

'If you do not appreciate this superb novel, I despair of you'
Illustrated London News

Volume 2 THE GREEN BRANCH

Young Harry Talvace, the son of Ralf Isambard's master-builder, has grown up in the court of Llewelyn, Prince of North Wales. Deep in his heart he nurses a desire for vengeance . . .

'A remarkably fine and historical novel'
Books and Bookmen

Volume 3 THE SCARLET SEED

The story reaches a strange and violent climax as the principal characters are drawn together in the final siege of Parfois under the towering shadow of the first Harry's master-work.

'It is immensely readable. A swinging, romantic yarn'
Sunday Telegraph

THE MARRIAGE OF MEGGOTTA

Edith Pargeter

Fatherless Richard de Clare, heir to the mighty earldom of Gloucester, was placed at the age of eight in the care of Hubert de Burgh. In the remote East Anglian fastness of Burgh he and Hubert's daughter Meggotta, the same age as Richard, met for the first time and quickly became inseparable. But two years later Hubert fell from grace with King Henry III and was faced with certain ruin and the threat of death.

By then aged ten, Meggotta and Richard were already deeply in love. Striving to protect them from becoming pawns in a vicious power struggle, Hubert's wife arranged their secret marriage.

They dared to defy the rigid conventions of the feudal marriage market. But the union was doomed and the young lovers paid a tragic price for their defiance.

'Touching story ... sensitivity and realism'
Mary Renault

'A very moving book'
Pamela Hansford Johnson

MOST LOVING
MERE FOLLY

Edith Pargeter

When Suspiria Freeland is charged with poisoning her
artist husband Theo, a scandalised country presumes her
guilty. What could one expect of a woman like that, with
her clever tongue and abrupt manners, those odd-shaped
pots she calls art and her ramshackle house – a woman
who brazenly admits her affair with a garage mechanic
fourteen years her junior?

Dissected in the full limelight of public courts and gutter
press, Dennis and Suspiria's already ill-matched liaison
seems doomed – and Suspiria's acquittal is only the start
of their real problems. Under the weight of popular
sentiment and censure, a world watching, misinterpreting
and taking possession of their every move, expecting and
hoping for disaster, how can their love survive? Worse,
the question the lovers dare not voice – if Suspiria did not
kill Theo, who did?

☐	The Heaven Tree	Edith Pargeter	£4.99
☐	The Green Branch	Edith Pargeter	£4.99
☐	The Scarlet Seed	Edith Pargeter	£4.99
☐	The Marriage of Meggotta	Edith Pargeter	£4.99
☐	Most Loving Mere Folly	Edith Pargeter	£4.99

Warner Futura now offers an exciting range of quality titles by both established and new authors. All of the books in this series are available from:

Little, Brown and Company (UK) Limited,
P.O. Box 11,
Falmouth,
Cornwall TR10 9EN.

Alternatively you may fax your order to the above address. Fax No. 0326 376423.

Payments can be made as follows: cheque, postal order (payable to Little, Brown and Company) or by credit cards, Visa/Access. Do not send cash or currency. UK customers and B.F.P.O. please allow £1.00 for postage and packing for the first book, plus 50p for the second book, plus 30p for each additional book up to a maximum charge of £3.00 (7 books plus).

Overseas customers including Ireland, please allow £2.00 for the first book plus £1.00 for the second book, plus 50p for each additional book.

NAME (Block Letters) ....

....

ADDRESS ....

....

....

☐ I enclose my remittance for _____

☐ I wish to pay by Access/Visa Card

Number ☐☐☐☐☐☐☐☐☐☐☐☐☐☐☐☐

Card Expiry Date ☐☐☐☐